Denise Welch was born in Whitley Bay in 1958. She is an award-winning actress and TV presenter. Her many credits include *Coronation St*, *Soldier Soldier*, *Waterloo Road* and *Boy Meets Girl*, to name a few. She is also an accomplished theatre actress.

Denise was a panelist on popular daytime show *Loose Women* for several years.

She is married to artist Lincoln Townley and has two sons, Matthew and Louis, and stepson Lewis. She now lives a quiet, party-free life in rural Cheshire.

Denise WELCH

If They Could See Me Now

An imprint of
Little, Brown Book Group
Carmelite House
50 Victoria Embankment
London, EC4Y 0DZ

An Hachette UK Company
www.hachette.co.uk

www.littlebrown.co.uk

sphere

First published in by Sphere in 2016
This paperback edition published by Sphere in 2016

1 3 5 7 9 10 8 6 4 2

A CIP catalogue record for this book
is available from the British Library.

ISBN 978-0-7515-6233-0

Typeset in Bembo by M Rules
Printed and bound in Great Britain by
Clays Ltd, St Ives plc

Papers used by Sphere are from well-managed forests
and other responsible sources.

MIX
Paper from
responsible sources
FSC® C104740

Sphere

Lincoln, Matthew and Louis.
For loving me unconditionally.

My mum, Annie. I miss you every day.

My dad, Vin. For your love and
encouragement always.

Acknowledgements

Maddie West and the team at Little, Brown, for your belief in me as a storyteller.

Gordon Wise at Curtis Brown, for fighting my corner.

Rebecca Cripps, for helping me bring Harper to life. I couldn't have told her story without you by my side every step of the way.

My best friends. You know who you are. You have enriched my life and have added colour to my first novel.

My beloved sister Debbie, for being my sister.

My stepson, Lewis, for being such a lovely addition to my already testosterone-fuelled family.

My nieces, Olivia and Alex, for being so kind, funny and caring and for being . . . female!

William, my nephew, who should write a comedy for his Auntie Nece to star in . . .

Duncan, my brother-in-law, for being a MUCH better dancer than your brother Lincoln.

And finally, my mum-in-law, Jenny, for welcoming me into the family and making your home feel like my home.

If They Could See Me Now

1

Harper Clarke stared at her reflection in disbelief. Her instinct was to scream, because the woman staring back at her was unrecognisable, a bruised and bloody mess. But she didn't scream, she didn't dare, it would have hurt too much. She didn't cry either. Her face was so painfully tender that she was scared to move even a muscle.

It felt like a fresh shock every time she looked. She seemed to be getting worse, not better. Oh my God, she thought, inspecting the damage for the hundredth time that day, I'm never coming back from this.

The raw, oozing cuts above and below her eyes showed no sign of healing. The bruises on her puffy cheeks, instead of fading, were getting darker all the time, creeping across her face like purple ink stains. Only the gash on her nose seemed to be improving. Beads of dried black blood were beginning to cluster along the scar, like tiny vampire ants.

She softly bit her lip as she tried to absorb the horror of seeing herself like this, so distorted, so unfamiliar. It wasn't just the blood and bruises that made her look so different from her normal self. Her whole expression had changed. The swelling around her eyes had pushed up her eyebrows and set them at a sad, surprised angle. Her puffed up eyes gave her an air of heavy-lidded stupidity. She was starting to resemble a zombie clown who had died first and then done ten rounds with Mike Tyson. It was a long way from her usual look, it had to be said. She was hideous.

It was weird, because she had never felt ugly before. She'd had her off days – who hadn't? – but she had never felt repulsive, or quite so much like a victim. Is it a good lesson to learn? she wondered. To feel ugly and vulnerable? The mirror wobbled in her hand as her eyes filled with tears. No, there was a different lesson to be learnt here. How could her marriage have come to this? How on earth did it end up this way?

She gingerly put her head in her hands and tried to think about something else. The faint drone of a vacuum cleaner was coming from upstairs. Betty was on the march, waging war against dust mites and anything else that obstructed her daily mission to keep the house immaculate. Betty was a one-woman army when it came to tackling clutter and dirt, which was fortunate, because otherwise Aaron would have sacked her long ago. He was very particular about cleanliness and order.

Harper listened as Betty moved from the landing to the staircase, thwacking the hoover against the skirting board at every step, methodically making her way down to the ground floor, where she would change the setting from mid-length to shagpile and carry on.

This was part of the deal she had made with Aaron when she married him, she thought. Someone else did the housework while she sat on her plush sofa looking at herself in the mirror.

And what a sight she was.

She had never thought this would happen to her. 'Not me. I'd walk away!' she'd insisted whenever her friends discussed it. She felt sorry for the women they whispered about.

'No man is worth it,' she'd say, shaking her head.

'Come on, you'd really leave that gorgeous husband of yours?'

Yes, she repeated. Even though being married to Aaron made her the envy of every woman she knew, she would rather grow old alone than endure *that*.

Yet here she was with cuts and bruises, just like all the rest of them. Harper Clarke, black and blue – it was unthinkable. What had changed? How had she gone from an assured, confident woman to a pulped and bloodied wife? She wasn't sure she knew the answer. Somehow, over the course of her marriage, she had lost herself. She had let herself go, given up and given in.

The whirr of the vacuum cleaner grew louder. Eventually the door of the living room opened and Betty's face appeared.

'Cup of tea, love?' she asked.

'Yes, please,' Harper whispered. Tears started to roll down her face. 'Oh, Betty, what would I do without you?' she burst out.

2

Six weeks earlier

'It's getting scary,' Harper told Betty when she came in from the gym, slick with sweat and frustration. 'He keeps flaring up. Every little thing seems to annoy him.'

Betty poured them both a cup of tea.

'He's constantly criticising me,' she went on. 'Last night, he'd barely hung his coat up before he started going on about the dark circles under my eyes.'

'For heaven's sake,' Betty said, crunching into a biscuit.

'First he accused me of looking worn out. Then he went on about my crow's feet. He got so worked up that I honestly thought he might hit me. I said we're all guilty of ageing. But he says I'm starting to look *ancient.*'

Betty tutted. 'Rubbish. He needs his eyes tested.'

'What can I do about it, anyway? I can't turn the clock back.'

'You can't,' Betty agreed.

Harper let out a long sigh. It was in Aaron's DNA to

be critical. Over the years, he had chipped and chipped away at her, making her feel smaller by the day, eroding her confidence and sense of self. He had found fault with her parenting skills, her choice in friends, the jokes she told and her drinking habits. He had attacked everything except her appearance, in fact. Until now.

'I suppose there's Botox and fillers,' she said despondently. 'Angela raves about them. But I hate needles ...' She shuddered. 'And sometimes Angela looks, well, a bit frozen.'

She stirred a sweetener into her tea. 'On the other hand, if it got rid of my crow's feet ...'

Betty leaned across the kitchen table and peered at her. 'You mean your laughter lines?'

'Well ...'

'He can't begrudge you those, love.'

Harper made a face. When he was in one of his moods, Aaron begrudged her everything, including laughter.

Especially laughter.

'You know how he is,' she said. 'It's like living in an earthquake zone – one minute everything is happy and calm, and the next the walls come crashing down.'

She sipped her tea and sighed again.

The irony was that, outwardly, he was the ideal husband. 'You're so lucky to have him,' her girlfriends told her, eyeing the expensive rings on her fingers. 'He's gorgeous.'

To them he was the ultimate silver fox, relaxed and charming. His animal grace thrilled them; his suave compliments turned them pink with girlish delight. It didn't seem to occur to them that he might have a dark side. Presumably they were too busy imagining him without his clothes on.

She had given up trying to broach the subject of his black moods. 'He's a man,' they said with a shrug, as if that explained everything. It was almost as if they liked to think of him as being perfect.

So they were unaware of his jealous rages, or the way he constantly chided Harper for being a helicopter parent around their two girls. They had no idea that he goaded fourteen-year-old Georgina about her weight, or treated his favourite, Taylor, as if she could do no wrong. They actually knew very little about him, she thought. His possessive, controlling nature was hidden from view, concealed by a ring of charm and the towering hedges that surrounded their large, comfortable home.

But Betty knew the truth, because every time Betty poured out the tea, Harper poured out her heart – and this outpouring of tea and heart had been going on for nearly twenty years, almost since the day Betty had answered Harper's advert for a mother's help. No one was a better listener than Betty. She was the living soul of tea and sympathy. With her small round figure and taste in floral dresses, she even looked a little like a teapot – and what's more, she exuded warmth and stability, other teapottish qualities.

'Sometimes he makes me feel so small, just completely powerless,' Harper continued.

Betty was at Orchard End every weekday, so she was fully aware of the tensions that ruled the house. She knew all about Aaron's temper – and how much Harper worried about the effect of his mood changes on the girls. She had witnessed how wonderful he could be, and how quickly he could switch to being casually cruel. Fortunately, she listened without judgement – unlike Harper's mum, who gave short shrift to her daughter's complaints.

'Look at the life you've got, your house, your car,' she'd say impatiently. 'Try smiling more and cook nicer food.'

As if, thought Harper. She couldn't cook to save her life, and her mother knew it.

'Don't worry, he'll mellow with age,' Betty said. 'They all do.'

Harper smiled. When it was raining in Betty's world, you put up your umbrella and waited for the sun to come out. Nothing could be simpler – and since this strategy had got Betty through several family dramas and a nasty brush with breast cancer, it definitely wasn't to be underestimated.

'How's Donna?' she asked. 'Has she got rid of the mice yet?'

She caught up on Betty's news – the daughter who lived next door, the son three streets down, and the scores of grandchildren who ran wild between their various houses. Betty's life fascinated Harper. She wondered how she managed to remain so contented, even when she was mopping up other people's mess. Betty's semi-feral grandchildren were always trailing mud and

God-knows-what-else into the house, being sick, or getting into trouble at school. Untold numbers of friends and relatives were in the habit of dropping by for a brew, any day, any time, most of them without ringing first. She and her daughter lived in each other's pockets. She hadn't spent a night apart from her husband, Jim, in forty years. It sounded less like a life and more like the seventh circle of hell to Harper, and yet Betty took it all in her stride, rain or shine, umbrella at the ready. She wasn't one for mood swings.

'The mice are gone,' Betty said. 'Now there's a hole in the roof. If it's not one thing, it's another.'

'It never rains but it pours,' Harper agreed, thinking of Aaron.

'Never mind, at least we managed to have a good Christmas.'

That was the amazing thing about Betty. She probably didn't have a pot to piss in, but it didn't matter as long as she had enough to feed her family and buy them something nice for Christmas. No doubt she smiled in her sleep, Harper thought, and yet you would never cross her. It wasn't that she was scary, but she was stoic and immovable, like a small, squat mountain. Or a teapot, in fact. Made of granite.

She glanced at the clock on the kitchen wall. 'Time for a shower,' she said, gulping down the rest of her tea. 'Got to get to the hairdresser's by ten.'

3

It took two hours to have her highlights retouched. Two hours in which she couldn't avoid the sight of her *ancient* face in the mirror, two hours in which she realised that Aaron was right – her crow's feet were multiplying like cracks across scorched earth and her dark circles spreading like poison. Perspective was an interesting thing, she thought morosely. Just yesterday she'd been thinking she looked pretty good for her age. Now, all she could see in the mirror was a wizened old witch.

I need a drink, she decided. A great big glass of chilled rosé to cheer me up.

Since it was nearly lunchtime – and since she rarely drank during the day, so there was nothing to feel guilty about – she popped into the wine bar along the high street, just very quickly. Then, feeling infinitely brighter and more optimistic about life, she breezed along to the nail bar two doors down.

'Mani-pedi?' the nail stylist inquired. 'What sort of colour were you thinking?'

'Pink,' Harper said, laughter bubbling up inside. 'Sort of rosé-coloured.'

'Lovely, so these are the tones we have . . . ' The stylist produced a palette that ranged from Cerise Sunshine to Summer Days.

'Have you got Tipsy Haze?' she said with a giggle.

The stylist frowned. 'Is it Chanel or Alessandro?'

She coughed politely. 'Don't worry. I'll go for Summer Days.'

Next, she bought a new dress – in blood-red silk – at her favourite little boutique on the corner of the high street. It wasn't much to look at on the hanger, but she loved the way the material flattered her curves when she tried it on. Proof that all those hated gym sessions had paid off.

'You look fabulous!' the shop assistant gushed as she emerged from the changing room.

'Well, no bulgy bits, at least,' she replied, getting out her credit card.

Gym, hair, nails, dress – she ticked them off as she drove home. It wasn't a hard day's work down the mine – she laughed guiltily, thinking of her poor Uncle Joe – but she felt a small sense of achievement all the same.

The feeling soon dissipated as she turned into the drive-way leading to Orchard End. Who am I trying to kid? she thought. I used to be a famous actress and I gave it all up to go shopping?

She stepped inside the empty house. Betty had left it immaculate, as she always did. Everything was in its place – it was spotless, neat, tidy, luxurious – but there was something soulless about Aaron's taste in interiors. If she'd had her way, the house would be decorated in a country style, using rustic colours and textures, with a big wooden farm table in the kitchen and vintage sofas in the lounge. There would be rugs everywhere, not wall-to-wall carpet, and she would make a bonfire in the garden and cackle gleefully as she watched the peach velour lounge curtains go up in flames.

But she didn't have her way, and never would. Aaron liked the house as it was. That was that.

An hour later she woke up on the sofa with a woozy headache, regretting both the wine and her frothy choice of nail colour. She realised that she hadn't asked Betty to prepare any food, so the girls would have to eat pasta again. Fortunately, they never seemed to tire of the local Italian deli's home-made sauces, but Taylor was bound to make some smart remark. Like Aaron, her eldest daughter could be very scathing about Harper's limited cooking ability.

She couldn't blame her. After all, most mums could at least make a decent spaghetti bolognese. But although she'd tried – she'd even had lessons from Betty – she just couldn't get it right, and the results of her cooking were invariably mushy, burnt or half-baked.

The phone rang – the house phone. She nearly didn't answer it, because the only people who ever rang the landline these days were her parents, Aaron's parents and Angela, none of whom she felt a particular urge to speak to right then. On the other hand, she reminded herself, her parents were in their mid-seventies. It could be an emergency. She looked at the number on the LCD screen. *Private number.* Could it be a hospital, or the police? She pressed to answer.

'Hello,' she said.

The opening bars of a song started up. Just a cold call, then, from someone trying to sell something. She was about to swear down the receiver when she recognised the song. It was a Marc Bolan track, a tune from her youth, and it meant a lot to her. Too much. It was not one of his hits and the lyrics were obscure, so she wondered what it could be selling. But when the track ended, the line went dead.

That's weird, she thought.

She jumped when the doorbell rang, a few moments after she'd put the phone down. 'Delivery!' shouted the voice on the other side of the front door.

It flashed through her mind that the phone call could be the prelude to being handed a box containing a severed finger or ear, but instead she signed for a couple of fitness DVDs that she'd ordered online two days previously. She shut the door and headed towards the kitchen in search of a piece of fruit, chuckling to herself. Before long, she was immersed in a leaflet about cardio abs.

She was on her iPad searching for cashmere throws when Georgie bounded into the lounge wearing her school uniform, a blue and grey ensemble that didn't do her plump teenage figure any favours. Harper's heart went out to her podgy little girl. She felt shallow for noting her appearance, but it wasn't to be helped, because Aaron was always going on about it. She desperately wished he wouldn't. She hated the thought of Georgie getting a complex about her looks.

'Mum, I got a part in the school play!' Georgie burst out.

Harper's heart swelled. 'That's amazing,' she shrieked. 'I knew you'd get something. Didn't I say you would?'

Georgie rushed over and hugged her. 'I wasn't even going to turn up for the auditions! Thank you for making me go.'

Harper squeezed her daughter tightly. 'I had a hunch you'd inherited the Walters' talent for performing,' she said. 'It comes from your great-granddad, Billy. Everyone said I got it from him – and now it's passed on to you.'

Georgie snorted, which she sometimes did when she was overcome with laughter. Harper found it endearing, but Aaron loathed it. 'Stop it!' he'd snap at his daughter. 'You sound like a great fat sow.' Which only made Georgie snort even more, because she assumed he was joking.

'Don't go over the top, Mum,' Georgie said. 'It's a school play, not a West End show. You and Billy Walters did it professionally. I'm just dipping my toe in.'

'We'll see,' Harper said.

Maybe Georgie would follow in her footsteps, she thought. After all, within a few years of her own first appearance in a school play, she had found herself at drama school in London, studying Chekhov with Angela.

Taylor arrived home at six, wearing a rose-pink fitted jacket, tight black leggings and fluorescent fuchsia trainers. She looked stunning, as always. Sometimes it seemed unfair that she'd inherited all the good-looking genes, but Harper loved her with the same fierce protectiveness that she felt for Georgie. Yes, Taylor had been born with the cutest of delicate features and a force field of charisma that made everyone want to pick her up as a baby and toddler. And yes, Aaron had helped her personality along by popping a silver spoon in her mouth and handing her everything else on a plate. But Harper didn't forget that Taylor might not have been born at all. The night she had haggled with Aaron for her survival was never far from her mind.

Even though she was constantly giving her a hard time. Today her first words were, 'Your hair, Mum! It's, like, *red.*'

'Chestnut, thank you. I had it done this morning,' Harper said, ignoring the suggestion that something might have gone wrong at the salon. 'How was your day, darling?'

'Good,' Taylor said. 'Andrew says I could be an account manager within a year if I go on selling ad space at this rate. I made my bonus again this month. He's going to take me out for a drink to celebrate.'

Warning bells sounded in Harper's head. She knew all about older, married bosses taking pretty, young employees out for a drink.

'Andrew is?' she said.

'Yeah, Mum, what's the big deal?' Taylor said, slightly too quickly.

'Oh, nothing.' She reminded herself that Taylor was twenty-three and old enough to make her own decisions.

Nevertheless, she thought, having children was confusing. People were always saying that kids grew up too quickly these days, but at Taylor's age, she had been living in regional theatre digs and doing all her own shopping, cooking and washing. Meanwhile, Taylor lived a pampered life at home, never lifting a finger, and although she was well educated, well travelled and worldly wise, she often displayed signs of emotional immaturity.

'Loving your new nail colour – very upbeat,' she said. It sounded like a compliment, but you could never be sure with Taylor. 'What's for supper?' she asked. 'Tell me it's not pasta 'n' sauce again, purlease! Have you ever actually cooked a meal from scratch, Mother?'

'Of course I have,' Harper shot back, throwing a heart-shaped satin cushion at her. 'Which is more than I can say for you, cheeky scamp.'

I'm treating her like a child again, she thought wryly. It's true what they say, kids never grow up in their mums' eyes.

4

That evening Harper and Aaron went for dinner at their favourite brasserie, 'because I want something half decent to eat, for a change,' Aaron snarled, having his usual dig at Harper's culinary skills. He spent the duration of the meal looking restlessly around the room, barely listening as she chattered about the children: how proud she was that Georgina had made it into the play; how well Taylor was doing in her sales job.

'What's the matter?' she asked him over dessert. 'Aren't you interested in what the kids have been up to?'

'Yes,' he'd said, with an exasperated sigh. 'Which is lucky, isn't it? Because it's all you ever talk about.'

Back at home, sensing that his mood was darkening, she suggested one last glass of wine.

'Didn't you have enough at dinner?' he said sharply.

She started uncorking a bottle of Merlot anyway. She

needed another drink to dispel the anxiety that was building inside her.

And then it started. 'I saw the way you were looking at that waiter,' he spat at her.

'Waiter?' she said, her heart rate speeding up. 'We had a waitress serving us. I didn't see a waiter.'

Aaron rolled his eyes. 'Don't play the innocent with me, darling. I saw you flirting with him across the room. He saw it too – and you know what? He was disgusted by it. Of course he was, a man in his twenties getting an eyeful from an old hag like you.'

Not this again, she thought. Please. Not now. 'Hey, I wasn't flirting with anybody,' she protested, trying to keep her tone light. Her hand began to tremble as she poured out the wine.

'Don't give me that!' he yelled. 'Do I look stupid? I know what you're like. You think you've still got it, don't you? But you're not a sex symbol any more, you're a sad, old has-been. The poor guy was probably puking into his wine bucket at the thought of having sex with you. If it wasn't so sad it would be funny.'

She reeled inwardly. He could be so vicious. But she knew better than to pull him up on it. She had been here so many times before. 'Please don't be like this,' she begged. 'Honestly, I don't know what you're talking about. We had a nice time at Pierre's, didn't we?'

'Nice? Only if your idea of a good time is watching your wife wear her knickers on her head. Can't you see how pathetic it is, an ageing crone like you?'

She took a deep breath. Experience told her to stay calm, but it was easier said than done. 'That's ridiculous,' she said. 'I've never even looked at another man, and you know it. What is wrong with you?'

'It's you that's wrong,' he shouted. 'You look old! You make me feel old.'

It was almost too much to take – jealousy, his oldest bugbear, crossed with his latest bugbear about her fading looks. A wrinkly, green-eyed, mongrel of a bugbear, staring her in the face.

'I'm fifty-three,' she snapped back, unable to control her anger any longer. 'What do you expect?'

He stiffened. 'I expect you to look your best,' he said in a low voice.

She braced herself. Aaron was so much more menacing when he spoke softly.

'That's why I give you an outlandish monthly allowance,' he went on, 'to make sure you look the best you can possibly look. But you don't look your best. You look fucking awful. So I'm saying, Do something about it. You've got the credit cards. Go and see someone.'

She frowned. This was a turnaround. His jealousy had completely evaporated. 'See who?' she asked, genuinely curious. 'I'm already best buddies with every beauty and fitness therapist in the county. Manicures, pedicures, waxing, threading, hydrotherapy – I'm constantly getting my hair done, I've had every facial under the sun. I'm at the gym every day, sweating my tits off to look good for you . . .'

'Spare me the details,' he said, cutting her off. 'Fifty per cent of seduction is mystery, remember.'

'Seduction?' she howled. 'That's a laugh. You've just told me how awful I look.'

'Well, do something about it and stop complaining,' he said. 'I'm sick of looking at you the way you are now.'

'What do you suggest, a head transplant?'

He smiled. 'Don't go over the top,' he said. 'An eye job would probably be sufficient.'

She gaped at him. 'Surgery?'

'Like I say, you've got the credit cards. But do your research. Get the best. I don't want my wife looking like the Bride of Wildenstein.' He laughed nastily.

'No, wait,' she said, panicking. 'You know I don't want to do that. I hate hospitals, doctors, needles. I . . . like my face. I don't want to change it.'

'It's not changing anything. You just won't look tired any more, that's all. People will think you've had a lot of fucking sleep in the last ten years. It's about refreshing your look.'

'Yes, how refreshing it would be to have a general anaesthetic and get my face slashed about by a surgeon!' she said. '"I'll have an eye job with that cool glass of lemonade, please, doctor. Super, how very refreshing!"'

But then Aaron had started wheedling, doing what he knew best, twisting the argument around to get his own way. He was bad cop and good cop rolled into one, and when he was good, he was excellent.

'Come on,' he said tenderly. 'I'm just trying to do what's

best for you, darling. Can't you see that? It's because I love you so much that I want you to be happy. And you haven't been happy for a while, my love, admit it. You know it's true. Something's been wrong.'

She felt herself relenting even before his arm snaked around her waist. With the tips of his fingers, his dangerously gentle fingers, he stroked her red silk dress in the space just above her pelvic bone. Despite everything that had been said, tiny ripples of desire spread across her body. 'You're a beautiful woman,' he murmured. 'I didn't mean to be harsh. You're stunning beyond belief, nobody's disputing that. All I'm suggesting is a little help, a minor lift to keep you beautiful.'

He turned his body towards hers and began to smooth her hair with his hands, planting kisses on her face, on her ears and neck. 'Will you consider it?' he whispered, his green eyes glittering as they met hers. 'As a gift to me? As a gift from me? As a sign of our love.'

'No,' she said, her breaths getting shorter. 'Definitely not.'

'Come here,' he said, pulling her towards him. 'Let me remind you of why it's better to do things my way.'

It was always the same, whatever the argument. She hated herself for giving in, but she would do anything to feel loved – and the only time she felt really loved by Aaron was when he took her in his arms. Only then did he lavish her with the tenderness that she constantly longed for. Only then, for a few luxurious moments, she could believe in Aaron and Harper, together for ever.

5

She started doing her 'research' the following day, muttering all the while how she wouldn't go through with it, yet strangely eager to browse endless cosmetic clinic brochures online. It was pure curiosity, that was all it was. It was good to find out what exactly was on offer. And maybe Aaron was right, she did look old and tired, so maybe she did need a boost to make her feel happier. Perhaps he would become easier to live with if she listened to him and took his advice. More importantly, he would go on wanting her. She couldn't bear the thought that he might stop wanting her.

Could there really be a fix out there? For an old, tired face? Half convinced that she was only really searching for a 'medically approved' miracle cream, she read up on every clinical procedure available, studied hundreds of before and after photos, and trawled newspaper articles and forums to get the names of the best cosmetic surgeons in Cheshire. Purely out of interest, of course. Just wondering.

She had assumed that all the eminent doctors would be in London, but that turned out not to be the case. The best eye surgeon in England happened to be right on her doorstep in Cheshire, so she booked a consultation. Just to see what it was all about. No harm in it, after all.

Meanwhile, she mentioned it to Angela. 'Just look at Helen, darling!' Angela exclaimed. 'Suddenly she's looking marvellous and we all know why.' Angela was still in contact with several of their old acting friends, some of whom were doing as well, if not considerably better, than Angela. 'She's definitely getting more interest, even though her acting hasn't improved.'

'But would you do it?' Harper asked.

There was a short pause on the line. 'I probably would if I were married to your delectable husband,' Angela drawled. 'You don't want to let him get away.' She sighed, and Harper steeled herself for a long tirade on the failings of marriage and middle-aged men, specifically Angela's pathetic, soon to be ex-spouse, James.

She glimpsed her marriage from a rosier perspective when she saw Aaron through other women's eyes – and the conversation that followed served as a reminder of how fortunate she was to be with him, despite his moodiness and flare-ups. Her mind wandered back to the previous night, editing out their argument and focusing on the passion and pleasure that had followed it. Aaron *was* delectable, and she still found him magnetically attractive, which was more than could be said for the way most of her friends felt about their partners.

'I never really enjoyed sex with him,' Angela now said of the hopeless James. 'I used to go over my lines while we were doing it.'

Several of her other girlfriends had almost completely shut up shop around the twenty-year anniversary mark – and one or two had even told their men to look elsewhere for physical satisfaction, which was unthinkable to Harper. It wasn't simply that she couldn't bear the idea of Aaron with another woman. Their sex life was a vital part of their relationship – it was the glue that kept them together – and she did her utmost to keep it fresh and exciting. Her top drawers were stuffed with beautiful lingerie; she subscribed to *Erotic Review*; she even had a secret stash of sex toys.

But, yes, they had problems. Who didn't? 'Every marriage is a trade-off,' she had found herself saying to Angela.

'And haven't you done well out of the free-market economy?' Angela said with a soft laugh. 'Your gorgeous husband pampers you rotten.'

Her friends never tired of pointing out how well provided for she was, from her colour-coded walk-in wardrobe to the platinum credit cards in her Burberry purse. The children wanted for nothing and they went on luxurious, five-star family holidays. She knew she should be counting her blessings.

'It's true,' Harper said. 'He's not easy to live with, though.'

'Who is?' Angela trilled. 'Must go, darling. Got a matinee today.'

Harper put the phone down thoughtfully. Did it matter that her marriage wasn't entirely happy? She had all the trappings of a contented life. There was none of the scrimping and saving that had characterised her Tyneside childhood, none of the painful choices and sacrifices. That was a relief in itself. But was it enough?

6

She decided not to mention the possibility of having an eye job to Betty or the girls. She wasn't thinking about it seriously, after all. She didn't tell them about her first consultation with Mr Golden, either, or how she had nearly walked out before she even saw him.

There was a huge, framed quote on his waiting room wall that really bothered her. It was so effing pretentious. *Love of beauty is taste. The creation of beauty is art.*

'Do us a favour!' she wanted to shout. 'This isn't about the creation of beauty. It's about sucking fat out of people's eye bags and sewing up the saggy bits.'

Mr Golden, when she saw him, had a tanned, polished shine to his face that reminded her of Aaron. She mentally renamed him 'Goldencheeks', and started to giggle.

'Delighted to meet you, Mrs Clarke,' he said, politely ignoring her laughter. 'How can I help?'

She stopped wanting to giggle. 'My husband says I look

old and tired,' she said flatly. 'He wants me to have an eye job. I'm not so sure, though.'

'Well, blepharoplasty can certainly make you look a lot more refreshed,' Goldencheeks said.

There it was again, she thought, that word, 'refreshed', that sherbety euphemism for 'younger' that Aaron had also used.

'But you need to want it too,' he went on, 'because it's not something to be done on a whim. It's a medical procedure . . .'

'An operation, you mean?'

He waved one of his smooth, manicured hands. 'If you like, yes, an operation – and during the relatively short recovery period afterwards, you will experience a wide spectrum of feelings. First you will hate me. Then you will want to kill me. Slowly you will start to forgive me. And finally you will adore me. So perhaps you can see why I need your fully informed consent, rather than your husband's.'

'So that I don't sue you?'

'Not in the least, that's not what I meant, but . . .' He looked nonplussed.

'You're not suggesting I'd fall in love with you and start stalking you?'

'Of course not,' he said.

Ha, she thought, glad to have ruffled his feathers. 'Well, I'm glad that's clear. So how will it change me? How will I look?'

'Not very different,' he said, visibly relieved to be back

blepharoplastry
euphemism

on familiar ground. 'My patients often say that somehow they feel more vibrant, like they've got their sparkle back.' He leaned back in his chair. 'I've done work on several actresses,' he added casually, 'and one thing I will say is that the camera loves what I do for them.'

She shifted in her seat. 'And you're saying . . .'

He smiled with his lips closed. Smarmily. 'Well, if I may be so bold,' he began. 'I mean, if you were considering a return to our screens, this would give you a terrific boost.'

She wasn't surprised that he knew who she was. Most people of a certain age did. She wished they would forget, though. She was a different person now, a million miles from the ambitious young actress who had changed her name from Harper Walters to Harper Allen to ensure that she got top billing in an alphabetical list of credits. She no longer lay in bed dreaming about winning awards and appearing on chat shows. She went to sleep worrying about her kids and the state of her marriage. Her priorities were different, and so was her perspective – but a lot of people didn't get that. They assumed she spent her days wishing she could have another bite of the cherry. Well, they were wrong.

'If you'll forgive me the indulgence of digressing,' Dr Golden went on, 'we never missed an episode of *Beauty Spot* in our house. I used to watch it with my children. What a brilliant comic creation Sandra was – and you played her superbly. We were all very upset when Sara de Clancy replaced you. She's a great actress – brilliant – but she wasn't a good Sandra. It was never the same after that.'

'It's kind of you to say so,' Harper said. An image of Sara de Clancy – weeping copiously while accepting her BAFTA lifetime achievement award two years previously – sprang into her mind. 'But I'm not going back to acting. I gave it up to be a wife and mother and it's a decision I've never regretted.'

'Ah,' he said, 'that's a pity – for us, if not for you. However, you didn't come here to discuss your acting career ... so, is there anything you'd like to know about the procedure?'

She flashed him a smile. 'No,' she said, picking up her Mulberry bag and coat. 'Thank you for your time, but I think you've just talked me out of it.'

7

She stopped off on her way home to pick up a photo of the girls at the framing shop. On the street outside, she bumped into Tiffany Bander, one of the mums at Georgie's school. 'Coffee?' Tiffany suggested. 'A hot black java Joe?'

Half an hour later, her super skinny latte had turned into a very welcome glass of Prosecco, soon to be followed by another. Even though they didn't have a lot in common beyond their daughters and a shared obsession with fitness fads, she and Tiffany always had a laugh, especially when there was a bottle of wine on the table.

'I can't believe I even contemplated it,' she said, beaming with relief. 'Did I say I hate needles?'

'Harps, I'll drop you the list of facial exercises my PT gave me,' Tiffany offered. She flattened her lips and stretched her mouth into a clownish downward curve. 'They work just as well as surgery.'

'Brilliant,' Harper said.

She arrived home an hour later, feeling nicely light-headed. There was no sign of Aaron, but she could hear the girls laughing in the TV room. She popped her head round the door.

'Look, Mum!' Georgie said, pointing at the television. 'They're showing reruns of *Beauty Spot* on Eat and Repeat. It's so weird seeing you on telly!'

Her heart flip-flopped in her chest. She hadn't seen an episode of *Beauty Spot* for twenty years or more, partly because copyright issues had got in the way of it being repeated. She glanced at the TV screen. There was her old friend Bill Milkley, camping it up as Tony, the sole male therapist at the eponymous Beauty Spot northern spa and salon, the focus of the series. When they weren't trying to sort out their convoluted love lives, Tony and his dippy female colleagues spent their days trimming, plucking and massaging their clients at Beauty Spot, with varying degrees of success – or failure.

Georgie squealed as Harper's character, Sandra, appeared on the screen, looking flustered. Sandra was a pathologically accident-prone buxom brunette, who had stolen the show with her unwitting sexual innuendoes and flair for jaw-dropping mishaps with hot wax. Her catch-phrase was, 'This won't hurt a bit . . .'

The camera closed in on her face as she said, 'Can you take over my client in Room Three, Tony? He's behaving like a great big baby!'

As the studio audience laughter rang out, Harper stared

at her old self, her young self, her beautiful self of twenty-four years ago, back when her name was Harper Allen. Not a line, not a wrinkle, not a crevice, she thought, swallowing awkwardly, her mouth suddenly dry. She looked exuberant in a way that she had forgotten she could look. Her complexion had a long-lost glow and freshness.

Her longing, in that moment, to be young again, felt positively painful. I want my youth back! her mind screeched. Where did it go?

'Mum looks like you, Tay,' Georgie said. She turned to Harper. 'You could be sisters.'

Harper forced a smile. 'I was twenty-nine, but I suppose I looked younger.'

'Had you met Dad then?' Taylor asked.

She looked back at the screen, where Sandra was struggling to put on a pair of latex hygiene gloves. 'I'm not sure. I think I met him a couple of episodes after this.'

In fact, she could remember it quite clearly, like a trauma. And in a way, that's what love at first sight was, wasn't it? Love's traumatic accident.

Crevice
exuberant

8

September 1989

Still exhilarated after recording an episode called 'All It Takes Is A Tiny Prick' in front of a live studio audience, the cast of *Beauty Spot* made their way to a meet-and-greet with several of the show's sponsors and their guests, which would kick off with a question and answer session.

Harper wasn't taking it particularly seriously. The live show had gone well and she'd already had a glass of Chardonnay by the time she took her seat on the raised platform reserved for the cast in the small conference hall at the studios. The stage was spotlit, so her view of the crowd was limited. Fine by me, she thought, peeping at her watch. Steve, their producer, had promised that he wouldn't allow more than twenty minutes of questions. With any luck, she would be in a taxi within an hour, heading back to her flat for a cup of tea in front of the telly.

A few minutes later, Steve asked for quiet. 'I'm sure I

don't need to introduce the actors sitting here this evening,' he told the audience. Peering out into the shadows, Harper estimated that there were around fifty people gathered around. 'They are, after all, the cast of the UK's most successful situation comedy,' he went on.

She drifted off as he listed the stats that would remind the sponsors of how privileged they were to associate their brands with *Beauty Spot*. Fifteen million viewers, a large chunk of them ABCs, audiences around the world ... It wasn't that she didn't feel happy and grateful for its success, but she'd never had a head for figures and, anyway, it was just a silly TV sitcom.

The questions began. Bill was asked what it felt like to be the only man in the principal cast. 'Heavenly!' he said. 'They've given me free rein of their dressing rooms. Is there a man, gay or straight, who wouldn't want to exchange places with me?'

Everybody laughed. The ice was broken and the Q&A was up and running. But, to Harper's embarrassment, the majority of the questions that followed were directed at her. Did she have any idea how famous she would become when she was first cast as Sandra? How much had her life changed? Did she enjoy the attention? Did she miss the theatre? Did she feel she'd sold out? Did she have plans to do more television?

It got so bad that she started to bat the questions over to the others. 'I'm obviously thrilled that the series has done so well,' she said. 'I felt sure it was a great script when I first read it, but you never know how something will be received until it actually goes out.' She turned to the actress sitting on her right. 'I think you had more of an idea, didn't you, Patrina? It was my first TV job, but you have so much more experience of this world . . . ' And Patrina took up the baton from there.

When she was asked about overnight success, she brought in the youngest cast member, Sharon. Questions about the theatre were deflected to Bill, who had squeezed in a successful West End revival between series one and two of *Beauty Spot*. And in answer to the one question she couldn't escape, Was she single? she replied, 'I've got a cat. Does that count?'

'Right, folks, we're going to start winding things up now,' Steve said, towards the end of the session. 'There's just time for a couple more questions.' He nodded at someone in the crowd. 'Yes, go ahead.'

'I'd like to ask Ms Allen how she deals with being the sexiest woman on television?'

Harper groaned inwardly. What kind of a stupid question was that? She couldn't see who had asked it, but it was a male voice and she wished he'd just drop dead.

'I don't know how to answer that,' she said with a coy smile. 'I think you'd better ask Joanna Lumley.'

'No, but really,' the questioner said. 'How does it feel to be lusted after by millions of men all over the country?'

She looked at Steve for guidance. He shrugged. 'That sounds like a vast exaggeration,' she said, laughing softly. 'Anyway, it's Sandra that people like, not me – because she's a very lovable character. If that comes across, then I feel I'm doing my job well, so thank you for the compliment.'

Steve looked at his watch. 'Time for one more question,' he said.

The same questioner jumped in before anyone else could speak. 'Ms Allen, what are you doing later?'

Who was this idiot? She put her hands up to her eyes to shield them from the light, so that she could see him. 'Who's asking?' she said, jokingly.

'I am,' said a man standing off to the side.

He wasn't what she was expecting. In one glance, she took in his wavy black hair, the chiselled nose and glinting eyes, the well-cut suit that accentuated his lean figure, the tanned complexion. He looked back at her with an amused expression, as if he couldn't care less what her answer was, and yet was certain that she would say yes.

'Um, going out to dinner with you?' she said.

'At last,' he replied, showing his white, even teeth as he smiled. 'A direct answer.'

9

January 2013

'I'm thinking of having a little bit of cosmetic surgery,' she told Taylor at breakfast.

Taylor frowned. 'What for?' she asked.

'For myself, of course – and your father suggested it, and—'

'So you're doing it to impress Dad,' Taylor said, folding her arms across her chest. 'What's the fucking point? You're already married.'

Harper couldn't help smiling at her naivety. It would be decades before Taylor had any sense of what a struggle it could be to sustain a long-term relationship, if she ever did. 'I said I'm *thinking* about it. I haven't decided yet. Your dad's keen on me doing it and I want to stay looking good for him . . .'

'Jeez, can't he accept that you're old?'

'Actually, fifty-three is not old, although it may seem it to you,' Harper snapped. 'Anyway, age is just a number,' she added, although she wasn't sure she believed it right at that moment.

Taylor sat back in her chair and smiled. 'My point exactly. Age is just a number. So why would you bother to have surgery to make you look younger?'

Harper fought the urge to slap Taylor's smug face and shout, 'You try getting old – it's harder than you think!'

Instead, she took a long silent breath. 'It's not really about trying to look younger – it's about enhancement. It's really just a step up from make-up.'

Taylor shook her head. 'Yeah, right. Tell me how having your face cut open just to please a man is "a step up from make-up"? Come on, Mum, it would be a pathetic show of insecurity, and it would set a really bad example to me and Georgie. Don't do it.'

'Well, that's told me,' Harper said with a brittle laugh, marvelling at her daughter's egocentricity. And yet Taylor had a point – she shouldn't do it just because Aaron wanted her to.

'Anyway, what difference is it going to make to your life – or your marriage to Dad – to have a few less wrinkles? You're old already. Get over it.'

'How nicely you put it,' Harper said. 'Have you ever thought about applying to the diplomatic service?'

Georgie rushed into the kitchen, half-dressed, and poured out a bowl of chocolate cereal hoops. 'What are you two talking about?' she asked.

'Mum's going to have a facelift,' Taylor said.

'Not a facelift, an eyelift,' Harper corrected her. 'And

I'm only thinking about it, darling. It's not a done deal.'

Georgie sat down at the kitchen table, her cheeks already bulging with cereal. She looked like a chubby little hamster. Harper wanted to reach out and stroke her.

'If it would make you feel better about yourself, you should do it,' Georgie said. 'Just make sure you get a good surgeon.'

Tears pricked Harper's eyes. What a gem her youngest daughter was.

Taylor stood up abruptly. 'Mum, I'm telling you, if you go through with it I will never, ever speak to you again,' she said, and she stomped out of the kitchen.

10

Ten days later

Aaron looked dumbstruck when he came to pick her up from Dr Golden's clinic. Well, who wouldn't be shocked to find that overnight his wife had been replaced by the bastard child of Mr Potato Head and Mrs Sausage Face? she thought. Yet for a man so skilled at disguising what he was thinking, she felt he could have made a better job of not reacting.

'Jesus,' he muttered, wincing. Not, 'Poor darling, how are you feeling?' Just 'Jesus.' Wince.

Although she was wearing sunglasses and had a scarf wrapped round her head, he hurried her into the Mercedes as if he was worried someone would recognise them. During the first ten minutes of their journey home, the air inside the car silently filled up with everything that had ever gone unspoken in their marriage.

It was like sitting in a pressure cooker. Harper wanted to shout, 'You made me do this and I hate you for it!'

But she said nothing. She was desperately hoping for some reassurance. She mentally listed some of the things he could have said to make her feel better. Why couldn't he reach out to her? She longed to hear him say something like, 'I expect you're feeling low and that's completely normal, darling. Don't worry, you'll be right as rain in a few days, and more beautiful than ever.'

He did eventually break the silence. 'Well, that was money well spent,' he said sarcastically.

She knew they were thinking the same thing. Her face looked butchered. 'The doctor said it went fine,' she assured him.

'I hate to think what you'd look like if it had gone wrong,' he replied.

Why did I agree to this? she thought, as they turned into the drive of their house. What the hell was I thinking?

Aaron saw her inside the house. 'I'm not staying,' he said, looking at his watch. 'I've got a business meeting in London. I'll be gone a couple of days.'

'What?' she said, panic rising. 'But the girls ...' She dreaded seeing Taylor, who was away at a sales conference in Manchester and didn't know she'd gone through with it. She hadn't dared tell her.

'Betty's here. She'll see to everything. Don't leave the house.'

'No!' she cried out, suddenly feeling cornered. 'Why can't you just drive me to Chesterton Manor? Who cares if anyone recognises me? I'm not a star any more, as you're constantly reminding me. It won't even make the news, and I can recover in peace there.'

'We've been through this,' he said, his face screwed up with impatience. 'You'll be papped, I'm telling you. You'll be called old and desperate. I don't want you to go through that, darling. I want to protect you from that.'

'By driving off to London?'

He looked at his watch again. 'Forgive me,' he said with a rueful half-smile. 'I can't be late. The deal on the table is a life-changer.'

'Oh, fuck off, then,' she shouted, turning her back on him and marching upstairs. From her bedroom window she watched him speed off in his Mercedes, spraying gravel in his rush to get away from her.

She snoozed fitfully in bed for a couple of hours, and then sat on the sofa downstairs checking her face in the mirror every fifteen seconds while Betty hoovered. She felt lower than she had ever felt before. The reflection staring back at her was grisly. Her marriage was a bloody wreck – and you could see it in her swollen, bruised and mutilated face.

Betty's offer of a cup of tea, half an hour later, couldn't have been more welcome. Her company never failed to be uplifting, somehow. What's more, if anyone understood why Harper was sitting around the house with a face like Rocky Balboa on fight night, it was Betty.

'Appalled isn't the word,' she said through half-closed lips, recounting the moment Aaron had come to collect her from the clinic. She took a tentative sip from her mug and instantly felt better. Her sense of humour was returning. She was still beaten, bruised and tender, but now she felt more like a battered ventriloquist than a battered wife. 'He was horrified. You should have seen his face! It was like a bad audition for a walk-on part in a slasher movie.' She attempted to grimace in mock terror.

Betty's eyes twinkled with amusement. 'I expect he was just concerned for you, dear,' she said. 'It's upsetting to see you like this.'

Harper raised her fists into a boxing pose. 'There ain't gonna be no rematch,' she said gruffly. 'I'm done with boxing.'

Betty laughed.

'Honestly, what did he expect?' Harper said. 'I had the weirdest feeling that he thought he was going to waltz in and find me lying in my bed wearing a lace negligee, suddenly looking twenty years younger. Goodbye, Ena Sharples, hello, Eva Longoria! I bet he hadn't given a thought to what this operation involved.'

'Although he doesn't strike me as someone who believes in miracles,' Betty observed.

'It was like the worst blind date you can imagine,' Harper went on, 'where the guy comes in full of hope and desire, only to find he's been matched with the cackling crone of Congleton!'

'The important thing is that you'll be as good as new in no time,' Betty said. 'Before you know it, all of this will be forgotten.'

'I really hope you're right,' Harper said.

The house phone rang. 'Shall I get it?' Betty asked.

'Can you say I'm tied up and take a message? Do you mind?'

Betty picked up the phone, smiled without speaking, and put it down again. 'Just one of those nuisance calls,' she said. 'But it was nice music, all the same.'

'Oh yes?'

'That Christmas song by Johnny Mathis. Although it seems wrong to be playing it in January.'

Harper's skin prickled. First Marc Bolan, now this. It couldn't be a coincidence, could it? Yet why would Mike be sending her cryptic messages after decades of silence? She shivered. Talk about a blast from the past. Why would he pick this particular moment to rattle her cage?

The clock in the kitchen chimed softly, four times. Taking a final sip of tea, she stood up. She had more important things to think about. Georgie would be on her way back from school and she needed to steel herself for her youngest daughter's arrival.

As Betty set off to do more hoovering, she caught sight of her reflection in the shine of the kettle on the kitchen worktop. Its concave mirror intensified the ugliness of her already distorted face, making her look like an ogre, a monster, a misshapen beast lumbering away from a bloody fight.

Dr Golden was right, she thought. She hated him. If he had walked into the kitchen right then, she would have knocked him senseless and eaten him raw – and it would be nobody's fault but his own.

She heard a key in the front door and stiffened. Here goes, she thought.

Don't cry, she told herself. Be strong. The last thing she wanted was to show Georgie how fragile she was feeling.

11

But it wasn't Georgie at the door. Instead she heard Taylor's voice, speaking on the phone to one of her colleagues at LED Advertising. '... yeah, the conference opened up some really interesting angles. I'll fill you in when I see you in the office tomorrow.'

Harper waited, listening nervously. She felt like a lamb to the slaughter. Already half slaughtered.

She heard Taylor hanging up her coat. Her bag dropped to the floor with a thud. 'Oh, hi, Betty,' she said offhandedly.

Harper couldn't quite make out what Betty started saying, but she heard Taylor's screeching response loud and clear.

'No waaaay!' The lounge door burst open and Taylor came striding in, her long blonde hair flying out behind her. 'I can't believe you fucking went through with it, Mum!' she yelled. 'I told you not to! Didn't I?'

'Darling . . . ' Harper began to plead.

Their eyes met. Taylor stood stock-still, as if she had been slapped. Then she screamed.

'It's not as bad as it looks, darling,' Harper said quickly. 'The doctor says it will heal within a few days and I'll be fine.'

'Oh my God, what have you *done?*' Taylor said, her voice dropping from a shout to a whisper. 'Your face, Mum, how could you? It's awful, you look like you've been beaten up. Are you even sure it will get better?'

She stared and stared, her hand cupped over her mouth, her eyes dark with repugnance. Harper returned her gaze, feeling frightened, guilty and hurt. 'Honestly, it looks far worse than it is. The doctor says—'

'Doctor!' Taylor shrieked. 'He calls himself a doctor? Doctors heal people!'

'Surgeon, then,' Harper said. Taylor looked as though she were going to shout something else. 'OK, cosmetic surgeon.'

Taylor slapped her hand to her forehead. 'I can't believe it. This is so pathetic. What the fuck are you trying to prove? Why can't you accept that you will never be young again? You will never be a TV star again. Why couldn't you just grow old gracefully, like other people's mothers?'

Tears of resentment stung Harper's eyes. 'We've been through this. It was your father's idea. You know what he's like. He wanted me to do it. He said I was looking old and tired.'

'You went along with it, just because a *man* told you to? So if Dad asked you to jump off a cliff, would you do that too?'

'No, but it's fast becoming a more attractive option than sitting here listening to you,' Harper retorted. 'Oh darling, can't you show a bit of sympathy?'

Taylor shook her head. 'There's no way you're getting any sympathy from me! You've only got yourself to blame,' she sneered. 'You should be ashamed of yourself. You disgust me.' She flounced out of the room, slamming the door.

Harper hung her head. Tears dropped from her eyes onto her lap, where they were quickly absorbed into the fabric of her fringed Marni skirt, leaving nothing but damp specks.

She heard another key in the front door. Georgie, she thought, straightening up. Another daughter, another onslaught – although at least Georgie knew what she was coming home to.

Making a supreme effort to hide her gasp of shock at the sight of her mother, Georgie rushed over to Harper and threw her arms around her. 'Oh, Mum, you poor, poor thing!' she cried, hugging her tightly. 'Don't worry, you'll get better soon. I read up about it online, during my lunch break. You'll look terrible at first, but it's a quick recovery. You'll be fine – better than ever, in fact!'

'Thank you, sweetie,' Harper said, clinging gratefully to her daughter.

At last, she thought. The one member of my family who actually cares about me.

She went to bed early, after forcing down a few mouthfuls of Betty's warming beef stew in the kitchen, followed by two strong painkillers. As she pulled back the white satin coverlet and slipped between soft Egyptian cotton sheets, she could hear the girls laughing at something on the telly downstairs. Taylor had eventually apologised for her angry outburst, prompted by Georgie, perhaps, or her own sense of decency. Taylor wasn't a bad girl, Harper thought. She just had strong opinions – and wasn't afraid of voicing them. She fancied herself as a bit of a feminist, which was a good thing, after all. It showed a sense of self-worth, something her mother could surely take some credit for.

She tenderly touched her swollen face, hoping it would be starting to heal in the morning. Yes, she thought, she hated Dr Goldencheeks, and right at this moment she didn't feel too kindly towards Aaron either. But she loved her daughters full to bursting, and always would. So she was glad she had given up her career – and everything that went with it – to be a mum. She had no regrets.

As her sore, swollen head sank into the Norwegian goose-down pillow beneath it, peals of laughter rang out from the TV room again, and she smiled. She had made her bed, she thought ruefully, and now she was lying in it. Thank the heavens it was so damn luxurious.

The phone rang. Go away, whoever you are, she thought, as she drifted into sleep.

A few moments later, her mobile phone bleeped. She picked it up drowsily and looked at the message. Someone had sent her a photo from an unknown number. A photo of Aaron kissing a woman outside the Savoy Hotel.

She magnified the image, just to be sure.

Yes, it was definitely Angela. Kissing. Her. Husband.

12

At one a.m. she was still staring at her phone, her eyes throbbing, trying to breathe her way out of a panic attack. How *could* he? After years of putting up with his jealous fits and rages – after years of being accused of doing everything under the sun with every male in the known universe – Aaron was the one being unfaithful? It couldn't be true. It was too absurd. Yet here was the evidence, right before her swollen, puffy eyes.

And with Angela? That seemed equally ridiculous. Aaron didn't even really like Angela, did he? It had always seemed to Harper that he just about tolerated her, for Harper's sake. But maybe that was part of the deceit. Maybe he had been pretending all along.

As for Angela, she had never made a secret of the fact that she fancied Aaron, but perhaps that was her way of being devious. She was committing her crime in plain view, hoodwinking everybody in the process.

Harper shook her head in disbelief. How *could* she?

A wave of anger rose up inside her and she looked around for something to throw at the wall. No, don't, she thought. It would be a disaster to wake up the girls, especially as this wasn't something she could discuss with either of them. Instead she took a pillow from Aaron's side of the bed and began to pummel it. When she was finished – when she had smashed his imaginary head to a pulp and broken every bone in his body, and then done the same to Angela – she picked it up and hurled it into the corner of the room, where it flopped lifelessly onto the floor.

Exhausted, she tried to lie down and rest, but there were too many questions buzzing in her head. When had the photo been taken? Tonight? She couldn't escape the thought that Aaron and Angela were quite possibly having sex at that very moment, having moved from a kiss outside the hotel to a bedroom inside it. The idea of their lips meeting – worse, their hips meeting – made her shudder to her core. She had already thrown up Betty's stew at the thought of it. She had also rung the Savoy to find out if they had checked in together, but they were either registered under false names or not there at all. Maybe they'd gone to the Ritz instead, she thought bitterly.

The bastard. She was tempted to send the photo to him, accompanied by a lone question mark in the text box. But what if he didn't reply? What if he was too busy having sex? Even if he wasn't, he usually switched his phone to silent mode when he went to sleep, so there was little point in trying to contact him. In the meantime, she would go mad. During the silent hours of the night, her imagination would obsessively generate images of them making love until her brain overloaded and exploded. Somehow she had to stop that happening. She needed to shut down her mind and get some sleep.

She felt a twinge of pain between her eyes. Dr Golden had told her to rest as much as she could in the days following the operation. 'Sleep aids recovery,' he'd said with one of his smug smiles. 'It heals the cells.'

Really? she'd thought. Tell me something else I don't know, Buster. Like how you get a healing night's sleep when you've just seen a photo of your husband kissing your best friend?

The answer was simple. You didn't.

God knew what it was doing to her bruised and bloodied face to be sitting up in bed all night in a stunned stupor, peering at the tiny square of light on her smartphone. Maybe it meant that she would never heal. She would be stuck like this, disfigured by scars and sadness, forever blighted by the pain that they had inflicted, wearing her misery for all to see. It sounded dramatic, but only the other day she had been reading about a group of doctors who thought that heartbreak could actually do physical damage – as bad as a broken leg, or worse. Mental anguish was not to be underestimated, they said. Since she was aching all over, inside and out – micro cell to nerve ending, heart and mind – she could well believe it.

She went back to staring at the photo. It had to be a

paparazzi shot, she decided, taken with a long lens, from across the road. And yet that didn't explain why it had been sent to her, unless it was a tip-off from one of the tabloids, which seemed unlikely. Was it blackmail, or a sting of some kind – a provocative gesture that would set in motion a chain of events that she couldn't foresee? It must have been sent for a reason.

She wished she were a detective in the operations room of a US police station, where she could blow it up on a huge screen and analyse it with her colleagues, searching for tiny, crucial clues. Perhaps, then, she would be able to get some detachment when she looked at it. Instead of feeling like she was plunging into a dark, infinite hole. She would discuss it with her work buddies calmly and forensically, listing the questions that needed to be answered while taking thoughtful sips from an enormous styrofoam coffee cup. Instead of sitting in bed taking deep, panicky breaths, as she tried to cope with the idea that Aaron and Angela might be having an affair.

Because this wasn't just a brush of the lips. No, what the camera had captured was what she and her friends at school had known as 'a proper French kiss', involving open mouths and tongues. It was something that only lovers did. It was the ultimate expression of intimacy. Oh God.

She got out of bed and slipped quietly down to the kitchen, where there was an open bottle of Sauvignon in the fridge. Dr Golden had expressly told her not to drink. 'Alcohol slows recovery,' he'd said. There was also a notice on the box of painkillers that he had prescribed, warning you *on no account* to mix them with alcoholic beverage. So she was thankful that she didn't have to open a new bottle. This way she could pretend that she was only having a taster.

Just a tipple. Because it was there. She downed half a glass in two gulps and poured another to take upstairs with her.

She lost her balance a couple of times on the way back to her bedroom. Good, she thought. It was a relief to be free of the heightened sense of awareness that had taken over her mind since she had first seen the photo. She didn't want to be awake and alert any more. She needed a break from the hurt and anger. Otherwise, she would combust.

Back in bed, she took another swig of wine and realised that she had stopped liking Angela years before, but never done anything about it. Why? Because you didn't actively end friendships as you did relationships, did you? So she had been waiting – or, at least, secretly hoping – for Angela to casually drift out of her life and not come back. Only, Angela hadn't gone anywhere.

Of course, she could have done the drifting herself. She could have stopped answering her calls and made excuses for why she was unable to meet up, until Angela finally got the hint. And yet she hadn't. It wasn't out of loyalty, either, even though they had known each other for thirty-five years. It was something else.

Once upon a time they had been great friends. They had clicked instantly when they'd met at drama school, two northerners amid a sea of people who took 'barths' instead of 'baths' and went out 'darncing'. They were soon sharing a flat together and spending their evenings drinking cheap wine and giggling about the prominent bulge in Darren Tolliver's stretchy trousers.

Back in those days she had told Angela everything, even her deepest, darkest secret. Was that why she had stuck by her, even though the friendship had become so one-sided? She had spent countless hours listening to Angela drone on about her problems, without once asking Harper how she was. Or was it because, very occasionally, they still had a really good giggle at life? She wasn't sure.

And now what?

She knew that she should warn Aaron and Angela about the photo, so that they could get their stories ready if it appeared in the press. Not that Angela was a big star or anything, but it would definitely be news if she were having an affair with Harper Allen's husband – the man Harper had given up acting for.

On the other hand, they deserved to be hounded. She wanted them to suffer. But she had to consider the impact it would have on the family, particularly on Georgie. It would be awful to see your father outed for infidelity and your mother humiliated in public. How would Georgie face her friends at school afterwards? She couldn't bear the idea of her youngest daughter being hurt in that way.

And yet . . .

She could feel the cocktail of wine and painkillers smoothing out the wrinkles in her thoughts as she began to slide towards unconsciousness. What did any of it matter? If it was the truth, why not let it out?

She would confront Aaron in the morning, she decided. She would send him the photo and wait for his response. Meanwhile, Angela could go to hell in a handcart. Once upon a time they had been closer than sisters, but somewhere along the line everything had changed.

—

13

September 1989

No one noticed Harper slip into Calypso's, her local wine bar just off the high street, wearing a shiny black mac, jeans and red court shoes. Angela was already sitting at their regular table in the corner, where Harper could pass a whole evening without being recognised if she sat facing the wall. It was a boring view, but perfect for a tête-à-tête with Angela. No one would bother them.

The head waiter's face lit up at the sight of her. 'Miss Allen! What a delight!' he declared in a loud whisper. With a sweeping movement he took her coat and bustled her across the room.

An enticing bottle of white wine was chilling in a silver bucket next to their table. Such a luxury, she thought. Although she'd been drinking it for most of her adult life, wine still spelt sophistication to her, perhaps because it had been almost entirely absent from her life as she was growing up. Her father drank only stout and ale, her mother

bustled

liked a spot of sweet sherry and her granddad's tipple was an elderflower concoction that he brewed in his allotment shed. One memorable Christmas when she was a teen, a cousin had turned up with a 'posh' bottle of Cinzano Bianco and hadn't been allowed to hear the last of it. To her knowledge, Chardonnay had never even darkened the door.

Meanwhile, Angela was already halfway through her first glass of it. She was looking predictably immaculate, her sharp dark bob as neat as ever, her make-up subtly perfect. Her oval face wore its usual expression of utter composure, which was often mistaken for haughtiness – and actually Angela could be a little bit superior, truth be told. But that was all part of her charm, in Harper's eyes.

'Sorry I'm late,' she said. 'I was on the phone to my agent.'

'Not to worry.' Angela lit up an extra-long menthol cigarette, took a deep drag and blew the smoke towards the ceiling. 'So what's the goss, then? You said you had something to tell me.' She held up her hand, as if to silence her. 'Let me guess. The phone call's the clue. Could it be that you've got the starring role in another cheesy sitcom?'

Ignoring the 'cheesy' jibe, Harper shook her head and beamed at her best friend, willing her to guess the momentous news she was about to impart.

Angela smiled back at her. 'Hmm, don't you look like the cat that got the cream? So, is it work? More TV?'

'I've met someone!' she burst out.

'Ah,' said Angela. 'And?'

She didn't blame her friend for her lack of enthusiasm. She had a history of passionate crushes that fizzled to nothing – and they had once drawn up a list of her exes and divided them into 'bad' and 'worse'. But this time was different, she thought – whether or not Angela believed her.

'He's really special,' she said. 'I think he might be … you know, The One. We're going to Paris on Friday.' The waiter appeared and poured her a glass of wine, which she eagerly raised to her lips. 'He's just so gorgeous.'

'OK,' Angela said doubtfully.

'Something tells me this could be *it*.'

'So he's great in bed, I presume.'

Harper's eyes sparkled. 'I've no idea! We've been on two dates and both times he's dropped me back at my flat, said goodbye with a smoochy kiss and left. It's weird, actually—'

'Didn't you ask him in?'

'I would have, but he didn't give me the chance!'

'You must *insist* next time,' Angela joked.

Harper giggled. 'His kisses – sweet Jesus, Angela! They're what my grandma would have called "knee tremblers". I can't wait for the sex, but on the other hand I can, because if this really is *it*, then what's the harm in drawing it out a bit?'

'True,' Angela agreed. 'As long as it's not a case of "All mouth and nothing in the trouser department".'

Harper laughed. 'Fingers crossed!'

'It wouldn't be the first time, let's face it,' Angela said with a smirk.

They locked eyes. 'Piers Longwood!' they said in unison, recalling a fellow student at drama school they had both had 'encounters' with.

'Such an unfortunate surname,' Angela said. 'Total misrepresentation of the goods.'

Harper shook her head. 'Poor thing, I couldn't get out of his flat fast enough! He was such a good kisser, too.'

Angela gave her a knowing look. 'My point exactly.' They chinked glasses happily. 'So, tell me more about this paragon of a man so that I can decide whether I want to steal him or not.'

Harper gasped. 'Hands off! You're married,' she shrieked. 'But strictly for curiosity's sake, his name is Aaron, and . . . what do you want to know?'

'Whatever you want to tell me, darling. How did you meet?'

She told her about the Q&A at the studios. 'He's quite a forceful personality, I suppose – and very confident.'

'So that makes two of you,' Angela said.

'But he's also very caring. He thinks everything through in advance – what time to pick me up, where to go for dinner and which bar is best for a late night drink. It feels kind of nice to let someone else make the decisions, for once.'

'You don't have to trouble your pretty little head about a thing?'

'It's not like that – but I'm not sure I would care if it was. My life is so mad these days that I probably need a firm hand. Anyway, this feels like love and I'm happy to go along with whatever he wants. Ange, his eyes have this glittering magnetic quality ... he's just so ... *compelling*.'

Angela looked amused. 'He's beginning to sound like a hero from a romantic novel. You'll be telling me he's got a square jaw and a muscular torso next.'

'You're right!' Harper said excitedly. 'He *is* like a hero. He's my knight in shining armour, come to save me.'

'And since when did you need saving, darling?' Angela drawled.

'Since always. My love life is a complete disaster, as you know.'

Angela didn't dispute this. 'So, where's he from? What does he do?' she asked.

'He's a businessman. Brought up in Essex. Now lives in London.'

Angela's eyebrows shot up. 'A businessman from Essex?'

'I know,' she said apologetically. 'But what can I do?' She shrugged. 'You can't help who you fall in love with.'

Angela topped both their glasses up. 'It's only been a couple of dates. You might still meet a nice creative lad from Oop North.'

'Yes, but it's time for me to settle down – and I think he's ready too,' Harper said intently. 'I'm twenty-nine, my clock is ticking. I want a husband and babies.'

'So you've always said. Still, it's not a reason to rush into things.'

'That's all very well for you to say. You've been married to James for ages. You can have a baby any time you want!

But I . . . well, you know why I'm so desperate . . . ' Her voice trailed off as memories flooded into her head.

'Because of what happened when you were at school, you mean?'

Harper nodded. Every time she thought about it, the images were the same, like a trailer for a feature film, on repeat – the first illicit meetings with her English teacher; the morning sickness a few weeks later; her mother's suspicions and horrified reaction; that bleak day at the abortion clinic. Actually, it was more like a depressing public information film than a teen movie, she thought.

She sighed. 'I'm not saying I shouldn't have done it, because the situation was impossible and I was only sixteen, far too young to even think about having a child. Anyway, he was married and I was just a schoolgirl. So it was the right thing, but, I don't know . . . ' She stared off into space. 'I've just always wanted to put it behind me, once and for all, by doing it again, in the right situation, properly. Can you understand that?'

Angela, who wasn't big on sympathy, gamely reached across the table and took her hand. 'Of course I can – and maybe this new man is Mr Right, you never know. But if he isn't, someone else is bound to come along soon. These things just happen.' She quickly withdrew her hand and looked in the direction of the bar. 'Let's order another bottle, shall we? I've got some news of my own.'

'Oh, yes?' Harper said, suddenly eager to change the subject. Angela was her only London friend who knew about the mess she'd got into all those years ago. She knew she could trust her never to tell anyone, but somehow talking about it, even mentioning it, made her feel exposed and vulnerable.

'I got the part!' Angela said.

'Which part?'

'Hedda!'

Harper's jaw dropped open. 'Hedda Gabler?'

'Yup,' said Angela, lighting another extra-long cigarette.

Harper's heart lurched just a little bit. Angela had been so snobby about her success in *Beauty Spot*, but she hadn't minded very much because Angela was still <u>schlepping</u> around playing small parts in regional plays. She was still putting in the hard graft that Harper had eventually found dispiriting in the years after drama school, so it was understandable that there had been a touch of sour grapes in her attitude to *Beauty Spot*. But playing Hedda Gabler was a game-changer. It was the part every serious actress longed for, even in a provincial production.

'Where?' she asked.

'The Bernhardt Studios.'

Harper gasped. 'The West End!'

'Yup.'

The waiter arrived to take their order. 'Champagne!' Harper said before Angela could get a word in. 'My friend here has got the part most actresses would kill for!' she explained. 'And I'm in love,' she added. 'So we've both got a reason to celebrate.'

14

January 2013

Through half-closed, swollen eyes, she watched Georgie creep into the bedroom carrying a breakfast tray on which teetered a tall mug of tea and a plate of toast and jam.

'Hi, Mum,' Georgie whispered. 'Don't worry about getting up. I'm fine having breakfast on my own. And try not to look in the mirror today. It says in all the threads online that people look their worst on the day after the operation – but by tomorrow you'll be starting to look like yourself again, only better.' She smiled tentatively.

Harper fought the urge to leap out of bed and hug her daughter tightly, because even the most level-headed person might be alarmed if their bloodied and bleary-eyed, swollen-headed beast of a mother suddenly sprang at them. Anyway, she didn't have the energy. 'Thank you, my darling. You're amazing,' was all she said, her voice still slurry with sleep.

'See you after school, Mum. Take it easy, spend the day

65

in bed.' Georgie walked out of the room, quietly shutting the door behind her.

Ignoring the tea and toast, Harper grabbed her phone and began to forward the photo to Aaron. Then she hesitated, uncertain of what to write underneath it. A lone question mark looked, well, kind of lonely and questioning, which wasn't the message she wanted to send. She wanted to pack a punch, to maximise the impact of the blow.

What the fuck? she wrote. That was better.

Wait, she thought, adding a few exclamation marks. She was about to press send when she hesitated again.

WHAT THE FUCK???!!!??? she wrote.

Much better.

Her phone rang three minutes later. 'Aaron,' she said coldly.

'Pussycat, what is going on?' he asked, sounding aggrieved. 'Please don't tell me you've got a private detective following me.'

He never failed to surprise her. Wasn't she the one who was supposed to be making the accusations? 'Are you having an affair with Angela?' she asked curtly.

He tutted angrily. 'Of course not,' he said. 'Would I be kissing her in full view of everybody outside the Savoy Hotel if I was?'

She gasped. 'So you admit you were kissing her?'

'You've just sent me the photo, Pussycat. I'm not going to deny it. But the shot must have been taken at a weird angle, because it wasn't how it looks. Our lips didn't even touch.'

'Don't lie to me, Aaron. I'm looking at the photograph right now! It's a full-on snog.'

'Don't be fucking stupid! I gave her a friendly hug and a peck on the cheek when I bumped into her outside the hotel entrance.'

'Really? That's not what it looks like to me!' She looked at her phone again. 'It's a proper clinch,' she said softly. 'You're holding her in your arms. I've never seen you do that to Angela. Ever.'

'It was all over in a second!' he said. 'She was in bits about James—'

'What do you mean?' she interrupted. 'She couldn't care less about James! She can't wait to get divorced.'

'Yes, but apparently he's got this younger bird, and she'd only just found out when I saw her.'

'So?'

'So she's worried he'll have kids – after all they've been through. Babe, you know what she's like. She said, "My fear is that she'll give him what I was never able to give."'

She stifled the urge to laugh, as she usually did when he imitated Angela's theatrical drawl. They had always found it funny the way Angela had slowly modified her accent until you could no longer hear the Durham.

She shook her head and tried to compose herself. 'Let me get this straight,' she said coolly. 'Angela was upset, so you *snogged* her – and you think that's perfectly—'

'It was the quickest way to get rid of her! She turned on the waterworks and said she felt unattractive – that no bloke would want an ugly old divorcee. This was all outside the hotel. It was embarrassing! I said of course they would want her, but then she cried even more and asked me to hold her because she was so cut up—'

'What did she say? "Hold me?"'

'Something like that . . .'

'And you took her in your arms? Because, for a minute there, you both thought you were in a scene out of *Brief Encounter* or *Dr Zhivago*? And then you kissed her, not because you wanted to, but to make her feel attractive and wanted again?'

'I gave her a quick peck because I felt sorry for her. Because she's your friend and I wanted to help her out. I did it for you, for your sake, even though I didn't want to. Because I love you.'

She frowned. Aaron didn't do compassion. He didn't feel sorry for people – he felt disdain for them – and he hated seeing a woman cry. So what was this all about? 'You're telling me that you stuck your tongue down my friend's throat because you love *me*?'

'Don't mention tongues again or I'll throw up,' he growled. 'For fuck's sake, I'd rather snog Betty.'

She couldn't help giggling silently at the thought of Aaron and Betty in a passionate clinch. Somehow he always managed to make her laugh, even in the direst circumstances. 'Were you going to tell me about it?'

'What is there to tell? I would have probably said I saw Angela and she was a fucking mess.'

She look again at the photo and tried to reframe it in her mind. It made sense that Angela would be devastated at the thought of James having children with another woman. Not because of James or the other woman, but because years of unexplained infertility and failed IVF attempts had understandably left her feeling sensitive. She probably did feel old and unloved right now – unloved and unattractive. But was that a reason to beg a snog off her best friend's husband? No, it wasn't. There was no excuse for it.

'So, why are you having me followed, hon?' he asked. 'That's the real question here. I've never even looked at another woman.'

It seemed an unfortunate turn of phrase in the light of what had just happened. 'I'm not having you followed,' she snapped. 'I was sent that photo anonymously last night. I don't know why. There was no text, nothing. Can you imagine how I felt when I saw it? You have no idea what I went through during the night!'

'You shouldn't have doubted me,' he said through gritted teeth. 'You know I wouldn't cheat on you. You're the only woman for me. Where's the trust?'

'Aaron, I was sent a photo of you kissing my friend!'

'Yeah, and who sent it? That's what I want to know.'

'Well, if it was a pap, then it's probably in today's newspaper,' she said with satisfaction.

He swore quietly. 'See what happens when you do someone a favour?' he said.

'Yes, terrible,' she agreed. 'Maybe you'd better think twice before you dole out your next mercy kiss, Mother Teresa.' The more she thought about it, the less believable the whole thing seemed. 'So, have you arranged to meet again?'

'Haven't you been listening? I couldn't give a toss if I never saw your friend Angela again. Like I said, I did it for you.'

Suddenly she felt very alone. 'When are you coming back, then?' she asked with a slight tremor in her voice.

She heard a click on the other end of the phone. 'I'm flying to Germany in a couple of hours, so I'd better shoot,' he said. 'I'll be back on Thursday.'

She felt like begging him to come straight home, but instead she said, 'I'll see you then, I suppose. Unless you've got somewhere else to go?'

'Of course I haven't, you daft cow,' he said. 'In the meantime, don't talk to the press. If anyone rings the house, say, "No comment," and hang up. Understood?'

'OK,' she said weakly.

Things had quickly returned to normal. The status quo had been restored. Aaron was issuing orders. She was agreeing to obey them. In a way it was reassuring, but in another way it made her want to scream. She had caught him out kissing Angela, but it hadn't made a jot of difference to anything.

15

On the fourth day after the operation, she began to look human again. It was too early to tell whether she was an improvement on her old self, but at least she was no longer shambling about the house with a head the size of a beach ball weeping pitifully into the sleeve of her Dior satin dressing gown. She had hardened over the last seventy-two hours, too, like a blobby lump of clay that had been sculpted and kiln blasted – although it wasn't her face that had toughened up, but her feelings.

After three days of fretting, she had come to the conclusion that Aaron wasn't telling her the truth about the clinch with Angela – at least, not the whole truth. It was also clear that she would never manage to extract it from him. He was too clever for her. He had a way of turning things around. The photo hadn't appeared in the papers, which might somehow have forced a confession in the ensuing media glare, so she was going to have to get it out of Angela, who was also clever, but not impossibly so, as Aaron was. It would mean seeing Angela face to face, and looking her in the eye, which she did not particularly relish. But it had to be done in person. It would be too easy for her to lie on the phone.

She was stretched out on her bed plotting how she would confront her, when Georgie popped her head around the door and said, 'Dad's back!'

Instinctively, she jumped off the bed and pulled the coverlet straight. Dashing over to her dressing table, she checked herself in the mirror, quickly primped her hair with the tips of her fingers and applied a subtle layer of lipstick. Her bruises were already half-covered by a thick slathering of foundation, in anticipation of his arrival.

She found him in the lounge, standing by the window, speaking on the phone. She could tell immediately from his tone of voice that it was a business call. Knowing better than to interrupt, even with a wave, she sat down on the sofa and waited. He had taken off his tie and loosened his shirt collar, which gave him a slightly scruffy, sexy, off-duty look.

Eventually, he ended the call. But he didn't come over to kiss her hello, presumably because she was still looking hideous. 'How are you feeling?' he asked.

'In need of a drink!' she said brightly, hoping he wouldn't question whether alcohol was a good idea.

'White?' He poured two glasses of Sancerre and handed one to her. She watched him inspect her face as he came closer. 'What's that shiny stuff on your skin?' he asked.

'You look like a waxwork model from the Chamber of Horrors.'

'That's nice!' she said, deciding not to admit that it was concealer. 'Actually, it's a post-operative moisturiser, to keep my skin pliant. How was your trip?'

He shifted from one foot to the other. 'Boring, but necessary.'

'Productive?'

He turned to look out of the window. 'Yes, in the long term,' he said, 'although I'm more interested in the short-term prospects.'

'Can't you have both? I mean, short term and long term?'

He looked pained. 'You see, that just shows how bleedin' ignorant you are.'

'Why? It must be possible, surely?'

'Do you have even the slightest idea of what you're talking about?' he asked.

She took a mouthful of wine, swallowed it in one gulp, and said, 'Actually, I do. I've got shares in a couple of companies that pay dividends in the short term and are also good long-term investments.'

Hark at me, she thought. Shares, dividends, invest-ments! I'm a woman of substance.

In fact, she didn't have a very clear idea of what Aaron did or how he earned his money, although she knew what to say when people asked her – 'He's the head of media management at Wallcro.' If they dug any deeper, she'd say, 'He builds relationships with media companies – you know, sponsorship, endorsements, that type of thing.' Hopefully, the questions would end there, because the nuts and bolts of his daily working life were mysterious to her, and she didn't pick up any clues when she listened in on his business conversations, either. Nothing much ever seemed to be said. She had to assume that one of his job skills was the ability to read between the lines.

'This is a different kind of business,' he said, with a dismissive wave of his hand.

'That sounds interesting. Bit shady, is it? Not quite legit?' she joked.

He didn't smile. 'Don't be stupid.'

'Well, I'm sure it's not totally above board, either,' she said defiantly. 'Look at football sponsorship.'

'Of course it's above board. Shut up now. You know I don't like talking about business when I'm at home.'

'Oh, and I suppose you were on the phone to your Auntie Deirdre just then, were you?'

He put down his wine glass. 'I was making money. For you to spend. Got a problem with that?'

'Hi, Daddy!' Taylor stood in the doorway, beaming.

His face lit up. 'Hello, gorgeous. You off out? Or are you going to spend a bit of time with your old dad, for once?'

The make-up on Taylor's eyelids sparkled as she fluttered them. She had a cosmetic shimmery sheen on her cheekbones too, not to mention her one exposed shoulder, which was poking out of her slashed pink top. Veritably dipped in glitter, Harper thought with amusement – and it suited her too. Everything suited you when you were young, even tacky glittery make-up and lopsided T-shirts with designer holes in them.

'My friend's picking me up in half an hour,' Taylor said. She wagged her finger at Aaron. 'Meanwhile, you're never at home. How are you, Daddy? I've missed you.'

'Come over here and give me a hug!' he said, holding out his arms to her.

Harper took a great big glug of wine as they cuddled and cooed. Only last week she'd been complaining to Betty about how excluded they made her feel. It wasn't deliberate – she just fell off their radar – and she wouldn't dream of resenting how close they were. But they didn't have to make her feel invisible. Right then, she could probably have taken off her clothes and danced a naked rumba without either of them noticing.

Georgie appeared. 'How did the play rehearsal go?' Harper asked.

'Great! Stella Bloxham's had to drop out because she's been selected for county gymnastics, so they've given me her role. It's a much bigger part!'

'Bigger meaning wider?' Aaron chipped in from across the room. 'Or just heavier?'

Harper frowned at him. Please don't go on about her weight! she thought.

Georgie laughed. 'It means more lines for me, Dad.'

He cupped his ear. 'More pies?'

'No, silly! You heard me.'

He looked his youngest daughter up and down. 'Just make sure the trapdoor's securely bolted, won't you, my little heffalump? We wouldn't want the earth to swallow you up halfway through your performance.'

Harper saw her chance to reroute the conversation. 'That happened to an actor in a play I did just after I left drama school! Luckily, he wasn't hurt, but we always suspected one of the stagehands of unlatching the trapdoor, because no one liked him. He was a theatrical old has-been who fancied himself as Laurence Olivier and treated us like a bunch of hams.'

'You probably were a bunch of hams,' Aaron said.

Taylor laughed. 'Cheeky!' she said, reaching out her arms to start tickling him.

'I bet Mum wasn't, even if the others were,' Georgie said, as Taylor and Aaron fell onto the sofa and began to play fight. 'She was great in *Beauty Spot*.'

Harper smiled. 'That came nearly ten years later. I'd done a long apprenticeship by then.'

'You've always said that people can either act or they can't,' Georgie argued, raising her voice to be heard over Taylor's shrieks as Aaron pinned her down.

Harper focused on Georgie and pretended not to notice the ruckus on the other side of the room. 'That's right, but you can learn a lot about technique through practice, especially if you trail around the country doing plays in regional theatres for as long as I did.'

'You must have loved acting to do it for so long.' As usual, Georgie was angling for stories about Harper's life as a struggling actor. She loved to hear about the missed cues, corpsing and backstage antics before she got her big break in TV.

'I honestly didn't know what else to do,' Harper said. 'I was a terrible secretary and an even worse waitress.' She took another sip from her glass. 'And I did love it. I lived and breathed it.'

Taylor jumped up from the sofa. 'So why did you give it up, Mum?' she asked.

Harper shot a glance at Aaron. 'You know why. Your father didn't want me to go on working once I had you,' she said.

'Really? How old-fashioned of you, Dad! And you just rolled over and gave up acting for him, Mum? If you loved it so much, you should have told him to fuck off.'

Harper didn't have to look at Taylor to see the sneer on her face. Out of the corner of her eye she could see her standing there, hands on hips, waiting for a response.

'I chose family life over acting,' she said. 'And I was in love. I didn't want him to leave me.'

Aaron rolled his eyes. 'I wouldn't have left you!' he protested. 'Look at me, the big, tough guy who forced your mother to give up her career. If you believe that, you'll believe anything.'

Harper stared at him. That was the thing about Aaron – he found it so easy to lie. She wanted to shout, 'You gave me an ultimatum!' But what was the point? She didn't want Taylor to know that she had bargained for her very existence.

She was sure Aaron remembered that night as well as she did. They had only known each other six weeks; everything was so fresh between them, so excitingly tentative, like an English holiday by the sea when the sun just keeps on shining, and you can't believe your luck, because it's never happened before. Well, not to you, anyway.

The ultimatum had come at the end of an anxious day, of hours spent waiting to be called on set while she fretted about how he would react to what she had to say to him. She hadn't the slightest idea what his response would be. She hadn't known what she was letting herself in for.

16

November 1989

Her nails were chewed down to the skin by the time he arrived to pick her up from the studios in his gleaming BMW. Her pulse began racing as soon as she saw him. Keep calm, she told herself. Don't blow it.

She took a deep pacifying breath in an effort to regain her composure, but the extra hit of oxygen set her heart pounding and she started to feel dizzy. Was she about to faint? Perhaps it would help if she did, she thought. A show of old-fashioned vulnerability might appeal to the gentleman in him.

She watched him as he walked through the green room towards her, all smiles for the cast, shaking hands with the director and slapping the backs of the executive producers. He worked for the show's sponsors, so of course they were glad to see him – he was Mr Money, Mr Fixit, and anyway he was naturally charming, with a knockout smile and a roguish glint in his eye. People were drawn to him – women, especially – and she couldn't help noticing that her female colleagues were looking at him as if he were made out of diamonds and chocolate.

Oh God, she thought, and her heart thumped louder. She couldn't bear the thought of losing him, especially now.

Somewhere she'd read that love was a form of insanity. It was true – she was mad about Aaron in the literal sense. He was all she could think about, day and night. Her brain was crammed with him. He dominated every aspect of her life. She went through her lines thinking about him and she cleaned her teeth thinking about him. That morning she had even seen the outline of his face in the grains at the bottom of her coffee cup.

She had never felt like this before – or if she had, it had been a very long time ago, way back in a distant past where some of her darkest memories were buried. She couldn't recall if that relationship had felt as intense as this did, but none of her other boyfriends had even come close. Compared to Aaron, they were just children, boys larking about playing silly love games.

'He's quite a bit older,' Angela said. She still hadn't met him, but of course she had an opinion. 'Doesn't it bother you that he's nearly forty?'

'No,' Harper replied. 'Nothing about him bothers me. He's perfect.'

'Has he got any money, love?' her mother asked suspiciously.

'Yup,' she said. 'And he spends it, too.'

He was smiling at her now, ready to whisk her out of

the green room and off to dinner at Quaglino's. He moved forward to brush his lips against hers and off went her heart again, hopping haphazardly across her chest like a tiny crazed Morris dancer. Her knees felt weak, her breath was short — it was a miracle she was still standing up.

Having promised herself that she would wait until they were at dinner to break her news, she instead blurted it out within a few minutes of getting into the car. 'What's new, pussycat?' he asked. It was one of their jokes. She was supposed to reply with a purr.

'I'm pregnant,' she said miserably. 'I'm sorry.'

He pulled the car over with a screech of tyres. She gritted her teeth as she waited for what would come next. He turned to her, eyes blazing. 'Is this a joke?'

A wave of nausea swept over her as she shook her head. 'It must have happened in Paris,' she said, hoping that the mention of their whirlwind weekend together would conjure memories of sex and laughter.

'But you don't want it?' he asked, frowning.

She hung her head and began to fiddle with the moonstone ring on her middle finger, a gift to herself on her previous birthday, her twenty-ninth. 'I do want it,' she whispered. 'But I understand if you think it's too soon . . .'

Of course he would think it was too soon, she thought. She stole a glance at him. He was nodding, as if in agreement.

'Did you do it on purpose?' he asked.

'No,' she said, wondering if that was really true. 'Did you?'

'You've got me there,' he said, breaking into a grin. 'Maybe I did. Who knows? So when do you want to get married?' He slapped the steering wheel. 'Next week? The week after?'

'That's not what I meant.' Her voice wavered. 'This isn't a trap. I didn't say anything about getting married.'

He laughed. 'I was going to ask you anyway, about six months down the line. But now you're pregnant, there's no need to wait, is there?'

It was too good to be true. She felt she needed to give him a let-out. 'We don't need to rush to get married,' she said. 'I don't mind waiting.'

The smile dropped off his face. 'Wait a minute,' he said. 'I don't want my child being born a bastard.'

Her hackles went up. 'What do you mean?'

His smile returned. 'I mean that I'm not interested in any of your actressy bohemian crap. Easy-come, easy-go – it's not for me. If we're going to do this, we do it right, the old-fashioned way.'

She watched in stunned silence as he undid his seat belt, opened the car door and got out. For one horrible moment, she thought he might be about to do a runner, which was one of the myriad scenarios she had envisaged earlier in the day. Instead he strode around the car to the passenger door, pulled it open and knelt on the kerb.

'Will you marry me, Harper Allen?' he said, smiling up at her. For the first time, she noticed that his green eyes were flecked with tiny shards of gold.

She had the strangest feeling then, as if she were holding

on to a helium balloon and soaring up through the night air into the moonlit clouds. High above the city, she looked down at a landscape that was littered with fragments of her past relationships, images of boozy kisses and rumpled sheets, pictures of hurt faces and slammed doors. They were strewn over the ground like pieces of bombed-out buildings.

'Yes,' she said simply. 'I will.'

He beckoned her and she stood up, as if enchanted, and fell into his arms. He held her tight, her face buried in his chest, while the evening traffic hurtled past them. Someone honked, and honked again, but she didn't care who saw them. She wanted to weep with happiness. Her baby was safe. She was going to marry the man of her dreams – the most attractive man she had ever met, the most astonishing lover.

'You're everything I could ever want,' he was whispering. 'Thank you for saying yes.'

She brushed her face against his cashmere sweater, her eyes filling with tears. 'I'm the lucky one,' she said.

They drove to the restaurant in exhilarated silence. The usual crowd of paparazzi were hanging around on the street outside the entrance and they sprang into action at the sight of Harper and Aaron, blinding them with a wall of flashing lights and calling out, 'Over here!' 'Who's the new man?' 'Is it love?' She was tempted to stop and pose but Aaron clamped his arm around her and propelled her inside, where they were met with unctuous smiles and compliments and whisked to a discreet corner table.

'Sorry about that,' Harper said. She couldn't deny that she loved the attention, but was well aware that other people found it a drag, particularly Angela, who tended to roll her eyes and tut whenever people came up to ask Harper for a photo or an autograph.

Aaron, too, had shown impatience with paps and autograph hunters a couple of times, but tonight he didn't seem to mind. 'They're just doing a job,' he said with a shrug. 'It'll be our first engagement photo.'

She looked at him flirtatiously. 'Are we engaged, then?' she asked.

'Course we bloody are,' he said, grinning. 'We'll get the ring next week.'

A thrill went through her, and she had a sudden recollection of her teenage self, of evenings spent staring out of her bedroom window dreaming of stardom, suitors, sparkling solitaires and posh London restaurants. She wanted to ask, 'What kind of ring? Where from?' but picked up the menu instead. It didn't do to appear too eager.

They giggled as they ordered their food. 'You'll have to learn to cook if you're going to be my wife,' he said – a teasing reference to the one and only meal she had made him, on the night they'd got back from Paris. The potato had remained lumpy even though she had mashed it to within an inch of its being, and she had over-fried the steak until it curled up like an embarrassed sandal.

'I will,' she promised, believing that she could, and would. 'I'll do a cookery course.'

He rubbed his hands together and picked up his knife

and fork. 'It'll be great for business if I can entertain clients at home. Ply them with Veuve Clicquot and caviar soufflé. Close the deal over a Cuban cigar while the wives chat about curtains in another room.'

'Or sex,' she said, laughing to mask her alarm at the thought of making a soufflé.

'Not sex,' he said with a laugh, stabbing his fork into the meat on his plate. 'Wives don't talk about sex. They chat about clothes and soft furnishings, harmless stuff.'

'OK, not sex. I'll regale them with juicy titbits about the world of showbiz instead.'

He put down his knife and fork. 'Not showbiz, either. They'll just think you're bragging.'

'But they're bound to ask,' she argued. 'Everyone watches *Beauty Spot*.'

'Yeah, but you won't be in it any more, will you? And people forget quickly. You'd better prepare yourself for that.'

She flashed him one of her trademark smiles, which were routinely described in the newspapers as dazzling. 'I've thought about that,' she said, waving her fork at him. 'They can easily write the pregnancy into the script. Sandra could have a rendezvous in the spa room while the boss is out and – Bob's your uncle – she's got a bun in the oven!'

She clicked into character and gave him a wide-eyed look across the table. 'I don't know how it happened, Stephen,' she exclaimed in Sandra's voice. 'He only came in for a rub down.'

Aaron leaned back in his chair and grimaced. 'Nah,' he said, shaking his head. 'You're not going to be fucking some geezer on TV while you're married to me.'

'It was just a thought,' she said, secretly pleased that he felt so possessive of her. 'How about if Sandra gets fat instead, from eating too many *sausages*, or *chocolate eclairs*.' She licked her lips and gave him an exaggerated wink.

He leaned forward. 'Are you telling me you want to work after our baby is born?'

'How about I take a break when the baby comes and see how it goes from there? Lots of actresses go back to work after having children. It takes a bit of juggling, that's all.'

'So, who looks after the kid when you're working?'

She shrugged. 'I don't know ... someone I trust.'

'Let me get this straight. You want this baby and you want me. But you'd be happy to swan off filming and leave me on my tod while abandoning your precious kid to a nanny?'

'Maybe not a nanny,' she said, dismayed at the speed with which the conversation was nosediving. 'But I'm sure my mum would help out – or perhaps your mother? Anyway, we'll manage. The life of a working mum is all about spinning plates, they say.'

She took a sip from her glass of water, wishing it were wine. 'And, believe it or not, I actually know how to spin plates!' She produced her winning smile again – anything to lift the mood. 'It was part of my research when I did that play in Wales about circus performers.'

He leaned towards her, his eyes boring into hers. 'Listen

to me and listen good,' he said in a soft voice. 'No wife of mine works. No child of mine goes near a nanny. You have to give me your word – or forget about it.'

'*Never* works?'

'Ever,' he replied.

'Not even—'

'Look at it this way – why would you want to? You don't need to. I can provide everything.'

'But what if my work makes me happy?'

He shrugged. 'You can book yourself into a clinic tomorrow, for all I care.'

She stared at him in horror. 'Just like that? Life or death. Nothing in between?'

He reached over the table and grasped one of her wrists. His expression had changed. His eyes were imploring her now. 'I want a *family*,' he said, his voice cracking. 'I want stability. I want happy kids and a beautiful life. And I want it with you, no one else, just you. Don't you want that as well? Please?'

Suddenly the world stood still. The waiters, the people eating at tables and drinking at the bar, the cutlery clinking, the glasses chinking – everything froze. All she had ever wanted in her entire life was for the man she loved to say those words.

'Yes, more than anything,' she said softly.

'So you'll give up acting.'

'If it's what you want.'

His grip on her wrist tightened. 'Is that a promise?'

'It's a promise, darling. Cross my heart.'

He let go of her wrist and clasped her hand. 'You won't regret it, pussycat. I'll look after you. I'll give you and the baby everything you need and more. You'll never have to worry about anything.'

Later, he'd taken her to the Savoy Hotel and booked them into a suite with a glittering river view, where they'd made love with such depth of feeling and pleasure that the intensity was almost too much for Harper to bear. 'It's you. You're the one. It's for ever,' he kept whispering as his body moved rhythmically against hers. If she were compiling a sensory dictionary, that hour would be her definition of rapture.

The memory of that night was one of her happiest, despite everything that had come afterwards. No one but she and Aaron would ever know that over dinner she had secured the future of her beautiful eldest daughter, Taylor – that she had saved her life before she was even born – and she had done it by sacrificing the thing she valued the most.

17

February 2013

There were several reasons why she was finding it hard to concentrate on what the woman on her left was saying. The most pressing of these was that Angela was on her right – and she hadn't yet found the moment, or the courage, to confront her friend until now. She felt prickly with heat and anticipation. What would she say, and when? The clock was ticking: Angela was heading back to London in a few hours.

Meanwhile, Angela was deep in conversation with the woman sitting next to her, so she could relax for the time being. Although *relax* probably wasn't the right word, because she had so many other things on her mind. Still, her worries would have to wait. First, she had to get through lunch without drinking any alcohol, so that she would be on her toes for the conversation with Angela.

She had forgotten how much noise a room full of well-heeled Cheshire ladies could make when they were gathered in the name of charity. There were at least a hundred ladies in Louboutins assembled in the airy ballroom of the White House Hotel, sitting at prettily adorned tables of eight, barely eating their avocado salads and going at the wine hell–for–leather. It was Friday lunchtime and the weekend had started early in this corner of the county. None of the mums would be doing the school run later. Their nannies and au pairs had been warned.

She bet that less than half of the women present could name the charity that they were here for, even though they had paid two hundred pounds for the privilege. It was irrelevant whether they were raising funds for a hospital unit or a new library. They hadn't come because they cared about any particular cause; they were here because they were the wives of affluent men who required them to mingle with the elite Cheshire set. And she was in no position to criticise them for it. She was here for the same reason. Or, at least, that was how it had all started.

Twenty years earlier, when Aaron's company had relocated to Manchester, he had made it very clear what he expected from their new life.

'There's a lot of money in this area,' he'd told her, his eyes gleaming. 'There's more champagne drunk per square mile than anywhere else in the country, and that includes London. It's a great place to do business and we need to make the most of it. I'll do the business. You do the networking.'

'Networking?' she'd stammered. It had sounded very corporate at the time, very American.

He nodded. 'Call it "socialising" if it makes you feel better. Get to know all the wives. Take them out for lunch. Spend as much as you like. I want to see invitations on the mantelpiece. I want to see our photo in *Cheshire Life.*'

She hadn't known where to begin. Where did you go to meet the cream of Cheshire society with a wilful three-year-old in tow? Taylor had a temper to match her father's and was liable to throw herself on the ground and kick her legs in the air screaming blue murder at any given moment. And who exactly were these 'wives' Aaron was talking about? It would help if he could at least give her a list of names and numbers.

She had started with a toddlers' group in Wilmslow, where she learnt about a 'strictly invitation only' kids' playgroup at the members-only Grange Club. She applied for membership to the Grange, only to be told there was a five-year waiting list, then had her cheque returned with a polite note when she attempted to book a table at a charity dinner dance there. Cheshire's top set was a closed set, it seemed. She cringed every time Aaron asked how her networking was coming along. How could she tell him she hadn't even reached the first rung of the social ladder?

She often wondered how long it would have taken to get anywhere, had she not by lucky chance found herself stuck in a department store lift in Manchester with Patty 'Party' Rendell. Stepping into the empty lift with Patty, she had been unaware that she was breathing the same air as the coiffured, fragrant queen of the Cheshire elite – and when the lift creaked to a halt between floors, she was none the wiser. It soon became apparent that the elegant stranger was terrified of broken elevators, however. 'Oh my days!' Patty said, leaning heavily against the wall. 'I think I'm going to have a panic attack.'

Harper, being no fan of confined spaces herself, had taken refuge in humour – and when the ordeal was over, Patty declared that she would never have got through it without her. As they waited thirty-five long minutes for the engineers to free them, her fear had dissolved into gulps of hysterical laughter at the stream of filthy jokes Harper kept cracking about shafts, pulleys and hoists. There wasn't time to panic, she said. She was too busy trying not to wet her knickers giggling.

'Try to maintain your pelvic floor, love,' Harper had advised. 'We're in enough trouble as it is.'

After the lift incident, Harper's social standing was assured. Patty got her into the Grange Club within two months and invitations started avalanching through the letter box. One thing led to another and soon she was buzzing around the charity circuit like a bee with pockets stuffed full of pollen. Once she'd found Betty to mind Taylor for the odd couple of hours – and keep the house immaculate for Aaron – she even joined a couple of the organising committees. It was then that she realised what charity really meant to the women of 'her' set, apart from the devoted few. Booze and mingling. Mingling and booze.

Sitting opposite her, Kelly Ponsett already had the tell-tale flush in her cheeks that said she'd had one too many. Kelly's husband, Micky Ponsett, did something with software, or in software – something softwarey, anyway. Harper liked to tease Kelly by asking her what exactly it was that Micky did. She never seemed to mind – probably because he was so rich – and it was funny to watch her complexion grow an even deeper shade of pink as she tangled herself up in computer jargon.

Kelly put down her wine glass and winked at Harper. 'Detox starts Monday,' she mouthed across the table.

'What kind?' Harper mouthed back.

'Grapefruit,' Kelly replied with a grimace.

Next to Kelly was Patricia Bloom, whose husband was the head of a company that fitted out super-yachts. The Blooms' house was a kind of interiors show home for clients – and they had recently lined their dining room with platinum wallpaper. Not platinum-*coloured* wallpaper, mind, but *real, actual* platinum wallpaper. Aaron loved it, but the room felt too much like the inside a bank vault to Harper.

On her left, Vicky Pacquard was midway through explaining what had inspired her to open a dog grooming parlour in Alderley Edge. Apparently, she'd had her light-bulb moment when she'd spotted a miniature pink poodle tied up outside Waitrose.

'It was so *adorable*, so *cute*,' she gushed, 'and I thought, What fun, how simply delicious.'

Harper smiled her brightest smile and did her best not

to stare too hard at Vicky's trout pout. It was anyone's guess what the beauty therapist had been thinking when she'd crammed ten years' supply of filler into Vicky's lips in one go. Instead of being plumped up, Bardot style, they were great big sausagey balloons. Still, Vicky didn't seem to mind them, and that was what counted, she supposed.

She was well aware that the scrutiny went both ways. While she was busy goggling Vicky's sausage lips, Vicky was likewise examining her for signs of artificial enhancement. She knew this, because Vicky and everyone else she had spoken to that day had declared how great she looked – and as they'd said it, each to a woman had left an invisible question mark hanging in the air.

She couldn't blame them for speculating. She was just as surprised as they were.

The eye job had turned out far better than she had expected. Two and a half weeks after going under the knife, despite a barely detectable puffiness around her eyes (which Vicky would doubtless have detected), she looked spectacularly 'refreshed'. Everyone was saying it. Several people had mentioned the fountain of youth. More importantly, Aaron had stopped switching the light off before he made love to her.

'And then it came to me in a flash: this area is crying out for a super-stylish pet spa!' Vicky continued. 'But don't tell anyone,' she added in a confidential tone. 'We're keeping it secret until the launch.'

'My lips are sealed,' Harper promised, instantly regretting her choice of words.

She was tempted to ask about Vicky's business plan and financial projections, if only to see the look of sheer puzzlement on her face. But she didn't want to be a spoil-sport. At least fifty per cent of the women in the room had started a business on a whim as flimsy as a miniature pink poodle. Bankrolled by their husbands, they'd had a ball dreaming up the name on the storefront and decorating their shops and showrooms. But that was usually where their entrepreneurial efforts had ended, because when it came to putting in the sheer bloody hard work that was needed to get a new business venture off the ground, most of them simply couldn't be bothered to get out of bed in the morning. And why would they? The incentive wasn't there. It didn't matter if they failed. Their hubbies could write it off against tax.

A few of the start-ups had taken off, of course. Lydia Blyton had done phenomenally well with her bridal wear business. But in general these women's goals didn't reach beyond shopping, having fun and going on holiday. Their lives flip-flopped between detoxes and binges. They had a lot of boozed-up lunches. Business was a sideline.

She gave Vicky's dog parlour twelve months, if that, and hoped it would be fun while it lasted. She had known Vicky long enough to have grown a little bit fond of her over the years. Saying hello and goodbye at the school gates had given them a comfortable familiarity – and they'd also got tipsy together a few times at the odd parents' gathering and charity do. All right, she would probably have preferred to be sitting next to somebody with more of a developed sense of humour, if only to take her mind off Angela, but it couldn't be helped. The table plans had been done by Patty 'Party' Rendell, who, now that she was more advanced in years, ruled the Cheshire set like a dowager duchess.

'We're going to make it an all-round salon and spa experience for socially advantaged pets,' Vicky was saying, taking a swig from her wine glass. 'We're offering animal reflexology, a canine dentist, even seaweed wraps! By the end of a day with us, your pet will be totally transformed.'

Harper giggled. 'In that case, can we drop off our husbands too?' she said. 'I'm sure I'm not the only one here who thinks their fella could do with a total transformation.'

Vicky looked puzzled. 'You can't mean Aaron?'

Harper laughed. 'Oh, haven't you heard? I'm married to Mark now,' she teased, half-wishing it was true.

'No!' Vicky swivelled her head frantically, looking for someone to confirm this earth-shattering news. 'Why didn't anyone tell me?' She turned back to Harper and realised she'd been had.

'Of course I mean Aaron, you silly,' Harper said, squeezing her arm. 'Any chance of booking him in for a brain peel and lobotomy?'

Vicky looked bewildered again. Along with almost everyone else Harper knew, she thought Aaron was the perfect man, so her 'joke' would need explaining – and some. Harper was relieved to be interrupted by a tap on the shoulder from Lauren Grayson.

'Just had to say how fantastic you're looking!' Lauren told Harper.

'You, too!' Harper eyed up Lauren's pregnant belly. 'How's the bump?'

'Great! But I've nothing to wear,' Lauren said, a statement in total conflict with the fabulous black and white halter neck dress she had on. She leaned closer to whisper in Harper's ear. 'Don't tell anyone, but I'm thinking of opening a maternity clothes shop.'

Harper mimed a zip action across her mouth, because she didn't want to use the phrase 'lips are sealed' in front of Vicky again. 'How exciting!'

'I've got so many ideas, you wouldn't believe it,' Lauren giggled.

Oh yes I would, Harper thought, as she beamed back at Lauren. Who hadn't imagined themselves to be an expert on maternity wear when they were pregnant? Who hadn't sat around thinking up clever names for the perfect maternity boutique? She certainly had, both times she'd been expecting, but especially the first time, with Taylor, back in the days when all that was on offer in the shopping centres were billowing tents with massive Lady Di bows on them.

In an ideal world, she thought, as she riffled through the rails of baggy sack dresses, Aaron would offer to be her financial backer. He would never let her return to acting, but perhaps he would allow her to run a little business.

Shop names began popping into her head. She started

waking up in the middle of the night and chuckling as she wrote down her ideas. I'm so brilliant, she thought, visualising a whole chain of Damsels in this Dress maternity wear shops.

The list was endless: Great Expectations, The Belly Boutique, Ladies In Waiting, The Whole Nine Months, Heartburn Hotel, The Waiting Dame, Bumpsadaisy and No Tents Please, We're British!

I must do this! she thought.

And then – both times – she'd had the baby and stopped giving a shit about what pregnant women wore.

The sound of glasses clinking brought an end to her reminiscences. Heather Beveridge, head of the organising committee for today's event, stepped up onto the ballroom stage to introduce the guest speaker, who was hoping to raise money for staff and equipment in a premature baby unit at a hospital in Manchester. 'Tragically, Jane's twins both died some weeks after they were born early,' Heather explained. 'She's certain they could have survived given the sufficient level of support, including vital equipment and specialised staff. But don't let me speak for Jane, because she's here in person to explain her campaign in more detail. I'm sure you'll find her story very moving, and I hope it will inspire you to put everything you can into fundraising for this very worthy cause.'

The room grew quiet apart from a few low voices, the audience sobered by the thought of what Jane had gone through. She took the mike, cleared her throat and began to speak. 'It's still very difficult for me to talk about what happened to my babies, Archie and Sophie,' she began, her voice cracking.

Soft laughter rippled across the room from one of the back tables and Harper bit her lip in annoyance. Why couldn't people show some respect? Why couldn't they honour this poor, brave woman by spending a few minutes listening to what had to say? But it was always the same at these functions. So much wine had been downed by the time the speaker got up that no one was really interested.

How did I get here? she thought miserably. She knew she belonged in the room, but a part of her genuinely wished she didn't.

Her mind drifted, perhaps as a kind of defence against the horror of what Jane had suffered. She didn't want to imagine what it would be like to lose a child, let alone two. Her heart contracted painfully at the thought of anything happening to Taylor or Georgina. She constantly worried about them, even when there wasn't anything wrong with them.

It was Taylor who was on her mind today, because in recent weeks Taylor's moods had been swinging drastically between a state of kittenish excitement and slumpy, red-eyed gloom. Harper had tried to talk about what was upsetting her, but Taylor wasn't telling, although her cagey responses had made it abundantly clear to Harper what was going on. It was no secret that Taylor was going out with her married boss – now separated, allegedly. She hadn't tried to hide it, because there was nothing to hide, she claimed.

So Harper had said nothing when she kept announcing that she was going out, then stayed in, or suddenly went out when she'd planned to stay in, or unexpectedly left the room to take a call, or went from happy to sad – or vice versa – after glancing at her phone for a nanosecond.

But the night before, she had heard loud sobbing coming from Taylor's bedroom, and she figured that the door would have been shut and the sobs muffled if Taylor hadn't wanted her to hear. So she knocked softly and went in.

'Hello, darling,' she said softly. 'Can I help?'

Taylor went on crying. She was lying on her bed half wrapped in her duvet, with her face buried in a pillow.

'Is it Andrew?' she asked, sitting on the edge of the bed.

Taylor shook her head. 'Andrew and I are fine,' she said into the pillow. 'But there are so many things getting in the way! I can't stand it. I just want to be with him.'

'Oh, sweetie,' she said, edging closer. She longed to stroke her head as she had when she was a child, but was worried Taylor would bat her away. Instead she gently rested a hand on her shoulder. 'Life can be complicated sometimes. Do you want to tell me about it?'

Taylor pouted. 'There's nothing to tell, really. He's having problems distancing himself from his last relationship, that's all.'

These had to be Andrew's words, Harper thought. 'By that, you mean his marriage?' she said. She didn't mean it to sound judgemental, but somehow it came out that way.

Taylor didn't bite. 'I know what it sounds like to you,

Mum,' she said, sitting up on the bed. 'But you really don't have a clue.'

'Don't forget that I had a life before I married your dad,' Harper said. 'As it happens, I know what it feels like to be in love with someone who can't give me what I want.'

Taylor tutted, Just like Aaron did when he was annoyed. 'But that's not how it is. He *can* give me what I want. It's just that, well, there are obstacles.'

'You mean, his marriage?' she said, trying to sound sympathetic even as she again pointed out the glaringly obvious fatal flaw in the relationship.

'Stop saying that, Mum!'

'Saying what?'

'"His marriage", like it was still happening. He's not in the marriage any more.'

'Are you completely sure about that?'

'Of course I am! Just shut up, Mum. You don't understand!'

Something in her tone irritated Harper. 'Just like his wife didn't understand him, I suppose?'

Taylor gave her a startled look. 'How do you know his wife didn't understand him?'

Harper's heart sank. Wasn't Taylor familiar with the clichés married men came out with? This was the problem with today's young people, she thought, conscious that she was developing an internal voice that sounded just like her mother's. Kids no longer sat down with their parents and watched family sitcoms that chewed over all the old hackneyed scenarios of life, warning them in the process of potential pitfalls, of philandering husbands and inter-fering mothers-in-law. 'Don't tell me he actually said that his wife didn't understand him?' she asked Taylor. 'Next you'll be saying they're separated but still living under the same roof!'

Taylor looked daggers at her. 'What do you know about anything?' she grumped, throwing herself back onto her duvet. 'You don't have a happy marriage! Oh, and by the way, Mum, there's a really unattractive glob of mascara under your eye that makes it hard to talk to you without wanting to laugh in your face.'

It was a silly thing to say but it had been meant cruelly, and the memory still stung.

God, she wanted a drink. Actually, what she really wanted was to have a good relationship with her beloved eldest daughter, but however hard she tried – and perhaps she tried too hard – things never seemed to gel properly between them.

She glugged down some water and looked over at Angela. Heedless of the speaker on the stage, Angela was still in earnest conversation with the woman on her right, albeit in a low whisper. 'Shhh!' Harper hissed at them. Angela stopped talking and gave her a mock-affronted look. Putting her finger to her lips, Harper responded with a pleading smile. Angela countered with an amused frown.

Harper shrugged at her, wondering how much longer they were going to play ping-pong using their faces as bats. It was difficult for her even to look at Angela right then, caught as she was between hatred for her friend, and pity.

Oh, sod it, she thought, spying the decanter of wine in the middle of the table. Sodding, sodding, sod it.

Soon her glass was half full – but only because she had emptied half of it – and she was gearing up for a good old spat with Angela.

Two hours later, she was back at home with a group of the girls from the charity do, drinking spritzers in the lounge. Angela was supposed to be getting on a train back to London in an hour, but she didn't look like she was going anywhere – she was lying the full length of one of the sofas in stockinged feet, holding forth about the hopelessness of men, with Tracey Gant kneeling in hushed reverence on the carpet beside her. It was all very Noel Coward in that corner of the room, Harper thought. Angela loved to play the actress.

Harper hadn't managed to catch her alone yet, so they still hadn't had their conversation. She told herself she was biding her time until the right moment, but in her heart she knew that she was bottling it. Literally. Now that she was sitting in a cosy armchair feeling comfortably hazy, she felt rather less inclined to have it out with Angela.

Her phone rang. It was Aaron. 'Everything OK, darling?' she said, instantly sobering up.

'Who's there?' He sounded annoyed.

She looked around the room. 'Tracey, Vicky, Angela, Kelly, Jocasta, Laura, Henny and Paula,' she said brightly.

Sensing what was coming next, she stood up and walked towards the kitchen.

'And the others?'

'No one else,' she said. 'Just a merry bunch of girls.'

'Don't be daft. I heard men's voices too.'

'No, you didn't.'

'Don't tell me what I can and can't hear.'

'I'm just saying there aren't any men here. If you heard a deep voice, it was probably Laura. You know she's always being accused of sounding like a man. She's got a low timbre, practically baritone. You should—'

'Don't get technical with me,' he snapped, and hung up.

'—hear her when she sings "Nessun Dorma",' she said into the nothingness.

She went back into the lounge smiling, as if nothing was wrong. 'Was that Aaron?' Kelly asked, looking more flushed than ever. Kelly was really making the most of her final countdown to detox.

Angela, having come to the end of her man moan, yawned and looked at her watch. 'Oh dear, I should think about leaving if I'm to get back to London in time for dinner.' She folded her elegant legs and swung them gracefully off the sofa onto the floor. 'Better freshen up first,' she said, picking up her handbag. She stood up, straightened her skirt and made her way out of the room.

Harper saw her chance. It was now or never. She waited a short while and then followed Angela upstairs to the pink bathroom. Angela always used the pink bathroom when she was at Orchard End. She had never been known to pop casually to the downstairs loo.

The bathroom door was shut when she got up there. While she waited, her heart pounded at a slow, measured pace. She kept seeing images of Angela as she remembered her at drama school – long-legged and beautiful, slightly awkward in her movements, a little shy around people she didn't know, but a huge bag of laughs if she was your friend.

In the second year, they had shared a flat that had walls as thin as cardboard and a kitchen sink that gurgled through the night. One evening, Harper had come in from the pub to find Angela sitting at the tiny kitchen table with a script in front of her and tears of laughter running down her cheeks. 'What's so funny?' she'd asked her.

Angela tipped her head to one side. 'Listen!'

A loud knocking sound was coming from the floor above, where their elderly landlord lived with his equally elderly, blue-rinsed wife. A woman's voice could be heard saying, 'Not like that, you silly oaf!' More banging. 'That's better . . . wait, let me turn around . . .'

'What's going on?' Harper asked. 'It sounds like they're building a boat.' Over the banging, she heard a sort of cooing noise, followed by a weird series of yowls and miaows. 'Have they got a parrot?' she asked, confused by the menagerie of animal sounds.

Angela started gulping and clutching her sides. She reached out her hand and tried to grab Harper's arm. 'They're . . . they're . . .'

The penny dropped. Harper burst into laughter. 'Of course they're not!' she exclaimed. 'They're over seventy!'

But, unbelievable as it seemed to a couple of twenty-year-old drama students, it soon became clear beyond doubt what the geriatric landlord and his wife were doing – and parrots and sex were evermore synonymous whenever Harper spoke to Angela.

She was standing at the top of the stairs when Angela came out of the bathroom. 'Hello, you,' Angela said warmly. 'Are you sober enough to drive? If not, perhaps you could call me a taxi.'

Under normal circumstances, Harper wouldn't have been able to resist saying, 'You're a taxi.'

Instead, she said, 'I know about you and Aaron.'

Angela smiled and looked her steadily in the eye. 'Me and Aaron? What can you mean?'

She was good. She was really good. But Harper was determined to be better. 'I'm not talking about when you met at the Savoy a couple of weeks ago.'

Angela's smile didn't waver. 'At the Savoy? Ah, you mean when we bumped into each other *outside* the Savoy. I'd totally forgotten. And no wonder, I was in bits.' She made a 'poor me' face. 'Aaron was an absolute darling,' she went on. 'He gave me a bloody great hug and sent me on my way feeling that at least I could count on my friends.'

Harper held her gaze. 'As I said, I'm not talking about when you met at the Savoy a couple of weeks ago, although it's weird you never mentioned it.'

Angela jutted her lower lip and made a 'poor you' face.

'No offence to Aaron, darling, but I blocked the whole day out. It was the only way I could cope with the darkness. You can't imagine how I felt, hearing about James's new woman—'

'Yes, but as I said, I'm not talking about that day,' Harper interrupted, resisting the urge to do a 'poor you' face back. 'I'm saying that I know everything. Aaron has been totally honest with me.'

Angela frowned and narrowed her eyes. 'Honest about what?'

'About you and him. We've been having relationship therapy. I asked him to come clean, and he did.'

Angela's evenly arched eyebrows shot up. 'Relationship therapy? Is your marriage in trouble?'

Harper shook her head. 'He told me about you, Angela.'

Angela's expression was one of genuine innocence. 'But what on earth could he have said?'

'Don't make me go over it,' Harper said curtly. 'It's humiliating enough to be standing here talking to you about it.'

Angela smirked. 'Then why are you standing here talking to me about it? Especially as there's nothing to say.'

Harper could feel her starting to get the upper hand. If she wasn't careful, she would soon be running rings round her. She went back to basics. 'Look, I know about you and Aaron,' she said with a sigh. 'Don't deny it. I'm not angry. I just want to hear your side of it.'

There was a pause. Angela looked deep into her eyes, searching for – what? The truth? She stared stonily back at her. Finally, Angela exhaled and said, 'It was nothing. It lasted less than a week.'

Harper reeled. She felt as if the air around her was being sucked away. She was being vacuum-packed by Angela.

She hoped her shock wasn't visible. 'That's it?' she said, keeping her voice steady against the odds. 'That's all you're going to say?'

'It was a mistake,' Angela said, lowering her eyes. 'It ended because we loved you too much. We got together because of you and we fell apart because of you.' She looked up at Harper again. 'What can I say? Sorry that we were both so angry with you that it happened in the first place. Relieved that you were too sick at the time to notice. Devastated that you've found out now.'

Harper thought fast, trying to make the connection. 'Too sick?' Then it came to her. 'When I was pregnant with Georgie ...' she said, trying to disguise the fact that she was only now piecing it together.

Angela's eyes filled with tears. 'Can you imagine how I felt when you told me you were pregnant again?'

Suddenly she was supposed to feel sorry for Angela? How had she done that? It was some kind of conversational magic trick.

'Yes, but—'

'You'd "had a little accident" and bam, you were having another baby,' Angela sniffed. 'Meanwhile I'd had ten rounds of IVF and it was all over for me. I was officially barren.'

'It must have been hard, but I can't see——'

'You were giggling about being an old mother, and I was just old.'

'Rubbish,' Harper said angrily. 'I was very conscious of how you must have been feeling. I did my best to play it down.'

'Yes, I noticed you doing that. It didn't help. You were obviously thrilled, but you pretended it was no big deal, when it was a huge deal to me. It just felt so unfair.'

'I felt bad about it, you know I did,' Harper said. 'But it wasn't my fault that you couldn't conceive.'

'I know. It's just that I would have given anything to change places with you.'

Harper felt her blood begin to boil. 'Was that what it was about? Changing places? Is that why you slept with my husband?' She couldn't believe she was saying the words. To Angela, her best friend. Her lungs did a weird contraction and she gasped. Using what felt like the last pocket of air left in her body, she said, 'Or was it to punish me?'

'No, it wasn't that,' Angela said quickly. 'It was ... more complicated. It takes two, you know – and Aaron was livid with you. He didn't want another child——'

'I'm not talking about Aaron,' Harper hissed. 'I want to know why you did it. My best friend.'

Angela winced. 'I think we were both looking for comfort,' she said at last, 'and expressing our frustration, perhaps. It was wrong of us.'

'Do you mean your sexual frustration?'

'It was more like grief – for me. I needed to reaffirm myself. I felt I couldn't be a whole woman—'

Harper stamped her foot. 'You could have effing well reaffirmed yourself as a whole woman with someone else's husband, couldn't you? It didn't have to be Aaron.'

Angela looked pained. 'I was depressed and confused. I wasn't thinking straight. I'm sorry.'

Harper bit her lip. Her right arm was shaking from the effort it was taking to keep it down by her side, as she fought the urge to leap on Angela and batter her. 'How did it happen? Where?' she demanded through clenched teeth.

Angela blinked several times. 'What did Aaron say, in your therapy session? You said you knew everything.' Now it was her turn to gasp. 'You didn't know, did you? Why, you— Aaron hasn't told you anything.'

'What does it matter? You'd better tell me everything, right now, or I'm going to punch you.'

'Look, if it's any consolation—'

Just then, Taylor came bounding up the stairs, taking them two at a time. 'Mum!' she called. 'Oh, sorry,' she said. 'Hi, Angela!'

Angela turned to her and smiled. 'Darling, I've got a train to catch in half an hour and your ma can't leave her guests,' she said. 'Would you be an angel and take your godmother to the station? Like, pronto?'

Harper stood watching them, unable to move or speak. She cursed the perverse quirk of timing that had just handed Angela her escape route on a plate, as if she'd simply snapped her fingers in a restaurant and asked for the bill. There was nothing Harper could say in front of Taylor. She felt as though she'd been tied up and gagged.

'Sure, no problem,' Taylor said. 'Everything OK, Mum?'

Harper smiled and tried to say, 'Yes, lovely!' But the words got mangled in her throat and came out in a hot, breathy, unintelligible blast.

Fortunately, Taylor didn't seem to notice. 'I'll just grab a couple of things from my room and then we'll go,' she told Angela.

'Wonderful, darling,' Angela said.

'It never happened again?' Harper whispered.

'No, we both knew it was a mistake.'

'I'll never forgive you,' Harper said. 'You know that, don't you?'

Taylor skipped back to them, jangling her car keys. 'Ready?'

Angela reached out to hug Harper. 'Bye, darling, thanks for a lovely time. Come and see me in London soon.'

'Definitely,' Harper said, stiffly returning the hug.

As Angela and Taylor went down the stairs, she turned her back on them and fled to her bedroom. Just before she slammed the door, she heard Kelly calling her. 'OK if we open another bottle of wine, Harps?'

'Be my guest,' she yelled. 'It's in the big fridge, in the utility room. I'll be down in a sec.'

From her en suite bathroom, she heard a car pull up outside the house. She peeped out of the window, hoping that she wouldn't be seen by whoever was arriving. Her eyes were red and puffy from crying hot, angry tears and her make-up was smeared.

She saw Aaron getting out of his car. The bastard had come to check up on her, as usual. He had driven from Manchester at breakneck speed just to make sure there weren't any men hidden under the sofa. It was pathetic, she thought. No, it was pathological.

The irony was that she had never strayed, so he was wasting his time with all this paranoia. The added irony – would that be a double irony? – was that she had been so busy trying to defuse his jealousy for all these years that it hadn't occurred to her that he might be the unfaithful one.

He was constantly crashing in on her unexpectedly, eavesdropping on her conversations and phone calls. 'Where are you? Who are you with?' These would be the words on her headstone if she died before him, she guessed. Perhaps she should write a codicil into her will, requesting an alternative: 'Ha! Got away!'

All the focus was on her. She was in the spotlight night and day. And it was her fault, he claimed. 'Remember the rose? It all started with that fucking rose,' he'd say bitterly.

'I remember,' she'd reply. 'But only because you never let me forget it.'

18

April 1990

She'd gone to meet him in Covent Garden, just around the corner from his office. He had suggested it, after she'd ventured that she might like to go and see Bill and the others on the *Beauty Spot* set. 'Just to catch up with the gossip and check out the actress who's come in as the new Sandra,' she said.

'Come and have lunch with me instead,' he'd said. 'Meet me in the piazza at twelve forty-five.'

It was a warm spring day and she arrived early so that she could browse the arts and crafts stalls. She bought Aaron a screen-printed silk tie with tiny naked women all over it, knowing it would make him laugh, and then wandered out into the sunshine to check out the street acts.

She was watching a clown blowing bubbles when she felt his arm loop around her waist. 'Hello, Pussycat,' he said, pulling her towards him for a kiss.

He took her hand and led her to the Trattoria Giuseppe,

where they sat at a table on the pavement, looking out across the cobbled piazza.

This is bliss, she thought, stroking her belly and closing her eyes for a moment to bask in the warmth of the sunlight on her face. She felt a little kick. *Utter* bliss, she thought.

A waiter came to take their order. 'Spaghetti carbonara,' she said, 'lots of it. I'm so hungry I could eat a syphilitic donkey.'

Aaron ordered an escalope and salad. 'You'd better watch it,' he said, eyeing her bump after the waiter had gone. 'Look at the size of you.'

She giggled. 'You think this is big? Wait till I get to nine months.'

He looked worried. 'Christ, how much bigger? If you swell up any more, you're not coming back, sweetheart.'

She shifted in her seat. 'Don't worry, I'm using your coconut oil every day.'

'Good girl. They say it makes all the difference.'

'Anyway,' she said defensively, 'the midwife says we're biologically programmed to spring back into shape. It just happens naturally.'

She crossed her fingers under the table. Aaron wasn't turning out to be the kind of New Age man who revelled in his pregnant wife's expanding body. Her lovely big boobs didn't seem to do anything for him, and he wasn't interested in caressing her belly. She couldn't help feeling disappointed. She had imagined there would be much more romance in it.

They were still having a lot of sex, but he was always behind her now, so as not to be obstructed by the bump. It was practical, she supposed, but it felt more like fucking than making love, and she would have preferred a gentler experience while she was pregnant. It was soppy of her to want to be face to face, kissing, laughing and stroking each other, but it just felt like a weird time to be having her hair pulled and bottom smacked while he whispered filthy nothings in her ear, even though it made her horny.

Perhaps she felt uncomfortable because it wasn't just the two of them any more. There was a baby inside her, and something told her that pregnant lovemaking should be adoring and affectionate, not raunchy and frenzied. She hadn't said anything to Aaron, though. He would either think she was being ridiculously fanciful or it would put him off – and she would rather have wild, banging sex than no sex at all. She smiled to herself. Aaron didn't have a New Age bone in his body, and that was fine. She loved him as he was.

'Just make sure you're eating for two, not ten,' he said, his eyes restlessly scanning the piazza. 'There's Graeme.' He got up from his chair. 'Give me a second. I need to talk to him.'

He walked briskly away and caught up with his colleague. They disappeared round the corner and she was left enjoying the sunshine alone, munching on ciabatta and watching people go by. Covent Garden was the best place in London for people-watching, she thought. Along with the hordes of office workers, it covered the entire spectrum of types, from American tourists on a whirlwind tour to local rent boys from Soho.

She started playing the shoe game, trying to judge people by their footwear. It was sparked by something Angela said. 'You can tell *everything* about a person by looking at the shoes.'

Was it true? Was a woman in wide-fit, cushioned slip-ons necessarily middle-aged and fashion blind? Or did she just have bunions? And what did red clicky-clacky heels signify? A sense of humour, or a desperate desire for attention?

People weren't so predictable, she told Angela, who wasn't having any of it. 'Show me the shoe and I'll show you the person,' she declared with authority.

It made Harper laugh. 'That sounds terribly profound, but does it actually mean anything?'

Angela would sniff haughtily. 'When I'm researching a character, the shoes are the first thing I decide on. They are the very essence of a person's outward expression.'

A pair of polished men's brogues caught Harper's eye and she watched them pacing in her direction. The shoes were sophisticated but the step was springy, and the man wearing them was younger than his footwear suggested. Tall and dark, with amused brown eyes, he was dressed in a stripy T-shirt and jeans. She decided that he had to be French or Italian.

Their eyes met and he came to a sudden halt. He stood stock-still, smiling at her, then raised his arm, twirled his hand and took a deep, flamboyant bow. She laughed in delight and then looked away, embarrassed. When she looked up again, he was gone.

How sweet, she thought, sipping her water self-consciously.

A moment later, he was standing in front of her table, holding out a pink flower. 'For you,' he said. 'You are the loveliest blossoming I have ever seen.'

She shook her head. 'Oh, no, I—'

'Please, yes,' he insisted.

'No, really . . . '

He smiled at her imploringly.

'Thank you,' she said, reaching forward and taking it from him.

He took a step backwards. 'Your husband is luckiest man *del mondo*.'

She couldn't stop smiling. 'I'll be sure to tell him you said so.'

'*Ciao, signora*.' He blew her a kiss and walked away.

Aaron got back just as their food was arriving. She was still holding the pink rose, having studied it for several minutes, wondering why her husband was more likely to compare her to a hippopotamus than a flower. Was it an Anglo-Saxon thing?

'Sorry about that,' he said, snapping open his folded napkin as he sat down. 'Nice flower. Where did you get it?'

Something told her not to tell. It was just an instinct, and she followed it. 'I bought it from someone doing the rounds with a basket of roses. It's silly, but I felt sorry for them.'

He turned and surveyed the tables around them. 'You're a soft touch, then. No one else fell for it.'

She pretended to look as well. 'No, they didn't. Bunch of meanies!'

'Why, how much was it?' he asked.

'Eighty pence,' she said, too quickly.

'A bargain! Let me see.'

He reached out his hand and she gave him the rose. 'It smells beautiful,' she said.

He took it, dropped it and squashed it on the cobbles beneath the sole of his Paul Smith shoe. 'Lying bitch,' he said under his breath, picking up his knife and fork and slicing into his escalope. 'Don't ever lie to me again.'

Was that really when it started?

She thought back to their wedding, which had taken place six weeks after his marriage proposal, just three months after they'd met.

'Let's keep it small,' he'd said.

'Really?' she asked doubtfully.

'We hardly know each other's friends and families. I don't want to be rubbing shoulders with a bunch of strangers on my wedding day.'

She understood, but the tiny guest quota put several noses out of joint among the people who didn't make the list. She seemed to spend whole days in the run-up to the wedding explaining that it would be a simple, intimate celebration, and she was sorry, but that was how she wanted it. Really, it was.

'Where's the fun in that?'

'But you're a TV star!'

'Very unlike you!'

Aaron kept his list to immediate family and a couple of old friends. Since his brother was in Hong Kong and couldn't fly back for the wedding, his grand total of guests added up to six people. Meanwhile, Harper was fretting about how to keep hers down to forty. He encouraged her to ask some of her Cullercoats gang – Janice and Lizzie, Christopher and Stu, and a couple of others – but he wasn't so keen on her showbiz friends. Fortunately, Steve and Bill from *Beauty Spot* got through the net, and Angela and her producer husband James, and a few of the pals she had made in various touring productions, so it wasn't entirely without a theatrical contingent, which was a relief. She needed to be around actors on her big day. She couldn't bear the thought of having a 'straight' wedding.

He wanted a registry office do, so that's what they had. She wasn't expecting to be overcome by emotion in the characterless ceremony room at the Newcastle Civic Centre, with its yellow walls and stiff, high-backed chairs. But when she came to say her vows and finally stole a glance at Aaron, he looked so swooningly gorgeous in his dark suit and white tie that she came close to bursting into tears of joy. He was handsome, he was rich, he was everything.

As their eyes locked, she felt a flutter in her belly, the first live evidence of her two-and-a-half-month pregnancy. Her heart leapt. The timing was miraculous – the baby was giving its seal of approval! If she'd had any doubts – which of course she hadn't – they disappeared in that moment. The marriage was meant to be.

They travelled by white limousine to a champagne reception and dinner at Ivy Lodge, a beautiful country house hotel outside Newcastle. Aaron had chosen it and it was very posh and terribly special. Everyone oohed and aahed when they walked into the grand, oak-panelled dining hall.

Harper adored Aaron's taste and extravagance, so she was surprised when she realised that she would have been just as happy having a knees-up at the Cullercoats Social Club. She didn't say so, but as she looked up at the stag heads and coats of arms on the walls, she knew in her heart that she would have liked a reet proper bash, with a cheesy disco and a DJ playing songs from the sixties and seventies, aunties, uncles and cousins everywhere, the entire cast and crew of *Beauty Spot* milling around, and lots of mess, chaos and inappropriate snogging in dark corners. That was how she had always imagined her wedding would be.

Instead it was a fairly quiet affair, more dignified than she would have liked and definitely a little bit awkward at times. It didn't matter though, because she was happy.

She and Aaron sat on the top table with their parents. His mother and father had only met her parents once before, and it had been a tricky encounter between south and north, a clash of aspiration and disappointment. Aaron's dad, Scott, had left school without any qualifications and built up a profitable fencing business in Essex against the odds. Monica, Aaron's mum, was suitably proud. They were big fans of Margaret Thatcher.

Harper's dad, Tom, on the other hand, was a staunch Labour voter who had been clever beyond expectation and destined for greatness – until he'd had the first of his funny turns after Harper was born. Neither wife had got what she bargained for. One had won, the other had lost. Harper's mum, Geraldine, was suitably disgruntled.

So there wasn't a lot of common ground at the top table, and the sound of eggshells being crunched underfoot could be heard throughout the meal. It didn't help that her dad was going through one of his up-and-down patches, nor that her mum was feeling pissed off with him for not being more like Scott or Aaron. Monica seemed a bit het up too, for no apparent reason, but perhaps it was because Scott kept rolling his eyes and saying things like, 'What do you know about it?'

'Lovely do,' her mother said after the starter. 'Must have cost a packet.'

'Our son certainly likes to have the best things in life,' Scott said – whether smugly or ironically, it was hard to tell.

'Don't we all?' her mother said with a wink.

Oh God, thought Harper, groaning inwardly.

Aaron got up to speak. 'How lucky am I?' he said, surveying the wedding party with a grin. 'Can you believe it, ladies and gentlemen? I feel like I've won the lottery. Just over a month ago, the most beautiful and talented woman ever born actually agreed to be my wife.' He turned to look at Harper, his eyes blazing. 'Thank you for saying yes, Pussycat.'

The guests breathed a collective sigh of pleasure. He paused for them to gather themselves before launching into his next charm offensive. 'Do you believe in love at first sight, ladies and gentlemen? The moment I saw her, I wanted Harper for my own ...'

She was in heaven as she listened – and a little bit amazed as he catalogued the qualities that had attracted him to her. These included her magnetism, her life force and the ability to make friends wherever she went. When he went on to describe her as clever, beguiling and captivating, she started to giggle. She was beginning to sound like a cross between Wonder Woman and Mata Hari.

'She's free-spirited, free as a bird,' he added. 'That's her essence, it's what I love about her, and I intend to nourish it – and her.'

'Thank you,' she said after the clapping and cheering died away. 'Especially the bird bit.'

She zoned out for a few minutes, thinking about how life could miraculously spin on a penny. Four months earlier, she'd had a flat and a cat. Now she was married and starting a family.

She came out of her daze as the main course plates were being cleared. 'Are you a member of a gym, Tom? A golf club?' she heard Scott ask her father.

'No, no, I don't do any of that.'

'How do you keep in shape?'

Tom smiled weakly. 'We live by the sea. I go for long walks along the beach.'

'Not quite the same though, is it? No drinks at the nineteenth hole?'

'He's a cheapskate,' said her mother.

'I've got the social club for all that,' her father said.

'But are you cardio healthy, Tom?' Monica asked earnestly.

Scott gave her a withering look. 'What do you know about it?'

The mood relaxed when her mother hit the red wine and cranked up her flirting with Scott, who flirted back. Even Harper could see that fifty-something Geraldine – known to all her friends as Gerry – was still an attractive woman. It was around then that her acting friends began breaking out of their straitjackets too. By the time the coffee and liqueurs arrived, everyone was joining in with impromptu speeches and sketches between the tables.

Gerry got up to regale everybody with the reason why she'd named her only child Harper, all because of her childhood passion for *To Kill A Mockingbird* by Harper Lee.

'What a book, eh? I'd never read anything like it. But me mates thought I was mad calling our girl Harper. "Who do you think you are?" they said. "Why don't you just stick to Sally or Susan, yer posh twat?"

'And I said, "Why don't you read the book first, before pointing the finger?" Oh, the horror! People started avoiding me in the street. They started whispering when they saw me. "Watch out for that one, she goes to the *library*!"'

The guests went into peals of laughter, and off went her mother into further tales of Harper's origins. Like Harper's dad, she came from a big, colourful, Tyneside family. Unlike Harper's dad, it had rubbed off on her.

When Gerry had finished speaking, her dad decided to get up and say a few words. He had turned down the chance to give a formal speech as the bride's father, but he obviously felt well enough to say something now. Harper's heart was in her mouth as he stood before the guests, nervously fiddling with his ear. Slightly stooped, with the last remains of a comb-over strung across his pale bald head, he had the air of a man whom life had defeated. But then he smiled, and his face lit up, and she remembered sunny summer picnics on the beach with Grandma Walters and the rest of the clan.

He cleared his throat. 'Picture this, if you will, ladies and gentlemen,' he said haltingly. 'A noisy social club in a northern seaside town in 1973, the bairn in a sequinned top hat and tails twirling her grandpa's silver-topped cane, and a crowd on the lash gearing up to laugh her off the stage.'

'Go, get 'em, Harper!' someone shouted.

'Now I knew that Harper loved to sing and dance,' Tom went on, getting into the swing of it. 'She was a reet show-off from the time she could walk and talk. But I didn't recognise the wee trouper who stepped into the spotlight on the rickety social club stage that Saturday night. She was thirteen going on twenty-five and she dazzled the daylights out of us.'

'What did she sing, Tom?' Angela called out.

The question appeared to throw him off stride. He shrugged and turned to Harper. 'What was it again, love?'

'I can't remember,' she lied. 'Something from *Sweet Charity*, I think.'

Her dad clicked his fingers, as if it had only just come to him. 'That's it, princess! It was always your favourite musical, wasn't it?'

A slight commotion at the back of the room drew Harper's attention. The next thing she knew, two hotel waiters were wheeling an upright piano towards her. 'Oh no!' she said, her hands flying to cover her face.

'Oh yes,' Angela said, taking over from Tom. 'It was your first public performance and I bet you can remember every word and every move.'

It was true. She could.

'Ladies, gentlemen and undecideds,' Angela went on, 'I give you Harper Allen, née Walters, now Clarke!'

'You monkeys,' she said, wagging her finger at them.

Tom grinned. 'Had you fooled, lass!' he said.

Steve from *Beauty Spot* sat down at the piano, cracked his fingers, and started into the first bars of 'If My Friends Could See Me Now'.

As she stood up and adjusted her dress, she made a split second decision not to give it the full Shirley MacLaine, as she had at the social club all those years ago, aged thirteen. Instead, to everyone's delight, she did a husky Marilyn impression, and Steve toned down his accompaniment accordingly.

There was much roaring and raising of glasses when she sang the line about eating fancy chow and drinking fancy wine. How prophetic, she thought when she sat down next to Aaron, still slightly out of breath. Had this really been her father's idea – or was Angela behind it? She could imagine Angela enjoying the irony.

Aaron clasped her hand and squeezed it so hard that it hurt. Leaning close to her ear, he whispered, 'You fucking slut.'

Shocked, she turned to look at him, wondering if she could have possibly misheard him. His mouth was smiling; his eyes were not.

'Didn't you like it?' she said.

'You're my wife now, not some performing slag,' he said. 'Don't forget it.'

She laughed, thinking that perhaps he'd had too much to drink. 'Of course I won't, darling. That part of my life is over now.'

She glanced over at the table where her Cullercoats friends were sitting. Stu was grinning at her, holding both thumbs up. Janice and Lizzie were whooping and clapping along with everyone else. Christopher was gazing at her thoughtfully. He'd always been a little bit in love with her, had Chris.

'Well done,' he mouthed. 'Hope you're happy.'

'I am,' she said, reaching for her champagne flute.

Next, Bill from *Beauty Spot* got up to impersonate Liberace, 'bestowing his deepest, most heartfelt well wishes' on the bride and groom. It was his party trick and he was spot-on funny. Before long, Harper couldn't breathe for giggling.

Aaron nudged her and whispered, 'I'm going upstairs now.'

She nuzzled his neck. 'Please can we stay just a few more minutes? It's been such a lovely evening, thank you.'

'I'm going *now*,' he said, taking her by the hand.

That was that. There were fresh tears of laughter pouring down her cheeks, but he expected her to go with him, and she did.

She missed the rest of Bill's take on Liberace. She missed three of her schoolfriends singing 'At Last' and ''S Wonderful'. And she missed Angela getting up, completely out of character, to tell off-colour jokes about one-legged jockeys and naked blondes.

She didn't mind, though. She was Aaron's wife now, expecting his child. She was his, and she was happy.

She could never be sure that the wedding was to blame, but afterwards her circle of friends seemed to shrink dramatically, and it continued to dwindle over the next few years. Maybe that was normal when you were a mum with a young child, but she knew it was partly down to Aaron. He didn't have time for a lot of the industry people in her circle. He was always saying that they weren't genuine friends – he called them 'liggers' and 'hangers on', which made things difficult for her. It was almost impossible to keep up a friendship with people your husband actively disliked, and so one by one they fell away, until only Angela remained. She still saw the Cullercoats gang once or twice a year, but it sometimes felt like they were in another country.

Aaron became more controlling after their Bahamas honeymoon, perhaps because he could – now that she was his wife and legally bound to him – or maybe he had always been that way. She would have liked the chance to ask one of his exes, but knew nothing about them beyond their first names. He was secretive about his past, an instinct she understood. It was better to live in the present, so everyone said.

Every day when he got in from work he rewound the answering machine and listened with his head close to the tiny speaker.

One evening he asked, 'Did you wipe over a message?'

'A message for you or for me?'

'Just answer the question, for God's sake.'

'Well, I deleted the one Angela left about her play. I wrote all the details down, so we don't need it.'

'I've told you not to wipe any messages,' he said softly.

'I don't see what difference it makes!'

'That's because you don't know. Leave the messages for me to hear – all of them. If the tape runs out, change it.'

She didn't dare to disobey. She always felt a tiny bit scared when he spoke softly.

Things worsened after the rose fiasco. She explained and explained why she hadn't told him the truth about the Italian man – and sometimes they spent whole evenings deconstructing what had happened – but he couldn't let it go. She'd cooked her goose, as her mother used to say. Aaron put it differently. She had stitched herself up like a turkey.

After that, he tested her to the limit. He rang the house throughout the day to check where she was – and was suspicious when she didn't answer the phone, even if she'd only popped out for some milk. He didn't like her to meet her friends for lunch, especially not male friends, not even gay male friends. Gradually he shut down all her social avenues.

She put up with it, though. She let go of her friends and turned inwards, happy to spend the final months of the pregnancy navel-gazing – literally, because she was enormous – and reading long family sagas set in turn-of-the-century northern mill towns.

When Taylor was born and she watched Aaron hold his little girl in his arms, bending over her in studied awe, with tears of wonder in his eyes, she felt that it had all been worth it – and she felt it would go on being worth it for the rest of her life. She was a mother. He was a father. Nothing else mattered.

Three years later they moved to Cheshire.

19

February 2013

She'd been caught in the glare of his headlights ever since, she thought, splashing water on her face. Meanwhile, what had he been doing all this time? While the light had been shining on her, he had been free to skulk about in the shadows, doing his own thing, unseen and unnoticed. So had there been others, apart from Angela? Watching him stride into the house, pulling off his tie as he went, she had a strong sense that there had. She turned away from the bathroom window. What did it mean? Was she going to leave him? She had absolutely no idea.

She decided she was probably in shock. Even though she'd been half prepared for Angela's admission about their affair, it had hit her hard, and now a numbness had come over her that reminded her of how she'd felt when her grandma had died. It was no bad thing, actually — it was useful. Feeling numb meant that she could reapply her make-up without crying again and calmly go downstairs.

Instead of falling on her knees and howling the house down.

Aaron was holding court in the lounge by the time she got down there. Vicky and the girls from the charity lunch practically had their tongues hanging out as they listened to his story of near-death and turbulence on a flight to South Korea. They were trying to outdo each other with their shocked reactions, gasping dramatically and saying things like, 'You're so brave!'

He looked so handsome it hurt. Desire flooded through her – uninvited, unwanted – and she nearly turned around and headed back to her bedroom. It was so unfair. He was still devastatingly attractive, perhaps even more so than when she'd met him. His wavy black hair had greyed, which had a softening effect on his chiselled features, and he wore it in a short, almost boyish style now. His green and gold eyes had lost none of their glint, and the ease with which he moved his lean, tanned body remained irresistibly sexy. No wonder her friends turned to mush when they were near him. No wonder they called him 'Cheshire's answer to Harrison Ford'. He was one of those men who didn't need to try. His air of relaxed confidence attested to his self-belief, which in turn radiated money and success.

She would have had sex with him there and then, if she could have. There again, so would all of the other women in the room, she suspected.

'No, not brave,' he was saying, smiling and shaking his head. 'But if I was going to die, I wanted to do it with a drink in my hand, so I asked her for a very large whisky.'

'And did she give you one?' Kelly asked.

'Oo-er, missus,' said Laura huskily.

'She tried to,' Aaron said, 'but we hit an air pocket and she lost her balance and tipped it all over the nun in front of me.'

This was greeted with gales of laughter. When it had died down, Kelly giggled and said, 'I've heard that there are some really naughty nuns out there.'

Harper took a sharp intake of breath. Was that a really embarrassing attempt at flirting, or was Kelly just pissed?

'Yeah?' Aaron said, looking perplexed. He glanced up and saw her. 'Sweetheart, where have you been?' He moved across the room to kiss her.

'Sorry, I had to take a phone call,' she said.

He laughed. 'One of your lovers?'

There was an outbreak of giggles among the girls. *As if*, they were thinking. As if anyone would want a lover when they had Aaron.

She alone knew he was being serious. It was a mistake to have said she was on the phone. He would interrogate her after the others had gone. 'Who were you talking to?' he would ask, again and again.

She played out the scenario in her head. 'I wasn't. I was just having some time out. You know what that lot are like.' She would show him the caller list on the landline and the mobile, to prove that she was telling the truth. Finally, once she had sworn on her daughters' lives that she hadn't been talking to anyone, he just might let it go. But then again, he might not.

She hadn't decided when she was going to confront him about Angela. Her instinct told her to sleep on it first. She'd like to thrash it out with Betty too – get her thoughts clear, find out what Betty thought about it all – but that would mean waiting until Monday, because Betty didn't work weekends.

She heard the front door opening. It was Taylor, back from dropping Angela at the station. 'Thanks for coming to the rescue,' she said, going into the hall. 'Did she make the train?'

'I guess so,' Taylor said coolly.

'Everything OK, darling?'

'Stop asking me that every five minutes, will you?' Taylor said, scowling. 'I'm not a baby!' She stomped up the stairs in the direction of her bedroom, leaving Harper wondering what she'd said wrong.

Aaron came into the hall. 'What's Taylor doing at home? Isn't Friday her big day at work?'

'I thought so too,' Harper said. 'I don't know what's going on with her. Maybe she needs to look for another job – and I definitely think she's too old to be living at home.'

'Don't be daft,' he said. 'Why leave, when she's got everything she needs here?'

'She needs her independence,' she replied. 'Which is something you can't have when you're living with your parents.'

'Only because you fuss over her so much.'

'Exactly,' she said. 'Fussing is what mums do, so if she doesn't like it, she should go.'

Just then, Georgie walked through the front door. 'Hi, Mum, hi, Dad,' she said, looking surprised to see them both standing in the hall on a Friday afternoon.

'Well, if it isn't Hattie Jacques!' Aaron said, turning to walk back into the lounge.

'Who's Hattie Jacques?' Georgie asked, looking wide-eyed.

'I haven't a clue,' Harper said, hoping she wouldn't follow it up.

'Mum, you haven't forgotten my play rehearsal tomorrow, have you? Ruby's mother can't take us, so I said you would.'

'I can't wait!' Harper said. 'As long as I'm allowed to stay and watch the run-through.'

'Yes, but, Mum—'

Harper laughed at the expression on Georgie's face. 'Don't worry, I won't embarrass you, love. I'll be as quiet as a wee mousy, invisible as a ghost.'

'Be serious, Mum, you're making me anxious already!'

'I'll be just like the other mums,' she said.

Georgie looked relieved. 'Thanks,' she said.

She went through the evening on autopilot. Taylor went out and Georgie went straight to her room after eating supper and didn't come out again. Aaron had work to do, so he spent most of the evening in his office. She was going to settle down and watch a film, but then Joyce from next door popped in to ask which company had gravelled their drive – and inevitably stayed for a drink and a moan about Walt.

Harper only half listened. There had been a constant buzzing in her head since the conversation with Angela, almost as if someone had placed a little fretting machine in there to agitate over the details while she went about the normal business of life. Only problem was, there weren't any details. She kept rewinding to the moment Taylor had interrupted them, shutting off her chance to pin down exactly what had happened. If only she hadn't bounded up the stairs when she had.

Joyce left eventually, after downing nearly a whole bottle of Sancerre. 'See you tomorrow night!' she said breezily.

'Lovely,' Harper said, her heart sinking at the thought of one of Joyce's dinner parties.

The buzzing got louder as she was taking off her make-up before bed. Where were the details to flesh out Angela's confession? All she had said was that they'd had an affair lasting less than a week – and she hadn't actually used the word 'affair'. She'd just said, 'It lasted less than a week.'

Presumably, 'less than a week' meant *nearly* a week; otherwise she would have said, 'just a few days.' So how many times would they have had sex in 'less than a week'? Five times a day for six days? Or once on the Thursday and once again on the Monday, when they'd decided to knock it on the head?

The not knowing would send her mad, she thought. Where had they met for their trysts? What was the sex like? Was Angela telling the truth when she said that nothing else had happened in the intervening fourteen years? Until she confronted Aaron, her mind would rattle and jar with questions and more questions, she realised. She felt a jab of lust at the thought of him.

It was time to put Angela out of her mind. Shut her out. Slam. She had other things to focus on right now.

She took a swig from the wine glass she had smuggled into the bathroom when they came upstairs to bed. She badly wanted Aaron tonight – she had wanted him from the moment she had come across him charming the pants off the charity girls. Desire was a sharp sensation, she thought, recalling the stabs of lust she had experienced as she watched him telling hero stories in the lounge. His powers of attraction were so strong they were practically superhuman.

Now it was time to get what she wanted – and what she needed. Aaron had never ceased to press the right buttons in the bedroom – and there was nothing as delicious as lying in his arms and being told that she was the sexiest, most beautiful woman in the world, the only woman he could ever love. Those words – along with the sheer heights of physical pleasure that he took her to – seemed to make everything all right.

She had no idea if she had nearly lost him to Angela, but she was determined to make sure he would never stray again. 'If you don't give him what he wants, he'll start looking elsewhere,' her mother had once told her. Well, here she was, giving him what he wanted.

Before dinner, she had hidden a new set of lingerie in

the towel cupboard by the door. She took it out and held it in her hands, all three hundred and fifty pounds' worth of it. It was a bra, knickers and suspender belt, three pieces of blue lace and silk so insubstantial they threatened to slither through her fingers and vanish, like magical water. She undressed and slipped them on, then opened a packet of sheer black stockings, rolled them gently up her smooth legs and fastened them to the suspender belt. Unhooking a silk wrap from the cupboard door, she draped it over her body and dug her feet into a pair of satin kitten heels.

Taking a deep breath, she walked into the bedroom.

20

The next morning, Georgie was up, dressed and ready to go at nine-thirty. 'Can you make me a packed lunch?' she asked. 'The canteen's closed at the weekends.'

'Er . . . ' Harper wasn't sure what they had in the fridge. 'Shall we pick up some sandwiches and snacks at M&S on the way?'

'Can't you just make me something?'

'Sandwiches, you mean?'

'And salad and fruit and stuff.'

'OK, let me see what I can rustle up,' she said breezily.

She wasn't fooling anyone. They both knew that she still hadn't got the hang of preparing packed lunches, even after all these years. But she was pleased that Georgie wanted something healthy in her lunchbox, for once. She was normally such a chips and sugar monster.

There was a large wholemeal loaf in the bread bin. She took it out and cut off a couple of slices. Well, they were wedges, really – what her mum would call doorstops, great hunks of wheat and roughage. She tried again, but produced another two slabs. Put together to make a sandwich with a block of cheddar between them, they looked like something only Worzel Gummidge would enjoy.

She peeled a couple of carrots and wrapped them in foil, then chopped some fruit into large, unwieldy pieces and crammed it into a Tupperware box. 'OK, what's next?' she said.

They picked Ruby up at ten-fifteen and arrived at the school ten minutes later. 'I'm so looking forward to this,' Harper gushed. Georgie and Ruby grunted politely.

As they walked along the quiet corridor to the assembly hall, she breathed in the unique atmosphere of an empty school. It felt wrong to be there, a little naughty, even – there was the ever-present possibility that you might burst into one of the classrooms and draw a willy on the blackboard while no one was looking. It was a sweet reminder of her schooldays.

She found it even more nostalgic to go into the hall and see the frantic activity of the stage crew as they prepared for the dress rehearsal. There may have been a technological revolution since she was at school, but some things hadn't changed. There were kids everywhere, labouring like worker ants, climbing, carrying and adjusting equipment. Meanwhile, Mr Nayar, the drama teacher, was issuing orders and clapping his hands every few seconds.

His face lit up when he saw Georgie. 'My witch has arrived!' he said.

'And your faun,' Ruby said.

'And my faun, of course,' he added, with another clap of his hands.

'I'm here to watch,' Harper said.

'Fine, fine, delighted,' said Mr Nayar, distracted by the sight of a boy carrying a wobbling ladder across the room. 'Any professional advice you could give us would be most appreciated.'

Georgie gave her a warning look.

'Oh no, I wouldn't know where to start,' she said. 'It's been so long now, and everything's so different.'

Once he was satisfied that the boy with the ladder wasn't going to knock the entire set over, he turned and met her eye. 'Could we have lunch together, at least? We're breaking for half an hour at one-thirtyish.'

'I'd like that,' she said. Georgie rolled her eyes. 'What?' she mouthed. It wasn't as if she had a choice.

While Georgie and Ruby went off to get ready, she settled into a plastic stackable chair and started reading the copy of *Vogue* she'd brought along.

Things began happening onstage about an hour later. She put the magazine down and steeled herself for what would inevitably be a long, drawn-out rehearsal of a not-very-interesting play. She didn't know much about it, but what she did know sounded like the opposite of entertaining. It was a modern production, written for schools, which meant that there were about fifty speaking roles – so that nobody got left out – and it drew heavily on the vampire movie genre, with a nod to *The Wizard of Oz*. It also featured songs. Oh God.

Georgie's part was bigger than most. She was playing the evil witch Malgosia and would be onstage for the entire second half of the play. Harper was worried that she had been miscast. Since when were wicked witches plump and rather sweet-looking? She suspected that Mr Nayar had deliberately cast her against type, but couldn't think why. Then she remembered that Georgie had only got the part after someone else had dropped out. Was she just a second-rate, make do, last-minute replacement?

Stop being so negative, she told herself.

She didn't think Georgie would have any problems getting up onstage. They had been through her lines several times and talked them over. The question was, could she act? Did she have stage presence? Harper glanced at her Rolex, wondering how long it would be before she found out.

As it happened, the play was pacier than expected and rattled along quite enjoyably. One of the lead boy vampires had a wonderful baritone voice and an excellent sense of comic timing. Harper wanted to clap after he'd finished his song, 'Me And My Fangs'. But she held back, not wanting to disturb the proceedings.

She sat bolt upright for the party scene that followed, knowing that the Georgie was due on any time. The sound of thunder and lightning made her jump and Malgosia appeared onstage wearing black rags and a witch's hat, looking nothing like Georgie. She emitted a ghastly cackle over the noise of the partygoers.

Great cackle, thought Harper, surprised at the power of her daughter's voice.

Next, Georgie launched into a monologue worthy of a Bond villain. Harper watched, transfixed. She dominated the stage, her curses ringing out as she damned the party guests to a life undead and lamented the disadvantages of being born wicked. Harper was impressed by the way she managed to combine murderous intent with vulnerability. It made her wonder how it would feel to look evil, and to be treated as if she were evil, even as a child.

Tears of pride sprang to her eyes. Risking Georgie's wrath, she stood up and cheered when they ran through the curtain call. Fortunately, Georgie seemed too dazzled, or too breathless, to notice.

Expecting her to rush round and ask her for feedback at the end, she thought carefully about what she would say. She had to get it right – too much praise might be crippling, as might too little.

But Georgie was nowhere to be seen. Eventually, she asked a passing stagehand if he could get a message to her. 'Who?' he asked, looking puzzled.

'Georgina Clarke. She's playing the witch.'

'OK, I know who you mean. I'll see if I can find her.'

She watched him sprint off. 'Anyone seen Jelly Clarke?' he asked three kids at the assembly hall door.

'In the canteen?' one of them suggested.

'Jelly on a plate, jelly on a plate,' another started singing.

The boy shushed them. 'Her mum's over there,' he said under his breath. Or that's what she assumed he said, because all three looked over in her direction. She pretended to be studying the cover of *Vogue*.

They wandered off, leaving her to wonder why Georgie was known as 'Jelly'. Was it affectionate or cruel? Was it because she wobbled?

Mr Nayar appeared. 'Lunch?' he said, swinging a small carrier bag back and forth. 'Shall we eat it here?'

'Why not?' she said. 'I was waiting for Georgina, but she's not come round.'

'Very good, isn't she?' he said, sliding a tray of sushi out of his lunch bag. 'Who knew? She's really blossomed since she took over this role.'

Harper grinned. 'Obviously I'd think she was brilliant if she were playing the back end of a pantomime horse – but, yes, she did seem to do pretty well.'

'She's got real talent,' he said lightly. 'If she wanted to take it further, I know a good acting agency in Manchester. There are lots of television roles for children her age and I'm sure she could cross over from the stage without too much problem.'

'Wow,' said Harper, fizzing with pleasure. 'That's high praise. I'll ask her about it when the play is over.'

'I'd be happy to help if she's interested.'

He separated a pair of wooden chopsticks and popped a dainty piece of sashimi into his mouth. 'Sorry,' he added, 'can I offer you some of this or did you say you'd brought a packed lunch?'

If she hadn't felt so hungry all of a sudden, she definitely wouldn't have produced her hulking ploughman's sandwich from her Waitrose bag for life. He affected not to notice as she clamped her teeth into the bread and ripped off a great chunk of cheddar and wholemeal, but it wasn't a comfortable moment, all the same.

In a flash, she rewound more than thirty-five years to another packed lunch in another school hall, with the handsome new English teacher who also happened to teach drama.

'You're very talented,' he'd said earnestly. 'I think you should consider becoming a professional actress.'

She had put down her sandwich in amazement. 'Do you really think so, Mr Smith?' She looked at him sideways, thinking how gorgeous and sophisticated he was.

'Yes, I do. And feel free to call me Mike from now on.'

That evening they went for dinner at Joyce's next door. Aaron had a spring in his step as they walked over there, no doubt generated by the prospect of Joyce's cooking. Joyce was a cook par excellence, to steal one of her favourite phrases. She'd done courses with cordon bleu, Leiths and the Four Seasons – or was it the Quatre Saisons? Harper could never remember and she didn't effing care. All she knew was that Joyce's fabulous cooking had been a source of irritation in hers and Aaron's marriage since they had first been to dinner with her, twenty years before. Because – as he never failed to remind her – despite her best efforts, Harper's culinary offerings were as slop in comparison.

'I hope it's boeuf bourguignon,' he said, rubbing his hands together.

'Really? Joyce's boeuf is always a bit rich for me. Takes at least a week to digest,' she said.

He didn't reply, preferring not to discuss such matters. 'I don't want to know things like that,' he had once said, when he'd overheard her telling a friend on the phone that she was bunged up after trying a new banana diet.

'I wasn't telling you,' she'd retorted.

She had forgotten to ask Joyce who else was coming to dinner and was dismayed to see Lydia and Harry Blyton standing on the doorstep as they arrived. Lydia had started a one-stop bridal business several years before and was unbearably smug about how successful it was. Now in her mid-forties, with a penchant for red lipstick and smoky eyeliner, she was a world authority on entrepreneurship – and had always been keen on Aaron. Her accountant husband, Harry, on the other hand, had a neck as thick as his head and was insufferably dull. Harper hoped against hope she wouldn't be sitting next to him.

'Darling man!' Lydia said frothily when she saw Aaron. 'I was hoping you'd be here.' She gave him a showy hug. 'And Harper!' she cried out. 'Wow, don't you look fabulous!' She gripped her by the shoulders and narrowed her eyes. 'What's your secret?' she asked, giving her a wink.

'Healthy living,' Harper shot back, breaking into a dazzling smile. 'Now give me a drink, someone!'

Lydia giggled and Harry chortled. Joyce opened the front door and welcomed them in. As usual, she attempted to greet everyone by kissing them full on the mouth. Harper swerved her lips and proffered her cheek instead, but Aaron got a full Joycey smacker. A whiff of boeuf bourguignon wafted into the hall as they took off their coats.

An hour later, Harper found herself trapped between Harry Blyton and a company lawyer named Mark Chambers. Harry was murmuring something about house prices in La Rochelle. Not only was he boring, but you had to strain to hear what he was saying. So much effort for so little gain, she thought, picking at her food.

Meanwhile, Mark Chambers was staring into the middle distance, or possibly at the enormous vase of lilies at the centre of Joyce's Danish rosewood dining table. Joyce, on his right, was forgetting her hostess duties, so rapt was she in conversation with Aaron. Lydia was listening avidly to Joyce and Aaron's conversation, ignoring Walt, Joyce's husband, in the process. Claire, Mark's wife, was also focused on Aaron, the wife magnet.

Mark started whistling under his breath, which Claire had once confided to Harper was a sign that he was angry.

'First they bubbled and then they locked it,' Harry was saying about the La Rochelle prices.

'You mean they doubled and then they rocketed?'

Harry raised one arm as high as he could get it, and nodded.

She turned to Mark. 'How's your home in the Algarve?' she asked. 'Has it doubled and rocketed?'

Mark took his time responding, but the mention of

the Algarve caught Claire's attention. 'We're so glad we bought when we did, but we would never sell,' she said, predictably. 'Why did you and Aaron never buy abroad?'

'We like to mix it up a bit, I suppose,' Harper said. 'Aaron didn't want to be tied down to one place.'

Claire appeared to stifle a giggle. 'That doesn't surprise me,' she said. 'He strikes me as the restless type.'

Harper wasn't sure she liked the not-very-subtle innuendo that was half buried in this remark. But if Claire thought she was a match for her, she had another think coming. Leaning towards her and smiling, she said, 'Believe me, he *is*. Lucky me, eh?'

Claire smirked and turned to speak to Walt.

Dessert was passion fruit mousse encased in a thin layer of chocolate, with a raspberry coulis drizzle and home-baked ginger snaps on the side. 'How long did it take you to make this, Joyce?' she asked, genuinely curious.

'Oh, a couple of hours, tops,' Joyce said dismissively.

'Piece of cake, eh?'

'Of course,' Joyce said with a laugh. 'Easy-peasy.'

A beautiful young Finnish woman named Tilda cleared away the plates. Joyce had introduced as her sous chef, but Harper imagined she was more of a hired help, because it would have been completely out of character for Joyce to let anyone help her in the kitchen. As she struggled to concentrate on Harry's explanation of France's archaic inheritance laws, she saw Joyce giving Tilda a discreet pat on the bottom as she carried the plates out of the room. When Tilda came back, Walt pulled up a chair for her and offered her a brandy. So it was like that, was it? Harper thought. Did Walt join in or just watch?

Out of the corner of her eye she saw Aaron leave the room. A couple of minutes later, Lydia Blyton followed him.

Normally, she would have thought nothing of it. But tonight she was on red alert. 'That's fascinating,' she agreed with Harry. 'Will you excuse me for a second?'

She headed out of the dining room into the hall. Neither Aaron nor Lydia were anywhere to be seen. She tried the handle of the downstairs loo. The door was unlocked. There was nobody inside. Had they gone upstairs? Her heart started to thump slowly and loudly, like the tolling of a funeral bell. Were they fumbling with each other's underwear in an upstairs bedroom?

Trembling, she began to climb the stairs. She couldn't bear the thought of discovering them together. But it would be worse not to know, she decided.

Just then, Aaron strode through the kitchen door, with Lydia skittering behind him. ' . . . not in a million years,' he was insisting, 'the margin is far too narrow.' Seeing Harper above them, he said, 'All right, Pussycat? What's wrong? Lost your way?'

Not only that, she thought, but I'm going mad.

She couldn't put it off any longer. She was going to have to challenge him about Angela tonight.

Georgie's bedroom light was still on when they got in. Harper knocked softly on her door and entered. Georgie was sitting sideways on a chair in front of her computer, swinging her legs nonchalantly. Her screensaver was a picture of a round-eyed kitten, innocent and sweet. Harper wondered what she had been doing.

'Still up?' she asked.

'Just shutting down,' Georgie said.

'You were brilliant today.'

'Thanks, Mum.'

'Everything all right at school?'

'Fine, thanks.'

Harper stepped towards her with arms outstretched. 'Give us a hug then, Sarah Bernhardt.'

'Sarah who?' Georgie asked, hugging her back.

Harper felt a wave of emotion as she held her daughter tight. How quickly her chubby-thighed toddler had grown up. Where on earth had all the years gone? A part of her wished that she could snuggle up in bed with her, but that would be impossible now, even weird. The days of cuddling little squidgepots were over until she became a grandmother, if she ever did.

Eventually, Georgie prised herself away. Harper noticed that there were tears in her eyes. 'Are you sure you're OK?' she asked.

'Yes, honestly,' Georgie assured her. 'What about you? Is everything all right with you, Mum?'

Harper felt a tingle at the back of her neck. 'Of course, darling. Why wouldn't it be?'

Georgie looked at her with sad eyes. 'I don't know ... it's just ... but as long as you're OK, I'm OK.'

'Well, I'm fine, really I am,' Harper said, giving her one last squeeze.

She felt worried as she made her way along the corridor to her bedroom. Something's not right with Georgie, she thought, wondering if it was anything to do with school and her 'Jelly' nickname. Or did the problem lie at home? And if it did, what the hell could she do about it?

She entered the master bedroom. Aaron, the wife magnet, was lying naked on the bed with an erection. 'It's like this, Pussycat,' he said with a grin.

'Oh, is it?' she replied, feeling a jab of resentment. 'Well, miaow.'

The conversation about Angela would have to wait.

21

She opened her eyes at seven the next morning to see Aaron standing over her wearing a sharp navy suit and crisp white shirt. She almost made a joke about being busted by the Feds, but the look on his face warned her off.

'Where are you going?' she asked, rubbing her eyes.

'Dusseldorf,' he said abruptly. 'There's a shirt missing from my case.'

She sat up. 'Really? That's strange.'

He kept a suitcase pre-packed for last-minute business trips. She was supposed to check that it contained everything on the list taped to the inside of its lid, but she usually left it to Betty.

She got out of bed, slipped on a dressing gown and went downstairs to the utility room, where Betty had left a rail of ironed shirts hanging up. She unhooked a couple – one white, one pink – and hurried upstairs with them. Aaron could of course have done this himself, she thought, but his emergency suitcase was Harper's responsibility – and he held her to it.

He was scowling when she got back to the bedroom, a world away from the playful, tender lover he had been the night before. 'I don't ask a lot of you,' he said, his voice seething with irritation. 'But somehow you always manage to fuck things up. How many times have I told you that I need my case ready to go at any moment? It's not too much to ask, is it?' He didn't wait for a reply. 'No, it fucking well isn't.'

She stood in the doorway, the shirts draped over her arm. 'I'm sorry, I don't know how it happened and I'll make sure it doesn't happen again.'

'You got that right, sunshine,' he said. 'Otherwise—'

'Otherwise what?' she jumped in. 'You'll go off and shag Angela again, or some other desperate housewife? In fact, how do I know you're even going away on business? On a Sunday morning?'

'Don't be stupid. I had a call at six this morning telling me that my only window for this meeting is today. It's not the first time it's happened.'

'Like it wouldn't be the first time you've shagged Angela.'

He grimaced. 'Don't start with that business about Angela again. I told you what that was about. Pack the white shirt for me – I'm leaving.'

She didn't move. 'I'm not talking about the photograph of you and Angela kissing. I'm talking about the affair you had with her fifteen years ago, when I was pregnant with Georgie.'

'What?' he said, screwing his face up.

'Yes, she told me all about it. Now I'm wondering how many other affairs you've had, Mr Possessive.'

He smiled wearily. 'Angela told you she'd had an affair with me? And you believed her? Come on, Pussycat, she's lying. She's a bitter, twisted old luv—'

'Don't say luvvie! You know I hate that word.'

'Woman, then. She's just a sad old—'

'And stop saying she's old! She's the same age as I am.'

'OK, just fucked up then. Whatever she is, she's lying, can't you see? It's so obvious what she's trying to do.'

'Is it? She didn't just come out with it – I had to force it out of her.'

His smile turned patronising. 'She's an *actress*, Pussycat!' He moved swiftly towards her and took her in his arms. 'Think about it,' he added. 'She's going through a divorce. She doesn't want you to be happy when she's unhappy, so she's dropped a bomb on you. She's a witch.'

'She wouldn't lie about something like that, Aaron!'

He pulled away from her, but kept his face close to hers, staring intensely into her eyes. 'You've forgotten who you're talking to, love. You're really accusing me of sleeping with that ugly mug? That minger? When I've got you? You're having a laugh.'

'Am I?' she said, beginning to wonder if he was the one telling the truth after all.

'Look in the mirror, darling. You're beautiful. Then picture Angela.' He waited a beat. 'I rest my case.'

'But it's not just about looks, is it? You both had your reasons for being pissed off with me. That's what brought you together, she said.'

'"She said,"' he mimicked. 'I wasn't so pissed off with you that I would have shagged a beast like Ange-fucking-la! I mean, how pissed off would a bloke have to be?' He laughed.

'To punish me,' she said simply.

'Then I would have told you about it, wouldn't I? Otherwise, where's the punishment?'

She could sense that she was losing. Or winning, depending on how you looked at it – losing against Aaron, winning against Angela. She gave it one last try. 'Maybe you had a drink, slagged me off and fell into bed together?'

He laughed again. 'Yeah, and maybe I give Betty one in the airing cupboard whenever you're not looking.'

He cupped her face in his hands and smirked. 'No, darling, it's not happening. I've never slept with Angela. I've never even looked at another woman since I met you. Now pack the fucking shirt and kiss your husband good-bye until tomorrow.'

Beaten.

She did as she was told.

Did she believe him? Only half. It was clear that she would have to go back to Angela if she wanted proof that something had happened. She couldn't imagine what the proof might be, though – apart from a photo, which surely wouldn't exist, especially after all these years. Aaron didn't have any distinguishing marks, so Angela wouldn't be able to point to a strawberry-shaped birthmark on his bottom or anything like that. What else could there be? She wondered if Angela would be able to come up with anything, when pressed. Maybe she wouldn't.

'I'm sorry, you'll just have to take my word for it,' she'd drawl.

Harper decided to save that particular phone call for later. In the meantime, she was going to try to have a nice Sunday. As soon as Georgie was up, they would go to the Grange Club and spend the morning by the pool and in the spa. Then maybe they would have some lunch, a selection from the huge choice of salads. She patted her stomach. Dinner at Joyce's had been rich and heavy. She was keen to stay off meat and carbs for the rest of the weekend.

She heard the sound of the front door. Wondering if Aaron had forgotten something, she made her way along the corridor to the top of the stairs and peeped into the hall. Taylor was taking off her coat and hanging it up. She was still wearing her clothes from the night before – her leopard print silk joggers, strappy heels and a sleeveless, black, glittery top – which suggested that she hadn't been to bed, although it was hard to tell.

'Hello,' Harper whispered.

Taylor looked around to see where the voice was coming from. 'Oh, hi, Mum,' she said.

'Is this a late night or an early start?'

Taylor pouted. 'What do you mean?'

Harper cocked her head and smiled. 'Well, do you fancy some breakfast, or are you still on the after-dinner brandies?'

Taylor rolled her eyes. 'Are you offering me a brandy at eight o'clock in the morning, Mother?'

'Of course not. It was a joke. I said it to make you smile, darling.'

'Well, it's not funny.'

Harper sighed. She fought the urge to ask Taylor if she was all right. The potential backlash wasn't worth it. 'How about a coffee, then?'

Taylor looked outraged. 'That's the last thing I need when I'm about to go to bed!'

It was time for Taylor to leave home, Harper thought. Really, really, *really* time – overdue already, in fact – and she wasn't going to listen to any more objections from Aaron.

'Well, it looks like I can't say anything right this morning,' she said. 'So I'll leave you to take yourself off. Georgie and I might be going to the club, if you want to join us when you wake up.'

Taylor shook her head. 'I won't be doing that,' she said. 'No way!' she added, under her breath.

Harper wanted to rush at her, scream at her and pull her hair. 'Since when did I bring you up to be so discourteous?' she wanted to shout. 'Where are your fucking manners?'

But she held her temper down. 'Suit yourself,' she said, turning away and heading back to her bedroom.

Georgie was still asleep at ten o'clock, her head twisted sideways on her pillow, big, brown curls spread around her face. If Harper half closed her eyes and blurred her vision, she could still see the little girl she had once been, the snub nose, pudgy cheeks and cherry-red lips.

Why do I keep wishing her young again? she wondered.

She knew a lot of mothers who felt nostalgic for the days when their children were babies and toddlers. One of the mums at Georgie's school was prone to saying, 'I begged my kids not to grow up, but would they listen?'

But Harper wasn't among the parents who looked back with a sense of yearning. She relished every new development in her children's lives, every step towards independence. So it felt odd to be experiencing this sudden wistfulness about Georgie.

As Georgie slept, she scanned her room for signs of trouble, or unhappiness. But all she saw was a typical teenager's bedroom, littered with pop posters, postcards and digital devices – an iPad, an iPod and a laptop. There was an empty banana skin in the bin and a plate covered in biscuit crumbs on the floor next to it.

On the wall above the desk was a slightly scrappy collage of family photographs that Georgie had cut out and glued for a school project a few months earlier. In the bottom right-hand corner was a favourite snap of Harper and ten-year-old Georgie, drenched and grinning under matching yellow sou'westers during a winter downpour on Cullercoats beach. Georgie's ice cream had blown away in the deluge and they'd laughed so much that they had barely felt the cold.

The focal point of the collage was a couple of photographs of Georgie and Taylor goofing around and hugging — something that didn't happen often, frankly — and another of Aaron with his arm round her, which happened even less. Harper felt a lurch of emotion as she looked at it. Poor Georgie.

'Wake up, sweetie pie!' she chirruped. 'Let's go for lunch and a swim at the club.'

An hour later, they were heading up the gravel drive leading to the Grange, a grand, ivy-covered Georgian house that had been remodelled into Cheshire's most exclusive sports club and spa. Aaron always whistled at the thought of how many palms must have been greased to get the planning permission. It was a fabulous place, decorated in the deluxe country style that Harper longed to recreate at Orchard End. The sight of the heavy burgundy damask curtains at the windows made her sigh with drape-envy. There wasn't a thread of peach velour to be seen in the whole building, not even the conference room.

As they got out of the car, she noticed Vicky Pacquard's Porsche. Two cars along from it, she spotted Patricia Bloom's Grand Cherokee. This was the only problem with the Grange — it was teeming with members of the Cheshire set. You could never get away from them. Still, today Georgie would be her protective barrier. 'Don't leave me alone,' she whispered as they walked up to the entrance. 'I'm not in the mood for chit-chat.'

Georgie giggled. 'But that's your life, Mum, that's what you do!'

Is it? thought Harper. 'Ha ha, very funny,' she said.

They picked up a selection of Sunday papers in the firelit lounge and went straight to the spa building, which had been built onto the main house in a sympathetic red brick style. Harper loved the pool area. It had a glass roof, a saltwater swimming pool and the world's most comfortable loungers. After they had changed in the locker room and found themselves a quiet corner to laze in, Georgie dived into the water and began to swim lengths of effortless front crawl. Harper looked on proudly. Both her girls were strong swimmers and had won swimming medals at school.

She flicked through the review section of the *Sunday Times* to see what was coming up on the West End stage. She still took the train to London for the occasional matinee and wondered if there was anything that Georgie might enjoy seeing too. She was reading an interview with Larry Lamb when a voice above her said, 'Snap!' Looking up, she saw Lydia Blyton smiling down at her, resplendent in a scarlet one-piece with matching lipstick, bag and FitFlops.

'So here we are on a Sunday morning, in a frantic attempt to swim off Joyce's dinner!' Lydia said. She groaned and patted her stomach. 'Mind if I plonk myself here a minute?' She dropped her bag onto Georgie's lounger.

Before Harper had a chance to reply, she was plonked.

Harper willed Georgie to get out of the pool and reclaim her place beside her, to no avail. Georgie was intent on swimming. Every few strokes she took a desperate rasping gasp of breath before plunging her face back into the water. She was oblivious to everything, even telepathy.

And so the chit-chat began. Harper admired Lydia's one-piece and Lydia admired hers. They talked about Melissa Odabash swimwear and a new boutique in Alderley Edge. Vicky's dog grooming parlour idea was discussed, as was the next charity lunch. Harper was losing the will to live by the time Lydia asked after Aaron.

'He's away on business,' she said, stifling a yawn. 'Left this morning. Back tomorrow.'

Lydia smiled knowingly. 'Harry's off on Tuesday. He's got a conference in Vegas. No prizes for guessing what he'll be getting up to in the evenings.'

'Does he like gambling, then?' Harper tried to imagine boring, thick-necked Harry calling the shots at a roulette table.

Lydia sighed. 'Funnily enough, that's not what I was thinking.'

'Oh,' Harper said, wondering what else it could be. Vegas equalled gambling, didn't it? Unless Harry was a Celine Dion fan.

'I sometimes wonder if he's got a number he calls from the airport,' Lydia went on. 'To say he's on his way.'

Harper was puzzled. 'Doesn't his office do that sort of thing for him?' she asked.

'I doubt it,' Lydia said, laughing softly. 'I can't imagine his secretary scheduling in his call girls.'

This remark merely added to the confusion for Harper. 'Sorry, Lydia, I'm lost. Is it Harry we're talking about?'

Lydia stared out across the pool. 'I saw it in a film once. At the start of every business trip the guy makes a call to an agency – and they set him up with a girl when he gets there.'

Harper laughed. 'I think I've seen that film. But you don't think Harry . . . I mean . . . surely you don't think Harry . . . ' She sat up straight on her lounger.

'I do,' Lydia said. 'Why not? They're all at it.'

'Who are?'

'Businessmen. The hotels are full of prostitutes, you must know that.'

'But it doesn't mean he sleeps with them, Lydia, come on!'

Lydia raised one eyebrow. 'He's a man, isn't he?'

'Not all men are the same,' Harper protested. Suddenly she felt as if she were defending Aaron, and her marriage. 'I just can't imagine Harry . . . ' She wanted to add, 'boring, thick-necked Harry,' but restrained herself. 'He doesn't need to stray, he's got you!'

'He has his cake and he eats it too, as my mum would say,' she replied.

Harper shook her head. 'You've got me totally confused now. If you think Harry sleeps with other women, why do you put up with it?'

Lydia shrugged. 'It comes with the territory. I knew

it when I married him. I love him. He's the father of my kids. And I don't believe in divorce.'

'OK,' Harper said uncertainly.

'Anyway, he'd ruin me if I left him. He's my main backer.'

Harper wondered what she could have possibly done to encourage Lydia to offload this sorry state of affairs. She reached over and gently touched her arm. 'I'm sure you're wrong, you know,' she said. 'Harry really doesn't seem like the type to play away.'

'Oh, I've seen his credit card bills,' Lydia said with a flick of her hand. 'Thousands of pounds, companies I've never heard of, all the usual. I've talked to other wives, I know the deal. I just hope he doesn't come back with anything nasty . . .'

'Nasty?' Harper asked. What did she mean? A threatening note? A pocketful of used condoms? A dead body in a suitcase?

Lydia stared at her coldly. 'I mean, a sexually transmitted disease. Look, either you're not taking me seriously, or you're incredibly naive. Hasn't it ever crossed your mind what Aaron might be getting up to when he's away?'

Harper bristled inwardly. 'Funnily enough, no,' she said.

'I'm amazed.'

'Well, there you are. Men, eh?' She forced a smile. 'Did you hear that Lauren Grayson is thinking about opening a maternity boutique?'

'Is she?' said Lydia, instantly taking the hint. 'What a fabulous idea!'

She tried to prevail upon Georgie to stick to salad during lunch, but Georgie wasn't buying it. 'I've been swimming for nearly an hour, Mum! I've earned my cheeseburger.'

'It's just so stodgy,' Harper said, taking a sip of Prosecco. 'Salad fills you up too, you know – without the bloated feeling.'

'Cheeseburgers don't make me feel bloated!' Georgie said with a grin. 'They make me feel great, because they're so delicious. But OK, I'll have salad – to please you.'

She came back from the salad bar with her plate piled so high that Harper felt embarrassed for them both. 'It's so unladylike! And people are going to think I starve you at home,' she complained.

'They won't,' Georgie assured her cheerily. 'They'll just think I'm really greedy.'

Harper didn't know what to say. She was terrified of mentioning Georgie's weight or size. Eating disorders were more dangerous to teenage girls than drugs and alcohol put together, according to the statistics, and she would rather have a plump daughter than a dead one. On the other hand, it wasn't easy, or healthy, to be over-weight. So, how did you help your children to get the balance right? She didn't have a clue. There had to be more to it than crossing your fingers and saying nothing, she thought, making a mental note to consult her GP.

She saw Lydia Blyton's BMW pull away as they headed into the car park after lunch. What was that all about? she wondered. Had the stuff about Harry been part of a ploy to plant seeds of suspicion in her mind about Aaron? If so, it had worked. She had imagined him dialling a secret telephone number from the airport about a thousand times already, damn her.

Back at home, she and Georgie settled down on the sofa in the TV room. 'Any requests?' she asked, pouring a glass of wine. 'Do you mind if it's in black and white?'

'Nothing too slushy,' Georgie said.

She chose *Double Indemnity*, and they watched in delight as Barbara Stanwyck sizzled, smoked and lured men to their doom. After which they defrosted a tub of Betty's legendary macaroni cheese, heated it up in the oven and polished it off between them.

22

'He totally denied it, of course,' she told Betty, the following morning. 'He didn't bat an eyelid, just said Angela was trying to make trouble. But why would she want to make trouble?'

'It doesn't add up,' Betty agreed, spooning sugar into her tea. 'Although some people are just troublemakers.'

'One of them must be lying, and you'd think it was Aaron. But I'm not sure. I mean, I know she fancies him, but I've never once had the impression that he fancies her back. Wouldn't I have sensed something in all this time?'

'It's hard to say, isn't it? One of my cousins was married to a man who had two separate families living in different cities.'

'So maybe I've been totally blind, then. After all, Lydia Blyton was amazed to hear that I don't worry about Aaron sleeping with prostitutes.'

Betty raised her eyebrows.

'I know!' Harper said. 'Like it's the norm! Like he's a freak if he doesn't.'

'What nonsense!'

Harper took a sip of her tea. She had never discussed Aaron's sexual inclinations with Betty, not because she thought Betty was a prude, but because she wasn't going to sit around the kitchen on a Monday morning, saying, 'We watched a lovely bit of porn last night and then he flipped me over and took me from behind. Well, what a climax, Betty! You should have been there!'

The fact was that there had never been anything to complain about, so there was nothing to discuss. She and Aaron had a great sex life. They seemed totally in synch – they both wanted a lot of sex and they had it when they wanted it, except when he was away.

Her heart turned over. Except when he was away.

She had always assumed that he did the same as she did when they were apart. Watched telly. Read a bit. Masturbated, maybe. Dropped off.

But perhaps she was being naive.

She knew that sometimes he took clients to high class girl bars, where they watched dancers twirl their pasties and gyrate around poles. She had never seen anything wrong with it. A few times she had gone along too and enjoyed the dark, glittery interior of the gentleman's club, watching the women flash their flesh while the men sat about like temporary sultans. Aaron assured her that it was all above-board, a harmless bit of fun. It may have been different in the less exclusive clubs, he said, but at the places he went to there was never any sex, it was just dancing, and most of the girls were doing it to help pay their way through college.

Only, what if there *was* sex?

Her thoughts were interrupted by Betty, who was finally responding to her comments about Lydia Blyton. 'I wouldn't listen to her, dear. She sounds warped.'

And this was the funny thing about Betty – gentle, benign Betty. She said 'warped' as if she were dispatching Lydia with a lethal flick of her fly swatter.

'You're right,' Harper said. 'I mustn't go down that road.' She drained the rest of her tea. 'But, Watson,' she said in her best Sherlock Holmes voice, 'this still leaves us with the rather thorny question of Angela.'

'Ah, Angela,' said Betty.

'Why would she want to break up my marriage by saying that she'd had an affair with Aaron, if she hadn't?'

Betty leaned forward expectantly.

Harper tapped her nose. 'We must eliminate the possibility that she hoped it would bring her closer to Aaron. It wouldn't, because he would know she had lied, and he would hate her for it.'

'True.'

'Then there is Aaron's theory that she is simply a jealous marriage-wrecker.'

'Hmm.'

'Or we believe Angela.' She slapped the kitchen table and stared intently at Betty. 'Well, what's it to be, Watson?'

There was a pause. 'I'm lost,' Betty said. 'What was the question again?'

Harper burst into laughter, which swiftly turned to tears. She put her head in her hands. 'You're right, Betty,' she said despondently. 'What *is* the question? Is it, "Do I trust Aaron?" "Do I love him?" Or, "Am I happy?" It's almost irrelevant whether he shagged Angela fifteen years ago.'

'*Are* you happy, love?' Betty asked.

'I don't know!' she said, breaking into sobs. 'It doesn't look like it, does it?'

'You've had a nasty shock, dear, and on top of your operation, too,' Betty said. 'It took months for Jim's sister to get over having her gallstones out. You need to take it easy.'

Harper snorted. 'I've been taking it easy for the last twenty-five years! I think I probably need to do something different now, before I make the final robotic transition into a Stepford Wife.'

'Now that would take some doing,' Betty said wryly, 'since you can't cook for toffee.'

'God, I'm not even up to being a Stepford Wife. Things are bad. What level am I at, then? A shop window mannequin? A blow-up doll?'

Betty stood up to turn the kettle on. 'Have a biscuit, love, and another cup of tea. Go for a walk in those lovely woods at the end of the garden. It's the simple things in life that bring us back to ourselves.'

Harper shook her head. A walk in the woods? What was Betty going on about? A woodland stroll wouldn't do her any good. But a comforting walk on Cullercoats Beach – now, that was more like it . . . Maybe she could bolt up there with Georgie, once the school play was over.

'You're a genius,' she said with a sniff. 'I need to remember who I am. I need to go home!' Her chest heaved – she wasn't sure if she was sobbing or laughing, or both.

'Now I'm starting to sound like Scarlett O'Hara.' She put on her best southern belle accent. '"Tara! Home. I'll go home. And I'll think of some way to get him back!"'

I'm becoming hysterical, she thought.

After Betty went off to dust the lounge, she wandered upstairs, only half aware that she was heading towards Aaron's wardrobe and suit pockets – until she entered his dressing room. It was ridiculous. She wasn't going to find any evidence of what might or might not have happened with Angela fifteen years ago, so what was she looking for? Invoices from prostitutes?

She went through every single one of his suits, but Aaron's pockets were empty. Typical, she thought. He was just too tidy to get caught.

His plane was delayed, so he said. She imagined him drinking coffee at the airport, waiting until it was too late to get to Georgie's school in time to see the play. He wasn't interested in Georgie's acting. He wasn't interested in Georgie. It broke Harper's heart.

She dreaded telling Georgie that he wouldn't be coming, seeing the disappointment on her face. Damn him.

He constantly teased the poor girl. He never had anything nice to say. Before the dinner at Joyce's on Saturday, he'd come across her eating a doughnut in the kitchen. 'Bulking up for your role in the school play?' he'd asked. 'What's the part, again? Bessie Bunter? Or Jake LaMotta?'

Georgie dropped the doughnut onto her plate and left the kitchen.

'Why are you so cruel to her?' Harper asked him.

He grinned. 'It's not my fault if she can't take a joke.'

'She probably didn't get it. She'll be thinking, Who the fuck is Bessie Bunter? And I doubt she's even heard of *Raging Bull*. Don't knock her like that. She's a super little actress and it's good for her confidence to be in the play.'

'I bet you love that, don't you?' he said with a sneer in his voice. 'Your darling daughter takes after you.'

'Why wouldn't I want her to do well? Wait until you've seen the play. You'll be amazed.'

But he wouldn't be amazed, because his plane was delayed. Taylor was also missing in action somewhere, with her phone switched off. The school assembly hall was packed with mums and dads, brothers, sisters and friends, but Harper was sitting alone, willing Georgie to do well amid the buzz of other families' expectations.

She found herself biting her nails in nervous anticipation, something she hadn't done for forty years. She instantly regretted it, not only because it played havoc with her manicure, but also because of the repulsive taste of pink shellac that lingered on her tongue as she waited for Georgie's big moment.

There was no telling whether Georgie would rise to the challenge of performing in front of an audience, or wilt in the face of it. Fortunately, she gave an earth-shattering performance as the wicked witch Malgosia and was cheered to the rafters when she came on for her final bow. As the audience whistled and clapped, Harper felt herself swelling up like a very large balloon – until she thought she would either float away into the ether, or pop.

After the curtain came down, she jostled her way through the milling crowds in her eagerness to get to Georgie and tell her how well she'd done. People kept stopping her to offer their congratulations.

'Didn't she do well?'

'Chip off the old block, eh?'

'Were you on the edge of your seat?'

'Didn't she?' she said, nodding and beaming. 'Can you imagine? Heart in my mouth! Absolutely thrilled.'

Mr Nayar was acting as an informal guard at the entrance to the corridor leading to the cast dressing rooms. She ran up to him and congratulated him.

'Thank you!' he said, radiating pride and relief at nuclear levels. 'We couldn't have done it without Georgina. She was brilliant, I'm sure you'll agree.'

Harper grinned. 'She did really well. Can I go through and see her?'

'Of course. She'll be in the dressing room at the far end of the corridor.'

She hurried along, brimming with excitement. As she neared the end of the passageway, she heard singing, or perhaps chanting, from behind the last door along, and remembered how great it felt to let off steam after a first night success. The singing became louder. She knew the tune, but couldn't put her finger on it. Then she recognised it.

'Jelly on a plate, jelly on a plate ...'

The song came to an end and the voices began shouting out numbers. 'One ... two ...'

Somebody was being given the bumps.

She didn't stop to think. She burst into the end room to find Georgie horizontal in mid-air, still wearing her witch's costume, legs and arms flailing, screaming for help, with a group of ten kids in a circle around her.

She had the presence of mind not to cry out until Georgie had been half-caught, half-dropped on the floor after her third bump. Then she yelled, 'Stop this now!' in the most authoritative voice she could summon.

The circle of kids turned to gape at her. She wanted to wrestle each one of them to the ground and throttle them senseless. Georgie scrambled to her feet, almost tripping on her ragged black hem. 'Mum? What are you doing here?' she asked.

Harper frowned. 'This is dangerous and against the rules. Now get out, all of you, or I'll report you to Mr Nayar.' She held the door open and the gang trailed out. She hoped that none of them could see she was trembling.

She looked over at Georgie, whose eyes were wide with shock. 'Are you OK, darling?'

'That was so, so embarrassing!' Georgie gasped.

Harper folded her arms across her chest. 'I'm sorry, but I couldn't stand around and watch you get hurt,' she said shakily.

'I wouldn't have got hurt! It was the bumps! We were celebrating the end of the play.'

Harper looked closely at her daughter. Did she really believe that, or was she scared to admit she was being bullied? 'I'm sorry,' she said. 'You'll just have to tell them your mum's a tyrant.'

'I can't believe it! I'll be slaughtered tomorrow.'

'Oh, darling, I hope not. You can't be the only one with an embarrassing mother.'

'That's true,' Georgie said, looking thoughtful. 'What are you doing here, anyway? I didn't think parents were allowed backstage. Where's Dad?'

Harper flung her arms around her. 'I came to tell you how brilliant you were! You were the best thing in the play by far – you brought the house down!'

Georgie smiled and lowered her eyes. 'Thanks,' she said, rocking on her heels.

'Mr Nayar let me come through. He says – and I agree with him – that you're talented enough to take this further, if you'd like to. He knows of an acting agency in Manchester that he thinks would snap you up. You could try out for TV, maybe. What do you think?'

Georgie looked surprised. 'Really?'

'Hasn't he said anything to you?'

'I'm not sure I'd like to join an acting agency.'

'Why not? Didn't you enjoy yourself tonight?'

'I did, but I don't think I'd like the pressure of trying to act professionally.' She hugged Harper back. 'Mum, I really love you, but—'

'Hey, Georgie!' a voice interrupted. They turned and saw Georgie's friend, Sophie, in the doorway.

'Hi, Harper,' Sophie added with a big smile that showed off her new pink braces. She looked at Georgie again and said, 'Did you ask her?'

'Can I go and stay with Sophie tomorrow night?' Georgie said.

'Of course. Where's your mum, Sophie? I'd just like to check it with her.'

Tiffany was in the corridor chatting to Mr Nayar. 'Did you really?' she was saying. 'Well, it was cooler than cool. You're totes amazeballs, as Sophie would say.' She giggled.

Harper went to stand with them. 'Harps!' Tiffany squealed, putting her arm around her and squeezing her. 'Georgie was awesome!' She'd obviously had a glass or two and her breath was warm and acrid – the breath of someone who'd been drinking wine on an empty stomach.

'Just checking that it's OK for Georgie to come and stay tomorrow night,' Harper said.

'And maybe the night after, too,' Sophie said, bouncing up to join them.

'Hang on, that would be—'

'Awesome! We love having Georgie. She's adorbs.'

'Mum! Embarrassing!' Sophie hissed.

'Well, great, then, thanks,' Harper said. 'Will you be able to take her home from school?'

'No worries,' Tiffany said, swaying slightly. 'I'll bundle her in the jeep and we'll bomb away like bats out of hell.'

'I'd like to see you bombing like bats at a steady thirty mph,' Harper said. 'Those speed cameras are everywhere. They're a nightmare.'

'If you go fast enough, they can't register it, so I've heard,' Tiffany whispered in a confidential tone.

Harper laughed, her mind racing to think up an excuse for dropping Georgie off herself. 'Well, if I hear a loud bang, I'll know it's you lot crashing through the sound barrier.'

Tiffany gave her a playful push. 'Only kidding. Don't worry, I drive like a granny on Valium, everybody says so.'

'Well, that's reassuring,' Harper said.

Tiffany pushed her again. 'You're funny,' she said, her eyes zoning in and out of focus.

In the car on the way home, Harper said, 'I might pay Grandma and Grandpa a visit while you're staying at Sophie's, love.' She looked over at Georgie. 'Or I could wait until the weekend and you could come too,' she suggested.

'I've got swimming club on Friday, and it's Ruby's skating party on Saturday.'

'Wow, a packed weekend,' Harper said. 'I'll go tomorrow then, as long as you'll be fine at Sophie's.'

'I'll be fine. Stop worrying about me.'

'Hey, you know why I worry, don't you?' Harper

teased. 'Because I love you THIS MUCH.' She briefly took her hands off the steering wheel and stretched them as wide as they would go.

'Be careful!' Georgie said, giggling. 'You're a crazy person, Mum.'

'Hashtag coolmum?'

'Hashtag deluded,' Georgie said. 'Sophie's mum thinks she's cool, but she's well over forty! What a saddo.'

Harper pulled up outside Orchard End, desperate for a glass of wine.

Aaron and Taylor were having a cosy drink on the sofa. Harper opened a bottle of white and poured herself a large glass. 'Georgie did so well!' she said as she joined them in the lounge. 'You missed out.'

'Sorry I didn't make it,' Taylor said, not sounding sorry at all. 'I was stuck in the meeting from hell.'

Harper doubted that. 'A sales meeting?' she asked.

'Yes,' Taylor said, avoiding her gaze.

'What were you discussing?'

'Strategy.'

'Strategy?'

'Yeah, planning and strategy.'

Georgie wandered in. 'What happened to you, Dad? I thought you were coming to see me.'

'My plane was late, plumpkin.'

'What time did you land?' Harper asked.

He shrugged. 'About eight.'

'Eight? What reason did they give?'

'Fog.'

'Fog?'

'Yeah, fucking fog.' He cleared his throat. 'It was good, was it?'

She sat in the cream armchair between the sofas. 'Amazing. Mr Nayar says Georgie should try out for TV. He thinks she's really talented.'

'Georgie is?' Taylor said.

Aaron's lips twisted into a sneer and Harper knew he was about to make a nasty comment about Georgie's weight. 'I thought I'd go to Cullercoats tomorrow,' she said, to head him off. 'Unless anyone wants to come with me, in which case I'll wait until the weekend.'

Taylor laughed. 'Not the fucking nostalgia tour again! How many more times can you drag us along that seafront with a cone full of mussels in one hand and a packet of winkles in the other, pointing out the places you kissed boys? Eurgh.' She wrinkled her nose. 'Anyway, I'm busy this weekend.'

Just the mention of mussels and winkles gave Harper a longing for the seaside. 'You used to love doing that walk,' she said. 'Looking out at the shuggy boats, playing the penny arcades.'

She went back to the kitchen and poured herself another glass of wine. 'Night!' Georgie called out on her way upstairs. 'I'm off to bed.'

'Off to Instagram, you mean,' Taylor murmured. She glanced at her phone. Suddenly her expression changed and she started yawning and stretching. 'Actually, I'm going to bed too.' She gave Aaron a tickly giggly cuddle and sloped off with barely a glance at Harper, who wondered again if she had done anything to upset her.

Aaron stood up and shook his legs. 'You're not really going north, are you? What brought this on? Don't tell me you're missing Tom and Gerry.'

Harper took a swig of wine. 'I need to clear my head,' she said. 'Anyway, I haven't seen them for ages. It'll be good to check up on them, make sure they're all right.'

'Bit sudden, though, isn't it?'

She sighed. 'It's been a long few weeks, Aaron.'

'Where are you really going?'

'Like I say, Cullercoats.'

'How long for?'

'A night or two.'

'What about me? What am I supposed to do while you're gone?'

She shrugged. 'The same as I do when you're gone, I guess.'

'What, hover round the kids? Get drunk with a group of silly, giggling women?'

'If you like.'

He strode towards her and grabbed her arm. 'What's got into you? Where are you really going?'

She tried to shake him off. 'Hey, let go!'

He tightened his grip. 'Which one is it? The waiter or the doctor?'

'Let go, I said! I don't know about any waiter or doctor. I'm going to see Mum and Dad.'

'You don't know, eh? You don't know who you're going to be fucking tomorrow night? Haven't decided yet?'

'Stop it!' she shouted. 'I'm not going to be fucking anybody! I'll be lying in my single bed at my parents' house, listening to the wind whistle down the street. And I'll be wondering why on earth I'm still married to you, the world's most jealous man – and why you still don't trust me, after all these years.'

He released her arm, leaving red marks on her skin, and smiled grimly. 'Because you're not trustworthy, sweet pea, and you never have been. Only, I found out too late, when you were already pregnant with Taylor.'

She stepped forward and pointed a finger in his face. 'Don't even think about bringing up that rose again! What about you and Angela? What about you and God knows who else? I've never suspected you of cheating because I would never dream of cheating on you. Whereas you can't stop imagining me with other men. What does that say about what you get up to?'

'Oh, very clever,' he said, narrowing his eyes. 'Fucking psychologist, are you now?'

'I wish I were, because you bloody well need one,' she replied. 'Listen to yourself! Where am I going? Why don't you put a bug on my car so you can trace my every boring trip to a charity lunch or shopping centre?'

'How do you know I haven't already done it?'

'Because if you knew what I was doing, you'd know how predictable my life is and you'd stop asking all these stupid questions. But go ahead, be my guest. Employ a private detective. Have me followed tomorrow. What a dull fucking job it'll be for the poor sod, hiding outside my mum's kitchen window listening to three people slurp their tea and talk about what her at number fifty-two has been doing to her front garden.'

'It's shrewd of you to call my bluff,' he said in his low, menacing voice, 'but it won't work. I want to know where you're really going, Pussycat, and you'd better fucking tell me now.'

She laughed harshly. 'Read my lips, boyo. I'm going to Cullercoats. You can ring me on the home number there a thousand times a day and I will still be in that kitchen, or in that single bed, wondering what the fuck is wrong with you.'

'I'll know if you're not there,' he said, in a barely audible whisper. 'And if you're lying, I will come after you.'

She wanted to scream. It felt like her head was on fire. 'Tell you what, why don't you just beat me up and kill me now?' she said. 'Save yourself the hassle of all those phone calls. Put me out of my misery.'

'Misery?' he said contemptuously. 'You call this misery? Living in a six-bedroom house? Credit cards galore? Four holidays a year? I'd like to see you try to live any other way.'

'I could easily live without it,' she said, although she wasn't sure if it was true. 'As long as I had a husband who loved and trusted me.'

She marched into the kitchen and poured another glass of wine, her mind whirring. Back in the lounge, she said,

'Actually, I don't think I want this life any more.'

'What are you saying?'

She frowned. What was she saying?

'Because, believe me, baby, if you tried to leave this marriage, I'd make sure you left without a penny.'

Her throat went dry. 'Why would you do that?'

'You're joking, aren't you? Would I give you cash to flash at other men? No, I fucking wouldn't.'

'Lucky I've got some money of my own, then, isn't it?' she said.

He gave her a look of contempt. 'Your pathetic little pot of savings wouldn't keep you going for more than a few months, babe – a year, tops. Especially as you've spunked most of it on treats for the kids and cruises for Tom and Gerry.'

She shook her head, still trying to put out the fire. 'This is ridiculous. We haven't even discussed splitting up and you're already talking about the divorce settlement.'

'You said you're leaving me.'

'Aaron, I'm going to Cullercoats for a couple of nights to clear my head and think things through! That does not constitute leaving you.'

'You said you don't want this life any more.'

'What I mean is that we're stuck. We have a great life, but we need to find a way to move forward, leave behind all the doubts and accusations. Maybe we should even think about going to couples therapy.'

'Therapy schmerapy,' he said. 'You need to know one thing, and one thing only. If you leave me, I will destroy you. That's all the talking there is to be done. Understood?'

She stared into his green glittery eyes. 'That's it? Can't we talk about what's going wrong with us?'

'Fuck you,' he said. 'If you go to Cullercoats tomorrow, I *will* have you followed.' He stalked off to his office and slammed the door.

23

The first place she went was the seafront. As she got out of the car, the smell of salty air brought tears to her eyes. I'm home, she thought. The sense of relief was overwhelming.

She found comfort in all the familiar sights – the golden horseshoe curve of Cullercoats Bay, the vast grey horizon beyond it, the church spire to the south, the Watch House to the north and the lone white cottage on the promontory. Against a backdrop of pale blue winter sky, a patchwork of clouds hung over the calm sea, which shone in the early afternoon light.

This is exactly where I'm supposed to be, she thought.

Half an hour later, she was standing in the porch of her parents' house inspecting their freshly painted front door. Silage green must have been on special offer, she decided, because surely it wasn't a colour you would actively choose to present to the world, even if you were in your mid-seventies and slightly depressed.

Her father answered her knock. His face lit up when he saw her. 'Harper, love.'

'Hi, Dad,' she said, giving him a hug. She stood back, looking for the cloud of gloom than generally hung about him, and was surprised to find it was absent. 'How are you?'

'All the better for seeing you,' he replied with a grin. 'You look grand. How was the drive?'

'Pretty good, three hours.'

'Is that the bairn?' her mother called from the kitchen.

'Here she is! Put the kettle on, love,' her father said.

Her mother came into the hall. She had a dishcloth slung over her shoulder.

'Hey, Mum,' she said. 'Hope I haven't disrupted anything by coming at such short notice.'

'Not at all, love. Only I forgot to tell you I've got me book club tonight, so I'll be out from seven.'

Harper laughed. 'Book club, is it? How times have changed!'

Her mother smiled. 'It's the *Richard and Judy* effect, isn't it? Say what you like about them, there's no denying they've done a lot to get people reading.' She ushered Harper into the kitchen, where the kettle was reaching boiling point.

'So "library" is no longer a dirty word in this town?'

'Only to the council. They're trying to shut them down all over the north-east. It's a scandal.'

'Yer mam's joined the campaign against the closures,' said her dad.

Her mother sighed. 'We need more publicity. If only you were still famous . . .'

Her words lingered in the air as she poured out the tea.

'I feel as if I should be apologising,' Harper said, 'but that would be silly, wouldn't it, since you were the one who encouraged me to get married and give up acting.'

'Nothing to apologise for, love,' her father said.

They sat down at the kitchen table and she was brought up to speed with the local gossip, deaths first. 'Remember Auntie Mabel? Doyenne of the social club?'

'Of course! She gave me my first spot, when I was thirteen. Don't tell me she's—'

Her mother nodded solemnly. 'Passed on last week, very sudden. The funeral's on Friday, if you can stay that long.'

'It depends . . . I'm not sure when I'll need to get back.'

Her mother bristled. 'I still don't understand what you're doing here when we're due down to you within the fortnight.'

'Is anything wrong, princess?' her father asked.

Tears pricked her eyes. 'Things aren't great with Aaron,' she said. 'He's very hard to live with.'

'Nonsense!' her mother said, as if she had just announced that the Queen was North Korean. 'He's the best provider I know. You've got everything you could possibly want, and more – and so have the children. What on earth have you got to complain about?'

'Mum, it's not necessarily the material things . . .'

'They count for a lot, let me tell you,' her mother said, with a note of warning in her voice. 'You need your comforts, especially when you get older. Not to mention the odd treat.' She shot a sideways glance at her father. 'I don't know where we'd be without our Mediterranean cruises, thanks to you and Aaron. And you love your trips to the Bahamas, don't deny it.'

'I know, I'm lucky – but it's not the holidays I'm talking about, it's the day-to-day living.'

Her mother made a face. 'You've still got Betty, haven't you? She does all the cleaning? The cooking, the washing?'

'Yes,' Harper said, realising how ungrateful she must seem, especially to someone who didn't have a house-keeper or a purse full of credit cards. On the other hand, she was sick of constantly reminding herself how fortunate she was to live in a nice house with plush carpets and a gravel driveway.

'But what about love?' she asked.

'Love?' Her mother spat the word out. 'It's all the same when you've been married for thirty years, believe me. After that, it's your lifestyle that's important – and I know people who would cut off their right arm to live like you do, so don't knock it.' She got up to refill the kettle, signalling that the subject was closed.

Harper looked across at her dad but he was engrossed in the local newspaper crossword. She smiled ruefully to herself. It had always been difficult to talk to them about her feelings – she couldn't suddenly expect things to change now. 'Sounds like a fair trade to me,' she said, trying to sound cheerier. 'They'd have to carry their hand luggage with their remaining left arms, but at least they'd be sitting in business class.'

Her father looked up and chuckled. 'Just 'aving a bit of 'armless fun.'

She and her mother groaned and soon they were back onto safer subjects – gardening, parking, Taylor and Georgie. They had three cups of tea each, one after the other. The sheer predictability of it was comforting. The only noticeable variation from the norm was that her father seemed in far better spirits than usual, and a far cry from the armchair lump she remembered from her childhood. Today he could almost be described as chatty.

'You're in good form, Dad,' she said with a smile. 'What's come over you?'

He leaned back in his chair. 'You know what, princess? I put it down to the new carpet in the living room.'

'Really?'

'Indeedy. I finally persuaded yer mam to get rid of that swirly monstrosity. It used to give me a headache just looking at it.'

Harper got up and popped her head round the living room door. 'Very nice!' she said, admiring the plain blue carpet. She could see his point. The room looked a thousand times less busy than it had with a floor full of green and red swirls.

'And that was all it took?' she asked. 'A change of carpet?'

He scratched his head. 'The new front door, of course.

Never could stand navy blue. And they've started up a photography club in town. I've been going there of a Thursday evening and—'

'He's on new pills,' her mother interrupted. 'We've finally got a GP who understands.'

Her father nodded. 'The heaviness has gone,' he said. 'At last. Fingers crossed.'

After an early tea of lamb chops with mint gravy, boiled potatoes and peas, her mum set off to her book club two streets away, threatening to return a little tipsy. 'We'll have a few sherbets,' she told Harper as she left. 'Gail's making some sort of fizzy cocktail and Moira's promised to give the ivories a tinkle.'

'Sounds like a reet proper literary soirée!' Harper said, feeling slightly envious that her mum was spending the evening with friends she'd known since her schooldays.

She herself had almost completely lost touch with her Tyneside mates now, although she wasn't entirely sure why. She had a feeling that time, distance and Aaron were the main influencing factors, but fame had also driven a wedge all those years ago.

She had never forgotten the time she'd been up in Cullercoats during the early days of *Beauty Spot*'s success. A group of them had been round at Janice's house and someone had suggested going to the pub. But after five straight days of filming the series, she hadn't been in the mood for a rowdy session at the Bird In The Hand.

'I'm that tired,' she'd said, 'I don't really fancy it tonight. I'll catch up with you lot tomorrow.'

'Oh, sorry we don't have a West End premiere for you to go to,' sniped Beverly Fisher, with a glinty gleam in her eye.

The remark confused her. 'Wait a minute, Beverly, all I've said is that I don't want to go to the pub.'

'That's all right,' Beverly replied. 'Don't worry about your old mates. You'd better get your beauty sleep, love.'

It still made her angry to remember Beverly's self-satisfied smile as she dished out her poisonous little nuggets. So she didn't miss Beverly Fisher one jot, but she would have liked to see more of Janice and Lizzie, her besties from school. She, Jan and Lizzie had gone around in a trio at Cullercoats High – and three was never a crowd as they moved through the different stages of girl-hood. Whether they were playing dolly dress-up, beach rounders or hiking up their school skirts to show off a bit of leg, they were all in it together, laughing as they went and endlessly taking the mickey out of each other.

They had gone on to get fall-down-drunk for the first time ever, during the long, hot August of 1975, when they had plundered a bottle of Jackie's mum's gin, only to be sick over her new crazy-paving. Since it hadn't rained in weeks and there was a hosepipe ban, Jackie's mum was more worried about how she was going to get the vomit out of the cracks than she was about their teenage delin-quency. So, after they'd done their bit with scrubbing brushes and Fairy Liquid the following morning, they hadn't even been grounded.

That whole summer had been spent listening to Lizzie's

tinny tranny and working out dance routines to tunes by The Stylistics, Hot Chocolate, Minnie Riperton and Disco Tex and the Sex-O-Lettes. The rest of the time they had giggled and sweltered over boys, in particular Robbie Harper, a velvet-eyed, tousle-haired hunk in the year above them. She couldn't count the number of times she had dreamt about marrying Robbie! Yes, even if it meant changing her name to Harper Harper, an idea that had made Lizzie laugh so much that she'd wet her knickers at the bus shelter.

Two years later, she had gone off to drama school in London, met Angela and started smoking gold-tipped cigarettes. It hadn't been the end of the trio, but things had definitely moved into another phase. At her wedding to Aaron, they had promised to stay in touch, tears streaming down their faces – and in later years, Janice, John and the kids had come to stay at Orchard End a couple of times. But she hadn't seen much of them in the last decade.

Had she seen them at all, in fact? Once or twice she had invited them to join her and Aaron for lunch at the Bird In The Hand – or maybe it had been the Coach and Horses – but they hadn't come. They hadn't snubbed her exactly, just made vague excuses. She'd had dinner with Lizzie at the Italian bistro in Whitley Bay that one time, but maybe it had been more than ten years ago, she couldn't remember. What had they talked about? It had been fun, anyway.

There hadn't been any falling out – they had just grown

apart, she decided. It was inevitable, since they lived so far from one another. It was a pity, but that was just the way things went. You couldn't expect to be friends for ever unless you lived in the same town for your entire life.

'Can I get you a drink?' her dad asked, once her mum had gone.

'Is the pope Catholic?' she laughed. 'I put a couple of bottles in the fridge earlier. But I don't suppose you'll have a glass of wine with me.'

'No chance, princess! Your mother has a drop from time to time, but I can't stand the stuff.'

He turned on the telly and they watched *Corrie* followed by a dreary detective drama, chatting over the dull bits. He told her about an exhibition of historic paintings of Cullercoats. He passed on news of random members of the family she couldn't recall. They reminisced about the social club when it was run by Mabel.

'So Georgie's got the Walters' genes, you say? Good little actress, is she?' he asked. Georgina had always been his favourite of the girls. He and Taylor rubbed along, but she was much more akin to her granny.

'Amazing. Her teacher says we should sign her up to an acting agency in Manchester.'

He frowned. 'So young? Is that wise?'

'She seems to like the idea.'

He grinned. 'Next thing you know, she'll be chomping at the bit to go to London – if she's anything like you were, that is.'

She didn't like to say that her desperate need to leave

home had been as much about getting away from her ma and da as it had been the lure of drama school.

'Actually, I'm not sure she's got it as badly as I did.'

'Don't push it, then,' he said. 'Let her grow up first.'

'I'm not *pushing* it,' she said. 'I'm *encouraging* it. I think it could be good for her. I'm worried she doesn't have a lot of confidence. She's a little bit on the heavy side, as you know, and ...' Suddenly her eyes filled with tears. 'I heard some of the kids at school calling her "Jelly" the other day,' she blurted out.

Her father tutted. 'Children can be cruel.'

'Aaron doesn't help,' she added, unable to stop now. 'He constantly makes jokes about her weight. He calls her "Ten Ton Tessie" and "Fatty Arbuckle" and says she should look into getting a career at Greggs. I know what you're going to say, that he's only teasing, but—'

He shook his head. 'Never liked him.'

'Who?' She looked at the telly. 'Jeremy Clarkson?'

'That husband of yours. You should never have married him.'

She was speechless for a few moments. 'Really, Dad? Why haven't you ever—'

'He's a right mardy bastard – and now you're telling me he's being hateful to our Georgie. No, I can't hold my tongue – that man deserves a dunking in the Irish Sea. But I'll say no more now. You get the picture.'

'I can't believe it,' she said. 'I had no idea.'

He put his hand up to stop her. 'I'll say no more. Your mother'll kill me. The arguments we've had, princess!

She's all in favour of him. Can't see for looking, some-times — that's yer mam. Wonderful woman, but she's got her blind spots, just like the rest of us.'

'But why—'

He turned away from the television and jabbed a finger at her. 'You should have stuck to your acting, princess. That's what yer mam never realised. It made you happier than bloody Aaron has.' He sat back in his chair again. 'But at least you've got your daughters.'

She held his gaze. It struck her that she could probably count on one hand the number of times she had looked her father in the eye without one of them looking away. 'Taylor and Georgie are the best thing that ever happened to me,' she said. 'So perhaps you're wrong about the acting.'

He screwed his face into a disgusted expression. 'You would have met someone else and had children with them,' he said. 'But you got to twenty-nine and you panicked.'

She felt a surge of anger. There was so much more to it — and he knew it, too. 'Or maybe I just wanted to be with someone who was the opposite of you!' she said, flaring up. 'Someone dynamic and go-getting — someone who achieved things, instead of sitting around in an arm-chair for months, barely saying a word.'

He sighed. 'That's as well as may be, and if it is, I'm sorry,' he said. 'I'm not saying I'm blameless. But you have to take into account the fact that I was ill. It's a shame. I was a shambles. You and yer mam had a lot to put up with.'

'It wasn't just your depression, Dad — if that's what it was. Actually, I didn't know what was wrong with you. All I knew was that you weren't like other people's dads, that you had what Mum called "bad patches".'

'None of us knew. If we had, I could have got help.'

'And there was never any money! All you two ever did was argue about money. So I chose someone who could provide. Only . . .'

' . . . it wasn't enough, princess. I know, and if I had anything to do with it, I'm saying sorry now. But don't worry, you'll sort it out, one way or another.'

'Thanks, Dad, I'm sure I will,' she said, feeling guilty for having a go at him.

They watched the regional news in silence. 'I think I'll go off to bed now,' she said.

'Right you are. Night, love.'

Up in the childhood bedroom, as she lay in her single bed flicking through *Tammy* annual 1970, she heard the sound of the front door. 'Where's the bairn?' her mother asked. 'Driven her to bed with your boring photography club stories, have you?'

She heard a low mumbling, the sound of her father recounting some of their conversation, presumably.

'What have you been saying to her, you old fool?' her mother screeched.

Her father said something else she couldn't hear. He had mumbling down to a fine art, she thought.

'You're full of nonsense, the pair of you,' her mother replied. 'Hearts and flowers, starry nights — well, life's not like that! Don't you dare start stirring things up, Tom Walters. She's got a lovely lifestyle down in Cheshire and she'd better know which side her bread is buttered. The furnishings at Orchard End alone are worth more than this house!'

Oh God, what am I doing here? Harper thought, trying to squash her head under a solid foam pillow to block out the noise. But it was no good. As her mother began pointedly totting up the many advantages of being married to a rich man, she got out of bed and stomped downstairs in search of another glass of wine.

They had lunch at Caesar's Café on the cliffs the following day. Her mother had mackerel, her father had sardines and she plumped for cod, chips and peas, which was delicious and worked wonders for her hangover. 'They're doing a brisk trade for February,' she said, looking around at the tables full of people. Most of the diners were of retirement age, but it was still surprisingly crowded, especially for a weekday.

'People love the seaside, whatever the time of year,' her father said.

She nodded and popped a final chunk of cod into her mouth. Some coastal towns could be depressing in winter, but Cullercoats off season had its own special appeal. The scent of candyfloss and ice cream was never far off, which in turn evoked memories of the Spanish City at Whitley Bay, and the funfair, and spinning on the Waltzer in the sunshine, screaming with fear and laughter.

'I've been to some places,' she said. 'But the fish and chips here just can't be bettered.'

'You mean, it can't be battered!' her father quipped.

She frowned. 'But it can be battered, Dad,' she said.

He chuckled. 'In one sense it can, but in another it can't.'

'So it doesn't really work as a pun, then, does it?'

'Oh, give it a rest, love,' he said in an irritated tone.

Her mother leaned forward. 'It's the silverback pound,' she muttered.

'What is?'

'All these people spending their pension pots. They call them "the lucky generation". Pity we missed out.' She leaned back and pursed her lips.

'We haven't a pension pot to piss in,' her father said with a hollow laugh.

They were examining the dessert menu when a woman appeared at their table. Harper looked up first. 'Remember me?' the woman said. Her short hair stood up like a brush and she was wearing very pink lipstick.

'Beverly!' she said, cranking up a smile. Of all people, she thought.

'On a flying visit to see the folks?' Beverly asked.

'Oh no, haven't you heard? I've left the hubby and kids and decided to move back in.'

Beverly laughed. 'You haven't changed. Still the same old Harper.'

'Less of the "old", please!' Harper said, running her fingers self-consciously through her hair.

'You haven't changed on the outside, either,' Beverly said. 'You look amazing.'

Harper was flummoxed. A compliment from Beverly Fisher? She felt like standing up and banging a gong. 'Well, thank you, Beverly, you don't look so bad yourself,' she said. 'We're doing OK for fifty-something, aren't we?' she added, in a stage whisper.

'Seen anyone else?' Beverly asked.

'Here, you mean? I only got here yesterday . . .'

'Because Lizzie's having a jewellery party for the girls at her house tonight, if you fancy coming along.'

'Really? Has she taken to robbing banks? Will she be divvying up the spoils?'

'Don't be daft,' Beverly said with a smirk. 'It's like a Tupperware party, but with jewellery. It's good fun, actually – but probably not your sort of thing.'

'Why not? Do you drink each other's blood as well?'

Beverly's smile became less smirkish. 'I mean, it's not going to be very glamorous.'

Oh, here we go, thought Harper.

'Why would you think I wouldn't want to come and have a night with a great bunch of girls, Beverly?' she asked.

Beverly's mouth twisted slightly. 'Well, your life is so grand, isn't it?'

'Oh, my life is grand, is it? What makes you think my life is grand?'

Beverly looked at her mother, who looked away. 'It's just what I've heard.'

'Well, I'd love to come! Thank you. Does Lizzie still live in the square? Should I ring her and let her know first?'

While her mother went to an appointment at the dentist, she and her dad had a walk along the Tynemouth Longsands. 'It's good to see you happier,' she said, breathing in the salty breeze.

'It's not been easy,' he replied with a thin smile.

She wanted to link arms with him, but hesitated. There had never been much physical closeness between them and she was worried it would feel awkward. Then he stumbled very slightly over a large stone and she took her chance, looping her arm through his and cosying up against his shoulder. Soon they were in step together. It felt a little bit weird, but she was glad to be close to him, and he was quite an effective windbreak.

She asked him about Grandpa Billy Walters, because she loved to hear about the days of music hall, the rowdy audiences, the way you had to sucker punch the crowd the very moment you stepped onto the stage if you wanted to avoid being booed, or worse. Billy had spent most of the 1920s and 1930s touring northern music halls, honing his act. In the end he'd been something really special, according to the people who knew him.

'Most of the variety acts were one-trick ponies, but they said Billy Walters could do anything on stage,' her father was telling her again, as they battled a sudden wind to reach the north end of the beach. 'He literally had people falling off their seats at his impersonations. I was too young to understand a lot of it, but I remember seeing rows of people crying with laughter.'

'I wish I'd seen him.'

'He stopped the show sometimes – and when I say that, love, I really do mean that he stopped the show. The other acts couldn't come on until he'd done his turn all over again, sometimes once, maybe more.'

'If only there was something on film,' she said.

Her father's eyes shone. 'You would have loved him,' he went on. 'After the war and his years in ENSA, he was even better, they said. He really had to stretch himself to make the wounded soldiers laugh. It was difficult. Some of them had half their faces blown off, but he still brought a smile. Then he was all set to get his own show on the radio . . .'

'It must have been awful when he died,' she said. 'For you and the others, for the whole family.'

'We just got on with it in those days,' he said stiffly. 'Your nanna kept the family together. She was an amazing woman, a stalwart.'

'I know,' she said, her throat closing around an unexpected sob. 'I wish she were here now. I'd really like to talk to her.'

'She'd tell you how lucky you are, no doubt.'

She nodded and looked down at the sand. 'Weren't you ever tempted to follow in Billy's footsteps?'

'No, lass, I was too caught up in the science of ship-building – and the romance of it too. I used to dream about building a ship and sailing away in it.'

She felt a twitch of resentment. 'But you ended up driving forklift trucks in the warehouse,' she said waspishly, as if her mother were speaking through her.

'That I did,' he agreed.

'Was shipbuilding just a childhood fantasy, then?'

'In a way.'

'A pipedream?'

'Not quite.'

There was a silence, and all she could hear was the soft crashing of the waves against the shore. 'Was it your illness that landed you in the warehouse?' she asked finally.

'That's right, princess. The company were going to sponsor me to do my studies, but then you came along, and we were only just twenty-one, yer mam and me.'

'But that wasn't young for those days, was it?'

'It was young enough.'

'And you were ill just after I was born?'

'I had a breakdown about a year later.'

'That's when you stopped studying.'

'I wasn't well enough to go on, and it would have meant trips away, which was a problem because I didn't want to leave yer mam . . .'

Didn't you? she thought. Aaron hadn't had any misgivings about it, especially after she'd had Georgie.

' . . . or you. A right gorgeous little bundle, you were.'

'But, effectively,' she said – and she was amazed that it was the first time she had fully realised it, 'your dreams came crashing down after I came along.'

He tilted his head from side to side, as if weighing up

her words. 'You could just as easily say that it happened after your mother came along – and there might be some truth in it. But it still wouldn't explain my illness, love. I have clinical depression. There doesn't have to be a reason for it.'

They left the beach and made their way up the cliff road. 'Does it run in the family?'

'I don't know, princess. Let's hope not, eh?'

'I'm thinking of the girls,' she explained.

'Of course you are,' he said.

Her phone rang just as they pulled up outside the house. 'You answer that, love,' her father said. 'I'll go inside and put the kettle on.'

It was Aaron, calling from the Orchard End phone. 'What is it?' she asked, her heart thumping. 'Are the girls OK?'

'I'm ringing to tell you how much I love you, Pussycat,' he said, his voice chocolatey smooth. 'I've never looked at another woman. You have to believe that.'

'OK,' she said hesitantly.

Was he going to apologise? He sometimes flipped moods after an argument, when he had been particularly cruel to her. There was a pattern to it. He would push her to the very brink, to the point where she almost jumped, and then he'd pull her back with lavish gifts and declarations of love. Her heart would soften then. She'd fall into his arms and forgive the viciousness. Why? Good question.

She looked down at the rings on her fingers. The

sapphire cluster on her right hand had arrived in a little white jeweller's box, the day after an all-night spat about whether or not she had smiled at a muscular pool attendant. The pink diamond next to it was his apology for a whole weekend of nagging about a low-cut dress she had worn to one of Joyce's dinners, allegedly to entice Walt into bed.

She felt like throwing them out of the car window. The usual pattern of things was unravelling. Her heart wasn't softening today.

'What are you doing at home?' she asked.

'Packing,' he said. 'It's the Frankfurt deal. We're finally closing. I'll be away for at least a week, I'm afraid.'

'Where are you going?'

'South-east Asia.'

'Ah.' An image of a glossy-haired prostitute appeared in her mind's eye.

'Will you come out and join me when it's over?' he asked. 'I'll book us into the Bali Oberoi for a few days.'

She inhaled sharply. Just thinking about the Oberoi filled her with longing – the villas with their own private gardens, the four-poster beds, the crisp sheets changed daily, languorous sex in the afternoon, the aquamarine sea, the huge orange sunsets, cocktails on the terrace . . .

'What about Georgie? I can't leave her in the middle of term time.'

'Come on,' he wheedled. 'She can stay with one of her little schoolfriends, can't she?'

It was so tempting.

But the pull of home was stronger. She thought quickly. 'I've just remembered, there's a Ladies of Compassion lunch in ten days' time. I'm on the committee. I can't duck out of it.'

The Oberoi visions faded, and disappeared.

'Anyway, we're going to Ibiza at Easter. That's only a few weeks away,' she added.

There was a pause on the line. 'Do you know how much I love you?' he said.

'Yes,' she replied automatically.

'You wouldn't ever leave me, would you?'

She thought about it for a second. Would she?

'No, of course not,' she said.

'Pussycat!' he exclaimed.

'Miaow,' she said obediently.

'I'll call you from the airport.'

'OK, bye!'

Talking to Aaron prompted her to call Angela. She left a message, because of course Angela wasn't picking up her phone. 'Would you give me a ring, please?' she said, in what she hoped was a subtly commanding manner. 'I need to speak to you about what we discussed last time. I'm up in Cullercoats, so I'm free to talk all day.'

She had barely disconnected when her phone rang again. It was Mr Nayar from Georgie's school, apologising for phoning her mobile and asking how she was. 'Remember the acting agency in Manchester I mentioned?' he asked.

'Yes?'

'The director, Ron Gover, rang this morning. They're doing a priority casting for a children's TV series next week. They've got a rush on to get it cast and I thought Georgina might like to try out for it.'

'Great! It'll be good experience for her, if nothing else. Will they send over some pages?'

'It's all being taken care of. Ron saw the video of the play yesterday. He singled out Georgina's performance.'

'How exciting! So, how do we go about setting up a meeting?'

Just then, her mother tapped on the car window. 'Who are you jabbering on to, then?'

'Sorry, I'm going to have to go,' she told Mr Nayar.

'"He said," "She said,"' her mother mimicked. 'Gossip, gossip, gossip, all day long. That Beverly was right. You haven't changed a bit.'

'Shut up, Mum,' Harper said with a smile as she got out of the car. 'You know nowt about nowt about nowt.'

24

She had a quick glass of wine to fortify her before setting off to Lizzie's. Then she phoned Tiffany to check that Georgie had survived the granny batmobile from hell.

Tiffany answered after thirty rings. 'Harps! How's it hanging in the north-east?'

'It's jumping, Tiff. All fine with Georgie?'

'Cool. YOLO!'

'What are the girls doing now?'

'I swear down I haven't seen them since we got in. They're in Soph's room, glued to her computer. It's all they do, these kids, right? Screen time!'

'I guess. So they're fine. Good. Tell Georgie to call me if she wants a chat.'

'Cool.'

'Thanks, Tiffany.'

'No worries, *bella. Ciao!*'

She drove the short distance to Lizzie's, figuring she

could leave her car and either walk or get a taxi back. As she stood outside the house, she stamped her feet to keep warm. It helped with her nerves, too.

Lizzie answered the door. Her face was wonderfully familiar. The high cheekbones, the twinkly blue eyes, the black mop of hair – none of it had changed.

'Harpo,' she said, grinning.

'Groucho!' Harper replied.

She wanted to fall into Lizzie's arms and weep for joy that she had finally reached a place where somebody really knew her – inside out and through and through.

'It's so great to see you!' she said.

'And you,' Lizzie said. 'You look amazing. Come in and have a drink.'

'I brought a couple of bottles with me,' she said as she edged her way along the narrow hall. She tried to hold up her Sainsbury's bag for life, but it was too heavy and so she dragged it.

'What've you got there, missus? Brought your laundry with you, did you?' Janice piped up from the lounge, where there was already quite a party going.

'Janno!' Harper called out. 'It's booze, mon. There was a two-for-one offer at the supermarket.' The bottles in the bag clinked as she took them into the kitchen. 'Is there room in the fridge?' she asked Lizzie.

Lizzie stared as she unpacked them. 'You brought six bottles of champagne with you?'

'Bling! It's a jewellery party, innit?' Harper said. 'Are the glasses already in there?'

'Wait, I might have some flutes in the cupboard.'

'Wine glasses will do!' Harper said. She grabbed two bottles and took them into the lounge. 'Now, who's for a glass of bubbly?' She looked around the room and picked out a familiar face. 'Beverly! Bubbles?'

'Wine's quite good enough for the likes of me, thanks,' Beverly said, raising her glass and smirking.

'Are you sure about that?' Harper said. How about a cup of bile? she thought.

Janice stepped up and gave her a hug. 'You still know how to make an entrance, don't you?' she said, her brown eyes fizzing with amusement.

'Well, if it isn't Janno Glasshouse!' Harper said, putting down the bottles and hugging her back.

Jan laughed. 'You haven't changed! "Your hair is burnt sienna, your eyes arc barley wine, my darling Harper Walters, when will you be mine?"'

'You remembered!' Harper said, her eyes wide with surprise. 'I never did find out who sent me that Valentine's card.'

'Are you sure?' Beverly called from across the room.

Harper felt irritated. Beverly had never been one of her inner circle and the Valentine's card had nothing to do with her. 'Gosh, Beverly, age hasn't withered your hearing, has it?' she said.

'I reckon it was our drama teacher,' Beverly said, coming closer. 'Who else would have used the word "sienna"?'

Harper reached for a bottle and started opening it. 'Mrs Manley? That's a joke. If anyone, it was that gorgeous

Robbie Harper!' She pretended to preen herself in front of the mirror.

'Mr Smith, I mean,' Beverly said doggedly. 'The sixth form drama teacher. He used to follow you with his eyes.'

'Mr Smith!' Harper said, as if she had completely forgotten about him. She popped the cork and poured out two glasses. 'You mean he used to watch me doing drama in the drama class, Beverly? Kind of like you would expect a teacher to do?'

'He used to watch you in the dining hall too.'

'Yes, because she was his star pupil,' Jan said with a chuckle. 'It doesn't mean he was sending her love notes!'

'Well, that's my theory,' Beverly insisted.

'I can't believe we're scrapping about a card that was sent ... what is it now?' Harper gasped. 'Oh my God, nearly forty years ago!' She leaned against Janice to say a silent thank you for backing her up. Only Jan and Lizzie knew about Mike Smith. She was certain they would never have told Beverly.

'And you barely even look forty,' Lizzie said. 'What's your secret? Had a facelift?'

Harper gulped down her champagne. 'Eye job,' she said. 'I didn't want it. Aaron talked me into it.'

She was astonished at how easily the truth came out. It happened naturally when you were among real friends, she thought, moving in closer to Jan and Lizzie, shutting Beverly out in the process.

They caught up on as much news as they could jam into seven minutes of party chat. Jan and John had just celebrated their thirtieth wedding anniversary with a week in the Canaries. Lizzie and Dan were fast approaching their twenty-fifth. Harper filled them in on Taylor's new job and Georgie's school play.

'So how would you feel if your Georgie went on to be an actress?' Janice asked.

'I'd be thrilled, of course.'

'You wouldn't feel a twinge of envy?'

'Not at all! I'm quite happy to live out my thwarted dreams through my children.'

It felt good to be joking around with old mates. 'I've missed you,' she told them. 'Why haven't we seen each other for so long?'

Jan and Lizzie exchanged glances. 'You can't say we didn't try,' Jan said.

'What do you mean?'

Lizzie grimaced. 'Well, I rang the house that time and spoke to Aaron ...'

'When?'

'On your birthday, about five years ago. And then on your fiftieth, of course.'

'It's news to me. He can't have passed the messages on.'

Lizzie's mouth turned down at the corners. 'Let's face it, Aaron doesn't like us much. Doesn't approve. We're not swanky enough for him.'

'That's not true!'

'We certainly can't afford to turn up to a party with a sackful of champagne,' Jan added.

Harper felt overcome by guilt, as if she'd been caught

eating caviar for breakfast while they rummaged about in her dustbins for scraps of food. 'I splashed out because it was a special occasion,' she said, in an attempt to sound less spoilt. 'It was cheap as chips, anyway,' she added. 'Only twelve quid a bottle!'

Jan and Lizzie raised their eyebrows and she realised her mistake.

'I just wanted to celebrate seeing you, after so long,' she said with a weak smile.

'It was a nice thought,' Lizzie said.

Harper felt a huge gulf opening up between them. 'You know me,' she said, nudging Jan. 'I'd be just as happy with a bottle of plonk.' She finished her second glass of champagne and went to pour another.

Lizzie looked at her watch. 'Right, I'd better go and sort my boxes out. I'll start the jewellery sale in about ten minutes.'

Jan was collared by another guest and Harper was left alone, no longer feeling on familiar territory. She surveyed Lizzie's lounge. It was crowded, so it seemed a little cramped, but it was beautifully done up using different paint effects in sea greens and blues. Lizzie and Dan obviously had a flair for interior decorating on a budget.

'I love the way they've styled this room,' she said to a woman in a dark trouser suit standing nearby, who looked a bit like Erin O'Connor on an off day. 'What would you call it? Distressed vintage? Shabby chic?'

'Don't you dare say that in front of Lizzie,' the woman said, giving her a hard look.

Harper giggled. 'No, no, shabby *chic*, I said.'

'Oh, go and drink some more champagne, why don't you?' the woman said under her breath, as she moved away.

'Good idea,' she said, resisting the urge to stick her tongue out at her behind her back.

She was about to go over and compliment Lizzie on her taste when someone else came over. This time it was a salt-and-pepper-haired woman wearing a white turtleneck sweater under a blue cardigan. She reminded Harper of Tabitha Twitchit.

'Well, then?' the woman said expectantly.

Harper blinked and smiled as she waited to hear whatever was coming next. She had a feeling she wasn't going to like it.

There was a pause. 'Don't you remember me?' the woman said at last.

'Er, I do . . . but . . . ' She tried to wind back time as she looked at her, stripping away the greying hair and wrinkles, pulling off the middle-aged clothes and replacing them with school uniform.

'The time I picked up your books when you dropped them in that puddle?'

'Oh.' She pretended that the memory was just out of grasp, but gradually returning. 'Was it during that huge downpour?' she said tentatively.

The woman rolled her eyes. 'You see, that's typical of you. It wasn't a downpour, it was a light shower, but you were screaming that your hair would get ruined. Drama, drama!'

Harper laughed. 'Had I been going at it with the curling tongs again?' She leaned forward, desperately trying to recall ever having spoken to this woman before. 'Sorry, I'm having a senior moment. My mind's gone blank and I can't remember your name.' She threw her hands in the air. 'How ridiculous is that?'

'April Wright, as was. I was two years below you at school.'

'April!' she exclaimed, none the wiser.

'Now you remember!' April said smugly. 'And I can finally ask you why you didn't mention me and my broken leg in that Tyne Tees interview you did about the school drama department.'

Harper had no idea what she was talking about. She couldn't remember being interviewed on Tyne Tees twenty-five years earlier, nor could she be bothered to go through the mental strain of trying to recall what she might or might not have talked about. What's more, she had no memory of April, or of April's broken leg.

But she hadn't forgotten how to bullshit.

'Oh, but I did!' she said. 'Believe me, April, I told them all about you and your poor leg. Can you believe they cut the whole segment out? I was furious, as you can imagine.' She shook her head angrily, and then shrugged. 'That's editors for you. You never know what angle they're going to take.' She took a glug of champagne. 'We are but celluloid pawns in the cutting room of life,' she added, for good measure.

April looked taken aback, as if she hadn't really

expected an explanation, and Harper wondered if they had ever, in fact, really known one another. Fortunately, she didn't have to waste any more time thinking about it, because just then Lizzie declared the jewellery bar open.

The guests gathered round a small table, where Lizzie had laid out an array of trinkets. Harper immediately saw a bracelet she liked and moved forward to pick it up. 'This is lovely,' she said, holding it up to the light. 'How much is it, Lizzie?'

Lizzie looked down at a price list. 'The tennis bracelet? It's twenty-four pounds.'

'Ooh, bargain!' Harper said. 'Do you take cheques or is it cash only?'

'I've also got a card machine,' Lizzie said.

'Brilliant! I'll go and find my bag.'

Lizzie followed her across the room. 'Please don't feel you have to buy anything,' she said. 'I realise it's all tat compared to the stuff you wear.'

'Don't be silly, I really like it!'

Lizzie grabbed her arm. 'Don't patronise me,' she said. 'There's a pink diamond on your finger, and it's not even your engagement ring.'

'Pink diamond?' Harper looked down at her right hand. 'You mean this piece of rubbish? It's just a zirconite, or whatever they're called. I don't like it much, actually. Hey, will you swap it for the bracelet?'

Lizzie stared longingly at the ring. 'It doesn't look like a zirconia to me, Harpo.'

'It's a good fake,' she said, slipping it off her finger. 'Please have it. I was going to chuck it away.' She pressed it into Lizzie's palm. 'What else have you got over there?' she added, walking back to the jewellery display. 'I'm a sucker for glittery things.'

She hoped she wasn't too obviously trying to compensate for their earlier exchange about the champagne. Either way, it was a relief to get rid of Aaron's ring. She felt lighter and freer without it.

She went on to choose a necklace for herself and a bracelet each for Taylor and Georgie. 'Their birthdays are coming up soon,' she told Janice.

'Wasn't Taylor a summer baby?' Janice asked, with a sideways glance.

She pretended not to hear. Heading back to the kitchen, she found another bottle of champagne and popped it open.

Beverly came in as she was pouring it out. Janice was right behind her. 'Yer mam says you go to charity lunches where the tickets are two hundred quid,' Beverly said. 'Is that right? Two hundred quid a ticket?'

'Sometimes,' she admitted, feeling sheepish. 'But don't listen to my mum. She's full of tall tales.'

'They must be amazing dos,' Janice said. 'Yer mam says it's all glitz and glamour, loads of women wearing Lanvin and Jimmy Choos.'

'I'm surprised my mum knows what Jimmy Choos are!' Harper said. 'Seriously, don't listen to her. She thinks the secret to happiness is having a rich husband.'

'Well, isn't it?' Beverly said, her eyes challenging Harper to deny it.

Harper took a swig from her glass. 'There's more to life than money.'

Beverly laughed shrilly. 'Next you'll be telling us that money doesn't buy you happiness.'

Harper took a deep breath. She was desperate to tell Janice what she really thought of the Cheshire set and their charity lunches. But she didn't want to share anything with Beverly Fisher.

She stepped closer to Beverly and put her face close to hers. 'Money is a bit like sex, isn't it?' she said coolly. 'It's not very important until you don't have enough of it.'

Beverly turned and walked out of the kitchen.

Bullseye! Harper thought.

Jan made a face. 'That was a bit harsh. Beverly's husband left her a few months back.'

'Oh, I'm sorry,' Harper said. Her head began to swim and she leaned against the wall for support. 'But I've had enough of everyone talking to me like I'm Elizabeth Taylor.'

'Come on,' Jan said. 'There probably isn't a woman at this party who wouldn't swap places with you.'

'You wouldn't!'

'I'd be tempted, though.'

'That's because you don't know what my life is really like.'

Jan flashed her an ironic smile. 'Yer mam makes it sound pretty good when I bump into her. She puts on a posh voice when she talks about you, says you live in the lap of luxury.'

'My mum is full of crap.'

'I wanted to ask you to my fiftieth, but when she heard I was having it in the village hall, she said, "Don't waste your stamp, love. I can tell you now, she won't be coming. She's got other fish to fry.'''

'Whaat! I'll fucking kill her. Of course I would have come.'

'But I'm happy to think of you living the life of Riley, you know. At least one of us is.'

Harper took another gulp of champagne. 'You're joking, aren't you? My husband is obsessively jealous, one of my daughters hates me, the other gets teased at school for being fat and my friends are all bored housewives who drink too much.'

'Still prone to exaggerating, I see,' Jan said.

'Sorry, Jan,' she said, shaking her head, 'it's just that sometimes I feel like I'm the only one holding this thing called family together.' Her eyes filled with tears.

Jan laughed. 'We all feel that way, silly.'

There was silence between them for a few moments while Jan ran the cold tap in the sink and poured herself a glass of water. 'But at least you've got the fabulous holidays and smart parties,' she said, turning back to Harper. 'You can't deny it's a charmed life – and you look great on it, too.'

Harper stuck out her lower lip. 'Looks can be deceptive.'

Jan sighed. 'Get over yourself, for fuck's sake. At least you're not struggling to pay your mortgage.'

'True, but you and John have a happy marriage.'

Lizzie appeared. 'Is this a private spat, or can anyone join in?'

'I'm not sure we can find a role for you right now,' Harper said.

'What do you mean, "a role?"'

She drained her glass. 'It's just that I seem to be turning into Sue Ellen Ewing—'

Jan snorted. 'Right down to the watery eyes and trembling lip!'

'And Jan here has morphed into one half of Pammy and Bobby. So who the hell are you going to be?'

'Not Miss Ellie. "Goddammit, Jock!"'

'Nothing else for it, then,' Harper said, slurring her words slightly. 'You'll have to be Kristin. Didn't she kill JR? Be my guest and get rid of my husband, please . . . and could you dispatch my mother at the same time?'

She closed her eyes, slid down the wall and collapsed on the floor with a bump. Just before she blacked out, she heard Lizzie say, 'More like Edina from *Ab Fab*, you mean.'

25

She drove back to Cheshire in a cold sweat. Images of the night before kept flashing through her head. She should never have taken champagne to the party. She cursed herself for drinking too much. She cringed at the things she'd said.

Her mistake had been to think that she could relax among old friends. But she couldn't relax. She could never relax. Not while she was married to Aaron.

She realised now that Lizzie and Jan were on another wavelength altogether. They had spent their entire lives among people who knew them and loved them, so they were used to being themselves, to speaking honestly about their feelings. They were down to earth, salt of the earth – all round earthy types. She must have seemed like an alien to them when she walked in to the party, fresh from her eye job, champagne coming out of her ears, rings sparkling on her fingers – only to moan about her life, get pissed and pass out. How fucking embarrassing!

Her forehead prickled. It was damp and cold. She wiped it with the back of her hand. 'Pigs sweat, women perspire.' That's what Aaron always said. Well, he was wrong. Unless she was a pig.

No, *he* was the pig.

Rain started to slash against the car windscreen. It was turning into an incredibly unpleasant drive. Little stabs of paranoia kept piercing her. It's the hangover, she told herself. Still, she was shocked by some of the things she had said at the party. She hadn't always been this unhappy, had she? Her marriage to Aaron hadn't always been this bad. When had it changed?

It was around the time she became pregnant with Georgie, she thought. Things had been so much better before that. Never perfect – because Aaron had always been moody and jealous – but their marriage had been a whole lot happier pre-Georgie. She had never really admitted it to herself. She didn't want to hang that on Georgie. But the truth was that Aaron hadn't wanted another baby, not at fifty. He had never forgiven her for going through with it.

Her mouth felt like it was lined with old pigeon's feathers. She reached for a bottle of water, wedged it in her lap and unscrewed the top. The radio was playing 'Sailing' by Rod Stewart. It reminded her of Mike Smith.

She took a swig of water, replaced the bottle top and put her foot down.

She was desperate to ring Angela, who had left a message around the time she'd been blacking out at Lizzie's.

'I'm on my phone now. Try me again. I'm happy to talk about it.'

I'm happy to talk about it. That could mean only one thing, surely. The affair had definitely happened. Otherwise she wouldn't be prepared to go into detail, would she? Even Angela wasn't that smooth. She wasn't a Bond villain, for godsakes. She wasn't a world class liar.

She would ring her as soon as she got home, It was the first thing she would do.

Fifty-two miles to go. The rain was still battering the windscreen. She took another swig of water and started thinking about Portugal.

26

Summer 1998

It was the best holiday they'd ever had. They stayed at a luxury villa complex in the Algarve and soaked up sunshine and rosé for two glorious weeks.

Admittedly, it hadn't started well. 'So, who was the guy in the suit?' Aaron asked her after dinner on the first evening.

She frowned. She still hadn't worked out the best way to answer this question. 'Sorry?' she said.

Aaron shook his head and smiled wryly. 'Don't play the innocent with me, sunshine. The young guy on the plane. It was obvious you knew him from somewhere.'

He badgered her for the next two hours, trying all his usual tricks to force a confession out of her. Eventually, she took off her clothes, lay on the bed and ate strawberries. That put a stop to it – and she had a feeling that Georgie had been conceived into the bargain, since she'd forgotten to use her diaphragm.

In the days that followed, Aaron settled down and started enjoying himself, playing tennis and swimming with Taylor, jogging along the beach at sunset and taking Harper to bed with him straight after dinner. He amused them with stories they'd never heard before – about his first job selling fire extinguishers door-to-door, and the time he'd been trapped in a New York lift with Chrissie Hynde – and charmed them with daily gifts of flowers and chocolates.

Taylor, who had been going through a whiny period, shook off her bad moods and basked in her father's attention. Meanwhile Harper sunbathed, read trashy books and drank wine at every civilised opportunity. All their meals were prepared for them by a local cook. Their housekeeper, Adelisa, did everything else. It was bliss.

The villa was draped in pink bougainvillea and enclosed by a jungly, sweet-smelling garden. After she had showered off the sand and sun cream at the end of the day, Harper liked to put on a floaty kaftan and do a tour of the plants and flowers, glass of wine in hand.

'It makes me want to completely redo the garden at home,' she told Aaron, sweeping her arm over a riotous patch of hibiscus. 'Get rid of the lawn and the borders. Replace them with something wilder, more overgrown.'

He smiled.

'What's funny?' she asked.

'I'm thinking that most people here would trade their kids for a neat English lawn. Not you, though.'

'It's all the colours—'

'Why do people always want what they haven't got?' he interrupted.

'I just thought it might be nice to do something different,' she said. 'How about I consult a landscaping company when we get back, just to see what they suggest?'

He shrugged. 'OK, but I like a neat garden. I'm into symmetry.'

She gritted her teeth. She had already made a couple of attempts to overhaul the house, to no avail. The peach velour curtains had been replaced by new peach velour curtains. The wall-to-wall cream carpets had been refreshed. Two pyramid flame outdoor heaters had been delivered to the patio. Nothing else had changed.

The first time Janice had come to stay, she'd looked around her, wide-eyed. 'What a lovely, spacious house!' she'd said.

'It's not me though, is it?' Harper whispered.

Janice kept her expression neutral. 'Well ... '

'It's not even Aaron,' Harper added. 'It's his parents. Their house is exactly the same, only smaller.'

So as twilight fell over the Algarve, she shelved her dreams of filling the garden at Orchard End with winding paths, rambling trellises, climbing creepers and scattershot shrubs and flowers. Aaron liked it neat, and it would stay neat.

27

February 2013

She pulled up outside Orchard End with a throbbing headache and a primeval urge to curl up and sleep. She felt as if she had just driven across the Siberian tundra in a blizzard. Turning off the engine, she rested her head on the steering wheel and sighed. She was home. But it didn't feel like home. It didn't feel like anywhere.

My life is a disaster, she thought. Everything is a mess.

Was it just the hangover talking? She always forgot that depression was only ever a hangover away. She liked to think of herself as a positive person, as someone who looked on the bright side of life. But hangovers stripped away the sunshine. They sucked the goodness out of everything.

Never again, she thought. I will never, ever get blind, blackout drunk again.

She tried to think nice thoughts, but kept coming back to Aaron's reaction when she'd told him she was pregnant, a month after the holiday in Portugal.

'Tell me you're joking,' he'd said. 'I don't want another fucking kid.'

He couldn't have made his view plainer.

She, on the other hand, was surprised to find that she did want another fucking kid. Even more of a shocker – and she had no idea whether it was down to the hormones or a suppressed secret longing – from the moment she'd seen the line across the dipstick window, she was prepared to put her desire for a fucking kid above her desire for a happy marriage.

'I'm not having a termination,' she said, folding her arms across her stomach.

His face twisted in disgust. 'How do I even know it's mine?'

'What?' she said, reeling. 'What the hell do you mean?'

'You tell me, darling. I was in Berlin for three days while we were in Portugal. You could have fucked any number of men while I was away.'

Her eyes filled with tears. 'You're not being serious, are you? It makes me feel sick even thinking about it.'

'Then think for a second about how *I* feel, you conniving bitch.' His eyes narrowed. 'You planned this, I know you did.'

She shut off the memory, only for another loop to start, this time featuring reruns of awkward scenes from the night before. Stop it! she screamed silently, but her brain whirled on – like hell's eternal carousel, playing the same tune on repeat.

Every memory made her wince. She didn't care what

people like Beverly Fisher and April Whats-her-name thought of her, but Janice and Lizzie's opinions really mattered. She sighed again. God knew what they thought of her after she'd got drunk and collapsed in Lizzie's kitchen.

She pictured them ringing each other up and giggling about her. She imagined Lizzie asking, 'Who does she think she is?' and Jan sighing and saying, 'It's been a long time. We're different people now.'

She wanted to yell at them, 'I'm the same as I ever was!'

But in the gloom of her mind's eye, they would look at her sadly and say, 'You know it's not true. You've changed.'

Were they right, these imaginary versions of her oldest, dearest friends? Had she lost the person she had once been, the girl on the Waltzer at Spanish City, the kid singing her heart out at the social club? She couldn't believe that her old self had completely disappeared. She was still in there somewhere, surely. Yet she hadn't surfaced for years now. So how could she be certain there was anything left of her?

She let herself into the house and limped upstairs to her bedroom. Drooping by the side of the bed, she could barely be bothered to wrest off her Chloé blouse and trousers before she toppled onto the mattress. With one eye closed, she set her phone alarm for ten to three and quickly sank into oblivion. It was a familiar routine. She couldn't count the number of times she had set her alarm for ten to three.

When she awoke, her headache had gone but she was

covered in a thin film of sweat. There were five missed calls and a message from Aaron on her phone. 'Where are you? Speak later.'

She bit her lip. He would ring on the landline at ten, as he always did, ever since he'd worked out that it was the perfect hour to fence her in. Because if she didn't answer the landline, he'd ring her mobile.

'Where are you?'

'Who are you with?'

'Why are you lying?

Frankly, it was easier to stay at home and talk to him there.

After a quick shower, she was in the car again, on her way to Georgie's school. Here we go again, she thought, her eyes still puffy with sleep. Sometimes she felt so bad after a night on the sauce that she went to bed after the morning drop-off and slept right through to the afternoon pick-up. She wasn't the only one. Everybody did it. Vicky Pacquard and some of the other mums even had a name for it – they called it the 'school run siesta'. Still, it wasn't anything to be proud of.

As she pulled up outside the school gates, her phone beeped, a text from Janice. *How's Champagne Charlie today? At least you weren't sick on the crazy paving! ha ha xx.*

For the first time that day, she smiled. She felt like a teenager whose mate had forgiven her for scratching her favourite David Essex LP. Jan was still her friend! She wanted to go on being mates after a ten-year gap and an excruciating reunion! Maybe things weren't as hopeless as she'd thought – and perhaps she wasn't such a train wreck, either.

Another text followed. *PS. Did we mention Justin Bennett's birthday party in two weeks? Hope you and your facelift can come. (Lizzie says you can stay at hers, cos yer mam wouldn't approve.) xx*

Justin Bennett? Apart from the unattainable Robbie Harper, Justin Bennett had been the best-looking guy at school. He had also been her first proper boyfriend, when she was seventeen. She wondered what he looked like now. Were his eyes as velvety brown? Was his hair still thick and flowing? Was he as tall and lean as ever?

Don't be stupid, she told herself. He's probably bald and fat and saggy.

She didn't think twice about her reply, even though she would have to lie to Aaron if she wanted to go to the party.

Me and EYE JOB (get it right, please) will be coming, she texted back. *PS Justin Bennett, whoo hoo! Race you to snog him!*

It was a joke, but you never knew – maybe Justin had aged well, and kept his hair, and she'd gasp when she saw him, and they would lock eyes, and the old feelings would flood back, and . . . stupid, stupid thoughts.

Ah, but you never knew.

Her phone started ringing. 'Are you outside?' Georgie asked, sounding stressed. 'Can you come in and talk to Mr Nayar, please? He wants me to go to an audition for a TV series – tomorrow! Help, Mum!'

'Don't panic,' she said. 'I'm just parking, I'll be right there.'

She took a deep calming breath and hoped that she no longer smelled of booze.

After squeezing into a tiny parking space amid the crowd of four-by-fours outside the school, she arrived in the drama room to find Mr Nayar wreathed in smiles and Georgie looking glum.

She gave Georgie a hug. 'Have they sent over the script?' she asked.

Georgie held up a sheaf of papers. 'Yes, but there's loads and if I've only got tonight—'

Mr Nayar stepped forward. 'It's absolutely fine, as I've told Georgina. She doesn't need to learn anything – she just has to read the pages through a few times.'

'We'll do it together,' Harper said, giving Georgie a squeeze. 'It'll be fun.'

Mr Nayar nodded. 'It's the sort of thing we do in class all the time.'

'What's it about?' Harper asked him.

His eyes lit up. 'It's a teenage drama, an intriguing web of friendship and rivalries.'

Georgie made a face. 'It's called *FOMO*, Mum.'

'What's that?'

'Fear Of Missing Out.'

She couldn't help smiling.

Georgie pouted. 'It's so unoriginal, it makes me sick.'

'What's the part?'

'The lead girl's best friend,' Georgie said.

'Hey, that sounds interesting!'

Mr Nayar beamed. 'It's a meaty role, with lots of humour and pathos.'

'She's fat,' Georgie said.

'Ah.' She searched for something to say. 'Well, it's all good experience.'

'I'll miss the last hour of school and you'll have to take me into Manchester.'

'That won't be a problem, but it's up to you, darling. Is it what you want?'

Georgie smiled wanly.

'That's the spirit!' Mr Nayar said, patting her shoulder.

Her headache came crashing back while she was sitting at the kitchen table, eating her last mouthful of pasta and deli sauce with Taylor and Georgie.

'Shall we start the read-through?' Georgie asked, drumming her fingers on the script.

She slumped in her chair, longing to go back to bed. 'Can we do it in half an hour?' she said. 'I'm feeling a bit poorly.'

Taylor pursed her lips. 'You always say that after you've had a big night, Mother.'

'Say what?'

'That you're feeling "a bit poorly". I bet you're just hung-over.'

'Of course I'm not,' she snapped. 'It was a Wednesday night in Cullercoats. We're not talking Magaluf here.'

Taylor rolled her eyes. 'I know what you and your mates are like.'

'Do you, now?'

'Bunch of pissheads,' Taylor said with a laugh.

Harper was tempted to laugh too, but something held her back. 'That's not fair,' she said.

'Mum, I've seen you off your trolley a thousand times!'

Harper bristled. 'Nonsense, the most I ever get is merry.'

Taylor snorted.

Georgie was leafing through the TV script. 'Wait, there's a page missing,' she said. 'I must have left it upstairs.' She skipped out of the kitchen.

Harper turned to Taylor again. 'What's got into you?' she asked. 'You haven't said a nice word to me in weeks.'

'Wouldn't you like to know?' Taylor sneered.

'Wouldn't I like to know what?'

'What's got into me.'

'What's that supposed to mean?'

'Maybe something *has* got into me.'

Her heart skipped a beat. 'Can you stop speaking in code, please?' she said sharply. 'This isn't the Enigma Project.'

Taylor smiled knowingly. 'I'm sure you can put two and two together – or one and one, I should say.'

Oh my God, Harper thought. She cast her mind back over the previous couple of weeks, trying to recall any telltale signs. Had Taylor's appetite changed? Had she looked tearful or worried? She sneaked a glance at her chest, and then at her belly. 'You're not ... pregnant, are you?' she blurted out.

Taylor raised her eyebrows. 'Now that *is* funny, coming from you.'

'Why do you say that?'

Taylor gazed at her coolly. 'I know your little secret, Mother.'

Harper's throat went dry. Her brain felt like it had come loose inside her head. Stay calm, she told herself. Shut this down.

'Well, good for you,' she said. After a few moments of grim silence, she added, 'So, are you pregnant?'

'Actually, it's none of your business.'

'Really? I think it is my business. You're living in this house—'

'Dad's house.'

'Not Dad's house, *our* house, and you're living here, and—'

'So?'

'Oh for godsakes just answer the question! Are you?'

Taylor shook her head.

Georgie came in, waving two loose pieces of paper. 'Are you what?' she asked.

'Nothing,' they said in unison.

Harper's head began to throb again. Someone had told Taylor about her teenage pregnancy. *Someone*. It had to be Angela. Taylor had given her a lift to the station on the day of the charity lunch. It must have been then.

She opened the fridge and pulled out a bottle of white Burgundy.

'Why don't you have a glass of wine, Mum?' Taylor said acidly.

'Yes, I will, thank you.'

She started feeling better halfway through the first glass, by which time Georgie was drumming her fingers again. 'Let's have a look at that script, shall we?' she said.

They went into the lounge, lit the fire and started reading the script aloud. Much of the dialogue made them laugh, especially the acronyms. 'But no one says LOLZ any more!' Georgie complained.

She wasn't too keen on some of her lines, either. Harper agreed with her that they felt a little stale, but between them they managed to freshen them up. 'This is great,' she told Georgie. 'We're really making progress.'

A couple of times they argued about where to put the emphasis in a sentence, which made her nostalgic for her acting days. She had always been in her element sitting round a table with a bunch of actors getting to grips with a new script. Apart from the terrible tea, what she remembered most about rehearsing for the first series of *Beauty Spot* was the giggling. Bill had loved camping up his lines. He'd had them in stitches at every read-through.

She tried not to steer Georgie's acting too much. It was years since she'd worked and, for all she knew, techniques might have changed completely. The last thing she wanted was to send Georgie into the audition sounding like the modern equivalent of Celia Johnson in *Brief Encounter*.

On the other hand, some of the slang in *FOMO* made her yearn for the elegant language of the old films.

'Please don't ever say, "Hashtag whatever!" to me,' she pleaded when they got to the last page. 'It's TFT.'

'What's TFT?'

'Too Fucking Teen.'

Georgie looked puzzled.

'I made it up!' she said. 'I'm going to start an acronyms Twitter feed for parents. I'll call it . . . Acromum!'

'What are you on about?' Georgie asked. 'Hashtag whatever! Can we get on and finish, please?'

They read it through a few times. 'You're good,' Harper told her. 'I'm really impressed.'

'But I'd rather play the lead girl,' Georgie said.

Harper gave her a hug. 'One step at a time, darling.'

Georgie yawned. 'Time for bed,' she said.

Harper went to the fridge for one last teeny-tiny glass of wine but, to her surprise, the bottle of Burgundy was empty. She contemplated opening another, just to have that one final snifter, and felt almost virtuous when she decided against it.

As she climbed the stairs to bed, she noticed that Georgie's light was still on. She knocked on her bedroom door and popped her head in to say goodnight. Georgie was sitting at her desk, with her computer on. Something flashed on the screen and then up came the cute kitten screensaver. Georgie turned and smiled, looking like butter wouldn't melt. She stretched and yawned and said, 'Just finding out my timetable for tomorrow and then I'll shut down.'

Harper wagged a finger at her. 'Don't stay up too late, young lady. Tomorrow's a big day.'

They sat in the waiting area of the Lippy Films offices listening to the receptionist field calls in a whisper. There were framed awards on the walls, alongside posters for a number of TV programmes completely unknown to Harper.

'*Gossip Vampires*?' she muttered. '*Once Upon A Tattoo*?'

'Shhh, Mum!' Georgie hissed.

'Georgina?' the receptionist said finally. 'The director will see you now.'

She led them into a bright room with large windows overlooking a patch of parkland. There were four people waiting for them, all of them under thirty, by the look of them.

Kids, Harper thought, recalling how Angela liked to complain that directors, like policeman, were growing ever younger these days.

One of the group stepped forward, a young man with messy brown hair and a fresh, honest face. He reached over to shake hands with Georgie.

'Hi, Georgina, I'm Adam,' he said. 'Thanks for coming in to read for us. Please take a seat.'

He turned to Harper, and she saw a flicker of recognition in his eyes. 'Hello!' he said.

'I'm Georgie's mum,' she explained. 'And are we waiting for your dad?'

A look of confusion crossed his face. 'My dad?'

'Just because you look about sixteen,' she said, laughing. 'Sorry, it's a joke my actress friend and I have about directors.'

'Oh, I see.' He smiled self-consciously.

He introduced Simon, one of the executive producers,

and Dwayne, who was going to film the audition on a camcorder. 'And this is Saskia,' he said. 'She's going to read the part of Cat.'

'I'm not an actress,' Saskia said apologetically. 'So don't expect much.'

Georgie leaned forward in her seat. 'Don't worry, I've only ever been in one school play,' she said.

Harper cringed. It was typical of Georgie to try to make Saskia feel better, but it was no way to sell yourself. She imagined Adam laughing afterwards. 'One school play! Just the one!'

Adam gave a brief explanation of the context of the opening scene. 'What's your impression of Cat?' he asked Georgie.

She looked back at him calmly. 'I think she's a bit of a cliché,' she said. 'Fat best friend dot com.'

Oh dear, Harper thought.

'Really?' said Adam.

Georgie cleared her throat. 'But I think I can add something fresh.'

He looked amused. 'Well, that's good news.'

They began to read. Georgie acquitted herself well, which was quite a feat considering that Saskia had not been understating her skills as an actress. The third time she mangled Georgie's feed line, Harper felt duty bound to say something.

'No offence to you, Saskia, but when we did that bit last night, it was quite funny when I said it like this, "Is that a *joke*?"'

'Right ...' Saskia said, looking up at Adam uncertainly.

'Mum!' Georgie whispered.

'I know, but if it's not right ...' Harper whispered back.

'Mum! Shhh!'

'Um, perhaps you wouldn't mind reading instead of Saskia?' Adam asked Harper.

'No, it's fine!' Georgie burst out.

'Hey, don't worry on my account,' Saskia said. 'I'm only the production assistant.'

'Nobody better than your mother to do it,' Adam said. 'I mean, especially if you've rehearsed it together.'

Georgie looked at the floor.

'OK,' Harper said.

It went much better the second time around, and Georgie got some laughs in the right places from Dwayne and Simon.

'Excellent, well done!' Adam said, when they came to the end of the scene. 'You've got a natural sense of comic timing.'

Harper beamed.

'We'll be in touch,' he added, looking at his notepad. 'It's the Gover Agency, isn't it?'

Harper leapt in. 'Georgina hasn't got an agent yet, as such,' she explained. 'It's fine to go through Gover's, but I can give you my number too.'

'Yes, great,' he said, without looking up.

She reached into her bag for a scrap of paper, fishing around for something, anything, and pulling out a florist's card. After jotting her mobile phone number down, she handed it to Simon.

'I'll take that,' Adam said, looking up and giving her a cheeky smile. 'By the way, I only wish there was a part in this drama for someone over twenty-six.'

She returned his smile and stood up to go. 'I don't act any more.'

'I know, and I was going to say that you could pass for twenty-six anyway, so it wouldn't be a problem.' His eyes twinkled.

He turned to Georgie. 'Thanks for coming in. We really appreciate it.'

'It's OK,' Georgie mumbled, following Harper out of the door.

They left the building in silence. 'That went well, don't you think?' Harper said, once they had reached the car park.

Georgie grimaced. 'It was fine, but you didn't have to flirt with him, Mum!'

'Flirt?' Harper said, with genuine surprise. 'It was just a bit of banter, darling. That's what auditions are all about.'

'It was embarrassing!'

Harper sighed. Georgie was getting to the age where everything her mother did was going to be embarrassing, even blowing her nose. 'Honestly—' she began.

'You gave him your phone number!'

She laughed. 'Only for your sake. Come on, he's not going to ring me asking for a date, is he?'

Georgie creased up. 'No ...'

'Well, then.'

Would I go if he did? she wondered.

It was an idle thought that came straight out of nowhere, and it startled her. Don't be silly, she told herself, instantly putting him out of her mind.

28

She got off the tube at Charing Cross and walked down the Strand towards the Savoy House Theatre. The afternoon light was beginning to fade and there were streaks of yellow and grey in the darkening sky. The street lights had come on, and the towering buildings and shop façades shone impressively in the twilight. Despite her dismal mood, she started humming an old music hall tune about sauntering along the Strand, gloves in hand.

Passing the Adelphi, she had a flash memory of queuing up for the revival of *My Fair Lady*, back when she was a drama student. Almost every show she had seen in those poverty-stricken days had been watched from the cheap seats, way up high or far at the back, where the people on the stage looked no bigger than mice. It hadn't mattered, of course. She'd always been thrilled to be there, watching bona fide, professional actors practise their craft.

Sometimes you could sneak past the ushers, or charm

them into letting you stand in the shadows behind a pillar off to the side – and if that didn't work, you could try strolling into the stalls for the second half, with the nonchalant air of someone who had been there for the first. Generally, though, you'd be in the row furthest back, behind the world's tallest man and a woman in a wide-brimmed hat, straining your ears to hear the lines and craning your neck to see the action. She felt exhausted just thinking about it. Would she carry on going to the theatre today if she had to go through all that palaver? It was hard to imagine, now that she could book the best seats in the house without a moment's thought.

When she arrived at the Savoy House Theatre, a blue-haired woman told her – rather brusquely, she thought – to wait outside while she rang up to Angela's dressing room. It was a glacial February day and she rubbed her hands together for warmth as she tried to psych herself up for the conversation ahead.

The narrow street was deserted apart from a couple of guys wearing skinny jeans and carrying satchels, standing a few feet along from her. She instantly pegged them as stage door hangers-on. After a couple of minutes, one of them said something about the Garrick Theatre, and left. The other came to stand beside her.

'Excuse me, did I hear you ask for Angela Stirling?' he asked.

She turned to look at him. His flappy ears were red with cold and there was an eager expression in his pale blue eyes. 'That's right.'

He emitted a weird whistling sound, like an old-fashioned hob kettle, and began to jig about, gasping with excitement. 'Oh my gosh! You're Harper Allen!' he screeched. 'Wow, I absolutely love you!' He put one hand out to shake hers, while fanning his face melodramatically with the other. 'I'm Alistair,' he said. 'I've been watching all the reruns of *Beauty Spot*. It's so, so brilliant – especially you, of course. Oh dear, am I going over the top? It's just that I'm so thrilled – *so, so thrilled* – to meet you!'

She couldn't help laughing. 'Carry on, I'm loving it!' she said. 'Although it's all ancient history, of course.'

He started to pile on the flattery and very soon she wanted it to stop. Once upon a time it might have meant something, but now it felt completely irrelevant, like praise for an exam she'd passed twenty years earlier. She steered him onto the subject of the play Angela was appearing in – one of the lesser Noel Cowards – which gave him the chance to gush about Angela instead.

'Oh yes, she's incredible,' he said. 'I've loved her for years and years. And we're quite good friends now, in fact.'

'Are you?' she said, only half-listening.

He seemed sweet enough, but he was a bloke in his thirties loitering in the street on a cold weekday afternoon, hoping to say hello to an actor. Meanwhile, she had serious matters on her mind. She craned her neck to see what was going on behind the half-closed stage door. What was taking so long?

'And we really have a giggle,' he said, putting his hand

up to his mouth and giving her a comic 'naughty-boy' look.

'I bet,' she said distractedly.

He seemed to sense her waning interest, but ploughed on anyway. 'We laugh at the same things,' he explained. 'She loves a practical joke – just like me. Only the other day—'

The stage door flew open. 'Sorry to keep you waiting,' said the woman with blue hair, in a different tone altogether to the one she had used earlier. 'Ms Stirling says to go straight up to her dressing room on the second floor.'

'See ya,' Alistair said wistfully, taking a step back. 'Give Angela a kiss from me.'

'I will,' she said, flashing him a relieved smile.

As she stepped through the door, she was hit by the smell common to every backstage area she had ever known. Asked to describe it, she would have said it consisted of the combined odours of dust, grime, a little sweat maybe, panic, haste and a trace of urine, with a lingering whiff of cigarette smoke. It wasn't necessarily pleasant, but it felt like home.

She experienced a twinge of nostalgia. The stage was her real love, she thought. Although she had never made it into the West End, she had played several leading roles in the bigger regional theatres, in front of thousands of people, for weeks on end. Eventually she had been thankful for her big break into television, but only because she was sick of doing shop work and catering jobs in the long 'resting' periods between stage roles. If she'd had constant work in the theatre, she might never have thought of going up for a TV audition.

She climbed two flights of stairs and knocked on the door of Angela's dressing room. Angela greeted her wearing a full length green silk dressing gown. Her hair was in rollers and her face make-up free, yet she still managed to look elegant, like a figure from a bygone age.

'Harper,' she said softly, closing the door behind them and motioning her to sit down in a smart, Louis IV style chair.

Harper remained standing. 'You know why I'm here,' she said, struggling to keep her composure.

'You've come to have it out about Aaron,' Angela said.

Harper glared at her. 'But first I need to know why the hell you told Taylor that I got pregnant when I was sixteen?'

Angela paled. She lit a cigarette, even though there was a clearly visible No Smoking sign on the wall. 'She told you? I didn't think she would.'

It was a typical Angela response. Harper gritted her teeth. 'Tell me why you did it, Angela.'

Her friend's eyes glittered. 'I couldn't bear the hypocrisy of it, darling. She said you didn't approve of her married lover and I thought, How unfair! I mean, we all make mistakes.'

Harper took a deep breath and looked down at her L. K. Bennet boots. She could see Angela's logic. It was a perfect case of, 'Do as I say, not as I do.' But Angela didn't know what it was like to have children. She didn't know that you would literally cut off your right arm to stop them making the same mistakes you'd made.

'You're forgetting that I'm very fond of Taylor,' Angela added.

Harper folded her arms across her chest. 'So you thought you'd encourage her to get her heart broken by some shit who probably hasn't got any intention of leaving his wife?'

Angela gave her a defiant look. 'I just thought it was a bit rich that she was getting lectures on morality from someone who'd done the exact same thing.'

'Lectures on morality?' Harper spat. 'Don't you know me at all?'

'Look, I blurted it out while we were talking in the car,' Angela said. 'I shouldn't have interfered, I'm sorry.'

'Wow, an apology,' Harper said. 'So you're sorry for fucking up my relationship with my daughter. What about with my husband?'

Angela's mouth twitched. Harper noticed that the veins on her neck were beginning to protrude – her 'Deirdre Barlow veins' as they always called them – which were always a sure sign that she was feeling tense. In any other circumstances, she would have pointed them out. But this wasn't the moment to bring up long-standing jokes.

'I've already said I was sorry about what happened with Aaron, and I meant it,' Angela said tersely. 'Although I'm not sure exactly how it would have "fucked things up" between you two.'

Harper gaped at her. 'You slept with him!'

'You think that made a difference to your relationship?'

'How can you even ask me that?'

Angela shrugged. 'I'm just putting it out there.'

But Harper wasn't interested in exploring possibilities. She wanted facts. 'Did it happen when I was pregnant with Georgie?'

Angela nodded and sat down. Her dressing gown flew open at the thigh as she crossed her long legs. 'It was by chance, really,' she said, exhaling a plume of smoke. 'That's the irony of it.'

'By chance?' Harper asked. 'Let me guess – you tripped over each other in an underground cave and suddenly found yourselves having sex?'

The ghost of a smile crossed Angela's face. 'No, but it was almost as improbable,' she said, stubbing out her cigarette in a large silver ashtray. 'We happened to bump into each other at the bar at Joe Allen's during a bomb scare in Covent Garden. The whole area was blocked off for more than an hour – although we didn't know it at the time – and we were both waiting for friends who'd been delayed by the chaos and police cordons.'

Harper listened carefully, alert to the possibility that Angela might be lying, as Aaron had so vehemently insisted she was. At the same time, she wondered who it was that Aaron had been meeting – whether for business, or for pleasure.

'Do you want me to go on?' Angela asked her.

She nodded.

'So we had a cocktail. I congratulated him on your

pregnancy, but he said he wasn't happy about it. Well, that sent me back to the bar for another drink. It seemed so unfair, especially as my latest round of IVF had just failed. To make things worse, I'd made the classic mistake of reading a bad review, the one that said that it was "impossible to fathom" why the leading actor in my play would find me attractive. That's why I was meeting Jonathan in the first place . . .'

'Jonathan?'

'Jonathan Brand. We were lovers for a while. Perhaps you didn't know.'

Harper tried to take this in. If she wasn't aware that her best friend had affairs, what sort of a friendship was it?

'So you went to meet your lover to boost your spirits, but found Aaron, and plumped for him instead?'

Angela held her gaze while she lit another cigarette. 'It wasn't *quite* like that . . .'

'Any old lover would have done?'

Angela shook her head. 'I know it's not an excuse, but we'd had too much to drink.'

'Didn't you think about me? About what you were doing to me?'

'I wasn't thinking at all. After two or three cocktails we were both pretty smashed, and it just went from there.'

'From there to where?'

Angela cleared her throat. 'To . . . a brief affair.'

'I mean, where did you go after that?' Harper asked, hoping that she wouldn't say the Savoy.

'To a hotel,' Angela murmured.

'Not the Savoy?'

'Look, the whole thing was a mistake. I've already said that. But if you ask me if I think it made a difference to your marriage, I would have to say it didn't.'

Harper shook her head. 'You betrayed me,' she said. 'And so did he. It changes everything.'

'It does now that you know about it – but you didn't know about it then.'

'You'd like to think that because it makes you feel better,' Harper said, jabbing her finger at her. 'But things were never the same after Georgie was born. I thought it was because of her! But it wasn't, it was because of *you*.'

'Garbage!' Angela protested. 'Aaron didn't want another child – and you know it. He was furious with you. I had nothing to do with it.'

Harper stood up again. 'No, you just fucked him!' she yelled.

'And I suspect I wasn't the only one,' Angela snapped back.

It felt like the knockout blow of the fight. Harper gasped. She felt winded.

'I didn't mean that,' Angela said, suddenly looking distressed. 'I'm sorry I said it.'

'What an absolute bitch you are,' Harper said, once she had regained her power of speech. 'I thought I knew you, but I don't know you at all – and I don't want to. I don't want to be polluted by you.'

Feeling nauseous, she put her hand over her mouth and retched. 'I thought you were my friend!'

She turned to the door, yanked it open and ran out of the room.

Back on the street again, she came face to face with Alistair. 'Did you see her?' he asked eagerly.

She nodded, trying not to cry. She wanted to march off purposefully, but felt disorientated and wasn't sure which way to go. What had Angela meant about not being 'the only one'? Was she just throwing another hand grenade over the wall – or was Aaron actually a serial adulterer?

'Where's the nearest bar?' she blurted out. 'I need a drink.'

'Well, there's the Savoy,' he suggested.

She shook her head. 'Not the fucking Savoy!'

He looked at her helplessly. 'What sort of bar were you thinking of?'

'The type that serves alcohol,' she said.

Five minutes later she was sitting in the snug of a traditional pub in the Strand, surrounded by American tourists drinking tea and coffee. She knocked back a vodka shot and picked up another. 'Bottoms up,' she said to Alistair, who was tentatively sipping a gin and lemon.

'Do you mind me asking if there's anything wrong?' he asked.

She grimaced. 'I've had some rather bad news about a dear friend. It came through on my phone while I was in the theatre.'

He looked worried. 'Nothing affecting Angela, I hope?'

'No, she doesn't know this particular friend.' She knocked back the second vodka and started to feel nicely numb.

'Do you want to talk about it?'

She wiped an imaginary tear from her eye. 'Actually, I'd rather not.'

'I understand,' he said.

She suddenly thought of a way to have a jab at Angela. 'Let's talk about you instead,' she said, leaning forward. 'Angela was ever so complimentary. She's obviously very fond of you.'

A huge smile blossomed across his face. He couldn't have been more delighted if she'd told him that Julie Andrews was on her way to personally serenade him. 'We do get on very well,' he said.

'Drink up,' she said. 'I'm having another, and so are you.'

Two shots later, it was time to go. She and Alistair had discovered a mutual love of Bette Davis and Joan Crawford films, but they were definitely running out of topics to enthuse about.

'Make sure you're there for Angela as much as you can be,' she said, putting on her cashmere coat. 'She really appreciates it. In fact, why don't I give you her number? She's been going through a hard time, what with the divorce and everything. She could do with a friend like you.'

He smiled knowingly. 'Actually, things are looking up for Ms Stirling,' he said, tapping his nose.

She detected the whiff of a secret. 'She told you?' she said, playing along. 'I'm amazed!'

'Only because I took a picture of them kissing in the street,' he whispered conspiratorially.

It took a few moments for the significance of this to

sink in. But when it did, she felt as if she'd been punched in the throat. 'How funny,' she managed to rasp. 'In the street, you say?'

'Just across the road, in fact,' he said. 'She thought it was hilarious.'

'I think she mentioned it, actually,' she said. 'Have you still got it?'

He gave her a coy smile. 'I'm not supposed to show anyone.'

She smiled back – one of her dazzlers. 'Ah, shame,' she said, keeping her tone light.

He cocked his head to one side, as if weighing the situation up, and she went on smiling as she fought the desire to seize him by his ears and head butt him.

'But for the wonderful Miss Harper Allen ...' he ventured. He picked up his phone and started scrolling through his photos. 'Just a peek, mind.'

One glance told her it was the shot of Angela and Aaron that she had stared at for so many hours in her bedroom. 'Cute,' she said.

'I know!' He smiled with delight. 'And we played a little trick on him afterwards.' He dropped his voice to a whisper again. 'She asked me to send it to his mobile phone. Anonymously!'

'But how?' she asked innocently.

'I used a pay-as-you-go phone, gangster-style. Just like in *The Wire*!'

'Ah,' she said.

'She thought it would create a big mystery, although it

was just a bit of fun, obviously. I'd love to know how he reacted.'

'Haven't you asked her?'

He looked at the floor. 'I've been over at the Victoria seeing my friend Zoë Wanamaker for a few weeks,' he confessed.

'So you have no idea that the man in the photo is my husband?'

He clapped his hand over his mouth. 'You're not being serious?'

'Of course I'm not!' she said, grinning at him like a mad woman.

29

Alcohol got her through the train journey back to Cheshire. Betty's leftover hotpot helped to sober her up at home. Taylor and Georgie didn't seem to notice that she was out of sorts, but to be on the safe side she said she thought she was coming down with something. Then she went to bed, turned out the light and cried herself to sleep.

The next morning, she woke up desperate to talk to Betty. But Betty phoned to say that she would be coming in late. She was taking Donna to see the people at the housing association.

'Is it the hole in the roof again?'

'Among other things,' Betty said grimly.

'You know you're fine to take the day off,' she offered. 'Anytime.'

But Betty was having none of it. 'I don't want to miss the next instalment!' she joked. 'I'll be in once I've dropped Donna back home.'

True to her word, she arrived just after eleven. Harper was sitting at the kitchen table, wearing a trackie, flicking manically through a copy of *Elle* – drinking in page after page of shoes, coats, lingerie and lipstick.

'How did it go with the housing people?' she asked, looking up.

Betty pursed her lips. 'It went.'

Harper snapped the magazine shut. Despite her restless page-turning, she hadn't managed to find the cover feature about the hazards of long-term friendship. Her eyes filled with tears.

'Are you all right, love?' asked Betty.

'I'm fine,' she said, trying her best to smile. 'What about you? Tell me about the meeting.'

'What's wrong?'

The tears started to roll down her face. 'I know what you're thinking, Betty,' she said, attempting to keep her tone light. 'Here we go again, old Droopy Drawers is back, dripping all over the kitchen.'

'Of course I'm not.'

'You're thinking, Where's that blooming mop? Before I have a blooming flood on my hands.'

'Don't be silly. What's happened?'

'You're thinking, What's this? The Wreck of the Hesperus meets the weeping women of Troy? *Again*?'

'Stop it, before I start laughing!' said Betty.

Harper wiped her eyes, stood up and put the kettle on. 'Sit down,' she said, her chest heaving. 'I'm going to tell you something that will blow your ruddy socks off.'

She warmed the pot and put in an extra bag for good measure. What was it her nana used to say? 'Where there's tea, there's hope.' Best make it strong, then. While it brewed, she filled Betty in on her meeting with Angela the day before – and the chance encounter with Alistair The Fan.

Betty was every bit as astounded as she thought she'd be. She kept shaking her head. 'I don't believe it!' she said.

If she hadn't been so horrified by what Angela had done, Harper might have enjoyed telling a story that had such a dramatic effect on her audience. Instead the tears started up again. 'I'm sorry,' she said miserably.

'Go ahead and cry, love,' Betty said. 'Better out than in. I expect you're still in shock.'

She sighed. It *was* a shock. But if she was honest, was it really such a surprise? It wasn't hard to imagine Angela's mouth twitching with amusement as Alistair showed her the photo of her and Aaron kissing. And it wasn't hard to imagine her eyes gleaming with mischief as she casually asked him to send it to her 'boyfriend'. Because, at heart, Angela was a cow. She wasn't generous. She didn't want her friends to succeed. She had been jealous of Harper since the day she'd rung her breathlessly to tell her she'd got the part in *Beauty Spot*. And now it turned out that she had deeply resented her second pregnancy and, in her bitterness, slept with her husband.

So the only real surprise here was that Harper had stayed friends with someone like Angela for all these years. OK, she hadn't known about the affair with

Aaron, but she had spent hours listening to Angela bitching about James, moaning about other actors' success and generally sniping at the world. Why had she put up with it? It couldn't simply have been nostalgia for their student days, she decided, although that was definitely a part of it. She bowed her head as she thought it over.

She didn't like to admit it, but she had probably stayed friends with Angela because she connected her with acting and the theatre, with everything she had given up for Aaron and Taylor – a world she had recently begun to miss much more than she ever thought she would. Angela kept her up to date with industry gossip, recounted ghastly auditions and amused her with tales of run-ins with directors and other actors. It was a vicarious thing, she realised. She had never regretted giving up acting, but her friendship with Angela meant she wasn't shut out altogether.

'Drink your tea,' said Betty. 'Have you eaten anything?'

Two fierce cups of tea and a ham sandwich later, she started to feel better. 'I just want to understand why she sent that photo,' she said.

'Goodness only knows.'

'I'm not sure it's a case for Holmes and Watson either. I'd say it was better suited to Cagney and Lacey, wouldn't you?'

Betty nodded. 'Good thinking.'

She switched to a New York accent. 'It's a *femi-nine* crime, very crafty. My guess is that she asked her fan to send me the photo because she wanted to jolt me into finding out about her affair with Aaron.'

Betty raised her eyebrows. 'But why?'

'Darned if I know! Why did she spill my biggest secret to Taylor already? Either she hates me, or she's one crazy broad on a toxic mission.'

She sighed. Linking her fingers together, she noticed the absence of the pink diamond ring that she had given to Lizzie. She was glad it was gone, even if it was worth a fortune. The irony was that she would be just as happy with a pink zirconia. She liked expensive designer clothes because they were well cut and made from quality fabrics – but jewellery was far easier to fake than dresses. As far as she was concerned, a synthetic gem in a good setting could be every bit as eye-catching as a Tiffany solitaire.

She slipped the sapphire ring off the middle finger of her right hand and slid it across the table towards Betty. 'Aaron gave this to me after an argument,' she said. 'I don't want it any more. I'd like Donna to have it. She could sell it and put the money towards repairing the house.'

Betty looked cheerfully at the ring. 'No, dear, Donna would think it very strange you suddenly giving her an expensive gift, out of the blue.'

'You take it, then. Sell it and give her the money on the quiet.'

'No thank you, love. It's a very nice gesture, though, and I appreciate it.'

They smiled warmly at each other, and it struck Harper that this was a smile of true friendship, a smile that signalled understanding and mutual respect, even love. It also struck her that she had never shared a smile like it with Angela. She went to put the sapphire ring back on her finger, but hesitated. Her right hand was unadorned now – a bit veiny, a bit wrinkly, a bit knobbly and totally naked. She had a sudden longing to set her middle finger ablaze with a great big gaudy piece of costume jewellery, something that Aaron would hate. She stood up and hooked the sapphire ring over one of the spikes on the wooden spice rack next to the cooker.

'I'm thinking of leaving him,' she said.

Betty looked at her cautiously.

'No, really, I am.'

'I'll make another pot of tea, shall I?'

'Go on, then – be a devil.'

Ten minutes later, the doorbell rang. 'Who's that?' she said. She looked at her watch. Tiffany was coming over for a run, but not for another half an hour – and Tiffany was never, ever early.

As she opened the front door, she caught a glimpse of a silver car pulling out of the drive. On the doorstep, there was a huge bunch of gladioli stems – about fifty of them by the look of it. 'Flowers?' she murmured, sensing something amiss. Firstly, it seemed strange that she hadn't been asked to sign for them. Secondly, they were inexpertly tied up with a ragged yellow ribbon. It definitely wasn't a professional job. As she picked them up, she noticed that there was a card on the step beneath them. It was printed with the words, *Don't Go Breaking My Heart*.

Were they for Taylor? She had totally lost track of what was going on between Taylor and Andrew, but she doubted the note was from him, since he was indisputably the heartbreaker in their relationship. It was a strangely worded message too, she thought. Would it occur to anyone under fifty that it was a song title from the seventies?

There was always the possibility that the flowers could be for Aaron, of course – if her growing suspicions about him were true. Only, she couldn't imagine him sleeping with someone who would leave such an unsophisticated offering on his doorstep.

She shivered in the cold air and went back inside the house. 'Where's the big Waterford vase?' she asked Betty.

Soon she was snipping stems and stripping away leaves. 'Thirty-seven gladioli,' she counted aloud. 'It's a bit over the top, isn't it? I wonder if they're all the same colour?'

So far, there wasn't a bloom to be seen. Betty unfurled a bud on one of the stems. 'This one looks very dark. Purple, probably.'

The doorbell rang again. It was Tiffany, in full make-up, dressed head to toe in Sweaty Betty jogging gear. 'Has hell frozen over?' Harper asked as she opened the front door.

Tiffany smiled. 'Why? Because I'm early?'

'Just kidding, come in!'

Tiffany took a step forward and looked closely at her face. 'I meant to say after the school play – you look amazing, Harps. Did you have something done in the end?'

Harper fluttered her eyelashes. 'I believe it's known as blepharoplasty.'

'Sounds painful, yo! Did it hurt?'

'Oh God, it was a nightmare.' She counted out the downsides on her fingers. 'Blood, pain, bruises, swelling, regret . . . but it's all forgotten now. I'm actually glad I had it done.'

'It's super subtle,' Tiffany said. 'You look . . .'

'Refreshed?' Harper said. 'Although I can't believe it right now. I've been crying all morning.'

Tiffany's face fell. 'Oh no, why?'

'Same old. Husband trouble.'

'Take a leaf out of my book and get rid!' Tiffany said.

'I'm seriously considering it, believe me.'

'Do you still want to go out?'

'Do I want to? No. Do I need to? Yes.'

They jogged through the garden and into the fields beyond, sticking to a scenic National Trust path. Harper noticed snowdrops and a couple of early primroses along the way. 'Can't wait for spring,' she gasped, puffing from the exertion of running for the first time in more than a month.

'Shall we take the shortcut back?' Tiffany asked, panting back at her.

'Let's not,' she said. 'I want to feel the pain.'

'YOLO!' Tiffany cried.

They set off again. As her feet pounded the soft ground Harper went over her conversation with Angela for the hundredth time. She couldn't shake the feeling that she was missing something. Angela had said the affair with Aaron had been brief – so why were they caught kissing outside the Savoy, fourteen years later? Had they revisited the affair, or did they just feel a lingering attraction? (She ruled out there being an enduring affection, neither of them being 'affectionate' types.) It didn't make sense – unless the affair had never ended. So, was Angela Aaron's mistress? Had she been his mistress all along? If so, why had she made the comment about there being other women? Was it the sort of thing a long-term mistress might say?

A tune popped into her head. It seemed to tally with the rhythm of her feet. 'Don't go breaking my heart,' she hummed. Elton John and Kiki Dee, number one for weeks and weeks, summer of 1976.

They got back to the house to find a pot of chicken noodle soup bubbling on the stove. Betty had gone upstairs to hoover. Tiffany licked her lips. 'Tell me it's wine o'clock, Harps.'

'There's a bottle in the fridge,' Harper said. 'The glasses are in the usual place. I'm going for a quick shower.'

When she came downstairs again, Tiffany was sitting at the kitchen table with Joyce from next door, chatting merrily.

'Harper!' said Joyce. 'Hope you don't mind me joining. Popped over to find out who did your decking – and what did I find? Tiff, here, opening a gorgeously chilled bottle of Sémillon!'

Harper studied Joyce's face for a moment. The way her cheeks were glowing, the slight glaze in her eyes, the hint of rictus in her smile – Joyce had 'alcoholic' written all over her face. And yet as far as she knew, she was only a social drinker – albeit a very, very sociable, social drinker. But perhaps she was, in fact, a raging dipsomaniac whose husband liked her to have sex with the Finnish au pair while he watched. Or maybe she watched? It was anyone's guess what went on behind closed doors – as Harper knew only too well.

Tiffany handed her a glass. She looked at it longingly for a moment. 'Actually, I won't,' she said. 'I always seem to be hung-over these days.'

'Babe, you've earned it!' Tiffany cajoled. 'Just one won't do you any harm.'

Harper gave in with a laugh. 'Remind me to stop seeing you at lunch time in future.'

They polished off the Sémillon and couldn't resist opening a bottle of Soave. After they'd eaten some soup, Tiffany went outside for a cigarette. Harper joined her on the doorstep. 'I'm going to ask you something,' she said, keeping her voice low, 'and I want you to answer me truthfully.'

'Sounds serious,' said Tiffany, flicking her fag end across the gravel.

'It is and it isn't,' Harper said. 'I'm not sure if I care what the answer is, but I need to know all the same.'

'I *totally* don't like the sound of this.'

'It's just one question, and all you have to do is answer

yes or no. To your knowledge, have you ever heard any gossip about Aaron sleeping with other women?'

Her question hung in the air for a few seconds. 'Before I come back to you, can I just ask one thing?' Tiffany said. 'Is this a make-or-break conversation? Does your marriage to Aaron depend on what I say?'

Harper started chewing her lip. 'You've kind of answered the question by asking that, haven't you?'

'No,' said Tiffany, staring out at the drive.

'Yes, you have. You're worried that I'll leave him if you say he's slept with someone you know.'

'What if I'm worried that you'll stay with him if I say he hasn't?' Tiffany said, turning to face her.

'Are you saying he hasn't?'

'Harps, I've never even heard a whisper of gossip about him.'

'But you think I should leave him?'

'I'd like to see you happy, babe – really happy.'

'That's not what I was asking, though.'

Tiffany shrugged. 'Maybe you were, without knowing it.'

Georgie was recalled for a second *FOMO* audition the following day. 'This time she'll be reading with the lead actress, so she won't have to deal with an amateur like me!' Saskia joked when she called to go through the details.

Harper drove Georgie to the Lippy Films offices after school. They were met by Adam, the director, Dwayne, who was filming the audition again, and an executive producer called Caroline. Adam, Harper noticed, looked different. His brown hair was still tousled, but he now had a five o'clock shadow, which made him appear less fresh-faced, a little older – even better-looking, perhaps.

He clapped his hands together when they entered the audition room. 'Thanks for coming back, Georgina! We're just waiting for Emma Beeson, the actress who will be playing Cat's best friend.'

'The lead role,' said Georgie.

He laughed. 'That depends on how you look at it, and who's playing the part – I'd say Cat's got a lot of the best lines.'

Harper had vowed to herself not to interfere, but she couldn't help saying, 'We've read the extra pages you sent over.'

'Great, what did you think?' he asked Georgie.

She looked at the floor. 'There's a lot about her being fat.'

'Are you uncomfortable with that?' he asked gently.

'A bit, I suppose.'

'I can understand why,' he said, 'but the way I see it, we're going on a journey with Cat. Here's the story of a girl who maybe is a little bit overweight, but what's crucial is how she deals with it – and of course she comes out the champion in the end.' He leaned forward in his seat. 'We're not trying to embarrass you. There are lots of girls who aren't stick thin and we want Cat to give them a voice. She's funny and clever. She's proof that you don't have to be thin to win.'

Harper was impressed. Most directors she knew would have said, 'This is the part. You're the right size for it. Either get on with it or get going.'

Georgie raised her eyes to look at Adam. 'OK,' she said.

Saskia popped her head around the door. 'Emma and her mum are stuck in a traffic jam. They're going to be another fifteen minutes.'

Adam frowned. Harper guessed that he didn't want to lose the momentum he had gained with Georgie. 'Would you mind reading for us, this one last time?' he asked her. 'I wouldn't normally ask, but since you're a professional ...'

'Was,' she corrected him. 'It's up to Georgina. Would you rather wait for Emma, darling?'

'No. S'fine,' said Georgie.

They read through several scenes. By the second page, Harper really started to enjoy herself. It was a huge leap for her – actually, it was downright ridiculous for a fifty-three-year-old mum to try to capture life from the perspective of troubled teenage girl – but she didn't care. Georgie seemed to catch her mood and they got into a rhythm that gave their banter a natural authenticity. Harper was surprised at how good they were together.

And so, it seemed, was Adam. 'That was amazing!' he said, jumping out of his chair when they'd finished. 'You were both fantastic!'

Harper felt herself flush with pleasure. She had forgotten how satisfying it was to pull off an audition.

'No need to wait for Emma,' added Adam. 'We'll be in touch within a day or two.'

Just then the door opened and in rushed a pretty blonde girl. 'I'm so sorry!' she said, gasping for breath. 'We've been sitting in the biggest jam you've ever seen for, like, two whole hours!'

Harper's heart sank. So this was Emma Beeson. A teenage girl with almond-shaped green eyes, a cute sloping nose and a rosebud mouth. Her hair was sleek and golden, her complexion dewy, fresh and flawless. She was around five foot six inches tall and probably weighed just under eight stone. The room filled with sunshine when she smiled.

Harper's heart went out to Georgie.

Adam wasted no time explaining to Emma that the audition had finished. Overriding her effusive dismay and repeated apologies, he managed to escort Georgie and Harper out of the room and through the reception area. 'You were really good,' he told Georgie again. He turned to Harper and took her hand to shake it. 'It's a real pity that you're no longer working. It seems a terrible waste of talent.'

'Oh, go on with you!' she said, too shrilly for her own liking. 'As if there aren't hundreds of actresses out there who can do better!'

He met her eye steadily. 'Believe me, there aren't. I'll be in touch soon.'

'Great,' she said, knocked off balance by the intensity of his gaze. She could have sworn he'd gently squeezed her hand, too.

*

Georgie was silent for most of the drive home. Eventually, Harper felt she had to say something. 'You were brilliant, darling. I don't want to get your hopes up, but I'd be surprised if you didn't get it.'

Georgie said nothing.

'What's wrong?' Harper asked. 'Aren't you pleased with the way it went?'

'I don't know, Mum.'

'But didn't you hear Adam say how amazing you were?'

Georgie sighed and turned her head to look out of the window. 'If I wasn't fat, I wouldn't mind so much. But I am.'

Harper smiled. 'Don't be silly, you're not fat! Anyway, who wants to be stick thin?'

Georgie didn't answer.

Harper tried a different tack. 'There are possibly two hundred girls who've gone for this audition. They will have recalled no more than five – and now you're saying you don't want to go for it?'

'Yeah, funny, isn't it? I mean, it's a TV series and everyone I know will be watching it. Why wouldn't I want them all laughing at me? Or, worse, feeling sorry for me? Can you imagine Dad—'

'Your dad would be as proud as I would!'

'Hashtag whatever, Mum! I haven't even got it yet. I don't want to talk about it any more.'

They drove the rest of the way in silence. As soon as they pulled up outside the house, Georgie got out of the car, slammed the door and marched straight up to her bedroom. Harper rushed after her. 'Please come back!' she called after her.

Taylor intercepted her in the hall. 'Dad's on his way from the airport,' she said. 'By the way, Mum, who died?'

'What do you mean?'

Taylor pointed at the vase of gladioli on the hall table. 'I didn't even know you could get black flowers,' she said.

Harper stepped forward for a closer look. The gladioli buds had started to unfurl and Taylor was right, they were black. Not purple, as Betty had suggested, but black. She recoiled. It was like some horrible omen. 'Neither did I,' she said. 'Eurgh, let's get rid of them.' She scooped all thirty-seven stems out of the vase and carried them into the kitchen, dripping water as she went. 'Get a bin bag,' she told Taylor, who had followed her in with a curious look on her face.

Taylor didn't move. 'A bin bag!' she yelled.

Finally Taylor obeyed. 'Where did you get them, anyway?' she asked, holding the bag open for her to stuff them in.

Harper grappled with the long stems, snapping them in half to make it easier to smash them down. A couple of ends poked her in the eye and she began to feel as if she were in a scene from *The Day of the Triffids*, fighting back extraterrestrial vegetation. 'Someone left them on the doorstep yesterday. I thought they might be for you,' she told Taylor. But as she said it, she had a terrible feeling that she knew who they were for – and who they were from.

Taylor smirked. 'For me? I don't think so.'

Harper heard a noise in the hall and jumped. 'What's this fucking mess?' a voice thundered.

Aaron, she thought. He was home.

Things quickly went from bad to worse. He asked about the flowers. Her explanation was, of course, unsatisfactory to him.

'You found them on the doorstep but you don't know who left them?' he sneered. 'Wasn't there a note?'

'No,' she said, glad that she had slipped the card into a drawer. She would get rid of it later.

He rounded on her. 'What is it with you and flowers?'

'Nothing,' she said, glaring back at him. The message in her eyes was clear, she hoped – if he brought up the Covent Garden rose again she would scream. 'We don't even know who they were meant for. They could have been for you.'

He shook his head in disbelief. 'You're clever, I'll give you that.'

'Wait a minute,' Taylor cut in. 'Who sends black flowers anonymously? Isn't it some kind of crime? Like intimidation or stalking, or something? Maybe you should call the police.'

Harper had forgotten that Taylor was in the kitchen. She and Georgie usually disappeared at the first sign of an argument between their parents, but for once she had stuck around.

Aaron ignored her. A switch had flicked and he'd gone into jealousy mode. His eyes scanned the room and lighted on Harper's phone. Picking it up, he began to check through the call log, muttering the names of the contacts listed. 'Betty. Sarah Trainer. Who's this? Lippy Films?'

Before she could say anything, he was ringing the number, with the phone on loudspeaker. Harper listened helplessly as the whispering receptionist answered. 'Lippy,' she said.

'I wonder if you could help me,' he said smoothly. 'You recently sent me some flowers and I'd like to return them.'

There was a pause on the other end of the line. 'I think you have the wrong number,' she replied. 'We're a production company, not a florist.'

He hung up.

'Dad, you're overreacting,' Taylor said.

'Shut up,' he snapped. 'You don't know your mother like I do. She's very secretive.'

Harper caught Taylor's eye. 'I'm no more secretive than anyone else in this house,' she said, keeping her tone light.

Taylor looked away. 'I'm getting out of here,' she said, heading into the hall.

'So are we,' Aaron said, still focused on Harper's phone, peering closer every time something new caught his attention.

She started to feel unnerved – as she always did when the green-eyed monster took him over. She racked her brains trying to recall if she had left any contacts or traces on the phone that would arouse his suspicions. She had deleted her texts to and from Lizzie and Janice. She had also wiped several internet searches – for Paul Smith shirts (he wouldn't believe they were for him), the top ten relationship self-help books, Angela Stirling, Joe Allen's, London bomb scares 1999 and how to hack hotel guest lists.

'The tea's already organised, so there's no need to go out,' she said, trying to distract him. 'Betty's left mint-marinated lamb chops.'

'Bin them or freeze them,' he said, matter-of-factly. 'Joyce and Walt are meeting us at the brasserie.'

'Since when?'

'Since I decided I needed to talk to Walt about intellectual property.'

'Business?' she said, her heart sinking. Two hours of chit-chat with Joyce loomed ahead of her. 'Can't you meet him tomorrow?'

'It's urgent.'

'What about Georgie? You know I don't like to leave her alone.'

He snorted. 'Sit her in front of the telly with a pile of doughnuts. She'll be as happy as a pig in shit.'

It felt like the last straw. 'Don't talk about our daughter in that way,' she snapped. 'Can't you see it only makes things worse for her?'

'If it bothered her, she'd lose some weight,' he said with a shrug, returning to her call list.

'Don't dismiss it like that! Don't you fucking understand?' she shouted. 'Every time you make a comment about her weight, she becomes more self-conscious. And the more food becomes an issue for her, the more she eats to comfort herself. So you, her father, are contributing to the problem that you keep criticising her for. You might even be the reason why she's eating too much, for fuck's sake!'

'What do you know about it?' he snarled, without even looking up. 'Teen psychologist, are you, now?'

'No, but it doesn't take a genius to work out that a girl needs her father's love and approval. And encouragement. And affection!' Her vocal pitch rose with every word. How many times had she said this, one way or another? But he never listened. 'Why can't you be a loving father to her?' she burst out in desperation.

He met her gaze, his eyes hard as steel. 'Do I know she's my daughter?' he asked. 'For sure?'

She stared back at him. 'What?' she whispered, tilting her head as if she had misheard him.

'I'll answer that myself,' he said flatly. 'No, I don't. She doesn't look like me, she doesn't act like me – she's nothing like me. And who knows what you got up to in Portugal when I had to take that trip to Berlin.'

Her knees buckled beneath her. She grabbed the kitchen counter to help her stay upright. 'Is this what you've been thinking all along? Why didn't you ask for a DNA test?'

She heard a noise coming from the hall, a bump followed by a soft crash. She darted out of the kitchen to see who was there, but the hall was empty. Perhaps it had been the sound of Taylor leaving – in which case, had she heard any of what had been said?

She guessed not. Taylor would have headed upstairs to

get her bag and keys before she went out. But, wait, Taylor had gone straight out after Aaron had told her to shut up, hadn't she? She couldn't be sure. She crossed her fingers and hoped that it hadn't been Georgie in the hall.

She went back into the kitchen. 'Take back what you said,' she demanded, 'or I will walk out of this house and never return.'

But the switch had flicked again. His suspicions presumably allayed, he was no longer holding her phone, no longer fixated on her call list. He stepped forward and put his arms around her. 'Just keeping you on your toes, Pussycat,' he said with a laugh. 'I only do it because I love you so much. You know that. You're my main source of electricity, my power. You can't blame me if I need to test the system from time to time.'

He pulled her close and pressed his lips against her neck. She shuddered. 'You're so fucking sexy,' he murmured. 'I want to fuck you right now.' He moved his lips up to her ear. 'Come upstairs.'

She shuddered again, but her eyes were wide open. For the first time in their marriage, Aaron had triggered an involuntary spasm of physical disgust in her.

30

It was only afterwards that she realised the significance of what happened next. It was then that she understood that she had just lived through the final evening of her old life. She couldn't have foreseen it, although she never stopped blaming herself for her stupid lack of insight. But by the time her old life ended, she had lost all perspective, or very nearly. By then she was practically sleepwalking through her days.

It was partly the drink, she guessed, although she hadn't been aware of it at the time. It was only drink, after all – something you drank and occasionally got drunk on. She hadn't questioned the fact that she was knocking back close to a bottle of wine every evening, or that she was always hung-over the next day, sometimes mildly, sometimes worse. Brain fog was an unremarkable feature of her mornings. She didn't mind it all that much. It meant she didn't have to think too hard.

It was really only during the afternoons that there was ever any potential for clarity, she realised – but three o'clock slumps and school-run siestas usually put paid to that, especially when she'd had a glass or two at lunchtime. It hadn't occurred to her that there was an alternative to living life in a blur. Wine was as much a part of her daily diet as pasta or salad.

Her lifestyle hadn't helped. As her mother was always pointing out, she didn't work, cook or keep house. When she wanted to buy something, she didn't weigh up the pros and cons of the purchase, or mull over whether it was value for money, or if she could do without it. She just bought it. Shopping was an automatic reflex. Pin number, zap. She didn't pay her own credit card bills. She didn't even look at them.

It wasn't a stress-free life, though. That was a laughable idea. While it was true that much of her time was taken up with relaxing beauty rituals – with hair, clothes, networking, dinners and charity lunches – ever present was the horror of living long term with a man who tried to control her every intake of breath. Added to this was the tension of trying to protect her children from within the psychological war zone that was her marriage, while at the same time trying to convince everyone they were living a normal existence. And then there were the peach velour curtains . . .

It was no wonder she was drunk half the time – or so she told herself in the rare moments when she tried to forgive herself.

The rest of the time, she just called herself names. Waste of space. Terrible mother. Fucking idiot. Wet rag. Doormat. Lush. Slave. Zero.

She went upstairs with Aaron because she couldn't think of a way to get out of it, since it wouldn't have seemed plausible to develop a sudden headache or a wave of nausea. They had sex. She went through the motions. He appeared not to notice. She felt sore afterwards.

There was barely enough time to shower and get dressed for dinner at the brasserie. 'You'll have to ring them and say we're going to be late,' she told him. 'I need to speak to Georgie before we go.'

He looked at his watch. 'We're leaving in nine minutes.'

She put on an Erdem silk blouse and skirt, changed her earrings to pale grey pearls, dabbed Tom Ford behind her ears and slipped on a pair of nude court shoes. What we used to call 'beige', she thought.

She knocked on Georgie's door and pushed it open a fraction. 'Can I come in, love?' she asked softly.

She waited until Georgie said yes, and then tiptoed into the room. As usual, Georgie was sitting at her desk in front of her computer. The picture on the screen showed a long-legged model in a bikini on a tropical beach.

'Are you all right?' Harper asked. 'I'm sorry about earlier.'

'S'OK,' Georgie said, looking down.

'I just got carried away by what a great little actress you are, darling. But if you don't feel comfortable with it . . .'

'I don't want everyone looking at me because I'm fat, Mum!'

'Georgie, you're not fat!' Harper said, trying to ignore her double chin. 'All I was thinking, I suppose, was that if you did well in this part, it might lead to other parts you liked better. That's all. But maybe you don't really want to be an actress.'

'I do want to be an actress!' Georgie protested. 'But I don't want to be "the fat one in *FOMO*", OK?'

'I understand, darling. It's just that one thing leads to another in this business.'

Georgie's face crumpled. 'You're trying to persuade me to do it!' she shouted. 'You're not on my side. You pretend you are, but you're not. You're just like everyone else. Get out of my room, Mum. Now!'

Harper shook her head, trying to clear her mind. What am I doing? she thought. This is madness.

She reached out her arms, but Georgie recoiled, a look of disgust on her face.

'I am on your side,' she said firmly. 'I love you very much. You wouldn't believe how much, in fact. I'm sorry, I got this totally wrong. I'll ring them tomorrow and say you don't want the part. We'll forget about it until you're older and . . . surer of yourself. The last thing I want is for you to be upset.'

Angry tears were running down Georgie's face, but she still wouldn't let Harper approach her. Meanwhile, Harper was conscious that Aaron would be downstairs pacing the hall, checking his watch every few seconds, cursing her. Better hurry this up, she thought anxiously.

'Dad and I have to go out for a couple of hours. Will

you be OK? There's a plate of food in the kitchen, ready for the microwave.'

'Go out, fine, whatever, I don't care!' Georgie blurted out.

'Sweetie!' Harper reached forward and clumsily embraced her, trying to hold her and kiss her, to comfort and reassure her. For a moment they were a tangle of arms and elbows, lips and cheeks. Then Georgie shook her off.

'It's fine, Mum!' she hissed, spinning her chair round and sitting on it the wrong way, using the chair-back as a kind of shield. She took a deep breath. 'I'll see you later.'

Harper heard Aaron calling from downstairs. Oh God, she thought. He sounds furious.

'Right, then,' she said. 'See you in a couple of hours, darling. Love you.'

She turned and left the room. As the door closed behind her, she heard Georgie whisper, 'Bye, Mum. Love you, too.'

That's all right, then, she thought. We'll discuss it again later.

Dinner was excruciating. She kept bringing up Angela. It was like a compulsion. Angela this, Angela that. Shut up about Angela! she told herself.

She glanced sideways at Aaron a couple of times, but he didn't react to the mention of Angela's name. All he was interested in, apart from his conversation with Walt, was why she needed to go to the bathroom *twice in one hour!* Was she hiding someone in there? he joked. Did she have a secret lover stashed in the Ladies? Meanwhile, Joyce got drunk and bored on about her childhood in Wales, and Walt rubbed his leg against hers under the table. By the time the bill arrived, she hated the lot of them.

When they got back at ten-thirty, Georgie's light was off. Harper popped her head round the door, but the room was in darkness and all she could see was the outline of her sleeping body. Taylor still hadn't returned. 'Night,' she whispered as she closed Georgie's door.

They went straight to bed. Aaron was tired from his trip and fell asleep instantly while she lay in the dark with a whole load of noise in her head. It wasn't voices, exactly – she wasn't going mad – but her brain wouldn't stop asking questions. 'Is this the end?' 'Is it finally over?' 'Are they still lovers?' Eventually she had to creep into the bathroom and take a sleeping pill.

Aaron demanded sex before he left for his breakfast meeting the next morning. He was running late, so it was mercifully quick. When he had gone she went down to the kitchen. 'Scrambled mush and bacon!' she yelled up to Georgie a few minutes later.

She served the food onto plates and called her again. 'It's getting cold! Where are you?'

When there was still no sign of her, she hurried up to her bedroom, muttering about the time. 'Come on!' she said, pulling open the curtains.

And then she stopped.

On Georgie's bed was a pile of cushions with a duvet carefully drawn over them.

That was when it began.

She rang Tiffany, her heart pounding. 'Is she with you? Did she come over last night?'

'Definitely not, Harps,' Tiffany chirped. 'What's she up to? I'll talk to Sophie and bell you back.'

She sat on Georgie's bed in a stupor, staring at her phone. Tiffany called back ten minutes later. 'Sophie doesn't know anything. I gave her the third degree and she says to look on Georgie's computer, but she doesn't know the password. She says the school bullies have been at her and she's been talking about wanting to lose weight.'

'Can I speak to her?' Harper asked, her voice trembling.

Sophie came on the phone. 'I'm sorry,' she kept saying. 'I really don't know anything. I hope she's OK.'

'Where could she be?' Harper pleaded.

'I don't know. Sorry!'

Tiffany took over the line. 'I'm going to take Sophie to school and come on over, right? Don't fret, Harps, she won't have gone far. I'll be there within the hour. Meanwhile, I'd call the police if I were you. Just to let them know.'

She nodded. Of course. The police. 'Thanks, Tiff,' she said.

Everything felt different, sort of watery.

She called Aaron. He didn't sound worried. 'I'll ring the police next,' she told him.

'Wait, don't get this out of proportion,' he said. 'So the girl needs a bit of space. Let her have it. She'll be back.'

'What do you know?' she said.

'Listen to me!' His tone became serious. 'If you hit the panic button, it could be bad news for all of us.'

'Meaning?'

'I don't want people thinking I've got problems at home. It doesn't look good.'

'I understand,' she said, biting back the desire to scream at him. 'Speak later.'

She left a message with Taylor, rang the school and the Grange. She telephoned her parents in Cullercoats, Aaron's parents in Essex and all the mothers of the kids in the swimming club. She searched Georgie's room. Some clothes were gone, and an orange backpack.

She rang the police, who gave her a reference number, and told her that it was extremely common for teenagers to disappear briefly. Ninety-nine times out of a hundred they were back within a few hours, at most a couple of days.

Days? she thought. She would be dead from worry by then. She could already feel herself dying.

She filled in an online form and emailed it to the police station. Betty arrived. They had a cup of tea.

'She'll be fine,' Betty said. 'She's done this on impulse, but she's a sensible girl at heart. My Donna ran away a couple of times when she was a teenager, but she never went far, or for long.'

'You must have worried, though.' Harper said.

'Frantic – I practically went grey overnight! But she came back, that's my point. They always come back. Even if it's just because they know Tuesday is shepherd's pie day.'

Harper burst into tears. Nobody in the world would come home licking their lips at the thought of one of her dried-out shepherd's pies.

Half an hour later, a police car pulled up in the drive. Two female officers came to the door and introduced themselves. 'Mrs Clarke? We're Nabila Karzai and Claire Wright. Is it all right if we come in?'

She led them to Georgie's bedroom, where they asked her a million questions about the days before her disappearance. 'I think there's been some bullying at school,' she said. She told them what Sophie had said, went over the fallout from the *FOMO* audition and touched on the tensions with Aaron and Taylor. 'She seems to spend a lot of time on her computer,' she added. 'Something tells me the answer could be online.'

'You mean, chatroom activity?' asked Claire.

'Yes, maybe. I don't know.'

'Is there anything missing from her room?' asked Nabila. 'If she planned her departure, she would have thought about what to take with her.'

Harper looked wildly around them. 'Her little green photo album – it's usually by her bed . . . but it's not there now. Nothing else leaps out at me. Wait – where's her lucky keyring?'

'Take your time. Have a thorough look around,' Claire said. 'Any idea where she might have gone?'

'I've checked with everyone I can think of and come up with nothing. Oh God . . . where is she? What happens next?'

'After we report back to the police station, your daughter's disappearance will be flagged up on the system and an investigating officer appointed. Don't worry, Mrs Clarke, we'll go on looking for her until we find her. And with any luck she'll be back before the end of the day. The reality of running away is often not nearly as pleasant as the idea of it.'

'I hope you're right,' Harper said, digging her nails into the palms of her hands. 'Thank you for coming.'

They left an hour later, just as Tiffany arrived, fully made-up, wearing a green pencil skirt suit and white stilettos. 'I read up about it on my phone on the way here,' she said, her eyes gleaming with determination. 'You tell the police, yeah? Then you get on social media. You get the word out on Twitter, Instagram and WhatsApp.'

'How?' she asked. 'I'm not even on Facebook. I tried, but Aaron . . .' Her voice trailed off.

Tiffany, it turned out, had seven hundred and thirty friends on Facebook and just under two thousand Twitter followers. 'Oh yeah, I'm on it, Harps,' she said.

She laid out the various routes they could go down. 'We could straight away send out a red alert saying Georgie's missing and asking for help,' she explained.

Harper lit up. 'Yes, let's do it. Quick!'

Tiffany looked thoughtful. 'But would that be the best way to get Georgie home?'

'Why wouldn't it?'

'What if she's already on her way back? Shining a

spotlight might scare her into hiding again. She'd hate the attention, wouldn't she?'

'She disappeared into the night! Wouldn't she expect me to freak out?'

Tiffany raised one eyebrow. 'Was there an argument?'

Harper nodded. 'But we made it up, I think ...' Her eyes filled with tears.

'Since we don't know what's going through that crazy teenage brain of hers, we're going to have to use our smarts,' said Tiffany. 'She'll come back but maybe we shouldn't try to force it. Not yet, anyway.'

Harper stared at her, feeling light-headed. The thought of Georgie somewhere out in the world – alone and unprotected – was unthinkable. At the same time, it was catastrophically vivid.

'In my mind I keep seeing her drowning, suffocating, screaming for help, being attacked ... you know ... horrible stuff ... Oh God, where is she?' she said, trying not to sob.

Tiffany put a firm hand on her arm. 'I know what you're going through. I'm a mum too. But you're going to have to pull yourself together. Get rid of those thoughts. Toughen up.'

Betty came in and made a pot of coffee. Harper added a glug of brandy to her cup. She took a deep breath and willed herself to be strong.

'Thing is,' said Tiffany, 'it's not news until she's been gone a day or two. So a red alert might not go viral. It might be better to build up your online profile first, so that you can reach as many people as possible if and when you need to.'

'I don't have an online profile,' Harper said.

'You used to be famous, right? We can work with that.'

Tiffany registered her on Twitter and sent her own followers a tweet. *Who loves* Beauty Spot? *I'm trying to persuade my mate @HarperAllen to start acting again #longshot #jointhecampaign*

Within half an hour, the tweet had been retweeted six hundred times and Harper's twitter feed had attracted more than a thousand registered followers, most of them talking about *Beauty Spot*. At any other time, she would have been surprised and flattered by the attention.

'But I can't see how this is going to help us find Georgie,' she said.

'A strong profile is a powerful marketing tool, trust me, babe.'

Harper accepted this somewhat mystifying assurance, because she didn't know what else to do – and frankly she would do anything if it would help to get Georgie back.

'Now you've got to respond. Keep the hype going,' Tiffany went on.

It was hard to know what to say. *What a set-up!* she wrote. *It's a nice thought, @TiffanyBander, but I'm a happy housewife/mother and I love my daughters, T&G #motherlove*

'Weak,' sniffed Tiffany.

But you never know, if the right project came along . . . #neversaynever she added in a second tweet.

'Now you're getting it.'

And one day when she's older I'd love to work with my talented, beautiful daughter Georgie, she wrote in her third tweet. *#can't wait for you to come home!*

'Bullseye,' Tiffany said. 'Let's move on to her computer.'

Upstairs in Georgie's bedroom, things turned surreal. 'Passwords,' Tiffany said, turning on the computer. 'What's her nickname or pet name?'

Harper listed the terms of affection she used with Georgie. 'Georgeous, Georgie-Porgie, Porgs, Babyface, Tweetypie, Munchkin, Tiggy . . .'

Tiffany tried them all – in caps and lower case, with numbers and without – but none of them gained entry to the computer. Harper kept spewing out suggestions. 'Aaron calls her Plumpkin. Taylor occasionally calls her Gee-gee.'

'Nope.'

'My dad calls her Fluffy,' she said in desperation. 'But it's—'

Tiffany's fingers bashed the keyboard. 'Fluffy 1234 – that's it!'

Harper peered at the screen, wondering why Georgie had chosen her grandpa's pet name for her, above all the others.

A few moments later, Tiffany started cursing. 'Crap! She's wiped her internet history,' she complained.

Harper watched as she pulled up various sites. 'What do we know? Bullying and weight loss. Let's try weight loss first.'

Tiffany steered them through a world of slimming

products – of dietary advice, stomach-shrinking vitamins, eating plans and thinspiration threads and forums. Harper thought she had tried every diet and detox known to womankind, but there were weight-loss sites and blogs promoting all kinds of stuff she'd never heard of, from fat-busting frogspawn sourced in the Amazon basin to something called the 'water loading strategy' and 'thindividual' self-hypnosis.

She imagined Georgie trying to navigate her way through all the information, looking for answers. It was unbearable. If she had only talked more to her about her body image. If only she had known what was going on in her mind.

'I don't know where I'm going with this,' Tiffany said, taking a break and flexing her fingers.

A familiar image of a model in a bikini popped up on the screen. It was the photo that Harper had noticed the night before. 'Georgie was looking at that yesterday!' she said.

Tiffany started tapping and clicking again. A new site opened up, and then another. Suddenly a disclaimer appeared. *This website does not promote harmful behaviour*, it said. *It is a support group for people who have an existing eating disorder. Do not enter this site if you do not have an eating disorder.*

Tiffany clicked.

Behind the disclaimer they found an alien world peopled by skeletal young women, all skin and bones, who had protruding ribcages and limbs that threatened to snap at any minute. Their bikinis hung off them like rags. They were smiling like zombies and posing like glamour girls.

Harper felt sick. 'What is this? They look like famine victims,' she said.

'It's a site for anorexics. I've heard about them. They encourage each other to go on starvation diets.'

The site was packed with tips on how to survive at subsistence level: *Half an apple and a cracker for lunch, one segment of orange . . .* There was advice on how to fool parents into thinking you were eating healthily: *Cram your pockets with crumbs when they're not looking, tuck the crusts up your sleeves.* There was a step-by-step guide to making yourself vomit: *Three fingers often works better than two.* In the corner of one page there was a space for confessing your worst sins, like eating the centre filling of a custard cream, or a whole bowl of peas.

Everything about it was wrong and confusing. Harper tried to remember her conversation with Georgie the day before. What had she said? 'Anyway, who wants to be stick thin?' Now she knew.

She started to feel dizzy. 'I've never seen anything so grotesque,' she said. 'This is suicide support, not diet support. Has Georgie been looking at this? Is there any way of telling?'

'I'm looking for her footprints,' Tiffany said.

While she explored the site, Harper stared sightlessly out of Georgie's bedroom window. What sort of bizarre world are we living in? she wondered.

'I've found something,' Tiffany said. 'Look at this.'

Georgie had posted a message on a thread entitled, *Taking Control!*

I'm new to this site. I wish I wasn't fat but I am. I've got big thighs and rolls of fat on my belly. Some of the guys at school have been laughing at me because my stomach sticks out further than my breasts. They say tits, but I don't like that word. Anyway it's true. About my belly. But I want to be thin. I want to learn how to starve myself. Where do I start?

Fluffy@Fattie

The question had been posted a month earlier.

There was only one reply so far, from someone called HollowCheeks. It said, **Stop talking fat and fatness! R U trolling? Fuck u and fuck off.**

Tiffany sighed. 'She was out of her depth in anorexic world, poor baby. The question is, where did she go next?'

Harper was crying again. 'She obviously needed to talk to someone. Why didn't she come to me?'

'You can ask her that while you're wringing her neck for giving you all this hassle,' Tiffany said. 'Harps, I'm starting to worry here. She's not keeping anything back and it makes her look ... vulnerable. Where the hell did she go next? Who's she been talking to?'

Harper's skin crawled. 'Do you think someone could have been been grooming her?'

'I fucking hope not.'

'I don't mean a paedophile. I'm sure she's too savvy for that. But—'

She broke off. Images of teen vampires, witches and werewolves swirled in her head. The idea of the 'evil teen' was one of society's obsessions. Hadn't she read somewhere that puberty triggered a complete rewiring of the human brain – and that hormonal changes could cause depression and madness? Could Georgie have got involved with other unhappy teenagers? So-called evil teens? While Tiffany tapped and scrolled, she thought about her father's 'funny turns', or bouts of depression, as they now knew them to be. She remembered asking him if depression could be hereditary. What had he said? That maybe it could?

I don't know anything, she thought. My daughter's mental state, starvation websites, what goes on in the teenage brain – why am I so completely and utterly ignorant of it all? Have I been asleep for the past few years?

Although Tiffany searched every chatroom she could find, they were none the wiser about Georgie's connections by the time she had to leave for a lunch appointment at twelve-thirty.

'Sorry, Harps, you need a techie to cut through all the crap,' she said when she finally tore herself away from the screen. 'Someone who loves their computer more than life itself, basically.'

'Maybe we're barking up the wrong tree. Maybe the answer doesn't lie online.'

'Who knows?' Tiffany said. 'But we've got to be real about this. She hasn't gone to see her French pen pal.'

Harper rubbed her eyes. 'Where do I find a techie, then?'

'You could try a private detective. The agency I used was totally high tech. My guy found everything I needed to know about where Doug was hiding his dosh . . . ' She bit her lip. 'I'm not supposed to talk about my divorce settlement, but I saved the family home, if you know what I mean.'

She picked up her phone and reeled off a number. Harper keyed it into her contacts list. They hugged and Tiffany left, promising to bell her later.

First she phoned the police and told them she had found evidence of chatroom activity – or at least, attempted activity. Then she called Aaron. 'I need a private detective on the case,' she said.

He laughed. 'This isn't a fucking episode of *Poirot*, woman. Calm down. She'll be back by the end of the day.'

'What do you know?' she said. Despite her pain and despair, it felt good to be throwing his favourite phrase back at him. Learnt from his father, and his father's father before him, it was the ultimate sexist put down. 'I'm doing it anyway.'

'OK, but if I find a strange man in my house when I get home I will kick his head in.'

She phoned the agency that Tiffany had recommended. 'I need a female techie,' she told them. 'If you don't have one on your books, I'll pay you to find one.'

31

She showered, dressed and spoke to what felt like a thousand people on the phone, including her parents, Aaron's parents and all the mums of the swimming club kids. 'I'm sure it's just a blip,' she kept saying. 'But please let me know if you hear anything.'

After several missed calls, she spoke to Taylor. 'Mum? I'm in Amsterdam. Andrew brought me here on a surprise trip. It's so romantic! Is Georgie back?'

'Not yet,' she said.

'OK, well, I'll be home tomorrow. Keep me updated.' Harper heard a faint giggle just before she hung up the phone. She didn't resent it. Taylor had no idea. She was in love. She was in another world.

Karin Hamasaki from RF Security Services arrived at the house at four o'clock. She was thirtyish – small, slim, bespectacled and dressed in monochrome colours from head to toe. She wore a black and white checked silk pussybow blouse, a black and white striped wool skirt – and black tights with white diamonds up the side. Her shoes were black and white patent. It was like looking at an optical illusion.

I've finally fallen down the rabbit hole, Harper thought.

Tiffany reappeared just after Karin arrived. 'Sophie's with her dad tonight, so I can stay as long as you need me,' she said.

'Thanks,' Harper said. 'I feel better when you're here.'

They had tea in the kitchen and filled Karin in on what they had found out so far. Karin had an air of reserve about her, but her eyes were kind and Harper felt safe with her. After she'd heard them out, she told them that she had worked on similar cases involving runaway teens. Although she couldn't discuss the specific details, online grooming had been at the heart of nearly half of the disappearances.

'Grooming by older men?' Harper asked hoarsely. Her throat felt drier than the Sahara during a sandstorm.

'In some cases, yes,' Karin said. 'If your daughter has been looking for peer support, she may have found it – or she may herself have been "found" by an older person posing as a teenager.'

'Can you trace her footprints across the internet?'

'I should be able to follow her trail away from the pro-ana site.'

They went up to Georgie's room and Karin got to work. Within twenty minutes, they were reading printed copies of a chat-room conversation between Georgie and a girl who called herself 'Fantine' and claimed to be sixteen, and an eighteen-year-old boy whose user name was 'Lil Papa Romeo'.

Harper felt her heart crack with every entry she read.

Fluffy: This is my first time here.

Fantine: Welcome Fluffy! U good?

Fluffy: Not really. Feeling fat today. Hate my dad.

Fantine: Parents suck! @complete fuckers.

Fluffy: ha ha. Fanks for making me laugh

Lil Papa Romeo: Wha bout ur dad?

Fluffy: Calls me fat. Jeez. Loves making jokes about it. Finks he's reely funny.

Fantine: Fathers hate their daughters. It's a psychological fact.

Lil Papa Romeo: I heard that 2

Fantine: What kind of jokes, @Fluffy?

Fluffy: If I eat a biscuit he says I'm stuffing my cakehole. He calls me Fatty Arbukle and says to tread softly or I could fall thru the floor

Lil Papa Romeo: What's Arbukle

Fantine: Your dad says that to you? He doesn't love you.

Fluffy: Been to Greggs again? Got a lift home on the pastry wagon?

Lil Papa Romeo: Not funny

Fluffy: Bet you're the biggest unit in your maths class

Lil Papa Romeo: Ur dad's an asshole

Fantine: Do you live with your mum as well?

Fluffy: Mum and older sis

294

Fantine: Your mum stays with him? She doesn't love you either.

Fluffy: D'oh – my mum does love me! :-)

Fantine: #delusional! Your mum's staying with a man who calls you all these names? FUBAR. She can't love you or she would of left.

Fluffy: Dunno. Maybe. Think she's scared of him.

Harper dropped the transcript and buried her head in her hands, horrified by the idea that Georgie might think she didn't love her because she had stayed with Aaron. And yet she could see Fantine's logic. He was an abusive parent, in a way. So why the hell hadn't she left him for the sake of her children?

It struck her, in that moment, that life would never be the same again. She vowed to leave Aaron as soon as she found Georgie. Taylor could come with them, if she wanted. She desperately wanted to things to be good with Taylor as well.

She steeled herself to go on reading.

Fantine: My mum hates me 2. My stepdad abuses me and she does jack squat bout it.

Lil Papa Romeo: Twisted. I'm home with my uncle @ bastard #cruel fucker. Sometime I wanna jump on the bus.

Fluffy: Where to?

Lil Papa Romeo: Up or down @nevercominback

Fluffy: Like Australia?

Lil Papa Romeo: Like oblivion. But don't want to go alone

Fantine: I cut my arms. #bigrelief. Any U do that?

Fluffy: POS. Gotta go. Back tom.

'POS?' said Harper.

'"Parent Over Shoulder,"' said Karin. 'Maybe you walked into the room during the conversation.'

Over the next hour Karin discovered reams of chat between Fantine, Fluffy and Lil Papa Romeo. They were a gang now. They told each other everything. It was clear that Georgie found support and comfort in their conversations. It was also patently obvious that the others were guiding her down the road to self-harm. Cutting herself, they assured her, would help to ease her worries. There was a lot of talk about 'ending the pain' and 'going where the peace was'.

'I don't believe this,' Harper said, trying to steady her trembling hands. 'It's almost as if they're trying to persuade her to kill herself.'

The cold, hard truth hit her like a mugger's iron bar.

Someone had been grooming her daughter to take her own life.

She felt the blood drain from her face. Her heart started thumping wildly, arrhythmically. 'I have to find her, before anything happens to her!' she said. She felt like a horse in a burning stable – trapped, panicked, hysterical.

Tiffany faced her square on and took her firmly by the shoulders. 'Listen to me, Harps. I know Georgie – she's a girl who's full of joy. Not in a month of Sundays would anyone be able to persuade her to kill herself.'

Harper felt herself starting to hyperventilate. 'What if she's with these people now?'

Tiffany poured her a stiff drink and made her put her head between her knees. By the time they found an extract of conversation in which Fantine suggested meeting up, she was breathing normally again, albeit into a brown paper bag.

Fantine: I need to get away from here.

Fluffy: Escapeeeeeee! And I can't wait to move out of home when I'm old enough.

Fantine: I mean now. Got get out now. @fucking hate my stepdad touching me. Thinking bout my cousin John's. He says I can stay anytime.

Fluffy: #lucky to have a place to go. I don't mind my home when my dad's away, but he's coming back in a couple of days.

Fantine: Say what? You could meet me there, have a break. Lil Papa Romeo, wanna come?

Lil Papa Romeo: Yur cousin wants 3 gests?

Fantine: There's a spare bedroom. We could all bunk in. Got sleeping bags?

Fluffy: Somewhere in the back of a cupboard! Where does your cousin live?

Fantine: By the sea @new horizons #sandy beaches!

Fluffy: Where? North or south?

Fantine: POS – Insta later when i get the address

Time sped up. Karin started searching for evidence that would lead her to Fantine and Lil Papa Romeo's real names and addresses, which would in turn lead to Fantine's cousin John, if such a person existed.

Then Tiffany found press reports of teen suicide pact sites in Europe and America. *Oh my God, oh my God, oh my God*, went the chant in Harper's brain.

She phoned the police and told them that she was certain that Georgie's life was in danger. 'We have to find her tonight!' she kept saying, trying to block out images of nooses, sleeping pills, syringes, booze and motorway bridges.

She clenched her fists. She had to believe that Georgie loved life too much to die. She willed her to stay alive. Please. I love you! she kept screaming in her head. I love you and I'll make everything all right. I promise, I promise.

She hoped that her brainwaves would be clear and strong enough to reach her. Tap into me, she begged the universe. Listen out for me, Georgie, she pleaded.

She got in the car with Tiffany and drove to the police station.

The duty officer perked up when he saw them. 'Can I help you?' he asked.

Two hours later they were back at Orchard End. Aaron tried to intercept her in the hall, but she pushed past him.

'Where have you been?' he called up the stairs.

'The police.'

'Did they tell you to stop fussing?'

She didn't reply.

'How did it go?' Karin asked, once they were back in Georgie's bedroom.

'They were helpful,' Harper said. 'They're going to make more enquiries and get everything ready to put out a missing persons alert. But we need to get to Georgie sooner than that. There's too much procedure with the police. What about you? Did you find anything else?'

Karin looked glum. 'I keep hitting dead ends and I'm getting suspicious about how careful they've been. It's almost as if they knew that someone would try to trace them.'

Harper looked at her stonily. 'They're not teenagers in fact, are they?'

Karin met her gaze. 'I don't know. Either way, I don't trust their motives.'

Harper checked her watch. It was eleven o'clock. 'I can't wait any longer. Tiffany, you've got to help me.'

Over the next half an hour, they bombarded social media with cries for help. Every message was accompanied by Georgie's latest school portrait and references to *Beauty Spot* and Harper Allen. They covered all the bases – Twitter, Instagram, Snapchat, WhatsApp, Tumblr and Facebook.

Just before midnight, the doorbell rang.

Aaron had gone to bed, so Harper answered the door. There was a man on the doorstep wearing a crumpled jacket and trousers that didn't quite match. He looked weary. 'Harper Allen, or Clarke?' he said. 'I'm Tom

Bayliss from the *Chester Chronicle*. Is Georgina still missing?'

Aaron came downstairs wearing a dressing gown. 'Is it the return of the prodigal fucking drama queen?' he said. 'At long last?'

Harper turned to face him. 'She's still missing, Aaron. I'm telling the press. You can't stop me.'

He raised his hands in mock surrender. 'OK, if that's what you want, I won't stand in your way.'

He didn't argue, she realised, because there was a journalist within earshot. But inside he would be boiling with rage that she had defied him.

She spent the night in Georgie's bed clutching a fluffy ginger kitten toy in one hand and her mobile phone in the other. Some of the time she lay on her back staring at the ceiling, but mostly she lay on her side, curled up, hoping.

Three feet away, Karin sat at Georgie's computer, searching the internet.

'Found anything?' she asked, every few minutes.

'Not yet, still working on it.'

While Karin exercised her high-tech powers of deduction, Harper's brain clicked and whirred like an antiquated knitting machine, fretting and agitating through the sequence of events leading up to Georgie's disappearance. There were a hundred different ways she could have prevented it, she realised wretchedly – and as the long, tortuous hours of the night crawled by, she catalogued them obsessively, blaming herself at every turn.

It was obvious to her now that she ought to have confronted Georgie with more force about being teased and bullied at school. This was her first fail. Her reluctance to tackle Georgie head-on had been cowardly. What kind of mother couldn't talk openly and honestly to her daughter about being bullied? A terrible mother, obviously. A stupid, drunken, gutless, distracted, self-centred, selfish mother.

Click, click. Whirr. But was Georgie's experience of school really at the core of her disappearance? She knew in her heart that it went deeper and further. After all, her ordeals at St Mary's High simply reflected what had been going on at home for her entire life. Even longer, in fact – because Aaron had treated her with disdain since before she was born.

'Found anything?'

'Still looking.'

His lack of love hadn't been too noticeable during the years of her early childhood. He had cautiously guarded the Clarke family brand – he wanted their lives to appear perfect – so it was only within the walls of Orchard End that he'd given rein to his contempt for Georgie – and Harper – at first. But the moment that Georgie had begun to let the side down by putting on weight, at around the age of ten, his attitude had changed. Suddenly she was a legitimate target for his scorn, no matter who happened to be around.

Harper understood what had gone through his head. He was ashamed of his podgy child and he wanted to distance himself – and his brand – from her. Unofficially, he had disowned her.

Several people who had seen them together in recent years had witnessed him taking potshots at Georgie. It was a sport for him, like squash or golf or clay pigeon shooting. She had tried to intervene – every time, all the time – but now she realised that she hadn't tried hard enough. Had she been in the mood to forgive herself – just a tiny bit – she might have acknowledged that Georgie had fooled them all by appearing untroubled by her father's routine cruelty, and perhaps the true gravity of the situation had escaped her as a result.

He never missed a chance to fire off a shot. When there were leftovers after a dinner party, he'd say, 'Dump them in a trough for the plumpster. She'll polish them off for breakfast, oink.'

'Lay off her, Aaron, don't be mean,' she'd say automatically.

But instead of wearily berating him for the hundredth time, she should have threatened in all seriousness to leave him. It was her fault that fat jokes about Georgie were a part of their everyday. She should have done so much more to protect her.

What kind of mother allowed her husband to bully her daughter? Only a terrible mother. Only a negligent, care-less, irresponsible, insensitive, sleepwalking mother.

'Found anything?'

'Not yet.'

She wished they were searching for a needle in a

haystack, because at least it was something you could do methodically. Cyberspace was just too enormous and too random for logical methodology – although she knew that Karin was doing her scientific best.

Until now, she had loved the internet. Information at her fingertips, online cashmere sales, a waterproof mascara that was only available at Harrods – she had thought of it as a dream-come-true shopping emporium with infinite, encyclopedic wallpaper. But now she hated it. It gave the appearance of being something new and positive, but it was a force for evil, a place where sick and twisted people preyed on the innocent and vulnerable.

Looking back, it was impossible to know why Aaron had refused to bond with Georgie. Had it simply been down to the fact that he hadn't wanted another child? Or because he actually believed that he might not be her biological father? Who knew what had gone on in that psychotic mind of his? She had very little idea, even after more than twenty years of marriage. However, she suspected it was a bit of both.

What she couldn't understand, and would never understand, was how the beautiful, trusting eyes of gurgling baby Georgie could have left him unmoved in the days after she was born. How the cute, chuckling ways of toddler Georgie hadn't prompted him to love her with every bone in his body. How he could have brushed aside the joy-filled five-year-old as she skipped off to school asking questions about the sky. Or the tutu-clad seven-year-old jumping merrily through their garden sprinklers on a summer's day.

She pressed the fluffy ginger toy to her chest. Georgie had been the most adorable of young children in a world where all children were adorable. Even today, at a difficult age, struggling with adolescence and issues of self-esteem, she was as loving and caring a daughter as a parent could wish for.

In a snap she would have given up her life for Georgie, gladly and willingly, without thinking, without blinking, without looking back.

Tears streamed down her face as she remembered a December day in Manchester when she thought she had lost her for good. Georgie had been three, maybe four – at the age, she reflected, when you were constantly losing sight of your child and fearing the worst, because they were so cute, so desirable and snatchable, in your eyes, at least.

After dragging her round the Trafford Centre on a Christmas shopping spree, she had taken her to a nearby playground so that she could let off steam. It was nearly four o'clock and the playground was packed with big, rowdy children, just out of school.

She had bumped into a friend and been distracted for moments – for forty-five seconds, maybe sixty, at most. Had it been news of someone's divorce that had diverted her? She couldn't for the life of her recall. It could just as easily have been cancer or a lottery win.

What she did remember, with horrifying clarity, was scanning the playground for Georgie and seeing her *nowhere*. And then tearing around the playground like a headless chicken, shouting wildly for her, her mind screeching in panic, going half mad with thoughts of kidnap and murder.

Running, looking, seeing nothing, her head swivelling like the demon in *The Exorcist* – thinking, Is that her over there? Is it her, is it her? Same height and curly hair, *wrong clothes.*

And then spotting her way beyond where she expected her to be, far outside the playground, sitting on a bench, all alone.

Talking to the pigeons. Perfectly fine.

Rushing out of the playground towards her, engulfing her, enveloping her, yelling at her not to disappear again, flooding with relief, sobbing with relief, crying tears of joy, shaking her and asking, 'Why did you leave the playground without telling me?'

'It was too noisy, Mummy. I wanted a bit o'peace and quiet.'

'Anything, Karin?'

'Not yet, still searching.'

Without realising it, she dozed off for a moment, and woke up in the middle of remembering. Oh, the relief, she had found her!

Where am I? she thought. Asleep or awake? The child, the teenager – which is it? What's happening?

Slowly it dawned on her that she was in a vacuum – not in a Manchester park hugging the little one she had found, but suspended in the gloom of her child's bedroom, waiting to hear from the teenager she had lost.

Blaming herself constantly, wondering if Georgie, the light of her life, was *even still alive*.

'Found anything?'

'Not yet.'

News of Georgie's disappearance appeared on several websites the following morning. It wasn't a big story, but she was grateful for the coverage in the local news sections. *Ex-sitcom star's daughter rumoured missing*, and Beauty Spot *star daughter appeal*.

The police called. An investigating officer had been appointed. Could she come to the station to coordinate plans for the missing person appeal?

'Yes,' she said in a soft voice.

They meant a live appeal on television, a press conference, she thought. Had anyone ever been found alive after one of those appeals? She blocked out the thought, determined not to lose hope.

She began to get calls from the press. 'I have to be careful what I say,' she told them. 'It's just possible that she's been groomed by older teenagers, or worse. We don't know much and the police have warned me against revealing any details. Can you say that I'm planning to make an appeal very soon?'

'How long has it been now?'

She bit her lip. 'Nearly forty hours, I think,' she said shakily.

'What about her father?' one of the journalists asked. 'Will he be part of the appeal?'

She hesitated. 'He will.'

She hoped it wouldn't put Georgie off if it was reported that Aaron would be involved. Problem was, if he wasn't, people would start having all kinds of suspicions.

Adam from Lippy Films called mid-morning, his voice full of concern. 'I read the news about Georgina,' he said. 'We're all very worried about her here at Lippy. Have you any idea where she might have gone?'

'Not really,' she said. She filled him in as best she could.

'We were about to offer her the part of Cat in *FOMO*, which of course is of no consequence now – unless you think it could somehow influence her decision to come home.'

'I'm not sure . . . '

'That's why I was calling – to find out if you'd like me to release the information that she's just been offered a lead role in a TV series. I mean, even if it means nothing to Georgina right now, it might help publicise her disappearance.'

'It's hard to know. She said she didn't want the part.' She felt guilty as she recalled how she had tried to persuade Georgie it was a fantastic opportunity. 'You're right,' she went on. 'It would be great publicity, but I don't want to complicate things.'

'I'd leave it, then,' he said. 'I really hope she comes home soon.'

'Thank you.'

He cleared his throat. 'If you change your mind, or if there's anything I can do to help, please ring me, any time of the day or night – any time at all. Please.'

'Right, OK.'

'Will you call me anyway, when she gets back?'

'Because of the part? I think you probably—'

'Not because of the part. I'd just like to know she's safe. Please.'

'OK.'

'Or if you don't have time, can I call you?'

'Of course,' she said, unsure of what exactly she was agreeing to.

32

Georgie's number appeared on her phone screen at three-thirty-five that afternoon, while she was sitting in one of the incident rooms at the police station. She nearly dropped the phone in her haste to press the answer button. It was like a hot potato in her hands, a slippery fish. She was all fingers and thumbs, clumsy and fumbling, as she grappled with it.

'Georgie? Are you OK?' she said.

'Mum?' she heard.

Georgie's voice sounded strangulated. Was there a gun to her head? A fist at her throat?

'Are you OK?' she repeated, her pounding heart in her mouth.

'Mum?' she heard again.

Her voice was thick, a bit muffled. Had she been gagged, tied up?

'Georgie?'

'Mum ... I'm so sorry, Mum!'

'Darling?'

'Mum?'

'Are you OK?'

'Yes.'

'You're not hurt, love?'

'No.'

'Are you coming home?'

'Yes.'

'Please come home, darling.'

'I am.'

'Please come now!'

'Yes.'

'Are you really OK?'

'Yes.'

'Can I come and get you?'

'Mum ...'

'I'm coming to get you.'

'You can't. I'm on on a train.'

'Just tell me where you are, love.'

'I'm on the train from Blackpool to Manchester ...'

'Are you sure you're safe?'

'Yes ... I'm coming now.'

'I'll be there to meet you in Manchester.'

'OK ... I love you, Mum.'

'I love you, too, darling.'

Harper stayed on the phone to Georgie throughout the journey back.

'Where are you sitting?'

'By the window.'

'How much longer?'

'About half an hour.'

'Thank God you're on your way.'

Pause.

'Georgie?'

'Mum, what's going to happen now?'

'Everything is going to be all right. That's all I know.'

She struggled to keep her voice steady. There was a lump in her throat and she was choked up with emotion, but she did her best to sound reassuring – even though she kept thinking she might collapse under the weight of her relief. Georgie was alive and safe. She was coming home. The wait was over.

They just about stayed connected until the train reached Manchester Piccadilly. Their voices kept zoning in and out, but the essence of what they needed to say made it through the splintered airwaves. Georgie needed her mum. Harper was waiting for her. All was not lost.

She met her off the train with a police escort and hugged her possessively, like a mother bear. Something had changed in Georgie's eyes, she noticed – a light had gone off. It made her heart crumple. She wanted to howl with grief. Her little girl had been hurt.

Please God make her better soon, she thought.

She bundled her off the platform and into the car, where they sat and talked as people came and went around them.

'What happened, love? What made you run off like that?'

Conscious that she needed to focus on every word that Georgie said in the rawness of the moment, she mainly listened, holding her tongue whenever she wanted to argue with her version of things. It was crucial to find out as much as she could about her state of mind. To help her put her life back together. To prevent anything like this happening again.

She shuddered.

In broken sentences and bursts of emotion, Georgie described how she had descended into despair over the previous few months. She couldn't pinpoint the start and wasn't sure if she could blame anything in particular, but it hadn't helped that the pressure had begun to pile up at school at the beginning of the year.

'The teachers went on and on about getting good grades. Like it was all that mattered!'

A series of minor disasters had got her down, falling in sequence like dark little dominoes. She had struggled with an English test, failed a maths test. Everybody laughed when she dropped a tray of food in the school canteen. Her school nickname was suddenly 'Jelly'. Jessica Tamworth had said something nasty about her dimply thighs. Some of the boys teased her about her big stomach. She'd enjoyed being in the school play, but it had brought negative as well as positive attention, perhaps a bit of jealousy. She felt that Mr Nayar had pushed her too hard to audition for *FOMO* – and that Harper hadn't fully taken on board her reluctance to play Cat.

Gradually her world became a mass of grey clouds.

She felt fat, weak and unlovable. But nobody seemed to notice. Or care. Dark thoughts rolled through her brain like mist and she didn't know where to turn. So she put on a smiley face and ate more. Which made her feel even fatter, weaker and unlovable.

'But you *are* loved. By so many people. *I* love you,' said Harper.

'I know, but you're my mum,' Georgie said. 'And you always seem, I don't know, so *unhappy.*'

That stung. Was Georgie basically saying that she didn't value her mother's love because she didn't admire or respect her?

'It's all going to change, I promise,' she said. 'I've let you down. But it won't happen again.'

She wondered how she could have been blind to her daughter's suffering. How could it have escaped her that her life had begun to feel hopeless? She had been living in her own emotional prison, she thought guiltily. She had been too focused on her own problems to realise that her daughter was dying inside.

She tried to suppress her feelings of terror as Georgie described how her online conversations with Fantine and Lil Papa Romeo had led to friendship.

'Fantine was totally blarg about living with her step-father,' she said. 'Romeo was bored of being bummed out the whole time. I told them I'd had enough of being fat and having a dad who doesn't love me. Don't try to argue, Mum. It's true.'

'Your father . . . can be mean, I know.'

'It's more than that, but whatever.'

'I know ... but ... how did you find these friends?'

'I went into a chat room. There was a thread about feeling negative, so I typed in, "Anyone feel as crap as I do?" Turned out Fantine and Romeo felt even worse.'

'It went from there ... to meeting in Blackpool?'

'At first it was just about talking to people who felt the same way. That's really all it was. Then they started to talk about "jumping on the bus". They'd heard about other teenagers doing it. You get a ticket to oblivion. You leave behind the troubles of the world.'

'And the wonders,' Harper said. But Georgie didn't seem to hear.

'Romeo found an online support group for people feeling suicidal,' she went on. 'They believe it's your right to take your own life if you want to.'

She paused, waiting for Harper to say something.

Harper took a deep breath. 'I suppose it is your "right", although it's a funny way of putting it,' she said carefully. 'But it's a terrible choice to make, and so sad – for you and everyone who loves you.'

'They don't see it that way.'

She knew they didn't see it that way. She had looked up cases of online suicide 'assistance', where teenagers had been 'supported' in their decision to take their own lives, often by people they had never met. Their farewell messages were full of hope and excitement. They said things like, *This is where the real adventure starts!* and *See you on the other side!*

It was impossible to know what they were really thinking when they wrote these cheery goodbye notes. Maybe they were trying to be brave and spare the feelings of their loved ones – or perhaps they actually believed that they were taking an extended gap year in heaven. She couldn't help feeling they didn't really understand the enormity or permanence of death. But she didn't say so.

'Did you find out their real names? Fantine and Romeo's real names?'

'They said it was safer to stick with our online names – and Romeo thought it wouldn't matter when we met on the other side.'

Her heart hammered in her chest. 'Were you going to Blackpool to kill yourself?' she asked.

'I don't know,' Georgie said. 'But when I got there, I knew I didn't want to do it.'

'Why not?'

Georgie started to gnaw the skin on the edge of her nails. 'They were ... it was ... kind of a let-down. Romeo's OK. But Fantine is really fucked up. It's like she's already dead.'

'Is she fourteen as well?'

'About nineteen, I think.'

Harper gasped. 'So much older!'

'She's nice in a way, but all she can think about is death. She goes round in circles talking about different ways of dying. And she talks really slowly, with this weird smile on her face. It's like she's wearing a sad suit, but she's happy being sad. It's ... kind of creepy.'

'It sounds *really* creepy.'

'She knows the best ways to do it. Like, hanging is quickest. And she likes the yucky details. She makes death sound really gross – the physical side of it. Romeo wasn't like that. He kept saying it would be exciting to venture into the unknown. But he was up one minute and down the next. I was a bit scared of him.'

'He didn't ... try anything?'

'No, Mum. Blech!'

'What was the house like?'

'It was a flat. The bathroom was pukoid. I didn't even want to go in there. There wasn't any food in the fridge. Blackpool's a dump, isn't it? Especially in the rain.'

'Actually, I'm fond of Blackpool. Well, I was until now. So what made you decide to leave?'

'I heard someone laughing – outside the window. In the street.'

Bless that person, Harper thought.

'It sounded like you, Mum. It made me miss you!'

'Did it, love?'

'You're uptight around Dad, but not the rest of the time. So I guess you're not really that unhappy. And you're funny when you laugh. It's just Dad ... he's so ... he's just an arsehole.'

'He's ... difficult.'

'Then I remembered you saying how upset you were when your nana died because you'd never see her again. I tried to imagine not seeing you or Taylor, Sophie or Grandpa again. I didn't like that idea.'

'Thank God! Because we love you so much!'

'Me too.'

'But were the others OK about you opting out?'

'Fantine wasn't. She said she needed someone to do it with. I felt bad, so I stayed another night. But when I woke up yesterday, I knew I had to get out. The front door was locked. I don't know if they meant to stop me getting away, but I panicked and climbed out of the bathroom window.'

'Well done.'

'I know she must be angry, but I couldn't stay.'

'You did the right thing, darling. You had to look after yourself.'

'I know, but—'

'Are you still thinking about . . . it?'

'No.'

'Do you think you can find a way to be happy?'

Georgie shrugged. 'I don't know. I've got to, I suppose.'

'Well, I'm leaving your dad,' Harper said. 'That might help for a start. We'll move into our own house. You can change schools if you want. I'll probably have to get a part-time job.'

Georgie gaped at her. 'All because I ran away?'

'Not just because of you. I've been thinking about it for a while. Now I've made up my mind.'

'Have you told Dad?'

'Not yet.'

'That's weird.'

'I know.' She put her arms round her again, tears

317

streaming down her face. 'But it's for the best, because this is where our new life starts. Thank you for coming back. Oh God—'

'Mum, I'm sorry!'

'It's OK. Everything's going to be fine now that you're back.'

At the police station, Georgie tried to keep her statement as vague as possible. She was unwilling to rat on her mates. Ria Desai, the investigating officer, was understanding – up to a point. She accepted that she hadn't found out their real names. But she wasn't prepared to accept that she couldn't give accurate physical descriptions of them. Or remember the address where she'd stayed. Or say with any certainty how serious they were about 'jumping on the bus'.

Harper took her aside for a moment. 'Darling, this is turning into a scene from *The Usual Suspects*, and it's not funny at all. Fantine and Romeo have parents too. If not, they have people who love them. You must help the police to find them and stop them doing harm to themselves.'

Georgie looked pained. 'But we made a pact, a promise ...'

'They need to see that there is help out there, and hope. One day they may be grateful to you for forcing the issue.'

Reluctantly, Georgie told Ria everything she knew. Harper watched her carefully. She may have come back from the dead, but she still wasn't right. They had a lot of rebuilding ahead of them.

33

'When are you going to tell Dad?' Georgie asked, when they got back in the car.

'I've got a few things to sort out first. Then I'll tell him.'

'Face to face?'

'By lawyer's letter.'

Georgie grimaced. 'Dad'll go mad.'

Harper sighed. 'I don't care, love.'

'Because of me?'

'No, because of him.'

She drove her to Cullercoats, to her parents' house, a place of safety and normality. Harper's mother greeted them with a late-night supper of lamb stew, mashed potato and carrots.

'Come here, bairn,' her father said to Georgie after they'd eaten. She squidged up next to him in his armchair for a good old cuddle and a bit of telly.

Harper sat down heavily on the sofa. She was asleep

within seconds. An hour later she stumbled up to her old bedroom. Georgie slept on some cushions on the floor beside her bed. Harper woke up in the night and silently stroked her hair.

The following morning she got up before Georgie and headed downstairs for a fry-up and endless cups of tea.

'Where did she go?' asked her dad.

'To stay in a grubby bedsit in Blackpool with the friends she made on the internet.'

'Bit grim at this time of year, I'd think.'

She smiled. 'It's not Lytham St Annes, but I don't think it was all that bad.'

'What brought her back?'

She burst into tears.

'Don't worry, love. I'm sorry I asked. It's too soon to talk about it.'

All she could do was nod and go on crying.

'I think the reality of going through with a group suicide must have hit home,' she said a little later. 'It all seemed a bit pathetic in the cold light of day.'

'As it would, especially in off-season Blackpool,' said her dad.

Teardrops splashed into her cup as she took a sip of tea. She was filling it up just as soon as she was emptying it, she thought. In the end there would be nothing in the cup but saltwater, which she had read sent you mad if you drank it. Or was it just seawater?

'You and the bairn are welcome to stay as long as you like,' her mother said. 'You know that.'

She blinked away her tears. 'Really, Mum? I thought you'd be telling me it was time to go home by now. To cook Aaron's tea and iron his shirts.'

Her mother pursed her lips. 'Well, I'm not. You don't cook or iron anyway, you cheeky sod, and I'm sure Betty can manage until you get back.'

'The thing is, I don't want to go back,' she said, putting her head in her hands. 'It's not just me who's unhappy there. It's all of us, especially Georgie.'

'That's up to you. I'm just saying that yer dad and I will stick by you, whatever you do.'

'Even if I leave him?'

Her mother nodded and smiled reassuringly.

The tears started up again. She hadn't realised how much it would mean to have her parents' support, but suddenly it was as if a weight had been lifted. It was ridiculous, she thought. She was a fully grown woman of fifty-three, and yet their approval still counted for everything.

Georgie appeared in the kitchen at eleven. 'Fancy a walk at Longsands, Fluffy?' Harper's dad asked her.

Harper cringed at the use of Georgie's online name, but Georgie didn't seem to notice.

'We could have fish and chips in town afterwards, if you like,' her father added.

Georgie's face lit up. 'I'd love it.' She turned to Harper. 'Is that OK, Mum? What will you do?'

Harper smiled to herself. 'No chance of tagging along with you two, then?'

'Of course, love!' her dad said. 'Georgie was only

321

thinking that you might have quite a bit to do today. Weren't you, Fluffy?'

Georgie looked mortified. Before either of them had a chance to dig themselves in any deeper, Harper said, 'You're right, there, Dad – just a few little jobs to keep me busy while you're out. Moving house, getting divorced, finding a job ... I'll have more than enough to keep me occupied until this afternoon, don't you worry!'

'Mum, I didn't mean—'

'Get yourself ready and off you go, love,' Harper said. 'Me dad's got a point. Anyway, he wants you all to himself, and who can blame him?'

She rang a top divorce lawyer in Manchester to make an appointment. Then she rang Tiffany.

'I owe you a thousand times over,' she said.

'Shut up!' Tiffany guffawed. 'You'd have done the same for me. I'm just thankful she's safe. So, how much did the tech detective set you back in the end?'

'Seventeen K,' Harper said. 'Worth every penny of Aaron's money, I'd say.'

'Paid already?'

'Signed and sealed.'

'Nice little earner for just over a night's work.'

'I know! But she kept me going through the longest hours of my life. That's priceless.'

'When are you back?'

'Not sure. I've got an appointment with a divorce lawyer the day after tomorrow, but I'll only come down for the day. That's what I'm ringing about. Is there anything I need to know before going ahead?'

Tiffany didn't even pause for breath. 'Listen to me, Harps, and listen good. Don't leave the family home. Not if you want to keep it. Even if you don't want to keep it, in fact. Stay there now, sell it later. I'll bet you anything you care to bet that he's hidden the rest of his money.'

'Hidden?'

'Offshore, tax-free, encrypted, securitised – you name it, he'll have a bank account with every kind of lock on it. And you won't have a gnat's chance of finding it. End of. So *do not leave the family home, babe.* Hear me? It's your future. It's your safety net. Read my lips. I am being mega serious here. Nothing is more important. It's the number one rule.'

Harper gulped. 'Bloomin' 'eck,' she said. 'I think I want you as my lawyer, Tiff. Sounds like you know your stuff.'

'I learned the hard way, babe. Believe me, getting through a divorce is like getting through cancer. You've got to fight for your life, every inch of the way. It's him against you. It's war.'

She walked down to Cullercoats Bay and sat on the pier, crying her eyes out. It was relief, mainly, she told herself. Relief that Georgie was safe. Relief that she was leaving Aaron. Relief that her old life had come to an end.

Once she had shed every last drop of liquid in her overworked tear ducts, she climbed up to the headland and walked along the cliffs thinking over how to help Georgie. She had an instinctive mistrust of psychiatrists – quite unreasonably, based on absolutely nothing, in fact – but it was time to overcome her prejudice and find someone who specialised in teenage depression. Maybe Georgie should go into therapy. She needed to find out more about it.

It might be helpful to seek out a parent support group too, she thought. Other mums must have been through similar traumas and come out the other side. She wasn't sure how to go about finding one, but knew she had to explore every possible avenue. This couldn't happen again. She had to make sure of that.

She turned her mind to what Tiffany had said. If her theory about Aaron hiding all their assets turned out to be true, there was definitely trouble ahead. Because even if she cleared out her current account, maxed the credit cards and sold off her modest portfolio of shares, there still wouldn't be enough money to buy a medium-sized kennel in Cheshire, let alone a house. She needed an income too. Her only hope would be to rent a flat in town and get a job. That was assuming Aaron took care of the school fees and paid child support. Some men didn't, she knew. Some men had to be chased down for the bare minimum.

She clicked her tongue and sighed. She hated the idea of being poor again, of scrabbling around trying to find the cash to pay for life's boring basics. But there really wasn't an alternative. After more than twenty years of pretending, she simply didn't have it in her to return to Orchard End and play housewife until the divorce came through. It would kill her. Anyway, the moment she filed for divorce Aaron would make her life there unbearable.

So that was that. She couldn't live with Aaron again – and neither could Georgie.

She rang him to tell him they would be staying with her parents for a few more days. His phone went straight to answerphone. She tried to sound normal in her message. 'I'll call later,' she said. 'Speak soon.'

Adam phoned while she was walking back to her parents' house. 'Yes, she's safe and sound,' she told him wearily.

'That's fantastic news!' he said.

'But I'm sorry, she doesn't want to play Cat. I hope you don't feel we wasted your time.'

'Not at all,' he assured her. 'In fact, that's partly why I was calling. We had a meeting this morning at Lippy, and we were wondering whether she might still like to join the *FOMO* cast, but in a minor speaking role.'

'I doubt it. Anyway, why . . . would you—'

'Our thinking is . . . ' He paused. 'When a novice actor shows talent and shines on the screen, it seems a shame not to take it further. Give it a try, so to speak?'

'What's the role?'

'Playing one of a gang of five girls at Cat's school. It's not a big part, but she delivers a few really funny one-liners about one of the teachers. We thought of Georgie because of her sharp comic timing.'

'That's nice! And does the actress who plays this part need to be a certain size too?'

'No, that's the thing. She just needs to be funny.'

'Look, I doubt she'll say yes. She's been through a lot. And I'm not sure I'd want her to do it anyway. We might stay in the north-east for a bit. Things are just … well, a bit all over the place right now. But I'll ask her.'

'Amazing, thank you. Although we're going to have to move quite fast with this, so … '

'I understand.'

'Could you give me a call later, just to let me know if it's a possibility? Or if she says no outright?'

'Of course. I should be seeing her any minute. I'll ring you after I've talked to her.'

'Great, and by the way I was wondering whether we could meet up to discuss your acting career sometime soon, as well.'

She came to a standstill in the street. 'What acting career?'

'The one you plan to resume,' he said. 'I saw your tweet about being persuadable, if the part was right.'

'Tweet?'

'Yes, on Twitter.'

She frowned. A vague memory threaded its way through the clutter in her mind. Yes, something or other had happened on Twitter – but she couldn't recall what it was, or if it was real or something out a dream.

'You wrote something like, "Hashtag never say never,"' he added.

'Oh that – I wasn't being serious. It was about building an online profile to find Georgie.'

'Ah,' he said. 'But have you seen how much activity it has generated in the Twittersphere?'

'No.'

'So you don't know that you now have seventy-five thousand followers on Twitter?'

Something went in her solar plexus. All the air seemed to escape from her lungs. Using her final inch of breath, she said, 'Go on with you!'

Great, she thought. How to impress your average hip, young director? Channel your inner Les Dawson.

She heard a boyish chuckle on the other end of the phone. 'And rising!'

'But what—'

'So I was just wondering if we could meet. And speak. Because this amount of interest in you makes you very bankable, if that doesn't sound too cynical.'

'Well, you see . . . ' She was still trying to get her breath back.

'I should confess that I've been watching the reruns of *Beauty Spot*. You're brilliant in it. So I guess I'm a bit of a fan. Hope that doesn't put you off.'

'Put me off what?'

'Meeting up for a drink.'

She couldn't help smiling, even though she felt winded. A drink now, was it? 'Don't be ridiculous,' she snapped. 'I don't meet men for drinks! I'm a married woman.' She crossed her fingers. Although hopefully not for much longer, she thought.

'Lunch, then,' he said. 'Something informal, away from the office, where we'll have the chance to chat. I want to get to know you better.'

A tiny thrill went through her. She did her best to

dampen it – and him. 'Why, what's your next project after *FOMO*? *Wolf Nana and the Teenage Vampires*, with me in the title role?'

He laughed nervously and cleared his throat. 'Actually, I've been asked to direct a touring production of *Who's Afraid of Virginia Woolf?* with a view to taking it into the West End.'

Her mouth dropped open. 'You are fucking kidding me,' she said. '*You are fucking kidding me!* But you're a teen TV director.'

'Yes. And? It doesn't have to be one or the other. Nothing's set in stone. Anyway, my background is in theatre. As is yours, I believe.'

'How do you know that?'

'Angela Stirling mentioned it.'

'Angela?' The conversation was getting weirder by the minute.

'Yes, she wants to play Martha.'

'Oh.'

Martha in *Who's Afraid of Virginia Woolf?* was the role every older actress in the English-speaking world wanted to play – and for the briefest of moments she felt herself gripped by a visceral desire to star in Adam's production. After all, she needed the work. She loved acting. It was a great part. And last, but by no means least, it would be a massive slap in the face for Angela fucking Stirling if she beat her to the role.

The next moment, reality slapped her back. It was ridiculous even to think about it. She hadn't acted in nearly a quarter of a century. She didn't know if she could even do it any more.

'Look, I don't think it's for me,' she said, feeling deflated all of a sudden. 'If you were even being serious, that is.'

She didn't care about Twitter or *Beauty Spot* – or acting, or working, or Angela, she thought. She already had everything she needed. She was determined to stay focused on the things that mattered. Georgie. Her family. Her friends. Getting away from Aaron.

'I was being completely serious,' he said. 'And FYI,' he added, 'I'm not a teen director, despite my youthful appearance. In fact, I'm thirty-eight.'

She laughed, despite herself. 'Not young at all, then!'

Karin Hamasaki from RF Security Services didn't charge her for finding out Mike Smith's telephone number and address – or for the additional information that he was retired and living alone in his semi-detached home in a village twenty miles outside Newcastle. She thought about calling him but changed her mind. She wanted to confront him face to face.

She remembered her mother slamming him as a coward nearly forty years earlier, unaware that Harper was listening at the door. 'He won't own up to it like a man! That's what I object to. Apart from the obvious. He's a disgrace.'

Her dad's grunted reply had further infuriated her. 'Why am I wasting my breath?' she complained. 'Any other sixteen-year-old's father would have gone round to his house and knocked the living daylights out of him! Not you, though, oh no, you're almost as spineless as he is . . .'

It was strange how memory worked, she thought. Her mother's opinion of Mike Smith had stayed with her, but she couldn't remember her own feelings very well. Had she judged him? She didn't think so. Yes, she had been upset that he didn't try to contact her during the summer holidays. She had done her share of heartbroken sobbing. But it was her parents who dominated her memories of the days and weeks after her mum discovered she was pregnant. Overwhelmed by shame, she had put herself in her mother's hands and obeyed her to the letter. She had been too scared to do anything else.

As she remembered it, all these years later, she'd endured a long run of boring evenings watching telly with her dad, wishing desperately that she hadn't got herself into trouble. And then it was over almost as soon as it had begun – in her memory, at least. When she'd finally emerged from the abortion clinic – feeling tearful and crampy, but otherwise unscathed – all she cared about was getting back to normal teenage life. The spell had been broken. She'd stopped thinking about Mike Smith. It was the hottest summer on record and she wanted to enjoy it with Janice and Lizzie. The whole episode had been swept under the carpet, as was customary in those days. Nobody spoke of it again.

She hoped that Georgie would be able to bounce back as easily as she had. Fingers crossed, she seemed to be moving on from her terrifying brush with danger. It was hard to be sure and she needed constant monitoring, but her depression appeared to have lifted. She was spending a lot of her time talking things through with her grandpa, and she was loving her grandma's cooking. Hopefully, she was beginning to feel glad to be alive.

What now, though? Was the answer to move back to Cullercoats? To be near her parents as they grew older, and closer to her oldest and dearest friends? It was probably unrealistic, she realised. If she was going to get a job and support herself and Georgie, it would most likely have to be in the Manchester area. Like it or not, she would need to tap into her Cheshire set network – turn on the charm and worm her way onto someone's vanity project payroll. A maternity shop, say, or a pet parlour – whatever it took, she would do it.

As she drove along the winding country roads to Mike's house, she went over her meeting with the divorce lawyer in Manchester.

Roger Silk-Cameron had given her the same advice as Tiffany. 'It would be preferable to stay in the family home,' he said, narrowing his eyes.

'We've already left. We haven't got a choice,' she replied. 'We can't take any more of my husband's bullying.'

He gave her a concerned look. 'Is he violent? That might help with securing the main assets.'

'Not physically violent, no.'

He sighed. 'Ah, we'll have to think again, then.'

She felt her cheeks flush in anger. 'It doesn't seem fair!' she said. 'I've been married to my husband for twenty-four years. I've done everything I could to make it a happy marriage. I've put up with his jealousy, brought up the children, entertained his colleagues and networked the hell out of the area we live in. I've tried to give him everything he wanted, including sacrificing my career to be a mother and having plastic surgery to make me look younger. I have been the model wife! And now you're saying I'll be out on the streets?'

'I've no doubt you've been an exemplary spouse,' soothed Roger Silk-Cameron. 'And of course you won't be living on the streets. If it's not possible to remain in the family home, we will just have to find a way to work around it.'

She pulled up outside the address Karin Hamasaki had given her, a pretty Victorian cottage with ivy growing up the walls. Mike Smith answered the door wearing jeans and a navy jumper. She wasn't expecting to see the twenty-seven-year-old man she had known nearly four decades earlier – of course she wasn't – but she was startled by his appearance all the same. Grey hair and jowls changed everything, she thought.

'Hello,' he said. 'Have you come to deliver the plants?' He smiled and in an instant she saw his young face again, the face she had fallen so crushingly in love with.

'No.' She fiddled with the collar of her Burberry trench.

Growing pale, he said, 'Harper? What are you doing here?'

'Don't you know, Mike?' she asked. 'Really? You don't know?'

He shuffled in the doorway. 'Well, I . . . you guessed it was me, did you?'

She folded her arms across her chest. 'I had my suspicions. But I knew for sure when your latest little surprise arrived. A Cullercoats postcard with a note saying, "Bye Bye Baby"? Who else was it going to be?'

'I see, yes. But it could have been a fan. Or someone else you—'

'Had an affair with, followed by an abortion? In 1976?'

He looked at the floor. 'OK, probably not.'

'What is it with all the cheesy song titles?' she said.

'I don't know . . .' He wouldn't meet her eye.

'Anyway, I thought we should probably talk before things get out of hand.'

He perked up. 'Of course, would you like to come in? Have a cup of tea?' He took a sideways step to allow her to pass.

She shook her head. 'I was thinking the village pub might be more suitable.'

He laughed uneasily. 'Why? Worried I might do something?'

She peered into the house. Everything looked immaculate. 'Well, you've been behaving very strangely, Mike.'

'But I wouldn't hurt you,' he said. 'You must know that.'

'How do you know you haven't already hurt me?' she asked crossly.

His face crumpled. 'If I have I'm sorry, I didn't mean to . . . I just wanted to reach out to you,' he added, with a pathetic smile. 'I think that's the modern term for it.'

She noticed that there was no apology forthcoming for

his behaviour all those years earlier. For taking advantage of his position as her revered drama teacher. For getting her pregnant during 'study sessions' in the department library under the stairs. For setting up a pattern of unhealthy relationships that had ultimately led her to marry Aaron, in fact. Still she would get onto all of that later. First, she wanted to know why he had suddenly taken to stalking her.

So she ended up going in for the cuppa. His sorry tale came tumbling out over tea and biscuits.

'Audrey and I stayed together,' he told her. 'It wasn't easy, but we managed to patch up our marriage after my "moment of madness" during that long, hot summer. Having children of our own would help us put the past behind us, we decided. It was always part of our plan, anyway.'

'Really?' she said sharply. What the hell were you doing screwing a sixteen-year-old schoolgirl, then? she thought.

He continued, oblivious. 'I moved schools – as you know – and we managed to settle down again,' he said. 'But then we found out that Audrey couldn't have children.' He took a sip of tea to disguise the break in his voice. 'Ironic, really,' he said mournfully.

Poetic justice, she thought, crunching on a biscuit.

'We muddled on, despite the disappointment,' he explained. 'We found contentment nevertheless – in gardening, holidays, visiting country houses, nieces and nephews, great-nieces and great-nephews. We were happy companions.'

She smiled.

'Then Audrey died, eighteen months ago.'

'That's awful,' she said.

'Cancer.'

'I'm sorry.'

'I don't think I've dealt with it very well,' he said. 'I've been dwelling on the past . . . as you can tell.' He put his hand to his mouth.

'But I don't understand why you're fixating on—'

'I just thought . . . I'm sorry, I don't know what got into me. You won't hear from me again. I'll stop.'

'You must stop, Mike. Otherwise I'll have to call the police,' she warned.

'I understand.'

'Maybe you should see a grief counsellor.'

'Maybe.'

She got up out of her easy chair. 'I'll be going now.'

'You could stay for lunch? Cold cuts and a salad?'

'No, thank you. And remember. No more notes or phone calls. Definitely no more black gladioli.'

She drove away, feeling sorry for him. Of course, life would be fine if you didn't want children, she reflected. How brilliant that would be! She thought of the anguish saved, the agony spared and the total frustration bypassed.

But if you wanted kids and didn't manage to have any, she imagined that the hole in your life would be bottomless.

Poor Mike, she thought.

Poor Angela.

34

She let herself into Orchard End feeling like a burglar. Although she had lived in the house for twenty years, it already seemed to belong to somebody else. The air was unbreathed, the carpets untrodden – there wasn't a speck of dirt, a trace of mess. Betty had left it how Aaron liked it – impersonal, pristine, like a hotel.

Her heart pounded as she walked into the kitchen. To her relief, her sapphire ring was still hooked around the prong of the spice rack. She dropped it into the zip pocket of her handbag. Hopefully it would bring in a couple of thousand.

She had seen the warning in her lawyer's eyes, earlier – if she wasn't careful, she would be on her uppers. And by 'careful', she sensed that he meant 'clever'. Otherwise there would be 'holes in the soles of her Manolos', as Tiffany put it. Her colour-coded wardrobe – and the rest – would be up on eBay.

So here she was, trying to be clever.

'Sneak in and nab what you can, after you've seen the lawyer,' Tiffany had urged. 'It might be your last chance. He's bound to change the locks when he finds out you're divorcing him.'

In the lounge, she did a quick scan for anything else worth having and scooped up two bronze figures on the mirrored mantelpiece. She had bought them in a flea market in Madrid before she was married and had grown attached to them over the years. But they weren't valuable, so it was pointless to take them – this was no time to be sentimental. Roger Silk-Cameron would definitely not approve. She placed them back on the mantelpiece and turned away.

As she left the room, she took one last contemptuous look at Aaron's beloved peach velour curtains. It was tempting to get a knife from the kitchen and slash them. But there was no time to waste on petty revenge, either. She needed to get out of the house as fast as she could.

The door to Aaron's office opened with the faintest of creaks. The noise would irritate him, she thought, however slight it was – he liked his hinges well-oiled and silent. Everything was neat and tidy inside the room. She found the key to his desk drawer in his pen holder. Unlocking the drawer, she took out a strip of paper with a set of numbers printed on it.

The safe was hidden behind a light sculpture on the inside wall. She slid away a panel of light bulbs to reveal a tiny dial. Working backwards along the line of printed numbers, she turned it left and then right, moving from 20 to 50 and back to 30. After seven revolutions, she heard a click. She waited three counts and pressed the centre of the dial.

The door to the safe sprang open. She reached inside and felt around for her jewellery box.

'Hello, Pussycat,' said a voice behind her. 'What are you doing here?'

For a second, she froze. *No, it couldn't be.* She had checked with his office. He was out to lunch with a client.

Forcing a smile, she turned round to face him. 'Hello, darling! I was just looking for my gold hoop earrings.'

He was standing a few feet away from her, looking sharp in a Savile Row suit. 'But aren't you supposed to be up north with Tom and Gerry and Fattypuffs?' he asked.

'Please don't call her that,' she said automatically.

'Georgina, then,' he said, deliberately drawing out the vowels. 'So, what brings you here, my little honey pie?'

'I had to drive down for a doctor's appointment,' she said lightly. 'Just something *gynae*,' she added, lowering her voice to a whisper. There was nothing Aaron hated more than hearing about intimate bodily functions. 'A little woman's problem, nothing serious.'

'But you should have told me,' he bellowed. 'We could have met for lunch!'

She shrank backwards, cowed by his booming voice. 'I rang your office, darling, but they said you were out,' she gabbled. 'And then I remembered my earrings so I popped in here. I thought I'd pick up a few clothes as well, since

I'm not sure how long I'll be staying with Mum and Dad. It depends on Georgie—'

'Oh dear,' he interrupted, shaking his head. 'Oh dear, oh dear.'

'What is it?' she asked. She felt a trickle of fear run down the back of her throat.

He rolled his eyes. 'Turns out my private dick can't tell the difference between a gynaecologist and a divorce lawyer.'

'No?' She tried to smile. Her mouth twitched nervously.

'I'll have to boot him. The stupid prick thought Roger Silk-Cameron was a solicitor, not a cunt doctor.'

She met his eyes. They were glinting green and gold. The game was up.

Her entire body turned cold, tip to toe, as if she'd been dipped in cryogenic ice.

'You've been having me followed?' she said, edging towards the door.

He smiled. 'Yeah, baby. Every step of the way.'

'But why?'

He stepped towards her. 'Because I didn't trust you.' He gave her face a light slap.

'Hey!' she protested.

He slapped her again, almost playfully – several times, on both cheeks.

'Stop it!' she said, backing up against the wall.

He smiled. 'Don't you like it? I thought you'd like it, babe. It's called bitch-smacking.' He slapped her again, with more force.

'No, hey! That really stings!'

'And since you're the biggest bitch of them all, as everyone knows . . . ' He moved his face close to hers. His eyes narrowed to slits.

'Stop it, you're scaring me,' she whispered.

He whacked her across the head. 'You deserve it, you fucking bitch. So, tell me, what did your lawyer say?'

Too shocked to reply, she made a bolt for the door, but he grabbed her and pulled her back towards him, holding her in a grip so tight that his fingers dug into her flesh.

He thumped her again, knocking her sideways. 'Answer me! What did your lawyer say?'

The room swayed. Her ears were ringing. 'Nothing! Stop it!' she begged.

He loosened his grip on her arm and she stumbled along the wall. Something sharp struck her leg. Her knees buckled and she fell to the floor. In slow motion she saw Aaron's shoe moving towards her. He kicked her in the ribs, with sharp precision.

'I've never trusted you!' he shouted. 'You're a liar! You've always been a liar.'

She scrambled to her feet, desperate to escape, but his fist sent her flying backwards again. She felt her lip split beneath his knuckles, her head crack as she hit the wall.

As she slid to the floor in a heap, she heard a voice in the distance say, 'Dad? What the fuck?'

She opened her eyes a fraction and saw Taylor standing in the doorway. 'Get out! This has nothing to do with you,' Aaron yelled.

'Mum?' Taylor wailed.

'Call an ambulance,' Harper murmured. 'Please, love.'

'OK . . . ' Taylor said uncertainly.

'Don't even think about it,' Aaron warned. 'Just get out!'

'Dad? Mum's got blood all over her face!'

He wiped his mouth on his suit sleeve. 'You're surprised?' he said, breathing heavily. 'You know what your mother's like.'

Taylor looked down at Harper in horror. 'Mum? Is it Walt?'

'Walt?' Harper mumbled, drifting in and out of consciousness. 'Just . . . get an . . . ambulance, please love . . . now.'

She stared at the mirror in amazement. Her face was totally black and blue. One of her eyes was so swollen she could barely see out of it. Her upper lip was a purple balloon. It was as if Aaron had done his best to cancel out Dr Golden's cosmetic surgery with 'a procedure' all of his own.

'I've had reverse blepharoplasty,' she imagined herself lisping at people. 'I wouldn't recommend it. It's really invasive.'

She was a bruised and bloody mess again, but strangely she didn't feel sorry for herself this time. She wasn't cowering from her reflection wondering if she would ever look good again. She didn't feel frustrated that Aaron wasn't being supportive. Because she knew from experience that her face would get better – and she was divorcing the bastard, once and for all.

'Who did this to you?'

'My husband.'

'Do you want to press charges?'

'Yes, and please make sure he stays away from me.'

'You can apply for an emergency protection order, or a restraining order.'

'Please, I'm terrified that he'll kill me. I need to feel safe in my own home.'

Aaron had made a monumental mistake when he had smashed her face to a pulp and broken three of her ribs. If he had kept his composure, he could have ruined her. Instead he had handed her Orchard End on a plate and inspired her to fight for a fair share in the divorce settlement. So she wasn't going to wallow in self-pity, even though the sight of her face was enough to make her weep, and she didn't intend to have a breakdown either, despite coming so close to death.

She got up off the sofa and walked gingerly into the hall. 'Cup of tea, Betty?' she croaked up the stairs to where Betty was dusting. 'I'm putting the kettle on.'

'I'll be there in a mo, love,' Betty called down to her.

She hadn't been telling lies at the hospital. She really was terrified of Aaron. She couldn't say for sure that he would have killed her if Taylor hadn't walked in, but it wouldn't have surprised her if he had. After twenty-four seething, simmering years, he had finally unleashed the violence within him. She didn't think it would be easy for him to put it back in its box.

And now he had disappeared. Not even Taylor knew where he was. She hoped the police arrested him soon. It was scary to think of him out there, prowling.

She heard a key in the front door. It couldn't be Aaron, because she'd had the locks changed when she'd got back from the hospital. And it couldn't be Georgie, because she was still in Cullercoats, unaware of what had happened. So it had to be Taylor ... striding into the kitchen wearing a tight red trouser suit, her hair swinging in a high ponytail behind her.

'Hello, darling, you look like someone off the *Mary Tyler Moore Show*,' she said.

'Mary who?'

'Never mind.'

'It's really hard to understand what you're saying.'

'I know. You may have noticed a slight problem with my lips. Any word from Dad?'

Taylor undid her jacket buttons and sat down at the kitchen table. 'Nothing, and I'm starting to get worried. You must have really pissed him off, Mum.'

Harper would have frowned if she'd dared, but her face hurt too much. 'Me, piss him off?' she said, lisping like a toddler.

Taylor poured out the cup of tea that was meant for Betty. 'I wanted to ask you at the hospital – why were you arguing in the first place?'

'I told you. He found out I wanted a divorce.'

'But you had an affair as well, didn't you?'

'Of course not!'

'Not even Walt? Dad was sure there was something going on with Walt.'

'Walt?' Harper said. It took every ounce of restraint

not to scrunch up her face in a pantomime expression of disgust and incredulity – although she wasn't sure if her facial muscles would be up to it anyway. 'You mean Joyce's Walt? The Walt who lives next door? Walt who quite possibly has threesomes with his wife and au pair?'

'You see, Dad said—'

'Come on, what do you take me for?'

Taylor bit her lip. 'But Dad's right when he says you're a secretive person. You do have a lot of secrets.'

'Bollocks!'

'He said you went to see your old teacher on Tuesday.'

Harper bristled. 'Well, I had to keep that quiet. Your father is obsessively jealous – or hadn't you noticed? He was having me followed by a private detective!'

'But why did you go to see him at all?'

'You mean the teacher? If you must know, I went to tell him to stop stalking me. But why are you talking like I'm the guilty one? I don't understand you, Taylor. Look at my face. Aren't you shocked by what your father has done to me?'

Taylor added milk to her tea. 'I've lost respect for Dad, if that's what you mean. But I'm not "shocked".' She scratched little speech marks in the air. 'You two have been at each other's throats for my whole life. The only surprise here is that it didn't turn violent years ago.'

Harper gaped at her, inwardly, because it was too painful to allow her jaw to drop open. 'That's all you're going to say?'

Taylor shrugged. 'I'm not saying it's your fault . . . but if you weren't happy, you should have left him, that's all. It's not rocket science.'

Harper thought of the myriad calculations that she had made over the years when dealing with Aaron's controlling behaviour, jealousy and temper. Of the many variables and potentialities she had balanced, one against the other, when trying to placate him and smooth out their life as a family. Of the complex equations she had written in her mind setting out the advantages and disadvantages of leaving him, all the while factoring in the possible impact on the children and his capacity for revenge.

'No, not rocket science,' she said, starting to grow hot with rage. 'More like quantum effing physics.'

'Oh, come on, Mum!'

'No, you come on! It's time you heard a few home truths, young lady. I gave up a lot to have you.'

Taylor rolled her eyes.

'Yeah, yeah,' Harper said. 'You've heard it all before. Why didn't I tell your father to fuck off when he tried to make me give up work? Well, if you really want to know, it was because he said that if I didn't stop acting I could forget about getting married – and get an abortion instead. It was that simple to him. But I wanted you so desperately that I agreed to give up the career I had worked for so hard and so long for.

'And I've never regretted it, even though your bullying bastard of a father has ground me down for all these years, and made me feel stupid and worthless – and half the time all I get from you is snidey sarcasm and contempt. And

345

you know why I've never regretted it? Because I love you with every bone in my body, Taylor Clarke, and I've always wanted the best for you and Georgie!'

Taylor stared at her. 'Dad wanted you to have me aborted?'

'I didn't say that. But it was a choice between acting and you – and I chose you.'

'I had no idea,' Taylor said, blinking in confusion. 'You should have told me. I hate all these fucking secrets.'

Harper reached across the table and tried to grasp her hand. 'Of course I wasn't going to tell you, darling. Anyway, your father adores you. He loves you more than anyone in this world. And I love you . . . so much.'

'What else haven't you told me?' Taylor asked accusingly.

Harper's shoulders slumped. Almost everything, she thought.

Taylor's phone rang. She picked it up. 'OK,' she said. 'I'll come and get you now.'

'Dad?' Harper said, her heart thumping.

'Georgie,' Taylor said. 'I told her what happened and she wanted to come home. I'm picking her up at the station now.'

Harper gasped. 'Why would you do that? After all she's been through?'

Taylor glared at her. 'I'm her sister. She needed to know what was going on, so I told her.'

Harper's eyes welled up. It was the first time in years that she had heard Taylor lay claim to Georgie as her sister. Was it possible that they would start to get closer, at last?

'But—'

'Anyway, she saw you like this when you had your operation! You didn't hide away then.'

'This is different. And I wanted to go to a spa then, but your father wouldn't let me.'

Taylor drained her mug of tea and jangled her car keys. 'No more secrets, Mother. It's time for a change.'

35

They were watching *Bridesmaids* and eating popcorn when the doorbell rang. Harper knew instinctively that it would be him.

'I'll go,' she told Taylor and Georgie.

She switched on the entry phone video screen. As he stood outside their front door waiting for her to open it, she studied her husband through her one good eye. It was probably her last chance to look him over thoroughly, she thought – to appreciate his strong features, the wave of his hair, the curve of his lips and his straight, straight nose. He was wearing an oversized cashmere overcoat with sloping shoulders, with a beautiful striped silk scarf looped around his neck. He looked effortlessly stylish and handsome, as ever – Cheshire's very own George Clooney, in fact.

Well, Cheshire was welcome to him.

He shifted position and his eyes glittered as they caught the outside light. *No, he couldn't be.* Yes, he was crying.

'I can't let you in. You know that,' she said through the intercom.

'Harper, I'm sorry,' he replied, choking back a sob. 'I lost my head. I fucked up because I couldn't stand being without you. What I did was fucking out of order. But it was only because I love you so much.'

'If you don't leave, I'll call the police,' she said softly.

He begged and pleaded, but she wouldn't open the door to him, even when he lifted a ring box up to the light.

Not another bloody ring, she thought. What was it this time? Blood diamonds around a heart-shaped ruby?

'I don't want it,' she said.

Taylor and Georgie came to join her in the hallway. 'Dad!' Taylor said.

'You'd better go – unless you want the girls to see you,' Harper told him.

He knelt down and placed the ring box on the doorstep. 'If you change your mind, Pussycat, I'll be waiting. For ever.' He turned and trudged across the gravel, towards his gleaming Mercedes.

When she was sure he'd gone, she opened the front door and picked up the ring box.

Well, you never know, she thought wryly. It might be worth thousands.

Epilogue

March 2014

Harper peeked out at the half-full auditorium. She was so nervous that her whole body was trembling. Even her eyelashes seemed to be trembling. *Don't be ridiculous*, she told herself. *That's not even possible.*

Stay calm. I know my lines. I trust my fellow actors. Everything's going to be fine.

She scanned the stalls and saw Lizzie and Janice and the rest of the Cullercoats gang. Lizzie's head was thrown back in laughter and the others were grinning at her. Suddenly she longed to be in the stalls with them, larking about, cracking jokes, looking forward to the show – instead of shaking like a leaf behind the safety curtain of the Duchess of Cambridge Theatre.

Stay calm. I know my lines. I trust the others. It's going to be fine.

Her heart began to race. It was a dream come true to star in a West End play – even more so to be playing

Martha in *Who's Afraid of Virginia Woolf?* It was something she had longed for as a young actress and never quite believed she could achieve. So this was a moment to be savoured, only ... why did the very thought of it make her want to do a runner to St Pancras and jump on the train to Paris?

She felt herself trembling again. It was fifteen minutes until curtain up. She should be yoga breathing in her dressing room. She should be warming up, mentally preparing – doing all the things she had learned to do on her long, difficult journey through workshops and rehearsals to reach this point. If she wasn't careful, her dream could implode into darkness. Despite all her hard work – despite conquering self-doubt and anxiety – she could find herself falling down the rabbit hole again.

She did another sweep of the stalls, searching for Georgie and Taylor. Where were they? She was sure her nerves would evaporate if she could just see their faces. After all, she was only standing here because of her daughters.

They had twisted her arm to go to the audition. They had chanted, 'Go, Mum!' when she'd got down to the last two. Georgie had made her endless soothing cups of tea during the long wait to find out if she'd got the part – and they'd danced around the lounge screaming with joy when her agent rang to say she had.

Even Taylor had been excited for her. 'It's great to see you actually *doing* something,' she'd said. Taylor remained obstinately unaware that inside her erstwhile boozy, gossiping, restless, bullied, overprotective mother there had lurked someone else altogether, someone desperate to express herself. She still seemed to have no idea that, in essence, her mother was still Harper Walters, the thirteen-year-old trouper aching to get onto the Cullercoats Social Club stage and wow the crowds with her Shirley MacLaine impression.

That was the way it was with kids, she thought with a smile. They couldn't imagine you even existing before they were born.

She scanned the auditorium again and saw Adam shaking hands with someone towards the end of the middle aisle – a producer, perhaps. They were expecting several industry heavyweights to show up this evening, which was such an alarming prospect that she didn't even want to contemplate it. Anyway, tonight was about Georgie and Taylor, not showbiz hotshots and VIPs. She wanted to make her daughters proud. That was all she needed to focus on.

Where were they? At the front of the stalls she spotted a few key members of the Cheshire set – Patty 'Party' Rendell with her doddery husband David, the Blooms and Kelly Ponsett. It was good of them to come, she thought, especially as she had so dramatically broken with Cheshire wife etiquette and chucked out her insufferable husband, instead of gritting her teeth and downing Chardonnay like the rest of them.

She watched Vicky Pacquard sidle into the seats beside Patty and David – and for the millionth time in a month she gave thanks that she hadn't ended up shampooing poodles at Vicky's pet parlour. But then the trembling started up again. It was a bit of a leap to go from helping out at Vicky's to standing on the stage of the Duchess of Cambridge Theatre, wasn't it? About to make your West End debut in one of the most challenging roles ever written for an actress?

She began to go over her lines, desperate for last-minute reassurance. But she couldn't get beyond the first three words, 'What a dump!'

What was next? She couldn't recall. She willed herself to think harder. Still nothing. Think! she told herself, trying not to panic. Tiny fireworks began to fizz and explode inside her head. Was she having a stroke? Her breath caught in her throat. A heart attack? What was the next line, for fuck's sake?

Stay calm. You know your lines. Everything's going to be fine.

And then it came to her, floating down a river of words, trailing the rest of the play behind it, and the fireworks stopped. A sense of calm descended. She began to breathe again.

She scanned the stalls and winced ever so slightly when she saw Justin Bennett joining the Cullercoats group. A series of unwanted images flashed before her eyes: a mortifying slideshow of mistimed kisses, misplaced elbows and underwear that pinged and refused to come off.

She had done her best to forget the events of their appalling one night stand, but here he was to remind her, thank you!

Still, the experience had taught her a valuable lesson.

First she had blamed the twinkle in his eye. Then she'd blamed the vodka martinis. Finally she had looked inwards and realised that getting completely hammered on your first date in a quarter of a century was a short cut to disaster – especially if you had a drink problem.

She glanced at Adam again. He was greeting someone else now, with another hearty handshake and open smile. Could he be any nicer? How different her second date in a quarter of a century had been to the first, she thought. After the cringe-fest with Justin, it had taken Adam three months to persuade her to go out to dinner with him – and the kiss they had shared afterwards, outside a Moroccan restaurant in the soft summer rain, had been chaste in comparison with her boozy snogs with Justin. And sober, too – because by then she had sworn off the sauce.

And dreamily romantic . . .

So much had changed in a year, she reflected in amazement. She felt fitter and happier than she had in years – and not just because she wasn't drinking any more. She was free of Aaron. That was a miracle in itself. She was seeing a good, kind man who genuinely cared for her. And she was working – acting! – which was beyond incredible.

How quickly life could spin around, she thought happily. But then her mood plummeted just as quickly as it had soared. She had a lot to prove tonight, she reminded herself, and it could all go horribly wrong.

The auditorium was filling up fast. She looked over at the entrance to the stalls and caught sight of her mum and dad, blinking in the glare of the house lights, stopping every few seconds to deliberate over the letters and numbers printed on their tickets, and eventually finding their places. Safely installed in her seat, her mother wriggled out of her coat to reveal a dazzling satin-sheen blouse in a startling shade of swirling fuchsia, the like of which surely hadn't graced the hotspots of London since the late nineteen sixties. Harper could only hope it didn't trigger an anxiety attack in her dad, bless him.

Mind you, her father was a different person, these days. There was a spring in his step, a sparkle in his eye – he smiled a lot and carried a camera. Things were clearly going well at his Thursday night photography club. Tears pricked her eyes. He had been a phenomenal support to Georgie, helping to set her back on the path to happiness with his patient listening and loving advice. She wished she had appreciated him more during her childhood. She would be grateful to him for ever.

Fortunately, the look of pride and pleasure on his face as he gazed around the auditorium – and on her mother's face too, amazingly – told her that perhaps she wasn't doing too badly in her parents' eyes. But where were Taylor and Georgie? Weren't they coming, after all? She scanned the stalls and entrances again.

Suddenly a figure in the crowd caught her eye. It couldn't be, she thought. But it was. Unmistakably. From the long legs to the neat bob.

Angela.

So she had come. Well, well. Had she casually accepted

an invitation tonight, or had she actively sought out a ticket?

One thing was certain – she wasn't here to see Harper succeed, not after she had beaten her to the role ten months earlier. No, she was here to see Harper fall flat on her face. Or, failing that, to *not quite* pull it off. Which would be worse, almost.

She imagined Angela coming backstage to 'congratulate' her afterwards. 'Bravo,' she would say, 'You did really well considering you've been out of the game for so long.'

Harper narrowed her eyes. Yes, the veins on Angela's neck were protruding, in true Deidre Barlow fashion. A stranger wouldn't notice them. A stranger would think how happy she looked. But someone who knew her could tell that she was smiling as if her life depended on it.

Harper clenched her jaw. I had better make this good, she thought.

She scoured the theatre again. There was Betty in a flowery dress, slipping into the seats next to her parents, and Donna beside her, dwarfed by the massive gold hoops in her ears. There were Tiffany and her new boyfriend, Kelvin, and Sophie . . .

Everyone was here now. Except the two people who counted most.

And then she saw them: her beloved girls – Taylor hurrying along in front carrying a handful of ice creams, Georgie rushing behind her with a big grin on her face. Her heart swelled at the sight of them. How beautiful they were!

She watched as they jostled their way through the crowds and skipped sideways along Row E – saying sorry to the people they passed as they made a beeline for their seats next to Betty and Donna. As they sat down, Georgie said something with a grin and Taylor bashed her on the head with a rolled-up programme, before handing over several small tubs of ice cream. Georgie passed one along to Donna, who passed it on to Betty, who leant forward and said something that started the whole row laughing.

Harper beamed at them. *My girls, my darling girls.*

Roger, the actor playing George, appeared by her side. Her heart began to pound and she started to tremble again. 'Why the fuck are we doing this?' she hissed at him. 'I could be on the settee at home with a cuppa and a bacon sandwich watching the box set of *Nashville*!'

'Because nothing will make you feel like this audience will when they see you in this,' Roger said. 'Go get 'em, girl!'

The lights went down. The audience chatter died away. It was time to go on.

She took a deep breath and stepped onto the stage.

Now read on for the beginning of
Denise's next book,

The Mother's Bond

Saturday, 19th April, 2015, Chester-le-Street, County Durham

As she wiped her feet on the welcome mat outside her front door, Kathryn Casey had no sense of the danger that lurked inside her house. Instead she savoured the feeling of coming home, as she always did, no matter where she'd been or for how long. This was her haven, her place of peace and safety – even when it was full of grumpy teenagers.

There was nothing grand about living in a modern red-brick semi on a residential development just outside town. You couldn't swing a cat in the upstairs rooms, at least two of the taps were leaky and the paintwork needed redoing. But after a decade of living there, it still felt like a palace to Kathryn. Compared to the cramped, boxy flat she'd grown up in, it was a bloody mansion.

Brett was always saying that a home was more than bricks and mortar. It was part of his sales patter, but it was true. In this house on Totteridge Avenue, their family had blossomed, the kids had grown up and she had matured along with them. In some ways it had shaped them. Maybe its layout had even influenced the ties between the children – the boys in their side-by-side bedrooms and Flora slightly cut off. In turn they had changed its structure to suit their needs, by extending the kitchen and adding a sun lounge off the living room.

Would they be the same family in a different house? she wondered. Would there still be a room known as 'Flora's rabbit hole'? There was no way of telling. All she knew was that, after ten years of Christmases, birthday parties and gatherings – after a decade of stories and dramas – who they were and where they lived seemed inextricably entwined, like a knot that could never be untied.

It only felt like yesterday that they had moved in. She would never forget the looks on the children's faces as they burst gleefully out of the back door into the garden. There had only been a small patio at their previous address, a house that Kathryn had never been fully able to consider her home. But when they moved to Totteridge Avenue, all of a sudden they had a lawn. They had trees and borders. They had space.

'Can we have a trampoline, too?' George had pleaded. Kathryn laughed at the memory. That boy never missed a trick.

Their new house had filled her with wonder. In the first days and weeks after moving in, she could happily have spent twelve hours a day at the kitchen sink, looking out of the picture window while she washed and dried the dishes, marvelling at their big green garden.

Ten years on and I'm even more of a homebody, she thought with a smile, unlocking the door and stepping into the hall. Thirty-six years old and already middle-aged, in attitude if not in years.

'I'm back!' she called out. 'Photos and all.'

She reached into her coat pocket and pulled out a small envelope.

They were going to laugh at her latest attempt to get a decent passport picture done. This one was even worse than the last, a proper criminal mugshot, grim and staring, with mad eyes.

She hadn't even said thank you to the Saturday girl-turned-photographer, who had snapped her in a booth off to the side of the pharmacy. 'That'll do,' she'd said, pretending she was in a hurry.

'Are you sure?' the girl had said, sensing her dismay. 'I can try again if you like.'

'Don't worry, love. You know what they say – if you look like your passport photo, you're too ill to travel!'

Hers was even worse than most, though. Was there anybody in the world less photogenic? She knew what George would say. 'Mam, don't take this the wrong way, because you're not bad looking – you know, for a mam – but the camera definitely does not love you.'

She heard voices coming from the kitchen as she hung up her coat. Better get the tea on, she thought.

'We're in here, love,' Brett yelled.

She made out George's voice and someone else's too,

followed by a burst of laughter. She frowned. 'Is Steven home?' she asked. Steven was supposed to be poring over his maths books at a school study session.

More laughter. He'd better not have come back early, she thought, steeling herself for a row.

She felt a gust of cold air around her ankles and whipped around to see if she'd left the front door open. But it was firmly closed. So where was that draught coming from? She checked the downstairs toilet, but the window was shut, and by then the draught had disappeared.

Brett and George were in the kitchen, tracksuits unzipped, beers in hand, faces glowing from cold air and exercise. Standing next to them was one of George's mates, who looked vaguely familiar beneath the shadowy rim of his baseball cap, although she couldn't see his face properly and God knew his name. The kitchen was always full of George's mates – it was hard keep track of them all. It wasn't Steven, at least.

'Kath,' Brett said, coming over to kiss her. 'They won! They're finally turning things around, can you believe it?'

'And here's the reason,' said George with a boyish grin. 'Mam, this is Ross, our new coach, the man who is single-handedly turning the Steelers into champions.'

'Ross?' she said hesitantly.

Don't be silly, she thought, it couldn't be him – even as she realised it was. Her heart started pounding. Her cheeks felt flushed and hot.

'He's studying sports management at uni,' George added.

George's mate stepped forward and took off his baseball cap in a gesture that could easily have been interpreted as old-fashioned politeness, if you didn't know what was really going on.

'Hello, George's mam,' he said, looking her boldly in the eye.

An electric charge of fear shot through her. She had dreaded this. It had kept her awake at night. It was a bad dream made real, a daytime nightmare. What was Ross doing in her kitchen, sharing a beer with her husband and stepson — as if he had every right to be here?

But I told you never to come to my home! she screamed silently.

Typically, Brett noticed something was wrong. 'Everything OK, love?' he asked, putting his arm round her.

She tried to keep her face blank as she groped around for an excuse. She had to remember that George had asked Ross into their house. Even though he was an intruder in her eyes, to the others he was a guest.

By a miracle, it came to her. 'I've only gone and left my passport photos at the chemist,' she said, giving her forehead a light slap to emphasise what a wazzock she was. She looked at the clock on the wall. 'If I nip back now, I might catch them before they close. Nice to meet you, Ross,' she added, hoping that no one could detect the tremor in her voice, the suppressed swell of liquid terror.

She swayed slightly as she made her way back towards the hall. The shock of seeing him there, in the kitchen of her home, had left her punch drunk. She grabbed her coat and keys and swiftly got into the car. In a blind panic, she turned on the ignition, over-revved the engine, shot along the road, braked sharply, opened her door, leaned out and was sick on the tarmac.

Ross had come to ruin her. He had come to destroy everything she had worked so hard to build, everything she held dear in the world. Somehow she had to stop him before he smashed her home and family to smithereens – if it wasn't already too late.

Chapter 1

October 1995, Byker, Newcastle

Kelly Callan wasn't surprised to hear a key turn in the lock, even though her nana wasn't due home for a couple of hours. She had been expecting a visit from Mo since the previous evening, when Jimmy Fry on the eighth floor had called her upstairs for a word, 'in private, like'.

As she'd climbed the grubby, flecked stone steps to Jim's flat, she'd felt sure he was going to impart some news or other about her mam. He always seemed to know where Mo was and what she was up to.

Nana said he was secretly in love with her. 'Poor shite, on a hiding to nothing,' she added with a bitter smile.

Jim's complexion was the colour of the tab smoke that fogged up his flat. He stared flatly at Kelly out of eyes that looked like a couple of week-old fried eggs. Nana said he was in his forties, but to Kelly he looked about eighty. His yellowish white hair and jowly cheeks said it all, she thought. He wasn't long for this world. He was on the way out.

'I saw yer mam in town yesterday. I thought you should

know,' he said, narrowing his eyes as he sucked on a rolly.

Even though it was what she'd been expecting him to say, Kelly's heart began to beat faster. It was her mam, after all. She hadn't seen her in months. 'Was she down the shops?' she asked.

He broke into a grin. 'You know Mo. Loves a gamble.'

'Hope she wasn't caught,' she said.

'If she was, she'll have given them the slip. That's all part of the buzz for her.'

Kelly didn't smile. Suddenly it felt uncomfortable to be discussing her mam's fondness for nicking stuff.

'Maybe we'll see her this time,' she said, with a hopeful note in her voice.

'If you do, tell her to come and say hello. Say Jim's got a present for her, something special.'

'OK.' She turned to go.

'How's the studies?' he asked.

She shrugged. 'The maths is hard, but I like Geography. I'm applying to uni now.'

'What's the course?'

'Travel, Tourism and Hospitality Management.'

'Good for you.' He stubbed out his tab. 'Get away from this stinking pisshole and make a life for yourself.'

She stopped in the doorway of his flat. 'It's not that bad,' she said.

'You say that because you don't know any different, lassie,' he said. 'Now get back to your books and make good your escape.'

*

She was trying to make sense of the Canary Islands' population statistics when she heard the scratch and rattle of a key in the lock. Next door had just stopped blasting Nirvana at full volume, otherwise she wouldn't have noticed.

Her pulse quickened as her mother came through the door carrying several bulging carrier bags.

'You see? I told you the bairn would be here to ruin our fun,' Mo complained, dropping the bags with a thud. 'Little Betty Bookworm, never leaves the flat.'

Kelly's heart sank. Typical, she thought. The first words I hear her say in nearly five months and she's not even talking to me. Hello, Mam, she said silently. Remember me, Kelly, your daughter?

Mo had a bloke with her, as per normal, although he wasn't her usual type. She tended to go for men who had dark broody looks and short tempers to match, but this one was pale and pasty, with a moon face and soft mousy hair. So hopefully he wasn't her boyfriend, because there was nothing worse than watching your mam sloppy-kissing her fella on the settee. God, it was gross. It didn't matter how many times she'd been there to see it, she couldn't get used to the sight – or sound – of it.

'What did I tell you, Paulie? She's like a piece of chewing gum stuck to the carpet,' Mo went on in her unmistakable rasp, the smoker's croak that Kelly would have recognised anywhere, even with her eyes closed.

Mo claimed it was a sexy drawl, a magnet for the blokes. 'Don't be daft,' Nana would say, creasing up. 'What kind of man wants to go out with a frog?'

Kelly inspected her mam's face for signs of wear and tear. Mo could be quite pretty when she didn't look like something the cat had dragged in – although she always had an unhealthy pallor. Even during the summer months her complexion was the colour of undercooked chips – and you could tell she wasn't one for eating vegetables, ever. Broccoli was for wimps, spinach was for tossers and if you offered her a simple glass of water, she'd push it away and screech, 'Fuck off with that poison!'

Today she wasn't looking too bad. A bit tired and hollow-eyed, maybe – and her scraped-back hair ended in a choppy bleached ponytail that hadn't been near shampoo or water for a while – but it was safe to say that she hadn't been up for three days on some insane speed-and-cider bender. Still, anything could happen at any time, Kelly thought. She didn't doubt that today's bloke had a little something stashed in his wallet.

Mo started feeling around in her pockets for her packet of tabs. She smoked without restraint, like a small industrial city in the former Soviet Union. 'How old are you now, our Kelly? Seventeen, eighteen?' she asked accusingly. 'Too young to hide away and shite, poring over your books. When I was your age, I was out on the town, having a laff, shagging myself silly.' She turned to the bloke and winked. 'I remember doing it in phone boxes when we couldn't find anywhere else. We all did it, didn't we, Paulie?'

Paulie squared his beefy shoulders. 'Phone boxes? Niver. Cramp my style.'

'Big man all over, eh?' Mo said, grinning.

Kelly winced. Seeing her mam flirt with a bloke was almost as bad as seeing her snog one.

Mo lit a fag and jabbed a finger at her. 'Look at you, sitting there with a face like a slapped arse! Aren't you even going to say hello to your own mother?'

Kelly smiled, despite herself. 'Hello,' she mumbled.

Mo rummaged through a Tesco bag and pulled out a bottle of wine. 'Get some glasses. Let's have a jar to celebrate the return of the prodigal mam.'

Paulie sat down heavily on the brown velour settee, which creaked under his weight. 'Careful you don't break the fucking couch, man!' Mo hissed. 'I'll be sleeping there tonight.'

He smiled and sniggered. 'Room for two?' he asked.

'That'd be telling,' she shot back.

Kelly went into the kitchen, where she found two water tumblers at the back of a cupboard. She gave the cracked one to Paulie.

Mo's lip curled. 'What, no champagne glasses?' she said. 'And where's yours?'

'Not for me,' Kelly said.

'Whaa?'

'I'm studying.'

'Well, stop fucking studying.'

'Mam, I need to complete this module by tomorrow.'

Mo popped open the bottle. 'Go and get yourself a glass or I'll nut you.'

She obeyed, because you never knew with Mam. 'Is it

real champagne?' she asked, holding out a pint jug that Mo had filched from the pub a couple of years back. She was being careful not to use Nana's best glass goblets, in case one of them got broken.

'As good as,' Mo said. 'Mouthful of bubbles. What's the difference?'

Kelly took a sip of the sweet frothy liquid and put her glass down.

Mo looked at her with narrowed eyes. 'You're a stuck-up little bitch, aren't you?'

Kelly said nothing. Had Mo already been drinking? It usually took more than half a glass to turn her nasty, but maybe champagne worked quicker.

'Hey, I got you something from town,' Mo said, as if she hadn't just insulted her. She went over to the carrier bags and pulled out a pink lycra mini dress. Kelly had seen something similar hanging from a peg in the Saturday market. She remembered thinking she wouldn't be seen dead in it – and that it was just the kind of thing her mam would wear, which was probably why she wouldn't be seen dead in it.

'Thanks,' she said.

Mo held it up against her striped T-shirt and jeans. 'You see, you just needed a bit of colour. Tart yourself up a bit. Live a little.'

Here we go, Kelly thought. Her mam didn't get her, never had, or she would have known that her daughter would as soon get tarted up in pink lycra as throw herself naked off the Tyne Bridge in winter.

But all she said was, 'I don't want to wear anything that's been nicked.'

Mo looked shocked. 'Who said anything's been nicked?' She slapped Kelly lightly around the head. 'You want to watch your gob, you cheeky bugger. Nicked, my arse!'

Nirvana started up again in the next-door flat. Kelly mentally cursed the paper-thin walls of their block. She knew every word of every Nirvana song without ever having owned one of their singles.

Mo wasn't keen either. She put Nana's radio on at full blast and turned the dial until she heard Motorhead's 'Ace of Spades'. 'Tune!' she yelled, and started dancing manically around the lounge.

Paulie took a small bag of powder out of his pocket and emptied it onto Nana's gleaming smoked glass coffee table. 'Blaster-bomber,' he said. 'Ultimate.'

'Come on!' shouted Mo, clenching her fists with excitement.

'Mam, you shouldn't,' Kelly said.

'Because of yer nana?' Mo said. 'She's not home until five, is she?'

'No, it's bad for you.'

Mo laughed. 'But that's where you're wrong, K. It's actually good for you – especially the likes of you booky wankers. All the students take this stuff in America.'

'How do you know?' Kelly asked.

'Don't they, Paulie?'

'Improves concentration,' Paulie said, using the edge

of Mo's fag packet to separate the powder into brownish lines. 'Try it for yourself.'

Kelly thought about the statistics she'd been struggling to decipher. She could do with extra powers of concentration. But wasn't a fool. A dose of Paulie's manky powder wouldn't give her brain an upgrade. 'What's it been cut with? What about the side effects?' she asked.

'Proper fucking doctor, you are!' Mo replied. 'It's no wonder you never leave this stinkhole of a flat. Where's your balls, man?' She passed Kelly a thin tube of rolled-up paper. 'If you don't like it, no harm done.'

Kelly shook her head. 'Except to my nose, heart and lungs, you mean?'

Mo guffawed. 'Fuck off, little Miss Clean-pants, and get some fucking drugs down you!'

Kelly shut her eyes and pretended she hadn't heard. Mo had been offering her this and that since she was about thirteen, and still she wouldn't take no for an answer. Where was the sense in it? Why would you deliberately lead your own child astray? Nana said it was pig-headedness, but Kelly sensed something deeper. Her mam was like a great empty hole of darkness that she was constantly trying to pull people into.

She hasn't changed, she thought, watching in silence as Mo dipped her head and sniffed a line of powder off the glass table. Why do I waste my time hoping?

She packed up her books and retreated into her bedroom.

*

That night she had her old nightmare, her 'scream dream', she called it, because it always ended the same way – screaming her heart out until Nana came running. It wasn't your usual kind of nightmare filled with monsters and quicksand, the sort that left you gasping with relief when you woke up. Those she could have coped with, because she wasn't a nervous wreck or anything. You gritted your teeth and got through nightmares like that. The terrifying thing about this dream was the way it stuck to real life, forcing her to live through the hours and days she'd spent in Bobby's bedroom, locked up with a potty and a packet of biscuits.

It always began with a feeling of dread. She and Mam would be climbing the stairs up to Bobby's room, and Mam would be giggling and saying, 'Do you want to see Bobby's bunnies, and all his lovely things?'

'Yes, Mam,' she'd say.

But at the top of the stairs, which seemed to go on forever, Bobby's room would be strewn with broken trains and mangled Action Men torsos – not a fluffy toy in sight.

'Where are the bunnies?' she'd ask, already fearful of what her mam might say in reply.

'Not bunnies, biscuits,' Mo would laugh, her eyes glinting with secret intent.

'No, Mam,' she'd whimper, as she felt Mo's hand slip out of hers and watched her dart out of the room. 'No!' she'd shout helplessly, as the bedroom door banged shut and she heard the key turn in the lock. She'd run to the door and hammer on it until she heard the front door of the flat click. Mam was gone.

Shuffling around to face the room, she'd notice a packet of fruit shortcakes on the floor and see Bobby in one corner, snot-nosed, smiling cruelly. And then she'd wake up drenched in sweat, screaming in terror until Nana ran in to comfort her.

Bobby and his dad were long gone, but they constantly returned in her dreams. Bobby's dad was called Si Crowther and he had once mistaken Mo for a prostitute in a pub on the Northumberland Road. Of course, Mo had turned round and given him so much jip at the very fucking thought that he'd finally bought her a drink to shut her up. They'd gone on to spend two nasty, drunken years together, fighting like bull terriers and boozing themselves rotten.

Si was a single parent, which was unusual for a man in those days. He claimed that Bobby's mam had upped and left the country with a Greek waiter, but Kelly had visions of him killing her and burying the body, because Si was the most frightening man she'd ever met. As tall as a doorway, with a sharp face and slit green eyes, he had such a short temper that even the soft creak of a footstep on lino could send him flying into a rage. Kelly often imagined him towering over Bobby's mam and strangling the life out of her. More than once she'd seen him beat Mo black and blue, so murder was probably second nature to him.

Mo and Si used to shut the kids in Bobby's bedroom while they went down the pub. 'Council house babysitting,' Mo would cackle. 'Safe and fucking free.'

Mostly it was for hours, sometimes a whole day. Twice – or maybe three times, Kelly couldn't be sure – she had spent a whole weekend trapped in Bobby's spartan bedroom, cowering in fear behind his bed. She had tried to block out the memories – the whine of her voice as she pleaded with him not to hit her, the sharp kicks that dented her legs and left huge purple bruises, and the biscuits they shared in the miserable stretches between his bouts of viciousness. She still felt sick every time she saw a packet of fruit shortcakes.

Nana came running in. 'Bad dreams again?' she said. 'Don't fret, love, you're safe now.'

'Nana,' she sobbed. 'Sorry to wake you.' She inhaled in a heaving gulp of air and her teeth began to chatter as the sweat cooled on her skin.

She had never told Nana what had happened at Si and Bobby's house. Mo had threatened her not to, or Si would come after her, or she'd get him to adopt her and she'd have to share a bedroom with Bobby for ever. It was all drunken babble, but the idea of Bobby becoming her brother, with a licence to do what he wanted – and of Si being her dad – scared Kelly so much, even all these years later, that although she knew Si was in prison and Bobby had left Newcastle, just thinking about them set her teeth on edge.

I'll never tell, she thought, just in case.

Nana sat on the bed and put her chubby arms around her. Kelly sank into her cushiony softness. Nana was the person who made everything all right. You felt safe when you were near her. The world started to make sense again.

'Is Mam still here?' she asked.

Nana pursed her lips. 'She's gone out with the fella – but says she's staying tonight, although there's not much more of the frigging night left now.

'I said, "Fine – you can stay on your own."' Nana went on. 'But I hope she doesn't come back – or if she does, that she'll be gone for good again soon. Even though she's my own daughter. I'm sorry, love, I know she's yer mam, but she's a wrecking ball, always has been.'

'It's OK,' Kelly said. She wanted to tell Nana that she felt the same, but she couldn't find the words. You were meant to love your mam, weren't you? Come what may? And she did. Only, it wasn't the kind of love she felt for Nana. It wasn't happy love, it was something more desperate, like having a lifelong crush on someone who didn't even like you, or longing for something you couldn't afford.

'Hush, now,' said Nana. 'Lie down again and I'll hold your hand until you fall back to sleep.'

'Reminds me of the storm night in Benidorm,' Kelly said with a sleepy smile, as her head sank into her pillow.

Nana chuckled. 'What a night that was! I thought the hotel was going to blow away. But we were still there in the morning, weren't we? Just like we'll still be here tomorrow, love. Nothing to worry about, Nana's here. We always get through.'

Kelly sighed softly and her breathing fell into a regular rhythm as she drifted off into a sunny dream about their one and only holiday abroad, in Benidorm, three years earlier.

Mo was flat out on the settee the following morning. Her mouth was open and she was gently snoring, loose strands of hair rising and falling over her face with every noisy breath. Her head was wedged in the crevice between cushion and settee back, her legs splayed and propped up over one arm. She still had her shoes on, a pair of red plasticky high heels.

Kelly popped her head into the lounge and scanned the floor for a sleeping Paulie, but he had obviously found somewhere else to crash, because he was nowhere to be seen. She wondered whether her mam had sent him away so as not to incur Nana's fury, or whether he had decided for himself that the chance of a shag wasn't worth the hassle. Kelly didn't care one way or another. She was just glad that there wouldn't be a scene about it.

As she washed up her cereal bowl in their tiny kitchen, she looked out of the window across a mass of grey houses and wondered where she would go when she finally left Byker. She had lived in Flat 14, Edison House for so long that it was hard to imagine what the world beyond held for her. But next year she would be leaving for good. First, to go to uni, and then, she hoped, abroad – somewhere carefree and sunny, where you could kick back in a clifftop bar at the end of the day and watch the sunset over the sea. Benidorm, maybe – although the travel rep who'd befriended her on their holiday had said that the Costa del

Sol was a hectic place to start a career in tourism, and she should try other parts of Spain first, or one of the islands, like Minorca or Ibiza. Just the sound of their names set her off daydreaming.

Nirvana started up next door, vibrating through the damp shared wall. Kelly heard Nana thumping her fists to get them to turn it down. She rinsed off the dishes. As usual, the foamy water wouldn't drain – the sink was bloody blocked again.

'Morning, love.' Nana came into the kitchen wearing her peach velour dressing gown and matching fluffy slippers, her hair done up in curlers. Somehow she always managed to look glamorous, Kelly thought, even first thing in the morning. It was a knack, almost a talent. If they had a version of Crufts for humans, Nana would win the 'best groomed' prize by miles – with a special commendation for her nails, which were amazing, every bit as pointed and polished as Joan Collins's.

'I've been through yer mam's pockets and found her front door keys,' Nana announced. 'I'm taking them back. I don't want her coming and going as she pleases any more, especially not while you've got exams to do.'

A tiny shock of fear went through Kelly. 'She'll go mad when she finds out,' she whispered.

'Not if she thinks she lost them last night while she was out on the rag. So don't say a word, love.'

Kelly saw a shadow cross the doorway behind Nana. 'Like a couple of old crones, you are. What are you plotting?' Mo asked.

'You up already?' Nana turned to face her. 'How's your head?' she added loudly.

Mo recoiled. 'Not too funny, Mam. I've hardly slept a wink. That settee's killed my back all night.'

'Oh, the settee, is it?' Nana said. 'Nothing to do with those bottles of wine you were drinking, or the company you were keeping till the early hours?'

Nana was the one person in the world who could snipe at Mo without getting shouted at, or worse. But Mo couldn't help answering back. 'I said I've got backache, Mam, not AIDS or fucking liver cancer,' she said.

'And no headache at all?' Nana asked, raising her voice again.

Mo winced and narrowed her eyes. 'Backache,' she insisted. 'Anyway, I'll slip into our Kelly's bed now, have myself some cushty while you're out,' she added, as if it was her territorial right to take over her daughter's bedroom.

'You've forgotten that I don't work on Fridays,' Nana said. 'So I'll be here doing bits and bobs until our Alan comes to take me for lunch.'

Mo's lip curled. 'Big Al's coming over? The golden boy, the apple of everyone's eye? Doesn't my little brother work on Fridays, either? Lazy bugger!'

Nana smiled. 'He's his own boss now. He can work the hours he likes – and believe me, he doesn't shirk.'

Mo made a face. 'I could have had a great job too, if I hadn't been saddled with a bairn,' she said defensively.

'Yeah, you would have probably been a brain surgeon

by now,' Nana said, nodding her head sarcastically. 'Only you gave it all up to be a mam.'

There followed a short silence, and Kelly wondered which of them was filling it with the darkest thoughts. The truth was that Mo had given up almost nothing to have her baby, at least when you compared her to other mothers. Kelly couldn't remember her infant years and a lot of the rest was patchy, but she knew what she knew, no matter what Mo sometimes claimed – her nana had brought her up.

Nana used to tell it like a fairy tale. 'Yer mam had you too young,' she'd say with a wistful sigh. 'She was a tot with a baby. You were just two bairns in the wood, lost and alone.'

Nana had saved them, the innocent children. But then Mo had gone astray, like the boy with the ice splinter in his eye in the Hans Christian Andersen story. That was the way Nana had originally told it to Kelly, anyway. In later years, when she thought Kelly was out of earshot, she'd tell people that Mo had 'always been a bad'un, from the day she was born'.

Kelly grew up worrying that an evil snow queen or fairy had put a spell on her mam. Which was probably better, she decided on reflection, than knowing that yer mam didn't want or love you. When she grew older and got into Catherine Cookson novels, she started hoping that the moment would arrive – perhaps when she 'came of age' – when Nana would sit her down and reveal that Mo was actually her sister, not her mother, and that Nana was mam to them both. But her sixteenth birthday came and went with no such announcement – and she wasn't sure it would matter by the time she was eighteen. After all, everybody apart from Mo agreed that Nana was her real mam, even though it wasn't a biological fact.

It helped that Nana had been at the hospital for her birth, and that she tenderly described their meeting just like a mother would.

'I fell in love with you on the spot,' she'd say with a nostalgic smile. 'You were the sweetest baby, so tiny and helpless that my heart swelled up every time I looked at you. There was something so familiar about your little face, something I don't think I'd even seen in my own kids. Was it traces of my mam? My own nana? I don't know, love, perhaps it was a mixture – but I do know that on the day that you were born, I swore to love and protect you for ever.'

'Like a fairy godmother?' Kelly would say.

That made Nana laugh. 'Yer fairy nana, love – that's me.'

From the other snippets she overheard, Kelly guessed that Mo had flitted in and out while Nana had been busy loving and protecting her. There had been a few times when Mo had come over all maternal and tried to make a go of setting up home with young Kelly, but then her man or her restlessness had got in the way, or the landlord had chucked her out, or she'd got drunk and stopped giving a fuck – it was never more than a few days – and then Kelly had gone back to Nana.

'Well, I'll be asleep most of today, so say haway to our Alan from me.' Mo yawned and walked unsteadily towards Kelly's bedroom.

'Wait, Mam,' Kelly called after her, 'I just need to get some books out of there first.'

'Don't mind me, you little swotbag,' Mo replied. 'I'll be dead to the world before you can say Mack the bleedin' Knife.'

CATCH UP WITH

Denise

WELCH

ONLINE

 @realdenisewelch

 /officialdenisewelch denise_welch

Join us at

The
Little Book
Café

For competitions galore,
exclusive interviews with our lovely
Sphere authors, chat about
all the latest books
and much, much more.

Follow us on Twitter at
@littlebookcafe

Subscribe to our newsletter and
Like us at /thelittlebookcafe

Read. Love. Share.